THE
SIX GIFTS

THE
SIX GIFTS

PART I: SECRETS

CHRISTIE K. KELLY

First Edition

Published in the United States by Bruce Farr Creative Publishing, a division of Bruce Farr Creative LLC, Westmoreland, New Hampshire.

Designed by Dave Lindberg Marketing & Design LLC
Cover art by Andrew Williamson
Author photography by christinegladephotography.com
Cover photography: Dreamstime.com

Library of Congress Cataloging-in-Publication Data has been applied for.

ISBN: 978-1-7325652-0-3

CONTENTS

꿈

For my dad

CHRISTIE K. KELLY

ACKNOWLEDGMENTS

It's nearly impossible to express the gratitude I have for my husband, Michael Murgo, who has been by my side, tirelessly cheering me on, since the day this story fell into my consciousness – and well, throughout our 40 years together. Without him, I would never have had the courage to take this journey. I love you, Michael.

Before the writing ever began, my dear friend, Valerie Badger, dug deep into the internet researching for months so that I could bring authenticity to a saga that crosses centuries. Her steadfast belief in this story along with her not-so-subtle prodding carried me through many a difficult slump. Thank you, Val.

Writing is a lonely trek best not done alone. I'm more than lucky to have a comrade in writing whose honest and encouraging words keep me tethered to the truth. Without all those lunches and dinners, it's possible both I, and the story, would've veered off the tracks. Thank you, Rose Cipriano, for your true friendship – and for your authentic Italian editing.

When Bruce Farr, editor extraordinaire, took this project on, I can only imagine how often he wondered what he'd gotten himself into. I was a greenhorn. But over the last years, his grace has never faltered. He has buoyed both my spirit and my prose. Thank you, Bruce, for the professional you are and for the friend you've become.

From book covers to business cards to my website and beyond, no one could be blessed with a more talented collaborator. I can't thank Drew Williamson enough for all he's done for me in the last 10 years. Many of my outlandish ideas have been brought to vivid life through his skilled hands and intellect. If there were an award for patience, he'd be the winner!

I went far out of my comfort zone when I took on Spanish dialogue throughout various provinces of Spain. Fortunately, I am honored to have a colleague who has lived in Spain. Gracias, Frank Gonzalez, for sacrificing many precious weekend hours on this project.

When a dream that has engulfed years of your life comes to fruition, there is a distinct feeling of enchantment when you feast your eyes on the final prize – at least for me. Thank you, Dave Lindberg, for your expertise in the painstaking process of bringing it all together.

Our poisons come in every guise
Their subterfuge to blind our eyes
And steal from us the little joys
That life bequeaths and time alloys

CHAPTER ONE

1964

O livia is slapped into consciousness—or more like punched—and comes to with her small, mystified face inches from the concrete, water erupting from her mouth in little spurts, like a fountain misfiring.

She senses no pain at all, just an overwhelming desire— an almost frantic need—to return to where she'd been just a moment before. She rolls her head toward the pool, her eyes darting from side to side, searching for the comforting blanket of light that, a second ago, had so lovingly enveloped her. The sun glints a harsh yellow off the pool's surface, not the same mystical white light she'd just been surrounded by.

A cacophony of voices rises and falls around her. Her tiny

body is lifted from the ground and positioned in a lounge chair. Many hands move over her, each frantic touch feeling like an interruption, an erasure of sorts, slowly washing away the sensation still fresh on her skin, the ecstatic feeling that she'd been drizzled with warm honey from head to toe. White honey, though, a kind so pure that it isn't really honey at all, but something else entirely.

Later, Olivia cannot sleep. She can't eat or drink or think of anything but the ecstasy of the white light. She holds vigil for it under her bed covers, behind her eyelids, inside her brain, just under her skin. She simply cannot let it go, can't allow herself to have lost it. She attempts with all her might to retrieve it. But, like a wisp of smoke through a window screen, it had slipped away.

The very next day, Olivia follows her older sisters to the next-door neighbors' pool; the only backyard pool in the entire town. With a soldierly determination, she marches in slow motion, as one does in water, down the pool steps and across its floor, seeking yet again, without hesitation, that which had swaddled her the day before.

This time, Olivia's sister spots her first, her hair floating in a sinuous, slow-moving eddy around her still, composed body. There is commotion, voices, more pounding on the back, another fountain of tiny spurts. But Olivia hangs on to the white light a little longer. And, this time, it is even whiter, warmer and sweeter, almost like the feeling of submerging into a steaming bath, or when, on an exceedingly hot day, a cool breeze seems to lift your body ever so fleetingly from terra firma. It is all of this and more. It is unexplainable, and then it is, again, gone.

Three-year-old Olivia is no longer allowed near water until

silence outside Olivia's head. But inside, she feels anything but at peace.

"Stop, will you!" she calls to Marco. "This is far enough!"

Marco plunges an oar into the water to break his momentum and then maneuvers his kayak around to face his wife. "You want to stop and float here?" he asks.

She doesn't want to float anywhere. She wants to fly like the loon she just saw take off across the lake. "Yes," she replies, as she attempts to catch her breath. Their boats face each other, Olivia's pointed west and Marco's east. Behind her sunglasses, she stares at the lines etched into her husband's eternally tanned face, and at his now salt-and-pepper waves of hair that used to be springy black curls. His looks haven't faded, though. He is still as handsome as ever. Although, as she notices, his face seems to have a blankness now, an expression void of even an inkling of passion. Instead, he has the appearance of someone who's keeping up a constant vigil against some amorphous fear.

"I can't stand it!" The words erupt from Olivia's mouth without warning.

"Can't stand what? I thought you wanted to come out here!" Marco replies.

"This isn't living," Olivia says. "We might as well be dead!"

Marco's head snaps back toward hers in shock. "Olivia! Don't say that!"

"Why not? We act like we're dead already!" She shoves an oar forcefully into the side of Marco's kayak. "I keep telling you that I don't want to live the rest of my life this way, you know, up here in the middle of nowhere," she says as she gestures with her elbows to the right and left. "But you won't listen!"

Marco's shoulders sink. "I don't know what you expect from

me, Olivia. We've gone over it a thousand times. You can't live in New Jersey because of the air and you don't want to live here. What the hell *do* you want?"

"Anything but this! I've got to do something, Marco! I can't just sit around and watch the time go by. You might be able to just sit there in your La-Z-Boy and watch life happen on the TV. But I can't. I want to live it!"

"Oh, so I'm the problem?" Marco sits up straight and twists the cap back onto the plastic bottle of water he's just taken a swig of.

"Well, you're the one that keeps me here like a prisoner!"

"Prisoner? Fuck you!"

Even in the glare of the sun, Olivia can see that the complexion on Marco's face has turned from olive to bright red. "Fuck you!" she hurls back.

Marco flings his half-empty water bottle at Olivia, grabs his oars and paddles past her. Olivia's natural reaction is to lurch her body away from the projectile. When she does, her center of gravity is thrown off-kilter, causing her kayak to tip to one side. She attempts to re-right the boat, to regain her balance, but it's too late. She slips into the water like a fish being thrown back. The icy-cold Vermont lake shocks her senses and stiffens her limbs. Having been a strong swimmer throughout her lifetime, she had foolishly chosen not to wear her life jacket. But her strength isn't what it used to be; she struggles to move her arms and legs against the weight of her wet clothes and shoes in the dark water that is pulling her downward. Her panicked open eyes see only black, but in her mind's eye she senses a hauntingly familiar bright white. The specter wrenches her from immobility and triggers her arms to scoop through the heavy water and her legs to frantically pump her back to the surface. She grabs onto her overturned kayak, pulls herself up and drapes herself over it, all before Marco has been able to turn and make his way back to her.

"Olivia!" he screams. "Olivia! Are you okay?"

The thought that she is dead-tired crosses her exhausted mind—dead-tired. She'd just got done saying that she might as well be dead. It appears the universe was listening. Scraping back the wet hair from her face, she treads water and lifts herself a couple of inches to peer at Marco. "Thanks," is all she says.

"I didn't mean to do that!" Marco says in a panic. "I didn't mean to knock you out of your boat! Olivia, I'm so sorry!" He maneuvers his kayak next to hers.

"I'm sure you are," she whispers sarcastically. But her voice is inaudible to Marco's hard-of-hearing ears.

"Do you think you can pull yourself into my boat?" he asks.

"Give me a minute," she replies through chattering teeth. Her eyes are now fixed on the soft mountains in the distance. She wishes the warm blanket of yellow-green could wrap itself around her and halt the bitter chill that has taken up residence in her bones.

Marco calculates while he talks. "I think if I shift all my weight to one side, you'll be able to pull yourself into my boat. If not, I'll get you in and I'll swim to shore."

Olivia knows there is no way Marco can swim in this cold water all the way to shore. To begin with, he's not a strong swimmer. She clenches her teeth and pushes off the overturned kayak, slipping herself back into the water. She feels the cold permeating her body, sending the sensation of little razors sliding up and down her skin.

Marco's boat is her salvation. She focuses on the red fiberglass in front of her, willing herself the strength to hold on. The kayak teeters as Marco adjusts his weight against hers. "Grab onto the paddle!" he instructs her. Somehow, she's able to grip the plastic oar while Marco pulls with all his might until she is draped across his boat. It takes a few minutes of rest before she's able to maneuver herself fully into his kayak.

Olivia shivers as she leans back against him, while Marco awkwardly paddles them toward the boat ramp. She sinks into her husband's warm body, but the gyrating motion of his paddling chafes against her wet clothes until she feels the friction scrape the skin raw on her upper arms. She grits her teeth against the rhythmic pain and focuses her attention on the distant shoreline. As Marco paddles, Olivia watches another loon fly across the surface of the lake. Her mind ping-pongs from thoughts of the deep, unforgiving lake to the beautiful creature that soars in front of her. She feels trapped in helplessness, and jealous of the loon.

CHAPTER THREE

PRESENT DAY

An hour later, Olivia wraps her chilled hands around a cup of hot tea while she waits for Marco, who has gone off to find someone with a boat to help rescue her overturned kayak. She has changed into warm clothes and stares at her cell phone as a distraction from the angst in her gut. She feels like she's swallowed a rock. Olivia's brain knows that falling out of the kayak wasn't Marco's fault, but logic doesn't seem to be in play in the pit of her stomach. Instead, the emotion of the event wraps around the rock in her belly like a layer of sediment.

Facebook presents her with a friend request. She stares at the name on the screen, Brenda Garrison. There have been others from her past who've tried to find Olivia—tried to entice her to hit the "friend" button. But Olivia hasn't taken the bait. Instead, she chooses to hang somewhere on the fringes of that social media program.

This name looks friendly, though; warmly familiar even. And in its familiarity, it demands more than a mere, dismissive "click" to hurry past, or a careless slam-down on the memories these requests tend to drag to the surface. After all, the name should look familiar. Brenda Garrison had been Olivia's best friend for 10 years, the girl with the long blonde hair, the big brown eyes and the even bigger boobs to match. The one who'd gotten all the boys in high school.

Olivia's curiosity rears up with a childlike insistence. She wonders if Brenda settled for one of those high school boyfriends, or if she ended up marrying some "bigwig" from the city. And she ponders whether Brenda had ever become a fashion designer like she'd dreamed of in those younger years.

Olivia lifts her head of dark-brown hair toward a corner of the vaulted ceiling, where a slender ray of sun is piercing through the high windows, illuminating a freshly spun spider's web. A fly, suspended in the sticky web, hangs entombed. A chill of recognition courses through Olivia, as if her skinny, ransacked, poisoned body shares a fate with the fly. Fucking fly, she thinks. Fucking poison. Fucking tomb.

Her eyes drift back to the screen and—on impulse and without the normal checks that keep her steady—she sets her cup of tea on the counter, clicks the "friend" button and maneuvers to the page.

Wow, her childhood best friend is still beautiful, still has that "come-hither" smile. A wave of nostalgia surges up in Olivia and she finds herself with an unfamiliar longing, a desire to know more. A Facebook comment pops up and she reads the post: "I was hoping it was really you I'd found."

"It's me. How are you?" Olivia types automatically, while her mind is still focused on how quickly her old schoolmate responded. She considers that the friendly and gregarious Brenda has become one of those people addicted to social media.

"I'm good. Would you mind if we took this to instant messaging?" Brenda asks.

"Okay." Suspicion begins to worm its way into Olivia's judgment. The familiar impulse to retreat and slam the door creeps along her still chilled skin.

"There. Better." Brenda continues. "How are you? You fell off the planet girl."

"Not really. Life just got busy." Olivia squeezes one of her hands into a fist. Steady girl, she tells herself; you can cut this off quick if you need to.

"Do you still live back east?" Brenda posts.

Olivia's slender, arthritic fingers open back up onto the keys. "Yes. I'm married with two sons. How about you, any kids?"

"Oh yeah, one boy, two girls—all out of the house. I'm a single mother now, thrice divorced."

"What? I always thought that when some lucky guy landed you, he'd never let go." Olivia's interest is piqued.

"Yeah well, I guess they all got their love for my boobs confused with their love for me, lol."

"Lol …" Olivia catches herself responding with the popular Facebook acronym. Where did that come from? It's not her style. "Just wondering," she continues, "was Bobby one of your husbands?"

"HELL NO!" Brenda interjects in all caps. "I dropped him

sophomore year in college and went onto bigger and better, if you know what I mean. Or so I thought, anyway, lol. Have you stayed in touch with anyone from back home?"

"No. I never seemed to have the time. You?" Olivia's brain begins a tug of war with her heart. Her brain says to end the conversation, but her heart isn't ready.

"Well yes. I'm still in touch with a few people. Tommy Johnson just e-mailed me this morning. He wanted me to know that Jeff was killed in a car accident yesterday. I thought you might want to know. Tragic, huh?"

Olivia reacts with a visceral jolt that spreads like electricity throughout her body, turning into an ache that pulsates just below the surface. A tear drops onto the keys of the laptop. She's surprised at her own reaction. After all, she hasn't seen this guy in over thirty years. He may have been her first love, but that was decades ago. Gathering herself, she types another question. "Was it sudden or do you know if he suffered?"

"I don't think so. Tommy said he was killed instantly. I guess his truck flipped and burned. He has two children. He married late. Dana Freeman. Remember her?"

Olivia scours her memory to put a face with the name, but nothing materializes. Instead, a visual of Jeff's kids and his wife, a neat little family of four, pops into her brain. How devastated they must be. "No, I don't think so. Was she in school with us?"

"She was a few years behind us, three maybe four. You knew her older sister Carrie. She was in our class."

The image of a mousy, quiet girl with her nose in her books eventually comes to Olivia's mind. "I think I remember her, quiet and shy. She sat in the back of Mr. Vreeland's class, right?"

"Yeah, that's her. Dana's a younger version. Jeff should never have married her. He should have held onto you."

Olivia shuts her eyes tight. Images of Jeff swell up; he was half Mexican on his father's side and half Irish on his mother's. Olivia remembers her attraction to his black hair and deep brown eyes. He was of medium height and had a muscular build—muscles gained from hard work on his father's ranch. The ranch where she'd first witnessed the miracle of a cow giving birth to its calf. And then Jeff's father saving it from sure suffocation after the mother rejected it when the birthing sac didn't break open and got stuck over its head. The same ranch where Olivia had learned to stabilize her stance, tuck her elbows into her sides, exhale, and, firmly, without hesitation, squeeze the trigger of a pistol.

She feels something well up in her throat, the vile taste of acid. Swallowing hard, she pushes it back down. "Where do you live now, and will you be going to the funeral?" But changing the subject only masks the churning in her gut. Memories have grit. They hang on, pushing with ferocity toward some reckoning.

"I live in Denver and I'm going to try." Brenda responds. "Tommy said it probably won't be until Monday. I don't know if I can get off work, though."

"What do you do?"

"I'm a loan officer at a bank. Do you think you might go? To the funeral, I mean?"

"Oh, I don't think so. It's been over thirty years. I don't know anybody there anymore, and it's a long trip. I don't fly." A murmurous hum begins to vibrate under her skin. Olivia inhales deeply in attempt to squelch it.

"Well, if you reconsider, let me know. I've got to run. The boss just walked in ... Oli, it's been great reconnecting."

"Yes, it has. I'll be sure to stay in touch now. Thanks for letting me know about Jeff."

The picture snaps into her brain like the trailer of a movie. *Olivia and her friends sitting on the bank of the Rio Grande where they always gathered to party. They had arranged rocks in a circle to build a campfire where they burned dried brush and driftwood, drank beer and deliberated what the future would bring. Brenda was there, blonde curls bouncing as she danced like a gypsy around her sexy but obnoxious boyfriend, Bobby. Jeff was sitting next to Olivia, his arm around her, beer in hand. The conversation is still crystal-clear. They were all talking about her. "So, Oli claims she's going to be a millionaire by the time she's thirty. What do you think Jeff, marriage material?" Bobby chided.*

Jeff just laughed and lifted his beer. Everyone else raised theirs in unison. "To healthy, wealthy marriage material," Bobby toasted, as he stuck his free hand under one of Brenda's breasts and gave it a heave. Everyone laughed, and Jeff bent down to kiss Olivia. She remembers the warmth of his breath and the tickle of his hair as the lock that forever hung over his eyes brushed over hers.

Jeff knew then—knew well—that he couldn't hold onto her, that there wasn't a chance in hell. He wasn't meant to leave that town and there was no way she was going to stay.

A million dollars, Olivia thinks, recalling Bobby's jibing. She's made her million, but it's all on paper, tied up in their business. Even if they were to sell the business, a million dollars wouldn't support them for the rest of their lives—if they're lucky enough to live another ten or twenty years. Hell, just the doctor visits, medications and chemical-free food they both need to survive would eat it up in no time. A million bucks isn't what it used to be. She tells herself she should've dreamed of being a billionaire.

Olivia's thoughts turn to Brenda, as she tries to conjure up images of what she imagines her life has been like. But, instead, a surge of old memories takes over: Brenda in her hot pink bikini, long blonde curls cascading over those formidable breasts, breasts that Olivia was so jealous of back then. Brenda never seemed to notice the jealousy, or, for that matter, even the stares from the other girls, or the boys' ogles. She was just an innocent, fun-loving girl with a heart of gold. A twinge of sorrow pinches Olivia's heart to think that she's missed out on years of making new memories with her old best friend.

Long-dormant images of her small, southwestern home-town, Alamosa, surface: smells of the dusty riverbank where she relentlessly walked, the warmth of bonfires in the town park on frigid winter nights, the regal peak of Mount Blanca standing like a sentinel on watch, and the steady flicker of the golden-yel-low aspen leaves that dot its ridges throughout the fall. Olivia wonders anew about the unstoppable, slow-motion progress through time, time in which she and her friends morphed ever so gradually from tiny curious beings into gutsy young adults.

After all those visions of grandeur she'd had as a teenager, how she ended up here in such a mundane existence on the side of a mountain in Vermont is the grand question now. Oh, she still has her ideas, but they're different at this point. She recalls one in which she and Marco conspire to rob a bank and drive across the country like Bonnie & Clyde, except, in Olivia's ver-sion, they throw money out the window to poor people while they're being chased. And then there's the idea that she'd grow weed in the basement like Nancy on the TV show *Weeds*, but they give it all away to sick people who need it for medical pur-poses. She'd tried to get Marco to buy into that one, but he'd just looked at her like she'd been smoking too much of the very stuff she was proposing to grow. And then there was the most diabolical scheme of all. She keeps this one quiet, not wanting Marco to think she's gone mad. In this plot, Olivia gets a job in the executive dining room at the chemical company, Monsanto. With all that corporate money, they've got to have an executive dining room. Olivia secretly injects measured but lethal doses of their own pesticides into those cretins' gourmet lunches and watches them get sicker every day until they die excruciatingly painful deaths, just like the bees, the birds and the human population that the company is so cavalierly extinguishing.

But reality always rears up and slaps Olivia in the face. She realizes that she'd probably die of a heart attack while she was in the act of robbing a bank. And, Marco's right, she'd no doubt smoke all the pot and her heart would stop from too much THC, especially considering that after being chemically injured she's now intolerant of chemicals. The executive dining room job is a far stretch, too. She doesn't have the stamina to hold down a job long enough to enact the scheme. But, without a doubt, she's got to do something. She is in her 50s and in poor health. She knows for certain that she has yet to find the answer to what she's referred to nearly her entire life as *The Why*. And the likelihood of finding it is slipping through her fingers.

CHAPTER FOUR

PRESENT DAY

The dirt coats Olivia's feet as she scuffs along the top of the riverbank, digging her toes into the loamy soil and kicking clumps of it into the air with each deliberate step. Her deep connection to the earth melts the world away and draws her into the warmth of its womb. Her fingers graze each tree within their reach, and she pauses occasionally to stroke a leaf or to admire the delicate intricacy of a spider's web.

The sun is warm on her tanned skin and her senses are tuned to the sounds of birds flitting from tree to tree, the rustle of the breeze through the leaves and the rushing sounds of the river. She stops and closes her eyes, listening intently to the water. It teases the corners of her mouth, causing them to turn up, and she sighs in contentment. She opens her eyes and continues along her path, faster now, anxious for the release the water so willingly provides.

She stops short when she sees a young man, a teenager maybe, sitting on a rock that juts out from the top of the riverbank. He's faced away from her, looking downstream, his knees pulled up to his chest, arms wrapped tightly around them. He is still, like a statue, the only movement about him that of some wisps of his dark hair in the warm breeze. He's wearing jeans, and his t-shirt is stuck to his back with sweat. Olivia peers downstream to try and see what he's looking at. There is just the river though, proud and roaring as it moves along its course.

She steps a few yards closer to him and sees a flash of movement out of the corner of her eye. Shifting her gaze down the bank and toward the river again, she notices a young girl with auburn hair standing on the shoreline waving her arms as if to beckon someone in the distance. The girl's heavy, long-sleeved dress hangs too fully on her thin little frame. It is impossible to see whom the girl is trying to summon. Olivia takes another step, moving past a stand of prickly bushes just below the ridge of the bank. In doing so, she can now see a woman a good distance beyond the young girl. The woman is kneeling in a shallow pool of water where the current has redirected itself around a sandbar, building a fragile, temporary dam that will wash away with the next storm. The woman's sundress billows in the water around her hips like an opened canopy. Her head is bowed, hands covering her face and her shoulders are shaking as if she is crying.

Olivia's first instinct is to go to the woman, but she looks again at the teenage boy and realizes he can clearly see the woman too. Yet he seems to be ignoring her. Olivia intuits that the young girl and teenage boy are the woman's children. But, if that's so, why isn't the boy responding to his sister's obvious gestures for help? The girl moves further downstream, still trying to flag someone's attention. The teen-

ager, however, does not move.

Not wanting to pass them—nor desiring to turn back—Olivia digs her toes into the dirt and squats down. Her eyes settle on the woman, who is clearly in distress. Going to her would be an intrusion, Olivia reasons. Then, suddenly, the woman slips down into the water. Olivia's heart leaps into her throat, and she jumps up. The woman sinks further into the water, almost as though she were in quicksand. The teenaged boy stands and climbs the few steps to the top of the bank, and he walks south, past the woman and the girl, his pace quickening with each step.

When Olivia sees the young girl running toward the woman, Olivia stands up and starts to pick her way down the bank. The girl screams for help. Heat prickles Olivia's neck and sweat begins to pour from her skin. She becomes tangled in the brush and struggles to get down the bank. The thorny bushes dig into her arms and legs, and the more she tries to free herself, the tighter the bushes hold her. She feels herself suffocating, her neck now choked in a tangle of brambles. Olivia can hear the girl's desperate screams and the woman's anguished choking, but she can't see anyone anymore. She panics—unable to breathe, move, speak.

ॐ

Olivia awakens with a start, gasping for air, drenched in sweat. It's the third time in as many weeks that such a dream—with all its urgency, its haunting characters, its sense of physicality—has invaded the recesses of her subconscious.

But this morning the dream has a mote of clarity, a revealing flicker of understanding. The river must be the Rio Grande. It must have something to do with Jeff's death. Always intuitive,

Olivia must have picked up a signal. It most certainly wouldn't be the first time.

Still lying in bed, the idea suddenly lands in her brain like a jet airplane touching down. She's got to go to Jeff's funeral. She wants to go. She ponders the idea for a minute. Fear creeps up. She pushes back the thoughts that she isn't well enough and that going back to Alamosa maybe isn't such a good idea. She convinces herself that there's nothing to be afraid of. The past is the past and the present is slipping away. Quick as a flash, the plane comes to an abrupt halt and the decision is made. In the same way she's made all her decisions, from the gut. It's only in the past few horrid years that she's foolishly varied from that practice. She is going and that's that. These essences of childhood that have been invading her subconscious have taken hold and are spilling into the dark chasm Olivia has kept closed-off and secure for all these many years.

She gets out of bed to let their two curly goldendoodles outside. Tucker, the protector, is the color of caramel and poodle-smart. Casper-white Boo, wily and goofy, is retriever through and through. They do their duty and then charge back inside, wrangling for position by the cabinet where their treats are stored, and sit obediently waiting for Olivia to dole out their score. She finishes with the dogs and finds herself lingering by her collection of carved wooden bears. They must have nearly thirty of the things, given as gifts to Marco and her over the years, primarily from their kids. Olivia pushes on the little wooden arm of the rocking chair bear and it begins to rock back and forth. Then she runs her fingers across the top of the whitewater rafting bears and up the tree of another, where a cub hangs for safety. She has looked at these bears a thousand times always wondering what it was that made her start the collection to begin with. She realizes she is using the bears as a stall tactic. So, she takes a deep breath and turns to Marco, who is sitting in his La-Z-Boy watching the morning news, the volume so low that there's no way he can actually make out what they're saying. It's something he does when he gets up before her so that he doesn't wake her. "Marco, something's happened." Olivia's voice is solemn yet strong. The murmurous pulsing of her blood is almost deafening now, but discernible only to Olivia.

Marco abruptly turns to face her. "What? What's the matter?"

"Well ... I had a Facebook conversation with an old friend from high school yesterday while you were recovering my kayak. She contacted me to tell me that my high school boyfriend was killed in a car accident." The words, now emerging from her own mouth, hit Olivia hard. Hearing them spoken out loud seems to make the circumstances more real. Her eyes widen, and she begins to tremble. Looking down at her hands, she notices that they are visibly shaking.

"Oh." Marco's face softens, the tragedy having too many degrees of separation for him to feel its weight. "That's awful."

"Yes, yes, it is. I think I want to go to his funeral," she blurts out.

Marco sits up straighter and shifts his body around. "Why?"

"I ... I don't know. I haven't been back there in forever. I just have this feeling that I should go." It feels like a magnet has attached itself to her skin, and it has a name engraved on it, "Alamosa." It's pulling her toward the small Colorado town.

"Oka-a-a-ay," he says, obviously having a hard time getting his head around the idea. "When's the funeral?"

"I'm not sure. I think Monday." The magnet tugs at her some more.

He stares at his wife for a long minute, his dark brown eyes processing the information. "You really think we should go?"

"Well, uh, I think I want to go alone." She waits for the baffled look on Marco's face to turn to hurt, but instead it twists into what she can see is sheer anger.

"Alone! Are you crazy? How? Fly?" She sees the veins pop out in his temple, a sign that the once cool and confident business owner will start to spiral from the confrontation and propel himself rapidly toward a migraine, a malady they both suffer from these days.

She takes a deep breath. "I'll drive."

He stands up and strides into the kitchen to directly address her, his head shaking back and forth with each step, dismissing the idea. "Alone? Drive across the country ... to some old high school boyfriend's funeral? Not by yourself!"

His rebuttal hits a nerve. Even though she knows she's thrown a bomb at him, she doesn't care right now. She realizes that this sudden desire to go to Jeff's funeral is a byproduct of her almost urgent need to escape, at least temporarily, this frozen ghost of a man she's been married to for more than 30 years. In New Jersey, when Olivia began having symptoms from the poisoning, Marco ignored her claims, dismissing them as hypochondria. That is, until the diagnosis from the allergist prompted him to recognize that he was experiencing the symptoms himself. It's the same thing now. She begs him to be more help to their son with the business, or to help her figure out a different business they can try and pursue in their current predicament. But he just stays stuck. His modus operandi is never to commit to a decision until either the answer knocks him on the head or he's given an ultimatum.

"I'll take Tucker with me. He can protect me." She can hear herself speak the words coming out of her mouth, and they sound crazy to her. She can't imagine what's going through Marco's brain right now. She knows she should give him time to process, but ever since the poisoning, the time it takes him to process anything feels beyond tolerable.

He snorts. "Ridiculous! You're not driving across the country alone."

He should know better. Trying to tell Olivia what she can or cannot do has never worked in his or anyone else's favor. It only fuels her fire. "It's not your decision."

He pulls his head back and glares at her, his lips pulled tight in defiance. They stare at each other, a stand-off. He averts his eyes away first. He always does. "I guess I can't stop you. Can I?"

"No. You can't." Olivia holds firm, her shaking hands grasping the edge of the counter.

Marco sets down his coffee cup with a deliberate thud, glares at her in disbelief and stomps off to the bathroom, slamming the door behind him.

Olivia gazes at Tucker and Boo who are at her feet, peering up at her as if to say, "What just happened?" She shrugs her shoulders at them, pulls her hands from the counter and reaches down to assure the dogs that all is okay. With that gesture, she feels a pop, a release of pressure, like that of a lid twisted from the seal of a jar.

CHAPTER FIVE

1966

Their movie-magazine-obsessed mother, Doris, named her daughters after Hollywood stars: Marilyn, as in Monroe; Elizabeth, as in Taylor; Grace, as in Kelly; and Olivia, as in de Havilland. At least four of them, anyway. Their oldest sister, Cari, is from their father's first marriage. Their mother always says she doesn't count. Doris swears, when out of range of her husband's ears, that she, herself, would be a famous movie star like Doris Day if she hadn't been saddled with all these kids.

Black-and-white photographs of Doris with colorized red lips, along with color Polaroids of her four girls, are displayed along built-in shelves in the living room next to the military headshot of their handsome father. To a stranger's eye, it would appear that the girls aren't related. They couldn't look more different, except that they all possess their father's captivating blue eyes. Marilyn is a blonde and wears a perpetual frown. Elizabeth has brown hair like their mother, and sports cat's eye glasses that she clearly isn't happy to be photographed in. Grace's long red hair appears translucent, and her eyes are always squinting against the sun. And little Olivia, with her pixie-cut light-brown hair that has yet to ripen into its true color, is the only sister that smiles. There is no picture of their step-sister, Cari.

Cari came to live with their family more than a year earlier, shortly after her alcoholic mother, comatose one night, had suffocated from her own vomit while passed out on her back. The intrusion isn't welcomed by Doris, who had always been jealous of her husband's voluptuous Italian first wife. But her four daughters are mesmerized by Cari's beauty, her shapely body and her Eastern accent. Experienced beyond her years, she's a 16-year-old girl from New York, with long, flowing black hair and olive skin that is eternally tan. The younger sisters, who range in age from 5 to 11, idolize her.

"Do the dishes. Scrub the floor. And no, you cannot have anything to eat. Dinner will be soon enough," Doris ceaselessly intones to Cari, who has become a perpetually hungry Cinderella without the glass slipper. But Cari isn't the only victim of Doris's sternness. The air in the house can be cut with a knife, and all five girls walk around on eggshells. They spend a lot of time in their bedrooms or in the rickety loft of the dilapidated, old white-washed carriage house where they hide for hours, not quite far enough away from the sound of their mother's spiteful voice prattling on between puffs on her Parliament cigarettes. If they've heard it once, they've heard it a thousand times: "If you dare complain to your father, your life will only get worse!"

Like hungry mice, Grace and Olivia, the two youngest, take to stealing food from the dinner table each night, fearful they'll be the next to fall prey to their mother's punishment of starvation. They sneak their biscuits, carrots, bites of fried chicken and even spaghetti from the table into their napkins and hide them underneath their mattresses, exchanging old, half-eaten morsels for new ones every night. It's quite a risky and elaborate scheme.

It's winter, and the ground in the San Juan Valley of Colorado is covered with fresh snow. Olivia hovers at the back door, staring at the multiple sets of footsteps that lead through the snow to the carriage house. She'd heard yelling and loud bangs and came running from her bedroom, stopping short of the door, her hand reflexively pulling back from the doorknob. The hair stands up on the back of her neck and she moves instead to the window.

Mr. Lewis, a short, round man with thick glasses and a combover—a colleague of their father's—emerges from the wobbly carriage house door, looking disheveled. One hand is tucking the tails of his half-buttoned shirt into his unzipped pants. The other is frantically patting his head in attempt to glue back into place a few strands of hair that have lost their place. He breaks into a near run to his car, all the while struggling with his shirt and his hair, not looking back even once. Olivia shifts her attention to Cari, who is standing a foot from Doris. They are just inside the door of the carriage house, but Olivia can see them clearly and she can hear their words, too.

"He was molesting her! I saw him!" Cari yells at her stepmother. She points a finger at the fleeing Mr. Lewis. "You can't just let him go! We need to call the police!"

"Shut up! Shut up right now! This is no concern of yours!

Go to your bedroom and don't come out until I tell you. Now!" Doris's voice sounds like thunder, and Olivia's body begins to shake.

Cari stands her ground. She stands and stares at her stepmother and then she boldly spits in her face. Olivia sees, as clear as day, the spray of frothy sputum hit her mother's cheek and forehead. And then she watches in utter shock as her mother slaps Cari hard across the face. Cari's hand flies to her cheek in reaction, and then she turns toward the house, toward the window Olivia is peering through, and runs for the back door.

For the first time, Olivia sees Grace. She is wrestling her arm from her mother's grip. In a second, she is free and running after Cari, tears streaming down her swollen face. "You go to your bedroom, too, young lady! I'll deal with you later!" Doris yells after Grace, as she wipes off Cari's spittle with the back of her hand.

Olivia drops beneath the windowsill and runs down the hall to her bedroom closet to hide before anyone knows she was watching. She remains there until dinner, listening to Grace, who is crying on the other side of the closet door. Olivia huddles in the corner of the dark closet, her knees up against her chest with her arms locked around them, repeating the new word over-and-over again in her head, molesting, molesting, molesting. She wonders what it means.

The resulting silence that pervades their house from that moment forward is interrupted the next afternoon by the discovery that Cari has not come home from school. She is nowhere to be found. The only clue to her whereabouts is from Marilyn, who confesses that she'd handed Cari her tapestry carpet bag filled with as many of her belongings as she could stuff in it out the window to her that morning when Cari was leaving for school.

The police are called. An APB is put out. Phone calls are made. Their father paces and cusses, and, like an army sergeant, drills their mother with probing questions. Their mother sits silent, lips pursed, her eyes throwing threatening darts at her daughters whenever their father's eyes are averted. Contrastingly, Cari's disappearance breeds a visible torture in their father's soul.

Olivia begins to have nightmares. The same one every night. They scare her to the point of immobilization, but she never discloses the dream to her parents or sisters. As time passes, the nightmares become less frequent, but they don't stop, not entirely anyway. Cari's face becomes harder and harder to recollect, but the eyes from her dream are branded in her memory, along with a clear image of Cari's tapestry carpet bag.

Cari is brushing Grace's hair. It is long and silky, the color of blazing maple leaves in fall. All the sisters, freshly bathed and dressed in clean pajamas, are watching and listening intently as Cari tells them about the boys she'd kissed when she lived in New York.

The front door bursts open with a loud bang like the sound of a bomb going off. Cari's story stops short. Intruders tear into the house screaming native war calls at the tops of their lungs. Their faces and chests are covered in painted streaks of red and black. They all have long dark hair and are wearing loincloths and leather ankle straps with fringe that flaps above their bare feet. One crowned with a headdress of tall black feathers grabs Cari by the hair and pulls her out the front door while the others stop just short of the rest of the girls and hold their tomahawks in the air, a warning not to follow.

In a second, the warriors are gone. The sisters scramble to the window where they watch, frozen, as the scene unfolds like a horror movie in the front yard. The one in a headdress—clearly the "chief," turns toward the window where the girls' faces are plastered against the glass. Olivia sees in a flash that it is their mother. Doris jerks Cari to her feet and twists her long black hair around her hand. Standing taut, Cari's eyes lock on Olivia's through the windowpane, her gaze intent and calm, as if she is trying to reassure Olivia, to will her strength, to give her hope. Until—the slice of the tomahawk cuts the air and carves a gaping red path through Cari's skull. Her deep blue eyes drain of light and her body falls limply to the ground, while her scalp hangs, dripping crimson blood, from Doris's fist. She turns and sneers at the frozen, deer-in-the-headlight faces of her daughters, who stand petrified behind the window glass. Olivia twists her head away from the unbearable sight, and then, a moment later, looks back to find that there isn't a soul there before her. Instead, the front yard is dotted with unmarked gravestones.

༶

The continual rush of the Rio Grande gives Olivia comfort. The ever-flowing water is in relentless escape, hastily racing south to an unknown outlet, and thence somewhere to the sea. Olivia imagines its destination as vast and mystical, an ocean teeming with possibilities. Every chance she gets she sneaks away, down the few blocks and over the double dikes, a five-year-old entirely unmissed by her family. She invariably sits on the banks, her knees tucked under her jacket, until the snow melts and the winds grow warm. Olivia imagines that it's autumn and the leaves of the trees are in full color. The dreamed-up leaves take a familiar form, they morph into the shape and color of Cari's tapestry carpet bag. She is sure she understands what Cari's eyes have been trying to tell her in her dream. Go Olivia. Find *The Why*. You can do it. You can do it for me.

On summer days, Olivia swims fearlessly in a shallow inlet of the river, blocked from the swift current by a sandbar. The local kids call her "Oli the Otter." She's taken to swimming as if she's grown fins. Under the water, she searches for *The Why*.

CHAPTER SIX

PRESENT DAY

It's the middle of May when Olivia sets off on her trek across the country, alone except for the company of her protective canine chaperone, Tucker. Marco's strong objections and those of their younger son—mild-mannered, level-headed Rio—hadn't convinced her not to go. "What if?" appears to be the common thread of their dissension. The same old reason for everything she shouldn't do these days. *What if* she's exposed to chemicals? *What if* she gets sick and can't take care of herself? *What if* someone takes advantage of her, because she's old and sick? "I'm in my 50s, damn it!" Olivia exclaims to Tucker. "I am not old!" From the passenger seat, Tucker swipes a sideways glance at her and then turns his head back to the road. She swears he just rolled his eyes.

As the miles slip by, reruns of Olivia's married life trail

through her thoughts. Snippets of her two sons when they were little, family vacations and abundant friends bring a smile to her face. But a thought of the friends Marco had chosen casts a shadow over the memories. He is a Gemini, a twin, a man who clones the personality of those around him. And the personalities he tended to be attracted to were those of men who chose to drown their sorrows in alcohol. It always irritated her to think that he needed booze to get through life. But then, it wasn't as if Olivia hadn't had her own vice. She just chose pot instead of alcohol. She misses smoking pot. For Olivia, it's a damn slap of reality that either age or illness has plucked one pleasure after another away from her.

It's the earlier years of her marriage that consume her thoughts until she pulls into a little travel motel just past Akron, Ohio. The room is nondescript, with old carpeting, metal blinds and thin bedding. She strips the linens, replaces them with her own and climbs into bed with Tucker curled up next to her. After a few minutes of texting back and forth with her old friend, Brenda, she considers calling Marco. But instead, she sends him a quick text telling him that they've made it to Akron without any problems. He texts back one word: "Good". Olivia falls asleep to memories of the slippery, satisfying sex she and Marco always made-up with after they fought. It's been a while since they've had one of those sessions, Olivia realizes.

She wakes with a hazy recall of sex dreams and a warm tingly feeling between her legs. Before opening her eyes, she attempts to recall the experience. The man had dark hair, but she's not quite sure he was Marco. She pushes the dreams away and begins the job of carrying everything back out to the car, a chore that drags on her more than she cares to admit.

The sky is dark with clouds today and she drives through bouts of rain followed by stretches of more clouds that threaten to unleash a deluge over the string of small towns she passes in Indiana and Illinois. The gray day turns Olivia's mood somber, and a crack of lightning in the distance summons a dream she had one night during the months that she was being slowly poisoned in their house in New Jersey. Alternating her hands on the steering wheel, she pulls on a jacket to warm her against the goose bumps spreading over her skin.

In Olivia's dream, there had been a sizzling crack of lightning and then a spirit-being who bellowed, "GET YOUR HOUSE IN ORDER!" The vision she had was of an old woman dressed in flowing white, a grandmotherly figure. At first, Olivia assumed it was a message to get ready for death, and so she had. She'd redone wills and sorted through pictures and prepared her family. But the old woman in her dreams hadn't meant that she was dying. Her words were literal. The grandmother spirit was speaking literally, trying to tell her that their *actual house* was the culprit. Thoughts of the mission-style house that had leaked poison turn to memories of her childhood home in Alamosa. She had left that house and town over 30 years ago, with a vow never to go back. She has no idea why she's so determined to return there now—especially to attend a funeral—other than she needs a purpose—any purpose.

They make it to Kansas City just as the sun slips below the horizon. "Pretty good, huh?" she asks Tucker, who is beginning to look disenchanted with the privilege of taking a drive. The long days are wearing on Olivia, as well. She stops at a Panera restaurant to pick up a salad, sends a quick text to Marco and another to Brenda, and then drags herself and her stuff into another old, dilapidated motel. The Hampton and Comfort Inns are much more appealing, she contemplates, but Olivia knows better than to chance a recent renovation with new carpet and drapes that will send her running from the chemicals "off-gassing." She sleeps like a baby, oblivious to the near-constant roar of tractor trailers zooming past her window on the interstate.

On the road by six o'clock the next morning, Olivia is anxious to get this trip over with. The sky is blue today, but the flat, boring Kansas roads and lack of greenery offer her brain nothing to focus on. She stares at the river of road that shimmers as if it were liquid, the mirage pushing out ahead of her just as she gains ground on it. Her thoughts turn to the dreams she's had over the last month. The woman that she conjures must be herself, lost in despair. The little girl, though, she isn't sure about. But the teenager, she is positive that he's a conjuring of her older son, tall lanky Mateo. He is a dark, consistent brooder, not unlike his father. Nearly five years earlier, during the months when she and Marco were being poisoned, Mateo had chosen to separate from both the business and the family. His choice piled pain on top of pain for Olivia and Marco. As a child, Mateo had pride in his family. But once he became an adult, he was never quite happy with any decision she and Marco made. Even now, it's agonizing for Olivia to admit that Mateo has become a person who seems to get a charge out of making his parents suffer. Add to that his flair for the dramatic, and his eventual break from the family played out like a "Lifetime" movie. It didn't take long for Mateo to get another job. And, in the blink of an eye, he and his pregnant wife, Julia, had moved to Boston. Since then, they've brought three little children into the world, grandkids whom Olivia, Marco and Rio have never met. Olivia aches to reunite with Mateo and to know her grandchildren. Her only salvation is that she's close to her son, Rio, his wife, Katie, and her three-year-old grandson, Leo.

Recent dreams of the river jockey for position in her brain amidst thoughts of family members. The pieces of Olivia's life have never fit together quite right. She'd wondered often whether she was truly meant to be with Marco, but, on the other side of those feelings, she would be overwhelmed with an intuitive sense that she was with the exact person she was supposed to be with. Friends would say that she and Marco seemed joined at the hip. None of them knew that she had left him many times, always coming back for the sake of the family. But look where that's gotten her; their sons must have felt the friction that existed between their parents—even more so when they came to work with them in the family business. When thoughts such as these surface in Olivia's brain, as they often do, the idea that it was she who built the tension and resulting wedge between their family members creeps into her conscious thoughts like spiders that have hatched a thousand babies underneath her skin.

The Rocky Mountains emerge in the distance, a display of majesty. A seemingly unending line of purple peaks shoot into the sky, like a solemn procession of sovereign kings calling her home. At the sight of them, tears sting Olivia's eyes and flow unchecked. She finds herself pulling off on the shoulder and leaning into the windshield with her arms hugging the steering wheel, like a child clinging to her favorite "blankie."

Tucker stands in the passenger seat and peers out the windshield, his gaze fixated on something straight ahead. "They're magnificent, aren't they, Tucker?" The mountains are just as she remembers them: the rock-solid foundation of her being, the monolithic background of her youth. She wonders how she ever thought she could escape them.

Pulling the car back onto the road, she races toward the mountains, excited now to get near enough to smell pine and feel the exhilaration. She snakes her way along roads that skirt the edge of rocky cliffs, with drop-offs that seem to extend for miles below her, into a vast wilderness.

In no time, she has her windows rolled down and notices that her ears are building pressure as she makes the steep climb up La Veta Pass. She welcomes the wind as it whips her hair into a frenzy, and she watches Tucker—his head out the window, his wind-whipped lips rippling into an unwitting smile. They climb to the summit and then drop suddenly in descent, ears popping from yawns, coasting for miles, no foot on the gas, like riding a bike with no hands. That is until the San Juan Valley comes into view, when Olivia's exhilaration seeps out of her like a slow leak in a balloon.

Olivia's SUV creeps along the valley floor with the still snow-capped peak of Mount Blanca looming behind her. The evening sun washes across the white foothills of the Great Sand Dunes National Park that ride the right edge of her field of vision, a vivid reminder of annual childhood field trips, when she would wade through what they referred to as "The Disappearing River" and, on snow days, launch saucers and sleds to race down one steep embankment after another.

Ranches and farms slip by, stirring more memories. She's not quite sure, but she thinks she singles out the one where she first learned to ride a horse, and then the farm where her high school science teacher was gored by his own bull, killing him.

She shudders to recall that he'd forgotten the cardinal rule and worn a red t-shirt out into the pen.

A roller coaster of emotions cranks up and glides over her as dusk blankets the sky, and she and Tucker pull up to the Inn of the Great Sand Dunes just shy of the bridge into town. For the first time since she left Vermont, it dawns on Olivia that she's made it across the entire country without incident, without a seizure, without a desperate call to Marco that she's made a huge mistake.

"We made it, fella. Thanks for being my wingman." Olivia takes Tucker's face in her hands and plants a big kiss on his wet nose. Tucker wags his tail, breaks from her hold and sniffs at the treats in the bag on the front floor. "Well, if ever you deserved a treat, it's now." She digs out a handful and lets him gobble them out of her hand. Pride overtakes Olivia as she struts into the lobby like a peacock with its feathered plume on display.

As soon as she swings her legs off the motel room bed, Olivia feels the familiar pounding, the gripping sensation coursing up the back of her neck that arches around to her brow like a c-clamp. Tucker looks at her and whimpers.

"Ugh. Okay, Tucker. Just give me a minute." The clock on the side of the bed reads nine fifty-four. "Jesus!" She hasn't slept this late in years. Olivia pulls on a pair of shorts, struggles into her sneakers and gazes in the mirror. "My God! I am not a pretty sight, Tucker!" He responds with a more desperate whine and an insistent scratch on the door. "Okay, okay," she assures him, as she attempts to tame the rat's nest on top of her head with a few strokes of a brush. On the way out the door, she notices for the first time what the motel room looks like, and that she'd forgotten to open the window, change the bedding or, for that matter, bring her oxygen inside. The c-clamp tightens.

A crisp, welcome breeze hits them both as soon as she opens the door. Tucker is on his leash hightailing it for a spot of grass, tugging Olivia haphazardly behind. The sun is bright and piercing, and she chastises herself for forgetting her sunglasses. A few deep breaths of fresh air prompt her to acknowledge the ferocious growl coming from her belly. She hadn't eaten dinner. Tucker pulls back in the direction of the room. He's obviously hungry, too. Alarm streaks up the back of her neck and radiates along her c-clamp-induced headache. She can't remember feeding him either. Olivia attempts to recall the events of the night before: entering the motel room, bringing luggage in, undressing. But nothing comes to her.

After feeding Tucker and securing him in the room, Olivia sits in the car and takes a few pulls from the oxygen tank, then makes her way into town, starving now for some comfort food. As she drives over the bridge, she glances down at the Rio Grande beneath her and is shocked at what she sees. The once roaring river looks more like a measly creek. The fact that the river isn't even half the width it was when she was young hits her like an arrow to the heart. She's heard that the west was suffering from drought but had no idea it was this bad. Her attention is diverted to the old steam locomotive that sits at the foot of the bridge, marking the entrance to Cole Park. Her shock about the river turns to surprise that the locomotive is still there, and she recalls with a smile how excited she always was to see it dressed in Christmas lights, its wheels flashing greens and reds as they whirled around, making the tons of steel appear to be chugging along in movement.

On Sixth Street, El Charro, the gem of a Mexican food restaurant Olivia was a regular at back in the day, is still there and open for business. The old neon sign flickers and the iron bars on the windows remain intact, protection against the unsavory elements of the south side of town. Inside, red-and-white-checkered table cloths cover old metal tables, and the walls are festooned with Mexican blankets woven in the bright colors of desert flowers and mellow sunsets.

A short Mexican woman leads her to a table while speaking Spanish to her young daughter, who is playing with her doll behind the counter, walking it along the edge and then casting it off in an elaborate dive to the laminate floor.

Enchiladas smothered in green chilies, no cheese, are set in front of her, but not for long. Olivia wolfs them down like she hasn't eaten in days. Forget breakfast, she'd decided. She needs Mexican food, a staple they have yet to get quite right on the east coast. The c-clamp weakens. She orders another plate, extra guacamole. Her phone buzzes. She picks it up to see a text from Brenda.

"I'm so sorry, but I can't make the funeral. My granddaughter is sick, and my daughter needs me to babysit."

"Shit!" Oliva says out loud. No moral support. She looks around the restaurant as if she'll see someone she knows who'll save her from going to the funeral alone. She doesn't recognize a single face. But, after 30 years, she doesn't know why she thinks she would.

"I'm sorry about your granddaughter. I hope it's nothing

serious." Olivia punches the keys on the phone a little too hard, taking out her frustration on them.

"I'll take her to the doctor tomorrow, get her an antibiotic. My daughter can't take off work. She's missed too many days recently and she knew I already had the day off. I really am sorry."

"It's okay. No need to apologize. I was just looking forward to seeing you." She truly was. It had been fun bantering back and forth over the last few days, like they'd never missed a step.

"Will you still be there next weekend? I could come down then, or maybe you could go back home by way of Denver."

"Let's see how the funeral goes. I'll text you tomorrow after it's over. Good luck with your granddaughter."

"Thanks. Make sure you tell me all the juicy gossip ... lol ... xo"

"I doubt there'll be any. But, if there is, you'll be the first to know. xo"

The c-clamp halted by fresh air and enchiladas with guacamole, Olivia now craves something else: to see her old house, schools, hangouts and Jeff's old house on 1st Street. Even though Jeff's dad owned a ranch, the family lived in town, just a few short blocks from the river and the one-lane bridge that leads north.

Olivia swings back out of town to pick up Tucker from his motel room jail and then doubles back to cruise the full length of Main Street. She detours up and down side streets, remembering them as if she'd lived here all along. Not that much has changed. Some new stores and restaurants, new schools and office buildings. But the houses are mostly the same, just older and smaller than she remembers.

Her old house, a white ranch, sits on a corner with a white

picket fence surrounding the yard. She and her sisters used to call it "The White House." Funny how, when you're a kid, everything seems so much grander than it is. The house has been renovated. A new dormer has turned it into a two-story, and an awning covers the extended front porch. Behind it, on the side street, the old carriage house has been re-sided and new garage doors have been installed. Two cars sit in the now paved driveway in front.

Olivia and Tucker sit in her SUV for quite a while. Memories flood her brain: her dad in the early years, teaching her how to ride a bike on this very street; her dad waking her up and taking her out into the yard at midnight to dig for night crawlers so that they could use them as bait the next day when he took her out to the lake to fish; her dad teaching her how to swim at the Adams State College pool. He taught her how to dive too, standing her on his six-foot-three-inch shoulders, encouraging her to fall forward as he guided her into the water. Oh, how she loved her dad, with his tall stature and his devious grin revealing the crooked eyeteeth that he passed on to his daughters. She suffers over these memories, the delightful vestiges of her youth that had been drowned out until they were rendered nearly silent under the roar of others less happy.

CHAPTER SEVEN

1966

The closet is dark but for a single stream of light through the crack that falls across the floor. Grace holds Olivia in place with one hand and works on her with the other, inserting the Barbie doll and then pulling it back out. There is no need to hold her. Olivia doesn't struggle. She knows that if she does, someone will hear. And if someone hears, Grace will be made to go away, and no one will be allowed to ever speak of her again.

Olivia doesn't blame Grace. She knows it isn't her fault. She's heard about demons at church and believes that one has crawled inside of Grace. It has taken her over and makes her sit for hours with her thumb in her mouth rocking back and forth on her bed. They all ache for Cari, ache to know where she is, ache for some bit of news or details. But not a crumb is dropped.

The stream of light becomes Olivia's solace. She stares into the crack where the white light shines, imagining the real white light, the one she saw in the swimming pool when she was three. After Grace is done with her, on days when the weather and circumstances allow, she runs to the river, strips herself down and lies naked in the swift current.

In the river, with her eyes shut, she imagines that a man appears. He's turned away from her, but Olivia can see that he is tall with dark hair. His confident, welcoming hand is stretched back, reaching for hers. She grabs hold and pictures him pulling her up and out of the river. But when she opens her eyes, he is gone, evaporated like fog on a car windshield when the heat first blasts. The sense of safety she felt with his presence vanishes.

Back in the closet a few days later, while Olivia stares again at the stream of light, the man appears in the misty glare. As before, Olivia can't see his face. He is turned away and forward, focused on something ahead. But his hand is there behind him, its long fingers and purposeful intent reaching for her. She closes her eyes, grabs his hand and holds tight while Grace shoves a hairbrush into her and swirls it around like a carnival worker twirling cotton candy on a stick.

This time, after running up the street and over the bank to the river, she pulls her clothes off to find drops of blood spreading like a dark stain in her underwear. Olivia submerges in the water, closes her eyes and lies still, waiting for the tall dark man to reach out and save her.

CHAPTER EIGHT

PRESENT DAY

E ntering Cole Park from Second Street, Olivia parks her SUV, and she and Tucker set out to walk the old familiar terrain. They start out clockwise on the now-paved path that circles the large, egg-shaped patch of grass. It's surrounded by trees: maples, oaks, elms and ash. She remembers the foliage being much denser than it now is. After living back east for so long, amidst such prolific foliage, Olivia now understands why this valley is considered a desert; it rings true. But, when she was a child, she couldn't comprehend how that could be. After all, it was nothing like the desert of Arizona where her family had traveled to see her grandparents.

Tucker sniffs frantically at every new scent along the way as they circle the perimeter. Olivia watches a man jog over a new footbridge that crosses the river on the north end of the park.

At the entrance on the south side, new buildings fill the lots and a skate park has been installed with concrete ramps and jumps. Olivia smiles at the small advancements that update the park. She is pleased, though, that the rustic, small-town feel is still intact.

Needing to rest, Olivia sits down on the grass near the playground. Her respiratory tract is grateful for the warm May air, and the fact that it isn't yet saturated with fertilizer and pesticides so abundantly sprayed onto crops in this area. Those chemical irritants clog her lungs like gunk in a car radiator.

Inhaling deeply, she feels the tension in her head ease even more, allowing her to relax and reminisce. She played softball in this park and ice-skated here countless times, when, every year, the town would flood an outdoor rink. All the town kids would play "crack the whip," skating in circles until one of them—usually Olivia, because she was the youngest—would fly off the end and slide to an abrupt stop against one of the logs flanking the rink's edge. But she'd pop right back up, over and over, ready to go again. She has always been a persistent little bugger, and she snickers at the belief that she still is.

Her eyes drift to the swing set, where she sees a young girl dragging her sneakered feet back and forth in the dirt as she glides forward a few feet and then back again, never letting her shoes leave the ground. She's a lovely little girl with long hair the color of a fawn, pulled back in a ponytail. But Olivia senses that there's something aloof about her, something off. She seems lost, sad. Her head hangs like the too-big, long-sleeved sweatshirt she's wearing. The little girl lifts her head and their eyes meet. Olivia averts her gaze away, toward the old locomotive at the entrance, not wanting the little girl to think she's been staring.

Tucker tugs his leash and pulls Olivia's attention back to him. And then, suddenly, the girl is standing next to them. Tucker is eager to sniff her and lick her outstretched hand.

"He's a goldendoodle," Olivia tells her, unbidden. "His name is Tucker."

The girl nods her head and kneels, taking Tucker's muzzle in her hands, showing no fear of him. Tucker springs forward and knocks her off balance, causing her to tumble backwards onto her butt.

"Oh, I'm sorry! He obviously likes you," Olivia apologizes.

"He's cute," the girl says meekly, pulling herself back onto her feet, "and soft."

"He is soft. It's one of the things I love most about him."

They sit in silence for a minute while the girl pets Tucker and he nuzzles her arm in gratitude.

"Do you have a dog?" Olivia asks.

A shadow passes over the girl's brown eyes and she shakes her head no. Olivia frowns and tries to think of something else to say.

"He died last year," the girl offers up.

"Oh, I'm so sorry. I'll bet you loved him. What kind of dog was he?"

"He was a golden retriever. His name was Mickey." Tears well up in the girl's eyes.

"It's hard to lose a dog. I've lost a few." Olivia looks off toward the riverbank and thinks about the dogs she and Marco had loved and lost over the years. "Maybe you'll get another one someday."

"I doubt it," the girl replies with certainty. "My dad said he was just another mouth to feed."

Olivia's eyes widen, and her jaw goes slack. She has no idea how to respond. The girl stands up, smiles at Olivia half-heartedly, gives Tucker one last friendly swipe, and then turns and walks past the swings. Olivia watches her as she makes her way slowly through the playground and out of the park, scuffing her feet in the dirt as she goes. Olivia finds herself wishing that she'd thought of something wise, something meaningful, to tell her.

Her cell phone rings and it's Marco. She hasn't called him since she got to town. Olivia's attention is drawn away from the girl as she steels herself to be chastised.

"Hello," she answers, her voice clearly on guard.

"Well, hello," he answers back. "I'm just calling to see if you made it there okay. I thought you'd get there yesterday."

"I did. I made it all the way here with no problems." She pauses, realizing that her *no problems* sounds more positive than she feels right now. "I'm sorry I haven't called. I slept hard last night and today I've been a little emotional seeing the old hometown and all. I was going to call soon." Olivia glances around to make sure no one can hear her.

"So, how is it? Like you left it?"

"Yeah, pretty much. How are you?"

"Okay. Boo is watching the window. He misses you and his partner in crime."

"We miss him too. What've you been doing?" She wants to tell Marco she misses him, but the words don't come.

"Not much."

Vibrations stir beneath her skin and she's irritated at his "not much." She guesses he's been sitting in his La-Z-Boy since she left. "Maybe you should work on one of the projects that need to get done around the house or read one of the books I've been trying to get you to read."

"Yeah, whatever. I just fucking called to see if you're okay."

Olivia knows it's her fault that he's angry. But maybe a little anger is good for him. Maybe it will shake him out of the funk he's been in for way too long. "I know, Marco. I appreciate it and I'm sorry I didn't call earlier. I just think maybe you could use this time to move forward, try to get unstuck." There is silence on the other end of the phone, a silence that Olivia is accustomed to. Marco has suffered from depression for most of his adult life, and silence has always been one of his symptoms. His first mid-life crisis was in his 30s, after his father, Vito, had summoned them to Connecticut to work for him and then, within a couple of months, banished them back to New Jersey. Olivia had always felt that Marco was never the same man after that. The entire episode had stripped him of his confidence. And then, in his 40s, just before Vito died of cancer, Marco mustered the resolve to go and see him. He asked his father if he had any regrets, and Vito's reply was to say that the only thing he regretted was no longer being able to work. The response wasn't what Marco was seeking, and it caused him to sink further into himself. And then, a few years back, when his beloved Uncle Leo died, it broke Marco apart. Olivia has been trying to put him back together ever since. Of course, being poisoned in their own house hasn't helped her efforts. She feels like all she's been doing for years is fighting for Marco's life and her own, and she's simply exhausted herself in the effort. She feels burned to a crisp.

"I'm just trying to get you out of your La-Z-Boy," she finally tells him. She can't believe those words just came out of her mouth, but she can't seem to help herself. "You know, we weren't spared death just to sit and stare at the television screen."

"Yeah. You have all the answers."

"I don't claim to have the answers. But I have ventured into town. I've made some friends, taken a couple classes. Even with my disabilities, I try to stay engaged with the world. What have you done to try to move on, to try and find some joy? It's unbearable to watch, Marco!" She knows she's probably gone too far. He's so sensitive these days. But Olivia can't stand it anymore. She misses the confident and charismatic man she married.

"I'm unbearable, huh? Is that why you left? So, you could be away from me?"

"Of course not, and I didn't say that. I didn't premeditate this trip either. I just felt the urge to come. That's all." She takes a deep breath. The c-clamp headache has started in again and all she wants to do is sleep. "I've got to go, Marco. I need to go back to the motel and feed Tucker. I'll call you tomorrow."

They hang up and she looks down at Tucker, who's staring up at her like she just stole his bone. "Don't look at me like that. Somebody's got to push him off that chair."

CHAPTER NINE

PRESENT DAY

O livia is wading in a pool at the shallow edge of the river—a spot where no current runs. Minnows surround her feet. She stands still and then pounces with her foot, trying to catch one between her toes, just to let it go free again. She's stripped down to her underwear, lacking any fear that she'll be seen there, alone in her thoughts and with the challenge of her pursuit.

There's a ledge a few feet out that drops off suddenly, just where the current picks up speed. She's careful not to venture out that far. There's nothing to grab onto between where she's standing and where the river rages, rushing so forcefully in its determined race southward.

She looks up to see a hawk soar overhead. It wheels in descending eddies, circling back and forth before perching on a limb at the top of a cottonwood tree, where it focuses its attention northward.

Instinctively, she turns around to look in the same direction.

A teenage boy with black hair is standing there on the bank a few yards away, dressed in jeans and a black t-shirt. He's got his hand above his eyes to protect them from the glare of the sun. He doesn't appear to see her; instead, something below has caught his attention. Olivia can't make out what it is he's gazing at so intently; the river bends and blocks her view just north of her, flowing from the west before it makes its mighty turn.

She wades quietly out of the water and slides on her t-shirt and shorts, careful not to draw his attention. Moving slowly up and along the river's edge, she takes cover in the low brush each time she feels too exposed, anxious to see what he's spotted. She spies a large boulder that juts out not too far from him, and she pulls herself up and around to the other side of it. Peeking over the top, Olivia spots a woman and a young girl working feverishly on what looks like a raft, weaving tree limbs together with reeds. They're busy tying them off in knots at the ends. The young, red-headed girl breaks away from her work every few minutes to gather more reeds, tripping frequently on a cumbersome, long-sleeved, sack-style dress she's wearing. She heads a few yards to the west, where a stand of river reeds wave in the slight breeze. The girl seems distracted each time she begins to hunt for more reeds, making a summoning motion with one of her arms, as if there is someone on the other side of the river that she wants to join them. But Olivia notes with a bit of alarm that there's no one there.

The woman is intently focused on her task. She doesn't look at or speak to the girl, or even seem to notice the boy, who is fixated on them, watching their every move. The raft grows wider with each added limb, finally becoming large enough to hold one person. When the woman sees the young girl walking away to gather another bundle of reeds, she pushes the raft into the water, wading out and crawl-

ing onto it. The boy drops his hand from his forehead and begins to move down the bank, his feet sliding and catching on roots and rocks. With the woman clinging to it, the raft floats farther out where it finally catches the current. The woman now sprawls across the raft face-down, her arms dangling in the water, surrendering herself to the current.

The teenage boy reaches the river's edge and the girl runs to him, dropping the armful of reeds she's carrying. They meet at the spot where the woman has just launched the raft, waving furiously to her. The boy wades out into the water and then stops short at a point just before the raging current will catch him. Meanwhile, the raft has reached the center of the river and picked up speed.

Olivia's foot gets tangled in a root, and she trips. She can't seem to get free of it. Sweat pours from her body, and she tries to scream for help, but no sound emerges from her throat. The woman on the raft is out of sight now, and the hawk has left its perch, gliding slowly and effortlessly, following the raft as it makes its way downstream more rapidly now. The boy wades back to shore and grabs onto the little girl, and they both drop to their knees and inexplicably begin to sob. Olivia is helpless and bloody now, with even more roots entangling both of her feet. She scratches and claws at them, trying to extricate herself from their vise-like hold, but their sinuous tendrils continue to move upward on her calves, encircling them in a tighter and tighter grip. Helpless, she falls back on the bank, unable to breathe, her hands now at her throat.

It takes a while for Olivia to pull herself from her troubled sleep. Her awareness of the headache that's crept from her ear to her eyebrow becomes more pronounced with each breath she takes back to consciousness. Then, the various, noxious motel room odors hit her with the same intensity as the smell of baking dough wafting up into your nose when you walk into a bakery, but, in this case, not so pleasant. Her eyes finally focus, and she takes stock of the freshly remodeled room and its malodorous scents; too many things "off-gassing" in it, Olivia realizes: carpet, polyester curtains baking in the morning sun, synthetic upholstered chairs, new furniture, the memory foam mattress. She can't believe she hadn't noticed it the morning before when she woke up with a headache or even later, when she'd finally changed the sheets.

Olivia forces herself to shower and dress, and then hastily packs and loads the car. After the funeral, she'll need to find a motel that hasn't recently been renovated. She is way too late for the church service, so she drives directly to the cemetery, parking a distance from the collection of cars assembled just yards from the grave. The sky is overcast, but the atmosphere is that distinct Colorado mix of crisp yet warm air. She ties Tucker to a tree near her car, grabs a bottle of water from the case she has in the back, fills his bowl with it and prays that he won't start barking.

A small crowd is gathered around the grave, with a priest before them speaking a few deliberate words. Olivia keeps her distance, hanging close to a tree several yards away from the service. She realizes that, in her gray silk blouse, black pencil skirt and strappy black wedges, she is overdressed for this assemblage. She spies someone that she thinks must be Jeff's wife, Dana, standing next to the grave. Her hair is a medium-brown and cropped short, and she is wearing a knee-length black dress that is a size too small. She's clutching a white handkerchief in her hand, but she isn't crying. Olivia can see Dana's face clearly, staring off into the distance, its expression more impatient than sad.

She shifts her gaze from Dana to a young man standing a few feet away from her. A shiver of recognition runs down Olivia's spine: he must be Jeff's son. He looks just like him—of medium height and with dark hair and a muscular build. The teenager has his arms crossed and is hugging them to his chest, indicating that he's cold. Olivia surmises that it must be his little sister by his side clinging to him, her legs fidgety, her face buried in the crook of his arm as if she wishes she could disappear.

Olivia scans the small crowd, searching for Jeff's parents, but she doesn't spot them. Instead, she notices his brother and sister, standing apart from Dana and her kids, surrounded by five young adults. Recognizing Jeff's siblings is easy, though their faces are more aged than when she saw them last, and his brother's hair has gone gray. There's only one other person that she can identify: Tommy Johnson, Jeff's best friend from high school. He's got the same shaggy haircut he had back then, but his black hair is now peppered with gray. He's still as good-looking, though, with the kind of rugged male physique that would catch most women's eyes. Olivia's heart skips a beat.

She hangs back until the ceremony is over and the small crowd begins to disperse. A girl that Olivia guesses must be Jeff's young daughter notices her and pulls on her brother's arm to stop. The girl stands stock-still, gazing back at Olivia with an expression of surprise on her face. Olivia realizes that it's the same girl from the playground whom she'd spoken to the day before. She wishes she'd known who she was then. Maybe she would have known better what to say.

Dana walks up to her daughter's side, and, when she spots

Olivia, stops short and cocks her head at her in disbelief. In just seconds, the expressions on Dana's face runs the full gamut of emotions before settling on disdain.

"Hi Dana," Olivia offers with hesitance. "I don't know if you remember me. I'm Olivia Alfieri—or, I mean, O'Keefe," she stumbles. "I'm so sorry for your loss."

Dana looks Olivia up and down and then fixes her gaze straight into her eyes, "I remember you very well. What are you doing here?" she demands.

"Well, I don't know really," Olivia stares back at her, challenging her accusing gaze. "An old friend contacted me and told me about the accident and, for some reason, I felt compelled to come."

Dana looks at Olivia for a long moment and then spits out, "Well, I'm sure Jeff is turning over in his grave."

The smell of alcohol blasts up Olivia's nose and she takes a step back. "Look, I didn't come here to hurt anyone or cause any trouble. There are other reasons I needed to come back, too. I guess this was just the catalyst." Olivia looks over at the teenager and the girl standing nearby and nods her head toward them. "I gather these are your children?"

Dana turns to look at them, hesitating in her response. "Yes, they are," she finally says. "This is Brian and that's Carly."

Olivia silently gasps at the name "Carly." Jeff had always teased her about how much she loved Carly Simon. Olivia had played her albums over and over. She was particularly fond of "Haven't Got Time for the Pain." It had become something of an anthem for her in her last year here. Olivia feels a flicker of uneasiness. Naming his daughter Carly hits a bit close to home. But then, Olivia reasons that she might simply be assuming something here. Maybe their daughter's name was Dana's idea.

Olivia reaches out to shake both the kids' hands and summons the doctrinaire response, "Nice to meet you." She holds on a bit longer to Carly's tiny hand than is customary.

Dana turns away silently and begins walking to her car, but then stops, turns back toward Olivia and blurts out. "Feel free to come back to the house. I'm sure Jeff would just love that." Olivia freezes from the sarcasm, feeling like she's on stage, has flubbed her lines and everyone is silently laughing at her.

Brian and Carly hesitate, looking at their mother and then back at Olivia. Finally, Brian grabs Carly's hand and leads her to the car. But Carly turns her gaze back to Olivia, training her eyes on the woman her mother has just had a few awkward words with. Jeff's sister, as well, has stopped to listen to the encounter. But making eye contact with Olivia is obviously more than his sister can bear. She snaps her gaze away and scurries off to follow her brother and the rest of her family to the waiting cars.

Olivia stands there, bewildered. Although she doesn't know what she expected, except maybe a warmer welcome from Jeff's sister. They'd been friends back when she and Jeff were dating. A hand skims across Olivia's shoulder and she turns around to find Tommy standing behind her. Without a word, he holds out his arms and they hug, giving Olivia the distinct sensation of rediscovering an old favorite sweater that was lost. "Don't worry about Dana," Tommy finally utters. "She's always had a chip on her shoulder about you."

"Me, why?"

"Well you've got to know it took Jeff forever to get over you." He cocks his handsome features into a "come on now" sort of expression.

Olivia looks down at the ground and sighs. "No, I didn't know."

"You did kind of disappear. Like, poof, off the face of the planet."

"Yeah, I guess I did, but I didn't mean to hurt him. I just had to go. I didn't belong here anymore."

"Hey, you don't have to explain yourself to me," Tommy says, throwing his hands up in the air, palms forward. "But, Dana, she's a whole other story. I'd probably steer clear of her, if I was you."

"Well, I'm definitely not going to her house, so I don't think I'll have to worry about that."

"Yeah well, I've got to go; obligations, and all. Wish I could say come with me, but, it's probably not a good idea. I'll brave it alone."

"Aren't you married?"

"Not anymore," he laughs. "The wife left me a few years back. It was my own fault, though. I always had a thing for the ladies, if you know what I mean." His dark, hungry eyes take in Olivia's body, head to toe, and then land back on her blue eyes.

"Jesus, Tommy! You haven't changed a bit." She feels a sudden tingle in her loins and remembers having the same sensations when she was around Tommy back in high school. But Olivia never pursued those "urges," if that's what they were. Tommy wasn't the kind of guy she wanted in her life. The string of girls he burned through back then parade through her mind. "Any kids?"

"One, he lives in L.A. I don't see him very often. He moved there with his mother when she left me. There's not much reason for him to come back here."

"I'd say you're a good reason."

"Well thanks. At least somebody still recognizes my charm."

Olivia chuckles and gives him a light shove on the shoulder. "Charm is not something you were ever short of." Tommy flashes a big, sexy smile. Olivia looks down at her shoes and scuffs the grass back and forth. The name "Carly" reappears in her brain.

"How about you? I heard you married some guy from back east."

She lifts her eyes back to his. "I did. And we're still married."

"Well, good for you. So, maybe while you're here you'll come to my restaurant for a bite to eat and we can catch up. I own 'Tommy's' downtown."

Olivia looks up, "Really? You own a restaurant? I would never have guessed that's what you'd do with your life."

"Oh yeah? What'd you think I'd do?"

"I don't know, something more playboy-ish, I guess." They both laugh at the word, and he extends his arm around her, guiding them toward the remaining cars.

"Sorry to disappoint you. I went to culinary school in California and then came back here and opened my restaurant. Been here ever since."

"Well, I can always use a good meal. But I've got to tell you that I'm gluten- and dairy-free, at least most of the time. It's a long story." She shrugs her shoulders in a way that conveys that she's tired of telling it.

"I can do that, no problem. Half the stuff on my menu is gluten-free and it's easy to keep the dairy out."

"My mouth is watering already." Tommy cocks an eyebrow and Olivia scowls at him. "But just dinner, Tommy."

He throws his hands up again, feigning innocence. "Okay,

okay, just dinner, but I have to say, Olivia, you do look really good for an old broad—skinny—but good."

"Old broad! Screw you!" She fails to tell him that most of the time she feels like she's 90. They both laugh and Olivia gazes back toward Jeff's gravesite, which is now empty of funeral-go-ers. "I think I'd like to hang here for a little while. I haven't talked to Jeff in over 30 years. I guess now's my chance."

"I understand. Olivia, it's been great seeing you. I hope you take me up on my offer. I'd like to hear about that lucky husband of yours."

They hug again, holding each other for what seems like min-utes. He smells musky, pure male. Olivia's eyes follow the sexy sway of his butt as he walks to his car and drives away. She turns and walks back to Jeff's gravesite and kneels on the soft ground. Staring at the flowers thrown onto the casket, she begins to talk to Jeff in a low whisper. She tells him about her life, her husband and her kids, about the years when they were growing up, the family business and about being poisoned. She talks to him freely, like she did when they were teenagers, back when he knew everything there was to know about her. Her tears come suddenly and rain onto the freshly turned earth. Olivia picks up a handful and sifts it between her fingers, the moist, loamy soil somehow connecting her to Jeff. She closes her eyes and prays for him, for Dana, for his family and for her own.

She sits back and lets the sun that has gradually emerged from the clouds drench her with its warmth, hoping it will relieve the headache looming on the side of her head. She closes her eyes and listens to the birds singing and fluttering about in the trees around her. A slight breeze brushes her face every now and again as she sits there, remembering her life then and thinking about what it would have been like if she'd stayed here.

Finally, she lifts herself from the ground and walks to her car, where Tucker is lying under the tree, snoozing. "Oh, Tucker boy, how about we go for a little walk?" Olivia offers, thinking maybe some exercise will make her feel better. Tucker obliges enthusiastically, and they walk around the paths and graves of the small cemetery, Olivia's legs intuitively steering clear of the south side. In contrast to the typical jam-packed cemeteries on the east coast, the short, neat rows of headstones shaded by trees seem sparse and spacious. She recognizes some of the names on the headstones and wonders if they are the relatives of her adolescent friends.

Thoughts of Jeff have attached themselves to her like needy children to their mother. Eventually, she feels like she needs to slough them off, along with the memories of her teenage years. She pushes her thoughts back into their proper hiding place, leads Tucker back to her vehicle and drives off down the solitary road leading into town.

CHAPTER TEN

PRESENT DAY

The pain that's been lying in wait crawls up and around the side of Olivia's head and she feels the sudden urge to vomit. Swallowing hard, she attempts to focus on the road, chastising herself for not realizing the motel room wasn't safe for her. She has no idea what took her so long to recognize it. Next thing Olivia knows, her SUV has veered off the road and—SMACK!—hits a tree head-on. Her chest slams into the steering wheel and Tucker flies off the front seat into the dashboard. No airbag deploys.

"Fuck!" Instinctively, she reaches over for Tucker. "Are you okay, boy? I'm so sorry!" He crawls back onto the seat and lets out a little whimper. Olivia examines him but doesn't see any blood, although he flinches when she touches his left front leg. Her breath is labored and she starts to panic, pressing her hands to her chest. The first thing she thinks of is oxygen—she needs oxygen. The tank she's brought with her is standing in the back seat and she reaches around, pulls the tube to her nose, twists the handle and sucks on the oxygen until her breathing regulates and she can turn her attention elsewhere, like to the throbbing in her chest. They sit, both stunned, until a voice in Olivia's ear startles her.

"You okay in there?" She looks up and sees a weathered old man with a hunched back standing next to her car. "I was drivin' by and noticed ya here. Looks like ya took the turn a little fast, eh?"

Olivia sighs. "Yeah, I guess I did. I think we're okay, just bruised a little."

"Good thing. You coulda killed the both of ya." He motions to the front of the SUV, which has smoke billowing out from the crumpled edges of the hood. "Looks like ya need a tow. I can give you and your dog a ride into town. On my way there now."

Olivia looks the man up and down and glances back at his truck. He seems friendly enough, and she doesn't have any other choice right now. She hooks on Tucker's leash, grabs her purse and crawls out the door, her chest throbbing with every movement.

"Name's Fred. I'll take ya to Jeb's. He's got a tow truck and he'll be able to fix your car, if it's fixable." He sticks out his hand. Olivia shakes it, wincing from the effort.

"Hi, I'm Olivia and this is Tucker. We can't thank you enough for your help." She says, as she gingerly walks over and painstakingly pulls herself up into his truck, urging Tucker to jump up and sit on the floor in front of her. Tucker pauses, and Olivia can see the pain in his face as he forces himself to jump. She glances back at her smoking SUV and silently reprimands herself for letting this happen.

Neither Fred nor Olivia speaks on the drive to wherever they're going. They just rumble along in his old pickup truck, while Olivia racks her discombobulated brain to figure out what she's going to do now. Fred pulls up in front of the service station, one Olivia recognizes from way back when. There are rusted-out cars flanking the sides of the lot behind newer ones waiting to be repaired, and old parts of every shape and size thrown into piles stacked as high as the station's roof.

"Well, here we are." Fred eases out of the truck and lumbers around the side to help them out. Olivia guesses he noticed that her hands were clutching her chest the entire way. "You want I take ya to the hospital?"

"No. No thank you. I'll be fine, really. Thank you for your help." Olivia doesn't do hospitals; too many dangers lurking behind those revolving doors, especially for a chemically injured person.

A burly guy with gnarled mechanic's hands, whom she gathers is Jeb, sends his bored-looking, twenty-something son to go get her car. She sits on a little chair out front of the old, grease-smeared repair shop, sipping a bottle of cold water and consoling Tucker, as she watches the boy maneuver the tow truck out onto the highway. Olivia pulls a fruit and nut bar out of her purse in an effort to calm the jumping beans in her belly. It does stop her stomach from growling but does nothing for her headache or her throbbing chest.

Jeb's son pulls up with her SUV hooked-up behind the tow truck, releases it back down onto the ground and pushes it into one of the service stalls. Jeb uses a crowbar to open the buckled hood and tinkers around for a while before he emerges from the service bay and walks over to Olivia with a grin on his face. "Looks like you did a number on the radiator. I'll have to order one. Don't have it in stock. You'll need a hood, too, and a few other parts. Probably take me a week or so to get this thing back runnin.'"

"A week or so! Really?" She panics over the idea that she's got to spend a week here with no place to stay and no car. Marco is going to love this. She grimaces at the thought of the inevitable conversation. "Can you fix the airbag?" she asks.

Jeb wobbles his head back and forth. "You'll need to take it to the dealer for that."

Olivia contemplates driving back across the country without a working air bag and finally sighs in acceptance of her predicament. "Do you know where I can rent a car?"

"Sure. There's a place out on the road to the airport. If you wait awhile, I'll get my son here to give you a ride." Jeb turns back toward the shop and lets out a little chuckle. Olivia doesn't get the joke.

She sits there for quite a while waiting on Jeb's son, whatever his name is, when she spies Brian, Dana's son, coming out of the convenience store across the street. Olivia ties Tucker's leash to the leg of the chair and crosses the street. "Hey Brian, remember me? I met you earlier at the funeral." Olivia reaches her hand out to shake his. But the pain in her chest makes her flinch and she withdraws it.

Brian stops and looks at her. He genuinely resembles his dad, from his shaggy black hair to the way he stands, right down to the toothpick he's rolling around in his mouth. "Yeah, I remember you."

She launches into her story, talking fast, like she tends to do. "Well, I've gotten myself into a little bind here. I wrecked my car on the way back into town and I need a ride to the car rental place out by the airport. Any way you could possibly give me a lift?"

Brian hesitates for a minute, looks over at the station, rolls the toothpick around with his tongue, and then shrugs his shoulders. "I guess so."

"I'll need to get some things out of my car. Do you think you could help me with that? I kind of hurt my chest in the accident and I'm not sure I can manage very well."

"Sure, whatever." He gets in his truck and follows her across the street. Jeb emerges from one of the bays and Olivia hears him tell Brian that he's sorry about his dad. Brian doesn't respond.

They make their way slowly along Main Street, in silence for a few minutes. "Dragging Main," they called it back in her day, when they'd cruise up and down, flipping a u-turn at the one dead end, and repeating it over and over all night long.

"What kind of dog is that?" Brian's question pulls her from her memories.

"He's a goldendoodle. His name is Tucker." The conversation with Carly about her dog dying creeps in. It's the first time she thinks about the fact that it was Jeff who told her that the dog was just another mouth to feed. That's not the Jeff she remembers.

"My mom hit our dog a year ago when she was backing out of the driveway." Brian utters this matter-of-factly, like he's talking about the weather or something just as banal. Olivia's surprised he's so forward with this information. Her tongue is tied just like it was the day before with Carly. She thinks about the smell of alcohol on Dana's breath and wonders if she was drunk when she hit the dog. Olivia changes the subject.

"So, Brian, do you have any suggestions where I might find a motel that'll take a dog? It looks like I'll be staying here longer than I expected, and I had a problem with the motel I stayed in the last couple of nights."

"Don't know much about motels." He scrunches his mouth up, moves the toothpick from one side to the other and scratches his head.

Olivia takes a long, sideways glance at him. He's a good-looking kid. She can't get over how much he looks and moves like Jeff did when he was that age.

Brian nods his head sideways toward Olivia, like he's acknowledging her stare. "Mrs. Capricci's had a 'room for rent' sign up for the last few weeks."

Olivia smiles at the thought that he thinks she's in need of a rental. "Well, I don't need anything for that long, just a week maybe, if that."

"I don't think she'd care."

"Okay ... So, who's Mrs. Capricci?"

"She lives a couple blocks from us. I've known her all my life. She's kind of known as the crazy old witch lady."

"Crazy old witch lady, huh? That's kind of scary."

Brian chuckles. It's a nice sound to hear from a kid that doesn't look like he laughs very often. But then, he did just lose his dad.

"Nothing to be afraid of. She's just, uh, different, that's all."

The throbbing in Olivia's chest gets louder as if to remind her it's there, and a queasy feeling rises in her throat. "Could you take me there?" She blurts out, surprising herself.

Brian looks over at her. "What about the rental car?"

"I'm feeling like I could use a place to lie down. I think the rental car may have to wait."

They continue down Main Street and then north on State,

driving a few blocks in silence. Then Brian asks, "How did you know my dad?"

She sighs, wondering what to tell him, but decides the truth is best. "I was his high school girlfriend."

Brian turns and looks at her, his mouth contorting into a sarcastic grin. "I guess that explains my mom's reaction."

Olivia doesn't say anything, but she can feel her heart beat faster and the throbbing in her chest pound harder. She wonders what he thinks of her. For some reason, it seems to matter to her. It's hard to read his face. She can't tell if he thinks that it's funny, her showing up, or just plain pathetic.

They drive past Jeff's parents' old house, where a few cars line the street. It looks the same as Olivia remembers it, except for the wood siding that's peeling and in desperate need of paint. Brian bears right onto Cascade and stops at the end of the street in front of a small and charming—if somewhat dilapidated—old house. Sure enough, there's a sign hanging from the picket fence, "Room for Rent."

CHAPTER ELEVEN

PRESENT DAY

The old house looks like a cottage from a Thomas Kincaid painting, covered in ivy and surrounded by gnarled old trees with branches that seem to reach out like arms poised to hug you. Brian and Olivia get out of the pickup, leaving Tucker to wait inside, and walk through the white picket gate onto a flower-bordered stone walkway that winds its way to the front door.

There is color everywhere: yellow alyssum, pink soapwort, clusters of blue flax and purple delphinium that stand tall above the rest, and even red and orange poppies. There are lilac bushes with rich lavender blooms, covered with butterflies gracefully dancing from one bloom to another, searching for nectar. An old lamppost stands a few yards from the front door, heavy with wisteria flowers drooping from a vine that has wound itself up and around the post, until all that's visible of the post is a piece of glass at the top, glinting in the sun. Brightly colored birdhouses dot the lower limbs of trees, and tiny thrushes flit from the branches to the birdhouses, pecking at the last few morsels of seed.

All the gardens along the front and around to the side of the house are shaped like circles, each boasting a fruit tree as its centerpiece. There is an apple tree, a pear tree, an apricot and cherry and even a plum and a peach tree. Olivia is amazed that she can name each one. The land around the rock-bordered tree gardens is either burgeoning with spring flowers or covered with low-growing herbs. Among them, Olivia recognizes thyme, oregano and mint. Slate stepping-stones have been placed strategically throughout. Olivia stops and bends toward some mint, breathing in the fragrant aroma, knowing it to be a soothing remedy for headaches.

The stone front porch is covered with clay pots filled with dahlias, nasturtiums, geraniums and, Olivia's favorite, pansies. Flower baskets overflowing with purple, pink and white petunias hang from the beams. Bumblebees buzz from flower to flower. There are towers of river rock cairns balancing in a row across the front of the porch and randomly situated between flower pots. Olivia gets a sense that each is positioned where it is for a distinct reason. Two battered old rockers creak in the gentle breeze, as if there are spirits in them, rocking through an afternoon tea. Olivia and Brian maneuver through the pots and cairns and find their way the few steps to the front door. Olivia's hand brushes the strands of an old, tarnished wind chime that hangs just to the right of the door. Its bell-like tone suffuses her with a peaceful joy tinged with nostalgia, evincing a temporary pause of the throbbing and nausea.

Brian stands with his hands in his pockets, looking somewhat uncomfortable, until the door creaks open. A woman, no more than five feet tall and with a large gray bun at the nape of her neck opens the screen door and steps out onto the porch. Her face—although it doesn't droop with severe, overlapping wrinkles like those of a smoker or drinker—does show deep, prominent creases across her forehead, at the corners of her dark eyes and on the sides of her European-looking nose and bony chin. These features, and her round, owl-like and deliberate eyes, doubtlessly reflect years of earned wisdom. Olivia immediately recognizes that she is in the presence of a bona fide "crone", one deserving of her reverence. Yet, despite her wizened appearance, the woman's clothing is youthful and whimsical: a purple t-shirt emblazoned with a large yellow sunflower, white cotton capris and Keds sneakers that surely must have once been white but are now dirt-stained the color of brewed coffee. Olivia notices that this intriguing soul has only one bit of jewelry, a single wedding band wound around her left ring finger.

"Ahh, if isa no da leetle robber baron," the woman utters in Brian's direction, with a mirthful twinkle. "Isa bout time you come by to see me." She laughs a prickly little laugh, and her dark eyes sparkle with delight as she pokes Brian in the shoulder. Then she turns her attention to Olivia. "When he'sa small boy, he'sa climb over ma fence to steala ma raspberries. One day I catch him and smack him on da behind with ma garden hoe!" This time her laugh is more pronounced, and she reaches up and pinches Brian on the cheek. "You always a cute leetle fella and now you grow up to be a good looker." She stops laughing and grows silent, her hand landing on Brian's arm. "I'ma so sorry to hear about you fodder." She squeezes his arm and Brian drops his eyes to the welcome mat that is so worn the only letters remaining are an 'L', a 'C', and an 'M'.

The old lady lifts her twinkling eyes to regard Olivia. "So, how are you, Olivia? Isa been a long time since I'va seen you around here."

Olivia takes a step back and grabs onto the weathered porch post as a small electrical charge courses through her body from head to toe. "How do you know my name?" she asks with a shaky voice.

"Wella, mia amore, you used to walka da banks of dis river like a clock-a-work and I always spend a lotta time in ma garden." She points a craggy finger toward the back of the house. "You were a strong head leetle one. That'sa fo shoo."

"But how do you know who I am, and how did you recognize me?"

The old lady bursts out with a cackling laugh. "You no remember me?"

"No. I don't think so."

"Oh, you no worry about dat. I'ma shoo you no foget me now. So, you need a place to stay?"

Olivia looks at Brian to see if he's got a clue about how she knows, but he just shrugs his shoulders. "Well, yes I do, but I'll probably only need something for about a week." She glances back at the pickup, where Tucker is hanging his head out the window, staring at them. "And I've got a dog."

"Wella, course you do." She slaps Brian on the shoulder. "Betta make youself useful, boy, and bringa her tings in da house." The old woman looks back at Olivia. "Whata you stand

der fo? Dat dog looka like he tirstier dan a fish in da desert!"
Mrs. Capricci eases herself back through the screen door and it
catches behind her. Brian and Olivia turn and head back down
the stone walkway, following her orders without question.

When Olivia shows up back at the door with Tucker, there's
a bowl of water sitting just outside of it. Tucker doesn't ask permission to slurp it down. The door has been propped open with
a watering can and once Tucker's had his fill, they venture in.
Brian is on their heels, hauling the oxygen tank and the few bags
Olivia had felt she needed. He drops them onto the old wood
floor with a thud.

They stand just inside the door waiting for Mrs. Capricci,
who has disappeared beyond the living room into the back of the
house. It takes Olivia a moment to get her bearings. The odors
in the room hark back to the days when Olivia would walk into
her beloved grandmother's old three-story boarding house in
Denver. It smells of dusty books and old tapestry throw pillows,
antique furniture, braided rugs and seasoned wood floors. There
is so much to take in. Her eyes scan the living room. The windows are full of plants: some hanging from the ceiling, others
sitting on the ledges and generally overtaking each other's space
like a jungle; spider plants and creeping Charlie, ivies and ferns,
a rubber tree, scheffleras, a weeping fig and even a lemon tree.
Philodendron plants wind their snaking tentacles around pots,
up walls and over curtain rods. The large south-facing bay window is covered with succulents, cacti and flowering bromeliads.
Two burro tails, teeming with long-trailing stems, hang on each
side. In the center of the wide shelf sits a crown of thorns, metic-
ulously twisted around and around into a thick circle, lush with
blood-red flowers.

There are books stacked haphazardly on shelves and in rickety towers on the floor. Collections of crystals and an array of polished healing stones in all colors and sizes lie about. The walls are decorated with frames displaying butterfly collections preserved in glass, ancient arrowheads and skulls, snakeskins and old rusted farming tools. An antique rocker sits in the corner on a round woven rug, a tall iron lamp with a stained-glass shade standing behind it like a sentinel. Dishes of feathers and smudging sage bundles, and silver plates filled with white candles of every height and circumference cover every available bit of remaining space.

With the weather outside unseasonably warm, a large fan is rattling around in the center of the room to cycle the air. Though it's early in the season for air conditioning, Olivia sighs in relief when she scans the room and sees no sign of vents or window units. Air conditioning makes her generally achy and unable to sleep. They never turn it on at home and she's kept it off in every motel room along her journey.

Mrs. Capricci emerges from the back of the house and motions to Brian, who is removing the watering can so that the screen door will close. "Bringa all her tings to da bedroom back behind da kitchen. You no wanna wounded woman to lifta heavy bags." Brian glances at Olivia. His eyebrow is cocked as if to say, "I told you," and immediately picks the bags back up. The two of them follow Mrs. Capricci as she shuffles through the living room and the kitchen, which also is packed with plants and treasures, then through a short hall and into the bedroom at the back of the house. For a short, elderly Italian woman, Mrs. Capricci's shape is much different than what you might expect. The old woman isn't round and loose, but, rather, lean and firm, with visible muscles that have been toned and maintained.

Mrs. Capricci instructs Brian to arrange Olivia's bags against one wall and then turns to Olivia, whose eyes are fixed out a large bay window on the backyard, which is a vision to behold. The window has a seat overlooking a massive, abundant garden that has obviously taken years and a loving hand to nurture.

"You can look in da garden tomorrow. Righta now you needa lie down." Mrs. Capricci pats her hand on the bed, coaxing Olivia to sit. Olivia is still holding Tucker's leash, but Mrs. Capricci takes it from her and hands it to Brian. "Take dis dog out to do his business and make a shoo he no do in ma yard." Brian walks back through the house with Tucker. The front door squeaks open, and slams shut behind them.

Mrs. Capricci pats the pillow on the bed, "You lie down. I'll be backa pronto wit a fix fo dat bruised chest and one fo da dog's front leg."

"How did you know about my chest? And how do you know about Tucker's leg?" Olivia's beginning to believe there's something about the crazy old witch lady story.

"He'sa favoring one leg. As fo you, don't aska how an old lady knows tings. She justa do." Mrs. Capricci leaves Olivia to get acquainted with the bed.

She is skeptical at how intuitive, or psychic, or whatever it is this old woman is. But right now, she doesn't care. She lies down with her head on the pillow, suddenly feeling the effects of the day wash over her like a tsunami. Looking around the room, she notices that all the fabric, curtains, bedspread and pillows appear to be cotton. She doesn't smell any unnatural smells, either. Instead, her nostrils are filled with the cleansing aroma of lavender. There are fresh-cut stalks jutting out of a cracked purple vase sitting on top of a scarred wooden dresser.

The room is a comfortable size and is painted a warm yellow green. Olivia notices now that there's a bathroom just through the door next to the dresser. She glimpses an old claw-foot tub with a showerhead hanging just above. The thought of soaking in a hot tub makes her muscles ache for the soothing release. But she knows her body needs rest first.

The front screen door creaks open and shut, and the click of dog's nails on the old wood floors fills the silent air. Tucker rounds the corner into the room and draws himself up onto the bed. Olivia notices that he doesn't take his normal leap but works his way up gingerly. The old woman knows what she's talking about. "I'm sorry, Tucker boy. I didn't mean to hurt you," Olivia tells him, her hand gently petting his leg in attempt to love his pain away. Tucker flinches and whimpers, his eyes lifting to meet hers. She pulls her hand away. "We'll get some rest and then we'll both feel better." She hears the murmur of voices in the distance, but can't make out the words, something about a rental car.

Just as Olivia is dozing off, Mrs. Capricci shows up carrying a tray bearing a steaming pan, some cheesecloth and a towel. Olivia rises onto her elbows, "Is that sage I smell?"

"Still gotta you sniffer, I see. Now justa lie back down and unbutton dat fancy blouse. I gotta work to do," Mrs. Capricci says in her old, crackly yet authoritative voice.

Unbuttoning her blouse, Olivia becomes aware for the first time of a half moon-shaped red mark that has formed on her chest. Mrs. Capricci gets busy with her callused hands arranging sage leaves that have been heated in what smells like vinegar into the cheesecloth and then folding it into a neat rectangle. The woman leans over and positions the poultice on Olivia's chest and covers it with a towel. A flicker of light catches Olivia's weary eyes as it reflects off a silver chain that is hanging around the woman's neck, but then disappears beneath her t-shirt. Olivia hadn't noticed it before and, for a split second, she wonders what the chain is suspending. But then the soothing warmth of the heated towel diverts her attention. The pervasive scents wash over Olivia's skin and waft into her nostrils with a healing quality. She moans and closes her eyes.

Mrs. Capricci doesn't say a word as she ministers to Tucker in the same manner, wrapping a similar poultice around his thigh, but using a piece of jute to secure it in place. Peeking through her heavy eyelids, Olivia sees that Tucker isn't even trying to remove it. Like Olivia's, Tucker's eyes are squeezing shut, his body surrendering to the same exhaustion as hers. The last thing she remembers is the sound of the bedroom door closing.

CHAPTER TWELVE

1970

Tlivia is still Grace's slave in the closet. The frequency of these episodes has decreased over the years, but Grace still holds her spell over Olivia, manipulating her through displays of thumb-sucking weakness and threats of hurting herself.

On this blue-sky summer day, Grace lures Olivia to the house next door, where she promises that the two teenage neighbor boys are showing off a new litter of puppies. Once in the boys' cluttered bedroom, someone locks the door behind them and the negotiations begin.

"Okay, 20 bucks," Grace declares to the older boy of 15.

"Ten is all we have," he replies with a smirk on his face.

"Where are the puppies?" Olivia asks, after searching the room with her eyes. The trio ignores her.

"Our deal was 20," Grace demands.

"Well, like I said, 10 is all we have." The younger of the two teens, a gangly 13-year-old wearing a Grateful Dead t-shirt, looks nine-year-old Olivia up and down with hungry eyes and takes a step toward her.

"Fine, but next time it's 20. Give me the money first." Grace holds her hand out and the boy slaps a wadded-up 10-dollar bill into her palm.

"What's that for?" Olivia asks, confused and now anxious.

The older, more muscular teen raises his eyebrow and curls his lip up to one side as if that were an answer to her question. The younger boy pushes Olivia onto the bed releasing a blast of his foul-smelling breath directly into her face.

"Stop it! Get off me!" Olivia protests, her heart pumping so loud she can hear it. Her words fall on deaf ears. The older boy joins in, pressing his arm against Olivia's chest to hold her down, while the younger one pulls at her shorts. Olivia begins to kick. The younger boy pins her with his legs to stop her from kicking. "Grace! Grace help me! Stop them!" Olivia is frantic. But Grace stands still and silent in the corner of the room, watching.

Frenzied, Olivia's eyes dart uncontrollably from the boys to Grace and then back to them, as their hands excitedly explore her body. Fear consumes her, causing her heartbeat to accelerate into a staccato thump-thump-thump. Desperation overtakes her. She finds herself uncertain if she should just let go and succumb to this attack, like she has to every one of Grace's, or if she should fight back. Confusion muddles her brain. The boys rip at her t-shirt and the younger attacker, having trouble pulling her shorts off, sticks his hand down the front of her pants. Olivia's eyes catch sight of a majestic bur oak tree through the window. One of its long branches hangs over the pool and appears to be moving, as if it's reaching out to her. The dark-haired man appears in her mind, the one from the closet and the river daydreams. He morphs to life from the tree itself, his body facing away from her. One of his hands is firmly holding on to a limb, while his other long arm stretches back toward her. He is attempting, with all his might, to pull her to safety.

A hot spike of pain travels up inside of her, from the bottom of her foot to the crown of her head. It feels as if she's been struck by lightning. It gives her strength—an explosion of white-hot intensity that seemingly comes out of nowhere. With one thunderous scream, Olivia frees her arms and simultaneously digs her fingernails into both of the boys' cheeks as they hover over her, cutting their soft facial skin like knives, carving crevices that immediately turn a shiny crimson.

Startled by her strength and resolve, the teenagers jump off Olivia and clutch at their cheeks, blood smearing onto their hands. They both turn to the mirror that hangs over their dresser to gawk at their wounds. Olivia takes the opportunity to flee from the room, but before she exits she shoots a look of piercing hatred at Grace. No longer the victim, Olivia wrestles with the door lock and finally escapes in a fury.

She runs blindly toward the river, sheer energy propelling her. No tears however; Olivia has been transformed. She is no longer the same girl she was that very morning. She walks along the top of the bank, feeling no need to wash herself clean. She continues along until the river turns south, picking up speed as she proceeds. A hawk high in a cottonwood tree catches her eye and she stops short, the rage roiling in her gut finally forcing its way out as she opens her mouth and releases a screaming roar. Startled, the hawk launches from its perch, and begins a wheeling flight, dipping down, hovering just yards from Olivia, exposing its red tail. The hawk appears to nearly stop in mid-air to make eye contact with Olivia before soaring off to follow the river south.

"Wella, I see you founda you power, mia amore," a voice speaks from behind her.

Olivia spins around in the dirt. A small middle-aged woman with long dark hair and fanciful eyes has suddenly appeared out of nowhere. She is just a few feet from Olivia, sitting peacefully on a fallen log on the side of the path, peering up at her with a knowing grin.

CHAPTER THIRTEEN

PRESENT DAY

What seems like days later, Olivia is aroused by the rejuvenating smell of chicken soup wafting through the crack of the bedroom door. The moon is in the night sky and there's a glow over the garden that spotlights the tiny insects whirling about. She looks down and notices that the poultice is gone, and her blouse is buttoned. She can't remember if she was the one who did it or not. She scratches her head, which wakes Tucker, who stretches and plops his paw onto her cheek. Olivia kisses his paw and he lets out a great big yawn that finishes with a deep canine groan. On that note, the door opens, and Mrs. Capricci enters carrying another tray in her arms.

"Isa time you getta some substance into dat skinny body of yous. I make you soup. Sit up now and eat some."

Once again, without question, Olivia does as she's told, her mouth already watering for the taste of salty broth. There's a small, hand-painted terracotta vase on the tray with a beautiful deep purple delphinium in it, and a white-linen cloth napkin wrapped in a tiny ring of grapevine. Sparkling water bubbles up in a hand-blown green glass, and a thick slice of homemade bread sits on a sturdy pottery plate next to a soup bowl.

"It looks absolutely delicious," Olivia tells her. "But I'm sorry, I can't eat the bread. I'm gluten-intolerant."

"Sure, you can. I bake it wit da almond flour. Just eat it, you see. You body needa substance. You mucha too tin—and no helty. You body no have nutrition. We gonna work on dat."

Dipping the rounded soup spoon sitting on the tray into the broth, Olivia slowly tastes the soup. It coats her throat and seeps down into her belly, warming her from the inside out. "Mmmm …" She doesn't remember ever having had such delicious soup. It's thick with parsley and reeks of garlic. She takes another spoonful, and then another.

"Slow down. You musta eat you food slow," Mrs. Capricci scolds.

Olivia puts down the spoon and hesitantly takes a bite of the bread. She hasn't eaten bread in ages. It tastes sweet, like a slice of honey. Her eyes roll around from sheer pleasure and land on Tucker. "Oh, I need to feed Tucker! He must be starving." She puts the bread back on the plate and starts to push the tray off her lap, wincing in pain. She notices, though, that it's subsided a little from the deeper, throbbing ache she felt that afternoon.

Mrs. Capricci holds up a callused hand to stop Olivia. "You staya where you are. He'sa food is in da kitchen. I can no carry it all at once. You keepa eating, but slow, slow." For emphasis, she pushes her hand down twice, like she's kneading a piece of bread.

"Wonder what's on the menu for you, boy," Olivia says, as Tucker mirthfully moves closer to her tray, sniffing.

Mrs. Capricci rounds the corner with another tray in hand. She sets it on the floor and turns to Tucker. "Here you go, boy; deener." Tucker slides off the bed and limps over to a bowl of soup and piece of bread, served on the exact same pottery as Olivia's. The only difference is that, instead of a glass of sparkling water, he has a pottery bowl filled with water. All he's missing is the napkin and flower.

"That's his dinner?" Olivia asks. "I've got food for him right there in the bag. He has a lot of allergies and needs special food."

"Baga, shmaga. I would no feed dat poison to rats. He eat what we eat." She moves her hands to place them on her hips and stares Olivia down.

Olivia bites her lip and looks down at Tucker, who is gobbling up his dinner, happy as a clam, and then back up to Mrs. Capricci. Olivia shrugs her shoulders. "I guess he likes it."

"Wella, course he does."

"I must say this is some of the best soup I've ever had, and well, I haven't had bread in ages."

"I can tell," the old woman scoffs.

Olivia savors every bite, while Mrs. Capricci stands guard. She wonders if the old woman is going to watch her every move. Strangely, though, Olivia doesn't want her to leave.

By the time she's licked the last morsel from her fingers, her belly is fully satisfied, and she realizes that she needs to go to the bathroom; she's sure that Tucker does, too. Olivia hands her tray to Mrs. Capricci and swings her legs to the side of the bed, pushing herself up. Unbelievably, the pain in her chest is just moderate. "I need to go to the bathroom," she tells Mrs. Capricci.

"And then I'll take Tucker out."

"No, no. Brian isa coming right now. He take a da dog fo da walk. I make a deal wit him. And he getta da rest of you tings froma you broken car, too."

Olivia hesitates and hangs by the bathroom door, really needing to pee. "What kind of deal?"

"No you worry you pretty leetle head. Now go on and do you business."

Olivia closes the door behind her and sits down on the toilet, wondering what kind of deal Mrs. Capricci has made with Brian. This kid is a teenager. Olivia's sure he's had more than enough of doing favors for some stranger lady, especially one that used to date his dad. She hears the click of Tucker's nails on the floor, the rattle of dishes and the squeak of the front door, all before she's able to get herself up and out of the bathroom.

Walking toward the kitchen, she runs squarely into Mrs. Capricci, who presses on Olivia's shoulders, which are almost a foot above hers, and turns her back around, "Oh no, no! You getta back in bed. Tomorrow is soon enough fo you to be up."

"But what about Brian? And Tucker?"

"I tell you, no worry about him. He happy to walka you dog and in da summer, I give him ma raspberries," Mrs. Capricci cackles. "He justa love ma raspberries. Like a fodder, like a son."

"I remember that. Jeff used to surprise me with fresh raspberries. I always wondered where he got them. They were from your garden, weren't they?"

"Like I say, like a fodder, like a son. He no always ask eder."

They share a laugh, the kind that only women share, and Olivia bends down gingerly to open her suitcase, searching for a t-shirt to sleep in. Mrs. Capricci retreats to the kitchen while Olivia changes her clothes, grabs her phone and slips back into the bed. She'd promised Marco that she'd call him today. She pushes the green "call" button and steadies herself for the conversation ahead.

"So, how did it go? Everything you expected?" Marco asks without saying hello.

"It's been a long day, Marco." Olivia sighs and continues. "Some unexpected things happened."

"What things happened, something at the funeral?"

"Well, not exactly. More like on the way back from the funeral." Olivia pauses for a moment before letting the cat out of the bag. "I wrecked the car."

"You what? Are you okay? Jesus, Olivia!"

"I'm sorry. I guess I was going too fast around a bend and I ran into a tree. But Tucker and I are okay; a little bruised, but okay. The car's another story."

"Well, I'm glad you're both okay. What happened to the car?"

"It needs a new radiator and a hood and a few other things." She cringes and waits for his response. This time it's is a little different: a few "shits!" and "fucks!"

"I know, I know. It was an accident. People have accidents. At least we're okay. Can you focus on that?"

"I guess I'll need to come out there now."

"No, you don't. I'm taking care of it. The car is at a shop and they're working on it. It'll just take a week or so." Olivia braces herself again.

"A week or so!" The words hang in the air while he attempts to come to terms with what he just heard. "Did you need medical attention?"

"Well, no, not really. I just bruised my chest on the steering wheel. But, well, Jeff's son gave me a ride and brought me to this old lady's house, and she's taking really good care of me. She let me rest and made me the most delicious soup."

"What are you talking about? You're at some old lady's house? And are you telling me the airbag didn't go off?"

"Yeah, I don't know why the airbag didn't work and the guy at the station said he can't fix it. He says I've got to take it to a dealer. And well, I was going to tell you that I had trouble at the motel last night and was going to look for a new one today. But then Brian told me about this room for rent and he just brought me here. I think she's a blessing in disguise. I already feel so much better."

"So, some old lady … in her house … making you soup?" Sarcasm drips from his accusing voice.

"Yes. Her name is Mrs. Capricci. She remembers me from when I was a young girl."

"Hmmm. So, you'll be staying with this … this Mrs. Capricci … the whole week?"

"I think so. We haven't really gotten that far. She seems kind of lonely, though, like she could use the company. And the room is perfect for us. It doesn't seem to have anything in it that's letting off any unnatural odors, and it has a bay window that looks out over the most beautiful garden that butts up to the bank of the river."

"Olivia, I hope you … I hope it … I hope you're okay. You know how fragile you are, right?"

"Yeah, yeah. I know, I know. But I'm not as fragile as you think I am. And I am careful." She's not sure if she's trying to convince Marco or herself.

"Yeah, so careful you wrecked the car."

"It was an accident. Come on, you can't talk. You've had enough of your own."

Silence ensues while Olivia imagines he's recollecting the various accidents he's had of his own over the years. "So, how was the funeral?" he asks again.

"Nothing to tell; really, I only saw one old friend, Tommy Johnson. Other than that, the only odd thing was that Dana, Jeff's wife, reeked of alcohol and wasn't very nice to me. But I guess I shouldn't expect her to be."

"Maybe she's just grieving. Sometimes alcohol helps."

"Yeah, maybe. Whatever." Olivia doesn't want to talk about Dana to Marco. The whole episode feels like it's from a totally different lifetime.

They hang up the phone after saying their goodbyes, just as Olivia hears Tucker scratch at the bedroom door. She gets up to let him in and to peek around. She gets to the kitchen and there's Mrs. Capricci, standing guard again.

"I tell you, you no get outta bed!" she says commandingly. "We talka tomorrow and really starta work on putting some meat on dose skinny bones." She extends a stubby finger in the direction of the bedroom and, without a word, Olivia and Tucker slink back in.

CHAPTER FOURTEEN

PRESENT DAY

Rays of sun stream through the window and fall across the bed, their warmth waking Olivia from a deep slumber. She's startled at first, not sure where she is. But her mind soon draws itself from sleep and into the day. She slowly remembers all the events of late, and she sits up to gaze out the bay window. The huge backyard faces east, just below where the river bends, and so it is drenched in sun. Delicate white honeysuckle blooms and bright blue morning glories capture her attention. Because it's so early in the season, the fact that they haven't just made a sparse appearance, but, instead, are abundant, is bewildering to Olivia. The richly colored blossoms wind their way up the trellis that borders the window, basking in the morning light. A patch of lavender catches her eyes, invoking a smile. Obviously, it's where the fresh cuttings on the dresser came from. She pulls a deep breath of the lingering scent in while again wondering how these plants could possibly be so far along in May. Tucker stretches and yawns, and then covers his eyes with one paw. Olivia peels back his paw and kisses him on the top of his nose, "Wake up, buddy." Tucker rolls over and spreads his hind legs, eager for a scratch.

She softly caresses the skin around his injury, gently massaging it back and forth and then around in circles. He doesn't even flinch. Olivia's hands instinctively go to her own injured chest. Astonishingly, it feels fine. She stands up in front of the mirror hanging above the dresser and lifts her t-shirt. Only a few faint red blemishes offer a hint that there ever was an injury. She raises her arms, moves them about and—nothing—no pain.

Olivia washes her face and brushes her teeth, pulls her long dark hair into a ponytail and slides her thin legs into a pair of shorts. Tucker's already at the door, sniffing the crack at the bottom. They make their way into the kitchen, where Mrs. Capricci is hard at work. "Good morning." Olivia greets her sheepishly, feeling guilty that this woman has been waiting on her hand and foot.

"Buongiorno, mia amore. You feela better, no?" Mrs. Capricci surveys Olivia with knowing eyes, nodding her head up and down as she speaks.

"I am. I'm feeling pretty good and I think Tucker is, too. I think maybe you worked some magic on us with those poultice remedies of yours."

Mrs. Capricci smiles and winks. "We all have a leetle magic in us, mia amore. Even you."

"Oh, I don't know about that."

A sumptuous spread of food is laid out on the kitchen table, and Tucker has begun lapping up his breakfast from a nearby bowl. Olivia's not certain, but she thinks he's eating granola.

Mrs. Capricci waves her hand toward the table, "Sit down—mangia. You needa you strengt."

Olivia pulls the chair out and sits down, wondering what Mrs. Capricci thinks she needs her strength for. There are fresh blueberries and a granola mixture that looks home-made, with grains, seeds, nuts, berries, some dried greens and two fresh nasturtium flowers sitting right on top. A beautiful, old, red teapot, with steam curling from its spout, graces the middle of the table, and a small pitcher of milk sits just off to one side.

"This looks absolutely delicious, Mrs. Capricci, but I'll have to eat the cereal dry. I'm lactose-intolerant and can't have dairy."

"Oh, bah child! Dat a goat's milk. I get it straight from da goat at Mr. Twill's ranch." She picks up the pitcher and pours it over Olivia's cereal.

Olivia hesitates, wanting to argue, but instead she picks up the spoon and begins to eat. Everything is as delicious as it looks, and she gobbles some down. She'll know sooner than later if the milk doesn't agree with her digestive system, but decides not to worry right now. Not a strategy she typically pursues.

"Slow down, mia amore, savor you food. Da body like it better when you take a you time."

Olivia stops mid-spoonful and rolls the granola around in her mouth, chewing slowly. Mrs. Capricci is right: it tastes much better this way. She smiles up at the old woman, who raises her hands in an "I-told-you-so" gesture. Olivia laughs, a little goat's milk spilling from the corner of her mouth and dribbling onto her chin. As if in exasperation, Mrs. Capricci shakes her head and pours Olivia a cup of tea. But a twinkle of satisfaction shines in the old woman's eyes.

Olivia scoots her chair back and sips her tea. She takes in the kitchen, overfilled as it is with stacks of cookbooks, kitchen gadgets that she's never seen before, and a full herb garden in the greenhouse window behind the sink, with three avocado plants bearing fruit in the middle of it. A collection of colorful god's eyes dangle from hooks in the corner of the window. Tied bunches of herbs hang in clusters from the ceiling. Pottery of all shapes and sizes fill the glass-front cabinets, along with stacks of little glass jars stuffed with dried herbs and spices. And there are vegetables and bowls of fruit freshly gathered from some garden, maybe Mrs. Capricci's own. In keeping with the abundant theme, there are plants hanging in macramé holders and flower pots competing for every available space.

Olivia's high-school bedroom comes to her mind. It was loaded with plants of all kinds. Jeff had gifted her a spider plant her freshman year and her love of plants grew from there. A memory of the then giant spider plant that Olivia had left for her dad when she'd moved out the day after graduation brings a smile to her face. It had been one of the delights Olivia could offer him, that every so often pulled him out of the despair he had sunk into ever since Cari's disappearance. Olivia had instilled in him a love of plants. Breaking away from her reverie, she suddenly decides that plants need to make a re-appearance in her home. She tries to remember when and why she ever stopped growing them, or why she hasn't ever planted the garden she'd always dreamed of.

Just as Olivia finishes her cup of tea, Tucker lays his head on her knee and wags his tail. "Oh Tucker, you need to go out." She stands up just as Mrs. Capricci hands her the leash. "I'll do the dishes when I get back, I promise."

"Just take a you time, child. Go tru da vacant lot and up da bank. A morning walk along da river will do you bot good."

"Thank you so much, Mrs. Capricci. Breakfast was wonderful, and I promise I will do the dishes when I get back."

"When you get back, we go out to da garden, okay? You can helpa me der."

Olivia begins to argue but abruptly stops. Instead, she bends down and kisses Mrs. Capricci on her wrinkled, rosy-red cheek. Their eyes meet for a moment. Olivia is sure she sees tears in the woman's dark eyes before Mrs. Capricci turns away and shoos them out the front door.

In the clear morning sun, Tucker leads Olivia up the bank and, when they reach the top, her eyes widen and her heart sinks. There it is, the Rio Grande, but not looking so grand anymore—at least not this year. They stand at the top of the bank and Olivia notices that the river sides don't even look the same. It's as if the banks on both sides have had their rounded tops sliced off. Olivia imagines it happened from the wear of weather and from people treading on them over time, but it doesn't seem natural; it's as though a bulldozer has cut across the top of them. She doesn't want to believe they're the same as she found them 30 years ago, and that her memory has tricked her into believing they were more massive than they were. She gazes back down at the river and knows for sure that it isn't the same magnificent rushing body of water it was when she was a kid. Back then, at the mere sight of it, the Rio Grande had the power to suck her in and grab hold of her soul. Now it just saddens her, looking as if it's dying a slow death. Olivia lets out a long sigh. Tucker turns to look up at her for a second and then tugs her forward and down the embankment.

Mrs. Capricci is right. Olivia used to walk this river as often as she could, even in the dead of winter. It brought her relief from the storm that was forever brewing in her house. All those girls stuck there, so unsure of how to move on, a father lost in grief and a mother in a constant, manipulative game to bury her actions and her daughters' reactions to them. Olivia used to believe that she was like the river, that she was meant to flow outward into the world, and that, once there, she would uncover *The Why*. But now, over 30 years later, her hopes are as bleak as she finds the river.

She unleashes Tucker and they trail along the river's edge, her sandals now dangling from her fingers, her toes digging deep into the sand. Tucker, now free to roam, frolics in the water, chasing minnows and biting at them playfully. Olivia darts back and forth with him, drenching her shorts in the chilly shallows, until the two of them finally wear themselves out. Olivia plops down on a log, arching her torso backwards to dry off in the sun. Her gaze turns upward toward towering Mount Blanca that, with its snow-white peak, stands like a watchtower at the edge of the valley. Olivia recalls the mesmerizing stories she'd been told as a child about how the Navajo people called it the Sacred Mountain of the East. The legend described how the mountain was covered in daylight and dawn and fastened to the ground with lightning. The stories invoked Olivia's awe when she was young, and they still do.

"Hi Tucker," speaks a small voice from the top of the bank. Olivia swings her head around to see who it is.

"Oh! Hi Carly. How are you?" Olivia rises and follows

Tucker up the bank, where he dashes to meet Carly, who doesn't immediately respond to Olivia. She's focused on the dog.

Olivia tries again. "Do you walk the river often? I was up here all the time as a kid."

Carly, her long-sleeved gray sweatshirt mottled with sweat, continues petting Tucker. She takes her time to respond. "Did you love my dad?" she finally asks.

Olivia doesn't hesitate. "Yes, I did."

"Then why did you leave him?"

The answer is sitting in the front of Olivia's brain. But she's unsure of how to explain it to a child. "Well, sometimes, even when you love someone, you have to leave."

"Why?"

"Hmmm. Good question. I guess because I wanted to leave Alamosa and your dad didn't. And, well, we were very young."

"Did you still love him afterwards?"

"Well, I cared about him." Olivia's eyes follow a squirrel scampering from one tree branch to another. "But we both fell in love with other people."

Carly casts her eyes downward. "He still loved you."

Olivia is taken aback by the words she's just heard, spoken by a child who doesn't know her or anything about her relationship with Jeff. "Why do you say that, Carly?"

Carly pulls away from Tucker and looks Olivia straight in the eye. "Because, sometimes he called me Oli."

Before Olivia can get her mouth to work, Carly turns and runs off down the bank, disappearing quickly between a couple of houses in the near distance. Olivia stands dumbstruck. She had no idea Jeff ever thought about her anymore. No wonder Dana has such animosity toward her. Tucker brushes against her leg to get her attention.

"Okay, okay. Let's go," Olivia says, with mild irritation. She clips the leash on Tucker and they head back. On the way, she tries to meld her memories of Jeff with the man she's learning he was today. Disenchantment envelops her, and she is over-whelmed with the feeling that she was stupid for coming to his funeral. When Mrs. Capricci's house comes into view, it stings Olivia with embarrassment to realize that she'd never offered Mrs. Capricci any money for the room. "Great job, Olivia!" she mutters to herself. "You're certainly batting a thousand!"

Olivia finds the perfect clothesline pole under the blanket of a maple tree, and she wraps Tucker's leash around it so he can dry off before going back inside. After scuffing the bottoms of her dirt-clad feet on the bristly mat, she swings open the screen door and heads inside to discuss rent.

Mrs. Capricci has taken off her apron and is sitting in her rocker wearing a big floppy sunhat, flipping through what looks like a medical book. "How was you walk, mia amore?"

"It was good I guess. We got a little wet. I tied Tucker up under the maple tree on the side of the house, so he can dry off."

"Perfetto. Take a him a bowl of water and I meet you in da garden."

"Before we go, there's something we need to discuss. I feel just awful. I never asked about the rent." Olivia lowers her eyes and shakes her head, disgusted with herself.

"Well, you no go nowhere. Der'sa plenty time fo dat."

"No, no. I need to pay you. You've already done so much. What do you charge for a week's rent?"

"Two hunnerd dollar a mont. Does dat sound okay?"

"More than fair. And even though I'll only be here for a

week, I'll pay you the two hundred. Most rents don't include food, you know? I'll need to pay you for that, as well." Olivia pauses, realizing what she's just said. "Um, that doesn't mean I expect you to keep feeding us." She blushes from what she senses her statement implies.

Mrs. Capricci smiles at her and waves her hand in dismissal. "I tella you befo, you needa put some weight on." She gets up and begins to walk back toward the kitchen. "And you be here longer dan you tink."

CHAPTER FIFTEEN

PRESENT DAY

rs. Capricci plops a large, floppy, bright-purple hat on Olivia's head. "You needa dis to protect you face from da sun."

Olivia's hands lightly skim the brim of the hat and she adjusts it on her head. Funny, her dermatologist had just told her a couple weeks before that she needed to buy a hat. He said the only skin that showed any sun damage was her face. She smiles quizzically at Mrs. Capricci, who smiles back with that knowing look on her face that Olivia is beginning to feel more than a little suspicious about.

"Let'sa go," Mrs. Capricci directs. "We gotta work to do befo lunch."

When Olivia emerges from the back door onto the stoop, she notices for the first time how truly magical this garden is. It is a sea of diverse greens and yellows, dotted with oranges and whites, purples and reds. The backyard plot is very large: the width of two normal-size lots. Laid out in two perfect circles, each probably 50 or 60 feet across, the circles bear a center and outer wheel divided into six equal pie-shaped slices around the outer circumferences, sort of like pizza slices with the points cut off. There are walking paths of crushed stone in between each slice and around the center circle. Both circular plots are surrounded by a foot-high stone border, each with only one entrance that is sited precisely on the west side. The garden circles are so perfectly designed that they remind Olivia of sacred geometric mandalas.

Mrs. Capricci gives Olivia a tour, beginning with the south circle and walking clockwise around the planted surfaces, explaining to her that the garden is like life, flowing in a circle that must be respected for the direction of its course. It is planted with low-growing herbs and vegetables, so as not to block the sun of its neighbor, the northern circle. They walk the gravel paths up and down each and every row as Mrs. Capricci points out basil and parsley, oregano and thyme, comfrey and sage, rosemary, bee balm and lavender. There are rows of multiple varieties of lettuces, kale and chard, onions, leeks and carrots, and there is summer squash and zucchini and eggplant. The northern mandala hosts broccoli, beets, cauliflower and peppers, peas and beans that are beginning to wind themselves around handmade trellises; and there are garlic plants and potatoes, staked cucumbers and too many tomato plants to count.

"What are these metal posts for?" Olivia asks as she grabs onto one of the uprights that stake out the inner and outer circles.

"Dey are da frames fo da greenhouses attach. Ramone put dem up in da fall and take dem down in da spring. Dat way isa grow all year. I use trays to grow da seedlings." Olivia visualizes what two large greenhouses covering these circle plots would look like, thinking that they must be as difficult to put together as a Rubik's cube.

Mrs. Capricci makes her way outside of the mandalas and to the perimeter of the garden. Olivia follows in a state of awe. Pumpkin, watermelon and cantaloupe patches line the southern-most section of the yard. There is a raised rock bed along the western side near the house that is packed with ornery strawberry plants. Raspberry bushes occupy a distinctive patch on the eastern side, segregated from its neighbors by a deep trench to thwart the raspberry plants' tendency to snake their roots underneath the soil. A horseshoe that wraps around the northern side of the yard and spreads part way down the eastern and western stretches is planted with stalks of corn and sunflowers, positioned so as not to block the sun as the stalks and stems grow taller than their neighboring plant species. It is highly evident that to design and create such a well-planned plot has taken the skills of not just a master gardener, but a mathematician, a horticulturist, a botanist and much more.

The entire backyard is bounded by a short wooden fence that apparently has never been painted or stained. Its warped boards and splintery surfaces convey a feeling that the fence sprouted up there unplanned, like a wild stand of saplings might. And at last, the perimeters are sprinkled with orange and yellow marigolds, presumably to ward off hungry predators.

Olivia stands in the presence of this great accomplishment and breathes deeply. The multiplicity of scents doesn't seem to bother her like strong fragrances typically do. Instead, she finds them filling her with vigor and the desire to dig her fingernails into the soil and nurture the plants that radiate such beauty and offer such nourishment.

Mrs. Capricci pushes a weed hoe into her hands and points toward the northern circle. "You pulla da weeds over der and I take a da harvest. Later, you helpa me fix da hole in da fence behinda ma raspberry bushes. Some animal pusha der body tru again."

Olivia looks back toward the raspberry bushes and strains her eyes to find the hole. She can't spot it, so she shifts her vision to the northern circle. "How will I know what are weeds and what aren't?"

Mrs. Capricci lets out a little cackle. "You justa know, dat's all."

Olivia heads over to the northern plots to evaluate the situation, poking around the plants with the hoe. She quickly realizes that there's little doubt which are vegetables, and which are weeds. It's not like she's never gardened before. Just not for years, not since her kids were small. She digs with the hoe, pulling her victims into a pile. But it doesn't take long before she abandons the hoe altogether and settles down on her knees and uses her hands to pull up the invaders.

She works around one plot and then another, beads of sweat eventually forming on her forehead and streaming down her cheeks and neck. She swats at a gnat now and again or pushes stray strands of hair back behind her ears. Her fingernails grow dark with dirt, and she smears it across her face as she attempts to wipe away the sweat. One large weed gives her trouble, its roots unyielding to her tugging, as if they're set in mortar. It makes her think of Jeff—stuck Jeff. But her thoughts turn quickly to Marco—stuck Marco—who's been immovable most of their married life.

Marco's father, Vito, was the culprit, Olivia reasons; one powerful, intimidating, unyielding man. He'd started his business back in 1970, when Marco was just 13, and he'd had little time left over to serve as a parent. So Marco rebelled.

Olivia disdainfully recollects the day Marco took her to meet his father. It was to a backyard family party where dozens of Marco's large Italian clan had gathered to celebrate a cousin's engagement. Marco walked her up to his domineering father and introduced her. Olivia promptly saw the resemblance between the two men and knew in that moment exactly what Marco would look like in 20 years. She also knew instantly in that moment that she would be by his side when he got there. Vito, however, thought differently, and wouldn't even acknowledge her. Instead, he spun around and walked away without a word. Olivia had never felt such humiliation, all those eyes on her, standing right in the center of them all. It was very clear. Even Olivia, who wasn't Italian, knew his father had thought her a *puttana*—a whore—for shacking up with his son.

Olivia had used that day as kindling, and she had used it all the way up until Vito was dead and gone and she was running their own company right next to Marco. She'd always stewed over the fact that she had taken the rejection from Vito and used it as fuel to prove her worth, while, conversely, Marco had used it as grounds to sell himself short.

From encouragement to ultimatums, Olivia had tried everything she could think of over the years to imbue Marco with some spunk and fight. But he always dwelled in a state of depression or resorted to alcohol, even before their son, Mateo, walked out of their lives, and before they were poisoned in their own home. The thought of that poisoning rears its ugly head in her consciousness. There's a reason Marco froze after that happened. Not only had he ignored Olivia's pleas about her symptoms, but there's also a possibility the crack in the sewer pipe was caused by a renovation he'd haphazardly begun in their master bathroom. Olivia certainly hadn't held back her beliefs about that.

"Ouch!" The weed she'd been struggling with while her thoughts were lost in the past has sliced her wedding ring finger. She'd been pulling with both hands, but the weed was stronger, more intent on saving its life than Olivia had judged. Mrs. Capricci scurries toward her and commands Olivia to follow her into the house.

"You have da artritis in you fingers," Mrs. Capricci tells Olivia, as she examines the finger she has just cut. "You no should eat da night shades so much."

"What are night shades?"

"Potatoes, tomatoes, peppers and eggplant. Dey cause da inflammation."

"But I love potatoes!" Olivia is distressed at the thought of more things she can't eat.

"You can still eat dem, just no more dan every fo days. You body needa time in between."

Olivia's concern dissolves. Four days? She can do that. "Your garden is remarkable," she tells Mrs. Capricci, as the old woman wraps a poultice of comfrey around her finger, securing it with plastic wrap to keep the moisture in. "There's so much going on back there. It's amazing that you can keep it all up." Olivia stops, feeling like she's just said the wrong thing. "I didn't mean you couldn't do it," She stumbles with her words, trying not to offend. "I just meant it's a lot for anyone."

"It feeda many. And it keepa me young, it do. Besides, I have a helper."

"Oh, I didn't know. I guess I just assumed …" Mrs. Capricci looks up at Olivia in the same way anyone might when someone says, I just assumed—like she's a jackass.

"Ramone will come by tomorrow to fixa da hole in da fence," Mrs. Capricci says, turning to wash the greens for lunch.

"I thought you wanted me to help you fix the hole. I can do it after lunch."

"No, you can't. And keepa youself away from ma raspberry bushes."

Olivia raises her eyebrow, knowing full well that she's allergic to them. "Why do you say that?"

"You allergic, no? And justa fo you knowledge, da roses are on da far side of da house, outside ma bedroom window."

"How did you know that I'm allergic?"

Mrs. Capricci stops what she is doing, turns from the sink and raises her eyebrows. "Da looka on you face when I tell you about da boys picking dem. And den again when I tell about fixing da hole in da fence."

"You figured out I was allergic from the look on my face?"

Mrs. Capricci raises her eyebrows again, cocks her head and turns back toward the sink.

"Okay, so then how did you know about the roses?"

Mrs. Capricci doesn't turn this time, but just keeps working at the sink, the cinnamon roll-size bun woven from her long gray hair highlighted by the glimmering sun streaming in through the window. "Dey go togedder, da same familia."

Olivia stands behind her, staring at her bun, contemplating the psychic knowledge this woman apparently possesses. Maybe she can tell Olivia why she wasn't allergic as a child but became so as an adult. Her eyes move to the window and the maple tree. "Oh, Tucker! I forgot about him. He's been so quiet. Do you mind if I bring him in? I'll be right back to help with lunch."

"Take a you time. I no needa you help." Mrs. Capricci wipes her hands on her apron, turns her back to Olivia and begins to search for something in the refrigerator. Olivia clearly hears her mumble. "Some time what we tink are allergies are justa something else in disguise."

Shaking her head in astonishment, Olivia's now certain that this woman can read minds. Still, she has no idea what that statement means. Olivia's need to share the events of the past couple of days with a confidante is increasing and becoming immediate. She grabs her cell phone, sits under the maple tree next to Tucker and texts Brenda, who instantly calls her for the scoop. The words spill out of Olivia, piling up on one another.

"Jesus! And I figured you'd already hightailed it home," Brenda exclaims.

"Can't. No car."

"Oh yeah. Well, I'm definitely coming down there now. I can be there Saturday afternoon. I'll stay with my cousin. Okay with you?"

"Fine with me. But, what am I going to do until Saturday?"

"Go see Tommy. He'll keep you company," she laughs.

"Yeah, just what I need." But she reasons that maybe it's exactly what she needs.

The words "keep you company" remind Olivia of the one man in her life who has always been there for her, Rio, her younger son and most trusted confidante. She quickly sends a text to fill him in on her trip. Rio texts her back, threatening to come get her. "Lol," she responds. "I don't need rescuing. But thanks." She unties Tucker and they head inside for lunch.

ॐ∿

"You ready to go?" Brian shouts through the screen, just as they're finishing up the colorful garden salad and freshly baked flatbread pizza that Mrs. Capricci has so skillfully prepared from gluten-free flour, goat cheese, fresh tomatoes and basil.

"Go where?" Olivia shouts back, as she walks to the door, wiping her mouth with a small linen napkin.

"To rent a car," he says with irritation, as if she should know why he's there.

"Oh. Okay. Let me just get my things and make sure it's okay with Mrs. Capricci."

"She told me to be here at two."

Olivia looks toward the kitchen and then back at Brian. "Okay then. Just let me get my purse."

Once underway, they turn left onto State Avenue to head through town. "So, does your family live in your grandparents' old house?" Olivia asks. She wants to break the silence, but also wants to confirm that they live there. The idea that she should visit Dana has just popped into her head.

"Yeah, we just passed it."

"I know. I was there many times as a teenager."

Brian looks over at her with his eyebrows furrowed up. "So, what was my dad like in high school?"

Olivia settles back in her seat. This she can talk about. "He was shy and quiet, but he had a great, kind of dry sense of humor, and everybody liked him." Olivia laughs before she adds, "As a matter of fact, I used to poke him with my finger all the time to get him to talk at all."

"Then why did you leave him?"

The second time today she'd been asked that question. She stumbles again, not really knowing what to say to this teenager she just met. "I—I guess Alamosa just wasn't where I was meant to be."

"That doesn't tell me why you left him."

She sighs and thinks about it for a minute. "Your dad didn't want to leave Alamosa. He always wanted to take over his dad's ranch, and I knew I couldn't stay here."

"Why not?"

"Well, to be perfectly honest, my family wasn't the happiest family to grow up in. I guess I needed to get away from them more than anything else." A sharp twinge of sadness pierces her to think that when she'd left Jeff and this town, she had also left her dad.

"Oh," Brian says, turning thoughtful for a moment, as he takes the right onto Main Street and shifts the toothpick in his mouth. "So, my dad was happy once?"

Olivia glances at Brian, not sure why he said "once." "I remember him as a very happy person, kind of a happy-go-lucky guy. I'm sure he was happy with you and your sister." She remembers that her dad was happy once, too.

Brian's eyes grow dark and he shifts in his seat. "Yeah, well then you didn't know him very well."

The sudden hint of anger in his voice startles her, shaking her free from the way her mind is shifting from Jeff to her dad. "You're right. I didn't know him at all as an adult. Maybe he was unhappy about the ranch or something. But I'm sure he was happy to have you and Carly."

Brian doesn't respond. He just waits for the light to change and then turns south onto the highway that leads to the airport. Olivia notices a tattoo on his arm; she'd seen it yesterday but hadn't really focused on it. There's a moose below an owl sitting on a branch with the moon behind it. It's very well done, she thinks, better art than most of the stuff you see on teenagers these days.

"Are you still in school?" she asks, trying to change the subject. She's sized up Brian and thinks that he looks like he's maybe 17 or 18.

"Senior. Graduate in a few weeks."

"Do you have a job for the summer?"

"At Tommy's place. I wash dishes and shit."

"Oh, my first job was washing dishes at The Campus Cafe. I loved it. Do you like working for Tommy?"

"Not really. Who likes washing dishes?" Brian throws her a look like she's a dishwashing freak. "I liked shoveling shit on the ranch more than washing dishes."

"So why don't you work on the ranch?"

"I did, until about a year ago. But then, my dad couldn't afford to pay me anymore. So, he told me to get another job."

"Oh." Olivia shifts in her seat. It sounds like maybe Jeff was having some financial problems. She thinks about the comment Carly made about their dog the day she first met her and changes the subject again. "Brian, do you think your mom would be okay with me stopping by your house. I'd like to tell her how helpful you've been to me." She has no idea why that just came out of her mouth. But she's suddenly compelled to go see Dana.

He looks over at her, his eyes a little wider, his mouth biting down hard on the toothpick. "I don't think you should do that."

"Why not?"

He pulls up in front of the rental car center. "Want me to wait and make sure you get a car?"

She hesitates for a minute, wondering if she should press him about going to see Dana, but then decides he's just a teenager with an attitude about his mom. She doesn't need his permission. "Yeah, that would be nice. I'll wave when it's okay for you to leave. Thanks for this, Brian, and thanks for walking Tucker last night. Well, just thanks for everything."

"Yeah."

Olivia gets out of the car to walk inside, but Brian stops her. "You want to put my number in your phone? You know, just in case—being that you're a foreigner and all." He throws her a sarcastic look, one that tells her she most definitely doesn't belong here. Olivia pulls her phone out of her purse and logs his number in her phone.

The attendant takes forever, and 20 minutes pass before Olivia waves at Brian that it's okay to leave. He waves back and rolls out of the lot and onto the highway. She watches him as he goes, wondering what he's got against his mother and his father. She remembers her kids at that age. They were damn moody. She shakes it off and turns back toward the attendant as he hands Olivia the keys to the snappy new Ford Fusion.

She opens the door and climbs inside, taking one breath and then jumping back out. "Oh shit!" She forgot about the canned "new-car" smell and the chemicals they use to clean these vehicles. There's no way she can drive around in this. Standing by the side of the car, she takes a few deep breaths in an effort to ward off the migraine or seizure that she usually experiences from this type of exposure.

She looks off down the highway, fumbles for her phone and dials Brian's number. He's back in two minutes. "Thanks so much for coming back."

"Didn't expect it to be this quick," he snorts.

"I have a problem with the smell in new cars. I forgot that I can't tolerate them."

Brian doesn't ask her any questions and she's relieved that he doesn't. It's always so hard to explain to people about her condition. Most look at her like she's crazy and then roll their eyes.

After Olivia turns in the keys to the now disgruntled rental agent, they drive back to town and by Tommy's restaurant on the way down Main Street. Seeing the sign prompts her to commit to go there for dinner one night this week. She's sure he's full of information about all their old friends, and Olivia feels a little surge of excitement at the prospect of hearing about their lives.

"So, Brian, can you drop me at your house, please. I'll walk home from there."

Brian glares at her, "I told you, it's not a good idea."

"I know. I just want to. I'd like to go see your mom."

"Well, I don't know why."

Neither does Olivia. But this time she avoids answering. "So, what's the possibility for a ride now and again? I mean, now that I don't have a car."

He switches the toothpick to the other side of his mouth and mulls it over. "Sure, whatever."

"Thanks, I appreciate it."

Brian turns the corner onto First, makes a u-turn in the street and pulls up in front of the old, non-descript two-story house that could use some upkeep. There are no flowers in the empty pots that sit on the stoop, just some straggler perennials in the front beds that are being overtaken by weeds. Olivia looks up to the dormered second floor, which she knows consists of one long, skinny, upstairs bedroom that Jeff used to share with his brother. It was in a twin bed in that room that Olivia experienced sex, in all its teenage confusion, for the first time. She gets out of the car, barely closing the door behind her before Brian rolls away from the curb.

"Good luck!" he shouts sarcastically through the window. Olivia watches him pull away and then turns toward the house.

CHAPTER SIXTEEN

PRESENT DAY

O livia walks up to the door and rings the bell. She notices that there's a car in the driveway, so she waits. She rings it a second time and knocks as well, but nothing. She walks around to the back of the house to see if someone is outside. As if by magic, the gate creaks open and Olivia suddenly senses something ominous. She spots Carly sitting at a picnic table in the back yard, her head angled up toward the sky, watching dark clouds roll in overhead.

"Looks like rain," Olivia says, to get Carly's attention.

A hesitant smile spreads across the young girl's face when she sees Olivia. "What are you doing here?" she asks.

"I came to see your mother, but no one answered the door. I thought I'd check to see if she was back here."

The smile fades from the little girl's face and she kicks at the grass. A few sprinkles of rain spit from the sky, dotting the ground around them.

"Is she home?"

Carly scrunches up her mouth, looks at the back door and then casts her eyes over the fence. She slowly nods her head yes.

"Do you think I could go in and talk to her?" Olivia's forgotten what it's like to talk to a girl this age. It can be like pulling teeth.

Carly shrugs her shoulders in an "I guess so" kind of way, but she doesn't budge from her spot to show Olivia in. A blanket of emotions drops over Olivia as she pulls open the screen door and passes the threshold of the back porch leading into the kitchen. This house had been her refuge, her safe house. It was the place where she'd pretended to be part of a normal, loving, laughing, bustling family.

But the house feels eerily different: instead of plants hanging in the kitchen window, family photos framed on the walls and fresh baked goods on the counter, there are dirty dishes stacked everywhere; cereal bowls littering the kitchen table, with stale milk in them; and pans of food that should be in the refrigerator laid out across the counters. The sink is barely visible through the piles of pots and pans, plates and bowls, all of them caked with dried-on food. Olivia's hands fly directly to her nose and mouth in an attempt to protect her from the stench. It's hard to believe that just yesterday Dana hosted Jeff's mourners in this mess.

"Dana! Are you here?" Olivia hears a moan coming from the living room. She steps through the archway to find Dana lying on the couch, a drink in one hand and a TV remote in the other, with some sort of letter unfolded across her sweatpants. She bolts upright into a sitting position when she sees Olivia. The letter falls to the floor.

"What are yo-o-o-u-u-u doin' here?" Dana slurs.

Olivia takes a deep breath and stands firm. "I came to pay my respects and to tell you how helpful Brian has been to me."

"Brian. What'd he do?" Dana sets her glass on the coffee table, wipes something off her dirty t-shirt and runs her fingers through her tangled hair in an attempt to look presentable.

"Well, for starters, he gave me a ride yesterday after I wrecked my car, found me a place to stay and walked my dog. He didn't tell you any of that?"

Dana squirms in her seat, glances at the glass and starts to chew on the inside of her lip. "Bri-i-i-an ... doesn't tell me much." She reaches for the glass and then pulls her hand back. Her eyes are glazed over and bloodshot. "How did he find you a pa ... lace to stay?"

"He took me to Mrs. Capricci's up the street. He was a lifesaver, really. I was having trouble at the motel. I have some health problems." No need to elaborate; Olivia doubts Dana will even remember this conversation.

Dana chews her lip for a minute and then stands up, teetering a little, but stabilizing herself on the arm of a chair. "Well, by all means, l-l-l-let me be the gra ... shus hostess." She continues to slur. "You want somethin' to drink?"

Olivia hesitates, wanting to run, but this woman looks like she needs some help. Brian's "good luck" comment rings in her ears. "Well, I guess I could use a glass of iced tea, if you have it."

"Follow me." Dana stumbles into the kitchen, fumbles around in the refrigerator, retrieves a pitcher and pours them both a glass of iced tea before falling into a kitchen chair from the effort. "Sit. Tell me al-l-l-l-l about yourself."

Olivia steadies herself to try and tolerate the odor and sits down at the kitchen table in the chair closest to the back door. She recognizes the table as the same one from 30 years ago. It's got a few more scratches and is a little rickety, but it's the same old wooden table and chairs. Olivia recalls that someone from Jeff's family was always sitting at this table, doing homework, rolling out cookie dough, laughing. "Well, what do you want to know?" Olivia asks apprehensively.

Dana leans forward, inches from Olivia's face and spits out, "I dunno, maybe why my husband never got over you!"

Olivia's heart leaps into her throat as she pushes her chair back. She runs her fingers through her hair and shakes her head back and forth. "I didn't know that, Dana. Jesus, I hadn't spoken to him in over 30 years. Why do you say that, anyway? What makes you think he never got over me?"

Dana peers at Olivia with her bloodshot eyes, "I dunno. What do you think, Ol-l-l-i-i-i?" she spits this question with a sneering curl of her lip.

Not one to shy away from confrontation, Olivia dishes it right back to her. "Maybe it was because of you, not me. Ever think of that?"

Dana sizes her up, like an opponent in the ring. "You think you're so-o-o-o smart, you and your fancy life." She waves her arm around awkwardly, an addled witch stirring her cauldron. "He threw you up in my face every chance he got. Only married me, 'cause I got pregnant."

Olivia exhales audibly. "Jesus, Dana, how was I supposed to know any of that? He was my high school boyfriend. That's all!"

Dana hangs her head and begins to whimper. "Yeah, that's all."

They sit without speaking while Dana cries and Olivia tries to figure out how someone can hang on to a high school relationship for 30-something years. Finally, Dana pulls her head up, takes a long look at Olivia and bursts into body-shaking sobs. On impulse, Olivia gets up from her chair and rests her hands on the top of Dana's shoulders.

"Dana, I'm so sorry. I'm sorry he did that to you and I'm sorry that he died." Not knowing what else to say, her brain lands on Brian and Carly. "He did give you two beautiful children."

Dana sobs even harder and her nose starts to run down and over her lips. Olivia looks around the kitchen for a tissue, finds a box and hands her one. Dana blows her nose, finally looking up at Olivia with soggy eyes. "They hate me, you know?"

"Oh, I doubt that very much. They're just hurting, like you. Brian is a great kid, you know. I mean, he's a teenager and those years are hard no matter what. But he showed me compassion when he didn't have to. That means he's got a good foundation."

Dana hangs her head again, "Well, its al-l-l-l-l shot to hell now!"

Olivia notices Carly peeking through the screen door. She's obviously been listening to them. Olivia smiles at her and Carly backs away, out into the yard again.

"Your kids still have you, Dana."

"Yeah, like I can do them any good now. I can't even provide them a place to live."

"You have this house, don't you? It's got to be paid off by now."

"We have two weeks to get out." Dana avoids Olivia's eyes.

"What do you mean, two weeks?"

"We're losing our house. I just got the letter from the bank. And so-o-o goes the fucking foundation." Dana scoots her chair back, walks gingerly to the sink and pours herself another tumbler of vodka, straight. She stands with her back to Olivia. "Maybe you should leave now."

Olivia doesn't know if she should stay or go. She shifts her eyes to the backyard where Carly is back sitting on the picnic table, in the rain. The poor girl: losing her father and her home, but this is none of Olivia's business. She suddenly feels uncomfortable and out of place.

"Okay Dana. I'll go. But maybe you should take notice that your daughter is sitting out there in the rain, alone." Olivia points to the backyard.

Dana suddenly swings around, piercing Olivia's eyes with daggers from her own. "So, now you're gonna to try to tell me how to raise my kids!"

"No, Dana. It's just an observation," Olivia states. "I'll let myself out."

"You do that."

The brief walk back to Mrs. Capricci's in the steady rain soaks Olivia to the bone. The heat from her body causes a visible steam to curl off her skin.

"Get out of dos wet clotes, mia amore! You catcha you det! Isa no matter dat isa warm outside!" Mrs. Capricci sets the teapot on the stove while simultaneously scooting Olivia down the hall with a towel. Tucker lopes along behind Olivia, stopping only to lick the drops of water she's shaking off onto the wood floor.

Later, the two women sit in the kitchen, watching the rain stream down the windows. "A much needa agua fo our dear garden friends," Mrs. Capricci utters. "My husband, he love da rain. He say isa bring us approval from da gods."

"Approval, huh? For what, I wonder?" Olivia is still hot under the collar over her run-in with Dana.

"He use to say dat we no know what until we know what." Mrs. Capricci replies, with a grin and a wink.

"He sounds like he was quite the character. If I may ask, how long were you married?"

"Oh, 50 years we were togedder, married in Palermo on da island of Sicily. We come across on da boat togedder."

"Wow. How did you end up here, in the San Luis Valley?"

"Oh, Mr. Capricci, he was a historian. He come here to look fo his ancestral heritage. You see, da great explorer, Juan de Oñate, who claim dis valley fo Spain in 1598; he was his ancestor." Mrs. Capricci's gets up to retrieve a picture of her husband—dark and handsome, and with gentle eyes. Her own eyes sparkle with adoration as she tenderly brushes her fingers across the photo.

"Did he find any relatives?"

"Oh si. Dey a few." She waves her hand in a whirl.

"So, wait. When did you say you were married?"

"I no say. 1943."

"So that makes you how old, if I may ask?"

"I am 95," she says, with obvious pride.

"Ninety-five! You don't look a day over 70!" Olivia is shocked that this woman could be 95 and still be as sturdy as she is.

Mrs. Capricci pats Olivia on the hand. "Tank you, mia amore. And you no look a day over 40, youself."

Olivia smiles at her, knowing full well that, by now, she must be aware of Olivia's true age—or at least her approximate age.

Then, sensing an opening to talk about it, Olivia launches into a synopsis about having been poisoned. Mrs. Capricci listens and nods, as if she already knows the story. "Maybe isa possible da poison was on purpose?" she interjects, with one eyebrow raised.

Olivia stops short in the telling of a story she has recounted to so many others, too many times. The thought had never crossed her mind. "Why would you think that?"

"One musta always explore every possibility."

"I don't see how that would have been possible. The poison gases came from a crack in our sewer pipe."

Mrs. Capricci shrugs her shoulders. "Maybe, you never really know how isa happen," she replies, as she rises to return the photograph of her husband to its honored spot on the mantel.

Olivia's thoughts are suddenly confused, like they've taken a turn into a labyrinth. No matter where her mind scrambles to, considering that she might have been purposely poisoned leads it to a dead-end. When Mrs. Capricci returns to the kitchen, Olivia changes the subject. "Do you have children?"

The quirky smile on Mrs. Capricci's face disappears. "We have one son. I no believe he ever marry or have children. He no speaka to me. And he no come to his fodder's funeral 20 years ago."

"So, you haven't seen him in over 20 years?" Olivia's mind flashes to Mateo and the thought of not seeing him for that many years.

"Tirty-five. We send him to college, paid fo it all from Mr. Capricci's earnings as a history teacher at Adams State. And den he go work fo dat monster company, Monsanto, making da chemicals dat will kill us all."

Thoughts of the executive dining room appear in Olivia's

brain. The one she had dreamed up in her elaborate scheme to slowly kill all the corporate bigwigs. If she'd have gone through with it, she could've killed Mrs. Capricci's son. She's glad now that her ideas were too farfetched to actually make happen. Except, if her son is one of those bigwigs, he probably deserves it.

"No, he no care about dis small town," Mrs. Capricci continues. He have no time fo what he call us, 'small-tinking parents.'" The old woman shakes her head back and forth. "No, we no see eye to eye." She throws her hands up in acceptance. "Isa okay, mia amore. You no can force da love."

Olivia is struck with a pang of guilt for so long ago having dismissed this town. But she had never dismissed her father. She had called him regularly over the years, each time having to threaten her mother to get her to put her father on the phone. Unlike Doris, her father took an interest in her family and career. He seemed genuinely thrilled that Olivia took the time to call and share her life with him. They had seen each other from time to time. He came to her wedding and met her in Denver a few times, brief visits where he would pick her up at the airport and they'd share a couple of days alone together exploring the city. Those trips meant the world to Olivia. But she never went to Alamosa. The thought of spending time with her mother brought on sleepless nights and intolerable anxiety. Her dad knew it, and so he chose not to tell Olivia when he got sick with cancer. Instead, he spared her and told no one. Even Doris was in the dark until very near to the end. Olivia was informed that her father had died via a letter from her mother, who wrote to tell her that her father had requested that there be no funeral and that, per his instructions, he had been buried in the cemetery beneath an unmarked headstone. These facts had shocked

Olivia. She couldn't understand why he'd want that. She even went so far as to ask Doris for proof, and so her mother sent her a copy of a document in which her father had written his instructions. Shortly afterwards, Doris moved to her old hometown in Nebraska, and Olivia has never heard from her again.

Olivia's thoughts turn to her son, Mateo. Deep down inside she knows his disdain is not only for the business, but for her as well. He and Marco had always been close. But his relationship with her had felt forced. Possibly, it was because Olivia's strong desire to create a family that was the opposite of her own had been a kind of suffocation for Mateo, one that he desperately needed to escape. Even though the final confrontation had been between Marco and Mateo, maybe neither of them is as much to blame as she is. Marco has always been a much gentler soul than Olivia has ever dreamed of being, and, well, Mateo is the son, not the parent. The thought that Mateo might feel about her the way she feels about Doris sends chills up her spine.

"You have two sons youself, yes?" Mrs. Capricci asks.

Again, Mrs. Capricci seems to read her mind. "I do. Our oldest is Mateo and our youngest is Rio. They are both in their 30s and married with children. Mateo has three little ones and Rio has one son, Leo."

The moments of her sons' births skim through Olivia's troubled mind, each different in its circumstances. Mateo's was traumatic. The placenta had torn away from her uterus causing a flood of bleeding and an induced birth, which in turn prompted the umbilical cord to wrap around Mateo's neck. He was saved by the nurse and Marco, both pushing frantically on Olivia's stomach as the doctor pulled Mateo out with a pair of forceps.

Rio's birth, by contrast, was natural and nearly painless.

Olivia remembers how she had insisted, without reason, that both boys be given Spanish names. In recollection, she thinks it may have been her way of connecting to the Spanish heritage of her hometown.

"So, you no talka to you older son?" Mrs. Capricci interposes.

"How do you know that?"

"From da way you say his name and talk of his children."

Olivia thinks back a moment to how she had recited their names and what her voice could possibly have revealed. "I guess we have something in common, huh?"

"More dan you tink, mia amore."

The rain dries up and the sun goes down. Olivia and Mrs. Capricci eat a quiet dinner of homemade soup that's thick with vegetables, herbs and chicken. In the silence, they hear Brian at the door, whistling through the screen to Tucker, who seems to have been waiting for him.

"I didn't know you were coming!" Olivia yells to him. "But thanks!"

"Yep." He and Tucker disappear quickly.

After dinner, Mrs. Capricci heads off to bed and, this time, Olivia cleans up. Afterwards, she settles herself into one of the old wooden rockers on the front porch to wait for Brian and Tucker, who slip in from the darkness just as she sits down.

The overhead porch light illuminates Brian's face, and Olivia can see that it's glistening with sweat. "Looks like you two got some exercise," she says, startling Brian, who hadn't noticed Olivia sitting in the dark.

He steps onto the porch and lowers himself into the rocker next to her. Tucker circles at his feet and finally plops down on top of Brian's sneakers, his panting tongue resting on the floor.

"I guess you've made a friend," Olivia says, gesturing toward Tucker. Brian pulls one foot out from under Tucker and begins to rub it back and forth along the dog's spine. Tucker responds by rolling over so that Brian can do the same to his belly. "Oh, you've done it now. He'll never let you stop."

Brian cracks a smile, revealing the trademark toothpick jutting between his lips. They settle back in their chairs, both watching the stars blinking in the now clear night sky. Olivia notices how much closer they appear compared to back east—even in Vermont. It's almost as if you can reach out and touch them, she thinks. Minutes pass with no words spoken; just the sound of the rockers as they creak against the wooden porch boards.

Brian breaks the silence. "Do you have any kids?"

Olivia cracks a barely noticeable smile. "Yes, I have two sons. They're in their 30s now."

"Oh. Are you married?"

"Yes I am. I've been married for 36 years."

Brian's head falls back against the rocker. He seems to be contemplating this information. Olivia is enjoying the energy between them. It's relaxed, like old friends. She decides to push the moment a little. "I lost my dad a few years back. I still miss him today. The pain goes away, eventually, but the memories are always there." She pauses. "You must be missing your dad."

Brian lifts his head and lets out a little snort. "Not really. I think maybe we're all better off."

Olivia can't believe he just said that. She snaps back at him. "You don't mean that, Brian! He was your father, and I'm sure he loved you."

Anger rises in Brian's throat and he pulls the toothpick from his mouth. "Yeah, he loved me alright! He loved me so much that he couldn't look me in the eye, or even waste any of his precious time talking to me! He loved my sister, too, if you can call that love! I don't know why my mom married him!"

Olivia sits with that for a minute or two, but then pushes onward, only a little softer this time. "There's always more to a marriage than meets the eye. Outside pressures tend to get in the way and we lose sight of what's important. Most often, time is the cure. Unfortunately, your dad ran out of that."

"Yeah well, I don't think all the time in the world could've fixed my parents' problems."

Olivia lets out a sigh, "Maybe not, but your mom is still here, and she needs you."

"Karma's a bitch."

"Brian! You don't mean that! She's your mother, and she's hurting badly. You should give her a break. Maybe you don't know everything!"

"Yeah, well, maybe you don't know anything!" He gets up out of the rocker, pushing Tucker to the side with his foot, and hurries down the steps, like he can't get away fast enough.

"Brian, stop! I'm sorry! I didn't mean to upset you!" Olivia calls after him.

Brian turns and glares back at her but doesn't utter another word. He climbs into his pickup truck, slams the door and peels away.

Olivia remains on the porch for a while, feeling like she'd bungled their conversation. The river dreams she'd had over the last few weeks pop into her brain. She flirts with a different hypothesis: It's possible the woman in the dreams is Dana. And, maybe, the teenager is Brian and the little girl, Carly. It's the first time she's even connected the two. It makes sense, though. Maybe her subconscious had foreseen that she would somehow get involved with Dana and her family.

She finds herself feeling swelled with excitement and, at the same time, deflated, like a full balloon with a pinhole in it, ever so slowly letting the air escape. Wherever her mind takes her, she can't seem to figure out how—or even if—she's supposed to help this family. She's having trouble enough with her own.

CHAPTER SEVENTEEN

1975

They are teenage girls forbidden to answer the constantly ringing phone or set foot near the family's mailbox. Any infraction of the rules provokes rage from their ever-vigilant mother. After months of enduring this odd behavior, the girls, who seldom interact with one another, seek some refuge outside of their home to discuss their suspicions.

"I think she's having an affair," Grace blurts out.

"Probably," Elizabeth agrees.

"It could be she's gotten herself into trouble somehow. Like stolen something or other," Olivia interjects.

"Whatever it is," Marilyn declares, "I don't give a shit. I don't live there anymore." Marilyn had married the first Mexican boy who'd have her. Olivia was quite sure she'd done it to piss off their prejudiced mother.

Suspicion, like a toothache, nags at Olivia. She sets out on a mission to find the motive behind their mother's absurd behavior. First chance she gets, while her mother is out shopping, she hunts through her closet and scavenges through her drawers. "I knew it!" she blurts out to no one. There, in an old wooden box, in between a pair of thick winter sweaters in the bottom of her mother's dresser, sits a stack of envelopes with a return address from someone named 'Carissa Della Torre, Scotch Plains, New Jersey.' Olivia doesn't recognize the name.

She counts five envelopes in total, dating back eight months, the oldest addressed to her father, the next four addressed to her mother. Olivia rifles through each, searching for the letters inside. Only one envelope—the oldest one—contains a letter. The other envelopes are mysteriously missing their contents.

Olivia pores over the one remaining letter, the hair standing up on the back of her neck as she reads. It only takes the first word, Dad, to realize that Carissa Della Torre is her stepsister, Cari. Olivia had never known her last name or that her full name was Carissa. After Cari ran away, Doris sternly informed her daughters never to mention Cari's name again. In the letter, Cari says she misses her dad and all her sisters. She says that she's decided to come see them. She asks if her grandmother—her father's mother who lives in Denver—is still alive. She wants to see her, too.

Olivia sits on the edge of her parents' bed, trembling. Visions of Cari and her long black hair invade her brain. Thoughts of the scalped dream, which she had just dreamt again a few nights ago, bring tears to her eyes. All these years, Olivia had thought Cari was dead. But she is still alive, and she wants to come back.

Olivia returns the wooden box to the drawer, tucks the letter and the envelopes underneath her shirt and storms out of the room in search of her sisters. They confer in Elizabeth's bedroom and agree that Elizabeth, the oldest left at home, should be the one to approach their mother about this issue. Later, Grace and Olivia linger near the open bedroom door while Elizabeth sits at the kitchen table, waiting for their mother to come home from the grocery store.

Elizabeth meets Doris as soon as she walks in the kitchen, shaking the handful of envelopes in her face. "Why didn't you tell us about these? This is why you wouldn't let us near the phone or the mailbox, isn't it? Why? Why did you keep these a secret?"

Their mother purses her lips and glares at Elizabeth, saying nothing, as she pulls cans and boxes from paper bags.

"Does Dad know about these? I'm going to tell him if he doesn't!" Elizabeth angrily persists.

"No!" Doris abruptly stops what she's doing and faces her daughter. "He doesn't know, and don't you dare tell him!"

"But she wants to come back! We want her back! How could you not tell him?"

"She doesn't want to come back. She just wants money. It would break your father's heart if he knew that." Their mother diverts her eyes toward some indefinite middle space.

"But the letter didn't say anything about money! And where are the rest of them?"

"I threw them away. Like I said, they would break your father's heart."

"She wants to see grandma," Elizabeth says in a meeker tone.

"Don't be so naïve," Doris retorts. "She just wants to know if she's dead yet, because she's fishing for some inheritance." Doris scoffs. "As if she'd get anything from your tight grandmother!"

Olivia and Grace hear everything. They catch a glimpse of Elizabeth in the doorway as she sinks in her stature, clipped short of hope, the fire she'd displayed a moment earlier clearly snuffed out.

"And don't you ever mention these again!" Doris rips the envelopes from Elizabeth's hand, spins around and disappears into the bathroom.

Elizabeth delivers the news to her sisters. "Cari doesn't want to come back. She just wants money."

"But the letter," Olivia counters. "Cari said she wants to see us."

Elizabeth shakes her head. "Mom is probably right. If Cari really wanted to see us, she would've come back years ago." Olivia wants to argue. She wants to confront her mother and write to Cari. But she knows she'll never see those envelopes again, and Cari's address along with them. "Fuck her!" Elizabeth says. "She left us. We don't need her." Olivia sits on the edge of the bed and watches tears stream down Grace's cheeks. And she sees Elizabeth take some pills out of her jewelry box and stuff them in the pocket of her jeans before she marches out the front door, slamming it behind her.

Even now, as a teenager, Olivia runs to the river to swim in the shallow inlet, safe from the thundering current. She lies floating on her back, her eyes closed. The pain of missing Cari, now opened like a fresh wound, weighs her down as if she's tied to a rock. She imagines her stepsister as a beautiful woman living somewhere in New Jersey. She can't remember the name of the town that was written on the envelopes—Scotch something. She conjures up visions of escaping to New Jersey and living with Cari. Eventually, the visions fade away and the mysterious man she frequently dreams about makes his familiar appearance, his dark image flitting in and out of her muddled stream of consciousness. As he always does, he reaches for her with his long arm and strong hand, pulling her from the water. And then he walks away, drifting toward the horizon. His alluringly confident, masculine sway stirs in her, as if a kaleidoscopic array of butterflies has been released down her throat to flutter inside her belly.

CHAPTER EIGHTEEN

PRESENT DAY

Mrs. Capricci and Olivia fall into a routine. The old woman cooks delicious nurturing food for Olivia, while Olivia returns the favor by working in her garden. This morning, the apprentice is shadowing the master while she harvests today's spring bounty.

Mrs. Capricci searches and picks, all the while teaching Olivia more than she can possibly retain: the reason why each plant species is planted where and how it is, with straight or cone trellises, what grows well together and what doesn't, and where she chooses to locate some plants to help shade their neighbors. The master gardener intones at length about fertilizer; how she recycles every little scrap from her kitchen into the compost pile in the far corner of the property; and how, on certain plants, she uses chicken shit from a rancher friend of hers who brings her a load twice each season. For the tomato plants, she collects coffee grounds, rich with nitrogen, to sprinkle on the soil beneath them. Eggshells are scattered about to enrich the earth with calcium carbonate and to ward off snails and slugs, which don't like them at all. Around the horseshoe perimeter, outside of where the greenhouses stand in the winter, the ground is dug down a foot. Mrs. Capricci explains that, in the fall, newspaper gets laid out in an overlapping pattern and covered with hay and grass to create a top coat of rich soil for the spring.

Olivia's head swims when Mrs. Capricci begins swinging her arms around like a windmill, pointing to different beds and explaining how she cycles them, planting ground cover on the non-harvesting plots to replenish the carbon in the soil. The old woman stops at the bean patch and gingerly kneels near each plant, demonstrating to Olivia with her dirt-caked hands how to identify the difference between each variety. Olivia just nods and smiles. She is way past paying attention. Her head is reeling with much more than thoughts about plants.

Like a bingo cage circulating lettered balls, she calls up names in her head; "M" for Marco and Mateo. Her lungs close. "R" for Rio. She takes a full breath. "D" for Dana, "B" for Brian, "C" for Carly—and Cari. She falls to her knees.

"Mia amore!" Mrs. Capricci shouts, dropping her garden shears and grabbing Olivia's elbow.

"I'm okay," Olivia assures her. But she's not sure at all.

"We stop now fo un poco, a leetle bit. You must needa some food. Oh me, I carry on so. I lose track a da time."

Olivia steadies herself and they walk back to the house arm in arm, leaving the baskets behind. The scalped nightmare from her childhood had reared its ugly head in her dreams the night before. That dream has continued to visit her every now and again throughout her lifetime. Like a pebble in your shoe that, over time, irritates the pad of your foot, Olivia's constant replay of this horrific scene digs at her as if the repetitive dream is punishing her for the fact that she failed to find Cari. Years ago, after Olivia moved to New Jersey, she'd tried to locate Cari by checking for her name in the phone books for every single New Jersey county, but nothing ever came of her search. After the internet came in to play, she'd tried searching for Cari's name and found a few matches, but none of them turned out to be the Cari or Carissa she was searching for.

Mrs. Capricci cooks them lunch—fresh trout from a local lake brought to her by Roman, the fence-fixer guy. Trout had been Olivia's father's favorite. She recalls how he'd taught her to fish for the rainbows they were both so fond of, and how to clean and cook them to perfection. She hasn't eaten rainbow trout in over 30 years.

"Sometime one musta go backward to go foward." Mrs. Capricci advises Olivia, as she busies herself at the counter, somehow aware that Olivia is currently fixated on her past. Olivia doesn't speak. She doesn't know what to say to that. Mrs. Capricci turns from the counter and smiles her knowing smile. "No worry, mia amore, you know whata do soon enough."

She has no idea what she's supposed to do or whom she's supposed to do it with. There are way too many dysfunctional relationships in her life right now. Annoyance travels through her network of nerves, lighting the ends on fire. Backward to go forward. Mrs. Capricci sounds just like Marco, who's been known to remark, "Sometime, you have to go west to go east." Olivia excuses herself from the table and heads to the river with Tucker.

They walk along the top of the bank, Tucker free of his leash and Olivia lost in thought, when she sees Tucker take off down the embankment. "Tucker!" she yells. "Get down!" The dog has found his buddy, Brian, sitting on a rock, sketching, and has jumped up on him and nearly knocked him over.

"He's okay. Hi Tucker," Brian greets his newfound canine friend, shifting his pencil and paper into one hand so he can use the other to scratch Tucker's head.

Olivia slides down the dirt bank behind Tucker and, as she gets nearer, catches sight of Brian's sketch. It's of a hawk perched on a limb above a river. Looking up, she sees his inspiration staring right back at her.

"You're good," she says, moving her eyes from the hawk to the sketch and back again several times. She means it. He is good.

"Thanks." He folds the sketch and stuffs it into his back pocket.

Olivia takes a seat in the dirt a couple of yards away, trying to gauge if he's still pissed off at her. She notices again the art on his arms. "Did you design those tattoos?"

He glances at his arms and then hugs them to his sides. "Yeah," he sheepishly admits.

Before he hides the tattoos, Olivia clearly sees that they're both representations of animals: one is of a dog lying down with a bone in his mouth, the other arm has a moose and owl in juxtaposition to one another.

"Is that one of your dog?" she asks, pointing to his arm.

"Yeah."

"Oh." He looks at her and she smiles a bit sadly at him. "And how about the moose and the owl? Is there any significance to that? I was thinking maybe the moose represents the high school mascot." Olivia can still recite the school song. It came into her mind the day she arrived, every word falling right into place, just like riding a bike.

"Everyone thinks that. But it doesn't."

"So, what does it represent, if you don't mind me asking?"

Brian hesitates for a moment as he rotates a toothpick around in his mouth, "It's for my grandpa."

"Your grandpa?"

"He used to take me camping up on Mount Blanca a lot. One night we were sitting by the fire and he spotted a moose just a few yards away. When we looked up there was an owl sitting on a branch just above the moose's head."

"Wow! That is really cool! Were you scared?"

"Nah, I was never scared with my grandpa. He was a big man."

"I remember." The hawk lifts off from the branch, causing it to shake as the majestic bird flies off and downward, skimming the river, its red tail visible. They both watch it as it soars and wheels effortlessly above the river.

"I used to come here every day when I was a kid. I miss it."

"Don't you have rivers where you live?"

"Sure, we do. But, this was the river of my youth."

"Mmmm."

"There used to be a lot more water in it," Olivia says.

"I know. I remember. It's only in the last few years that it's dried up like this."

"And what's with the sign I saw over by Cole Park—if you see a mountain lion, fight back?" Olivia's eyes widen, and she claws her hands like a lion might.

"Yeah, they're around. You have to be careful."

"I don't remember having to worry about mountain lions when I was a kid."

"Yeah, well, times change."

A gust of wind whips a strand of Olivia's hair into her mouth. She peels it out. "So, are you going to stay here, or are you going away to college?"

Brian lets out a huff. "Yeah, right, college."

"You're a really good artist, Brian. I'm not just saying that. There are scholarships, you know."

He sneers at her and stands up to leave. "College is the furthest thing from my mind."

"Brian! Don't leave. I'm sorry. I know you have a lot to figure out. I guess I just wanted you to know how good you are."

"You really have no idea, do you? College isn't even on my map. Who do you think is going to take care of Carly and my mom?" He stands firm, glaring at her, challenging her to answer a question he knows she's incapable of answering. Olivia closes her eyes and hangs her head.

"I told you. You have no idea." He starts to climb the bank; Tucker follows him. Olivia hustles to catch up. She knows she doesn't have an answer for him. She just doesn't want him to feel so lost and alone.

Brian doesn't protest when she pulls up beside him to walk along the bank. He doesn't bolt, either. That's a good sign. When they get to the cutoff to Mrs. Capricci's, he stops, and Tucker does too, shifting his line of sight down the bank and then back at Brian.

"I'll see you later, when I come to take Tucker out," Brian says.

"Thanks," Olivia replies, grabbing his tattooed arm for a quick squeeze.

He nods and walks off along the bank and around the bend. Tucker and Olivia both watch until they can't see him anymore and then make their way back to Mrs. Capricci's. Olivia's heart feels like it's going to break. No kid his age should have this much weight on his shoulders.

Suddenly, Olivia is possessed by a desire to go see Tommy. She needs a man to talk to. She strolls into the house and plops down on the couch. Mrs. Capricci is sitting in her old chair with the worn upholstery.

"I was wondering, Mrs. Capricci, does that old Ford in your driveway still run?"

The old woman lifts one eye from the book on Native American herbs that she is obviously engrossed in. "Acourse."

"Do you think I could borrow it? I was thinking that I'd go visit an old friend tonight."

Mrs. Capricci lays the book on her lap and rests her head against the back of her chair. "I say isa bout time."

Olivia shakes her head in amusement of the old woman, leaving her to nap while she dresses for dinner. In her room, she notices a set of car keys on the dresser next to the purple vase of lavender stalks. She swears they weren't there before.

On her way out the door, she receives a bit of advice from Mrs. Capricci, whom Olivia thought was asleep. "Watch out fo dat one, Olivia. He be a wily one." Olivia rolls her eyes to herself and lets the screen door creak to a close behind her.

The pungent aromas hit her as soon as she enters the restaurant, creating a stir in her belly and stoking her hunger for something she probably shouldn't eat, something greasy and spicy. Tommy greets her like a relative who has miraculously appeared after being lost at sea. Olivia's got to admit to herself that the tight hug feels good.

"I wasn't sure you'd come," he intimates to her, as he leads her to a booth.

"I wasn't sure I would either." She scans the dimly lit room, impressed by the ambiance and striking decor. It's very modern, like a decorator had a hand in designing it. There are booths clad in blue and orange fabric with high backs for privacy, larger tables in the middle and even a small bar with a bright blue top that's lit from underneath by fiber optics. Bright, colorful canvas art lines the navy walls. Labels adjacent to the paintings indicate that they've been done by local artists.

"So, no gluten or dairy, right?" he asks, pointing his finger at her.

"Right."

"How would you feel about letting me select your dinner? I have some things in mind." Tommy rubs his hands together to encourage her.

"Okay. I'm game. Something spicy, but not too spicy."

Tommy laughs, "I've got it covered. Give me a little time. I've got some things to finish up back there and then I'll be out to join you."

"Really? That would be great. I was hoping we could get some time to talk." Olivia feels more than hunger pangs churning in her gut.

While she waits at the table, Olivia texts Marco and then Brenda. She pushes down the nasty thoughts she's having about Tommy while she checks in with Marco, and lets Brenda know she's at Tommy's restaurant. Brenda texts back, "Handsome as ever, isn't he? lol."

When dinner finally shows up, it's to die for: braised short ribs with caramelized kimchi, cauliflower mashed potatoes and sautéed mushrooms. Olivia is swooning, and Tommy knows it. "The fastest way to a woman's heart," he says sexily, "is through a man who can cook."

"Is that why you became a chef?" Olivia grins, suspending her food-laden fork in mid-air.

"It doesn't hurt the cause." Tommy slides his hand down and along Olivia's thigh.

The hair on her skin stands at attention, and she takes a deep breath before she swallows her food. His hand moves up her thigh and stops uncomfortably close to her crotch. Heat builds and releases itself in tiny spots of perspiration on her forehead. Tommy's hooded eyes meet hers, like a predator who's ready to pounce.

Olivia reflexively shoves his hand off. "Come on, Tommy. You know I'm married."

"Never stopped me before."

"Maybe it should have." Olivia shakes her head in attempt to get rid of the fantasy that's just hatched in her mind. She has never cheated on Marco in three and a half decades. Though, right now, she's tempted. "I thought you learned your lesson. Besides, that's not why I'm here."

Tommy puts a few inches between them. "Oh, I see, an ulterior motive, huh? And here I was thinking you came to see me."

Olivia smiles and pats him on the shoulder. "I did come to see you. And this place …" Her eyes take in the walls, the bar and the front window, all so tastefully modern. "Tommy, it's fabulous, really."

He lightens up. Same old Tommy, she thinks, still rolling

with the punches. "This old place?" He smiles more sincerely. "Oli, no joking around, it's great to see you, too. So, what's on your mind?"

She shrugs her shoulders, scrunches up her lips and dives into a different subject, all while she fights to suppress her carnal thoughts. "I was just thinking you might have some insight on Dana. She told me she's losing their house."

"So, you went over there anyway, didn't you? Couldn't stay away."

"I know. I know. It's just that Brian's been so helpful to me. I wanted to tell Dana. But, once I got there, jeez! All hell broke loose. Has she always been this big of a drinker?"

"I heard about your little car accident," he chuckles. "Brian told me. You know he's back there doing dishes, right?"

"Oh shit. I forgot. Do you think he can hear us?"

"No, of course not, he's elbow deep in dishwater."

"Okay good. Did you know they're losing their house?"

"Yes. It's a small town." He looks around to make sure no one is listening. "The ranch, too."

"What? What happened?"

"I really don't know. It all seemed to go south pretty quick. There's something else, Olivia. You sure you want to hear it?"

Olivia braces herself. Why she doesn't know. "Yes. Tell me."

"They're doing an investigation into Jeff's death. They don't think it was an accident."

"Well then, what was it?"

Tommy looks down at his plate. "Well, let's just say ..." He looks back up and into Olivia's eyes, "... that they're not ruling out suicide."

Olivia slouches back in the booth. "Suicide?"

"He was in a lot of debt, Olivia. He knew he was losing the ranch and the house. But I don't think he told Dana."

"So, she didn't know? Jesus! No wonder she's drinking."

"Yeah, well, that didn't just start."

"Oh." Olivia takes a deep breath, "So, you got any suggestions on how to help her?"

"Not really. I'm not so good at that kind of thing; been somewhat of a drinker myself over the years."

"I didn't mean about that. I meant about her house."

Tommy shakes his head. "From what I hear, it's a done deal."

"Aren't there any relatives willing to help? What about her family, or Jeff's?"

"Don't think so. No love lost there in either direction. He and Dana, they kind of alienated themselves from what I understand, especially after his dad died."

"I noticed his parents weren't at the funeral. Are they both dead?"

"His mom died like 10 years ago. But his father only passed a year or so ago. He had a heart attack out on the ranch."

"Oh. That's too bad. They were good people." Olivia's heart wrenches from memories of the warm, loving parents who had welcomed her into their family.

"Yeah, they were."

"So, weren't you and Jeff still friends?"

"I think I was his only friend. But he still didn't tell me anything. He'd stop in every now and again for a drink. But you know Jeff; he was never much of a talker."

The door to the kitchen swings open and out walks Brian with a mop in one hand, pushing a bucket full of water with his foot. Olivia looks at Tommy, who scoots out of the booth and begins to clear their dishes. "Coffee?"

"No, no thanks. I didn't realize it was so late." She glances around the restaurant. "We're the only ones left in here," she states in disbelief. "Hi Brian," she calls over to him.

"Hi," he says from behind his back, while he scoots his bucket closer to her, mopping the floor as he goes.

"Oh shit!" Olivia grumbles. A strong whiff of bleach has wafted up her nose. Fuzzy black dots immediately appear in her range of vision. She lurches up and careens out the front door.

"What the hell was that?" Brian asks Tommy.

"Hell, if I know. Let's go!" They run after Olivia, who is now sitting on the sidewalk, her back against the front of the building, wheezing.

"You okay?" Tommy asks as he kneels by her side.

"I, I just … need … fresh air. The bleach … I can't … tolerate it." She continues to gasp for air, her hands clasping her throat.

"Do you need to go to the hospital?" Tommy asks.

"No. No. No hospital … just home."

Tommy grabs Olivia underneath her arms and lifts her up. "Brian, go get your truck. We'll get her in and you can take her home. Oli, you okay?"

"I'll … be fine." Her breath is still uneven as she wobbles to her feet.

They get her into Brian's pickup. "We'll get that car back to you and I'll call you tomorrow to make sure you're okay," Tommy says through the window before Brian peels away.

"I'm sorry for this Brian," Olivia apologizes. Another c-clamp headache is creeping up and around her head, making it hard for her to focus.

"Why are you sorry? I should be the one who's sorry. I didn't know about the bleach."

Olivia mumbles a reply as she rolls down the window and gulps the fresh air. "How could you?"

CHAPTER NINETEEN

1977

It's early Saturday morning, and Olivia's bedroom door bursts open with a bang. "Get up and come out to the living room!" her father bellows. "We have something to discuss!" He moves on to find Grace, the only other sibling still living at home, and shouts the same command through her bedroom door.

In the living room, the girls see their mother crouched in a chair, crying. She doesn't make eye contact with either of them. Grace and Olivia sit down on the couch, very obviously wanting nothing more than to go back to bed.

"Your mother has nearly bankrupted us!" their father blurts out. "Almost all of our savings are gone! She says she's spent it all on you!" The way he's looking at them lets them know that he doesn't believe his wife's story.

All the O'Keefe girls had begun working as soon as they could get a job washing dishes or bussing tables, and before that they had babysat every chance they got. Olivia herself had been working restaurant jobs since she was 14, putting in as many hours as possible. It got her out of the house and gave her a way to save for her future escape. At no time had she ever asked her mother for money, and she suspected it was the same for Grace.

"I've decided it's up to you whether she stays or goes. She's almost ruined us." Her father scratches his head as he shakes it back and forth, his body towering over his daughters as they sit fidgeting on the couch.

"Well, what do you think?" He directs his question at Grace.

Grace eyes her mother with disgust. "Look, I don't care what you do with her. I'm out of here in two months." With that, she gets up and stomps back to her bedroom, slamming the door behind her.

Their father redirects his question to Olivia. "And you?"

Olivia takes a deep breath. Her mother still hasn't looked at anything but her hands. She just continues to sob. "Dad, you can't expect me to make a decision like this." She looks at her dad with sympathetic eyes. "I'm sorry, but you have to figure this one out for yourself."

Back in her room, Olivia listens to her father lecture her mother, who has no defense. She doesn't hear her mother utter a single word. The one-sided argument ends abruptly when her father sternly announces, "I'll take full control of the checkbook. You'll never have anything to do with our money again. I will give you a strict allowance and I want every receipt for everything you purchase. Do you understand?" Olivia imagines her mother meekly nodding her head yes. Her father then pounds the floor back to his bedroom and slams his bedroom door.

Olivia, on her bed, stews over what just occurred. She has a good idea where the money went. But did Cari ask for it or did her mother bribe her to stay away? Olivia deduces that it's got to have been the latter, and the idea that she is correct about it burns inside her as if she has been branded with an iron. She dresses quickly and escapes through her window.

She runs to the river and down along the bank, fury building as she makes her way to Jeff's house. She wants to tell her father what she knows in her heart is true. She wants him to shake the truth out of her mother. But she knows that, either way, whatever the answer is, it will cause her father more grief, more despair than he's been living with for all these years. She knows she can't tell anyone.

Jeff isn't at home, but his Irish mother welcomes her son's tearful girlfriend inside, hugs Olivia against her bosom and rocks her back and forth. Olivia doesn't utter a word of explanation as her tears soak the woman's clothing. Jeff's mother strokes Olivia's hair and, every few minutes, repeats the comforting words, "Whatever it is, dear, it'll be okay."

CHAPTER TWENTY

PRESENT DAY

Mrs. Capricci is up, waiting for Olivia with a mustard plaster concoction. As she explains, "Dis worka wonders on da respiratory tract. We put dis on you chest first and den on you back. As fo you headache, I gotta coconut and peppermint oil diffusing in you room. I make a da oils myself. You belly already full. Dat good fo da inside absorption. Just wait, mia amore, you feela better in no time." The wise old woman talks comfortingly to Olivia while she arranges the poultice and then covers her with a heavy blanket.

Olivia doesn't question how the old woman knew what had happened and to be prepared. Instead, she breathes in Mrs. Capricci's medicine gratefully and collapses into a deep, welcome slumber that isn't disturbed even as she's rolled over and a fresh treatment is applied to her back.

When she awakens, Marco is the first thing on her mind. She misses him for the first time since she's left. Mrs. Capricci's remedies have worked their magic and Olivia feels refreshed and ready for another day. She's decided it's time to start writing down these miracle potions for future use.

"It's me. I thought I'd call to check in," Olivia tells Marco, after she works up the nerve to call him. She's more than a little tentative about his reception.

"Hey. How's it going?"

"Good. Just biding my time until the car is fixed." She fails to tell him about the bleach incident or about her thoughts of infidelity. She convinces herself that neither will serve any purpose. "What's going on there?"

"Been reading that book you've been trying to get me to read; you know, *Beyond a Shadow of a Doubt.*"

"Really?" She's not sure this is Marco she's talking to. He's reading a book, and one about psychology at that. Wonders never cease. "So, what do you think?"

"I think I should've read it a long time ago. I guess I've been stuck in the left wheel, huh?"

Olivia laughs. "We all get stuck. It's recognizing it that helps us get through quicker."

"Yeah, well, I guess it's not my forte."

"Yeah, not your forte." Olivia's thoughts turn to an image of the stuck Marco wheel.

"So, how are you feeling?" Marco changes the subject.

"Good, Good. Just getting ready to go out into the garden for the morning."

They exchange a few more words about the dogs and the weather and then hang up, leaving Olivia with mixed emotions.

She should feel happy that he's taking a step to help himself. Instead, she's aggravated that it's taken her leaving to give him a kick start.

She and Mrs. Capricci work in the garden side by side today, underneath a sky of billowy clouds. They weed up one row and down another. The old woman's weathered hands skillfully twist and pull, stopping occasionally to reach up and carefully wind a vine more securely onto its trellis.

"Refresha ma memory, Olivia; who you say take you out from you poison house befo it take a you life?" Mrs. Capricci asks without breaking her stride.

"Well, I guess it was Marco who finally got us out of there."

"I see."

"Why do you ask?"

"I'ma old lady. I just wanna make sure I have da story straight in ma mind."

Olivia turns the question over in her own mind. It may have been Marco who had saved them. But he'd almost let her die before that happened.

"Der are two sides to recovery, you know," Mrs. Capricci continues. "First, one musta let go of what is dead to eliminate, den dey musta find fertile soil to sow da love again. We all figure dis out in our own time, and often no on our own."

Olivia wonders if Mrs. Capricci is directing these statements at her, or if she's talking about Marco. Because, for some reason, she feels like she's just been scolded. They finish the remainder of the morning in silence. In her mind, Olivia pulls Mrs. Capricci's sentences apart and puts them back together again and again. Possibly, she'd been talking about them both.

Mrs. Capricci again prepares a fresh salad from the garden with various vegetables, nuts and grilled chicken that not only tastes great but infuses Olivia's compromised body with energy. Shortly after they're done eating, her phone rings and Tommy's name flashes on her screen. She smiles at the fact that he was thinking about her. "So, how're you feeling? You gave us quite the scare last night," he says.

"Much better, thanks." She gives Tommy a short recap of her poisoning and subsequent health conditions. "I'm sorry to have put you through that."

"Don't be sorry on my behalf. I'm just happy it wasn't worse. So, what's on your agenda for today? Going to meddle where your nose doesn't belong?" Tommy laughs, but it sounds more like he's egging her on.

"Well, I wasn't planning on it. But, now that you suggest it—"

"—Yeah, right, same old Oli," Tommy interrupts. "Let me know how it goes. Maybe you and Brenda can come to dinner at my place tomorrow night and fill me in on the juicy details. It's on me and, I promise, no bleach this time."

"We'll see." Olivia's attention has already moved on, lured by the pull of Jeff's wounded family. After hanging up the phone, she leashes up Tucker and heads for Dana's.

This time when Olivia knocks and shouts out Dana's name, she gets an immediate response. "You again?"

"Me again. Can I come in?"

"Can I stop you?"

"Funny," Olivia replies, as she walks in the door with Tucker. "I was thinking maybe Carly would like to take my dog, Tucker, for a walk. They seem to like each other."

Dana is on the couch again, glass in hand, but, apparently, not yet slurring her words. She gives Tucker a once over and then motions to the backyard. "Knock yourself out."

Tucker leads the way, already sniffing Carly's scent. He bounds out the screen door, nearly knocking Carly off her feet in the process. She lets out a squeal and a full belly laugh. It's a great sound to hear from a little girl who appears to be wound up as tightly as a jack in the box.

"I thought you might like to take Tucker here for a walk."

"Really?"

"Yes, really. Maybe take him over to the river and back? Be careful, he likes to tug."

Carly and Tucker make their way through the gate, letting it squeak shut behind them. Olivia braces herself and heads back inside.

"I thought you were here to bug Carly, not me," Dana flings at her.

"I'm just waiting for Carly to come back with Tucker and thought maybe you could use some company."

"Do I look like I want company?"

"Look Dana, I get it. You don't like me. It's just—I was thinking about what you told me about the house the other day and it got me wondering. I know it's none of my business, but did Jeff have any life insurance?"

Dana looks up, suddenly interested in Olivia's words. Her eyes shrink into a narrow squint. "Well, I don't know. Hadn't thought about it, I guess." She bows her head and jiggles the ice around in her glass. "Do you think Jeff would've thought to buy life insurance?"

"I don't know. But it's worth checking into, don't you think?"

"And how would I do that?"

"Well, where does he keep his important papers?"

"At the ranch, I guess. He never brought any kind of paperwork home. Everything was a fucking secret with him."

"Okay, so you want to go to the ranch and look?"

Dana peers at Olivia, calculating whether she's being set up or offered genuine help. Olivia can see it in her eyes. She gives her time to think it through. "You'd go with me?" Dana finally poses.

"I'll go with you." Olivia's pulse revs up a notch. Now she's getting somewhere. "I'll be here tomorrow at two."

"Olivia?"

"Yes?"

"How would he be able to pay for life insurance if he couldn't even pay the mortgage?"

"I don't know. But, it's worth a try, isn't it?"

"Well, I'm not going to get my hopes up. It'll probably end up being just one more way he's screwed us."

Tucker bounds through the kitchen and into the room pulling Carly behind him. The young girl stops short, letting go of the leash when she catches her mother's last words. Carly's face goes white. She backs up around the corner and into her bedroom, quietly closing the door behind her.

As Olivia and Tucker walk back to Mrs. Capricci's house, she trains her eyes on the clouds overhead rolling across the sky, above and below each other, disappearing and then emerging again a few moments later, as if they're playing a game of hide and seek. She trips off the curb and nearly falls into the street, regaining her balance from the tug of Tucker's leash behind her.

Luckily, he'd stopped to sniff the street sign pole.

A few minutes later, she opens the creaky screen door to find Mrs. Capricci sitting in her raggedy chair with a book in her lap. But her eyes are closed. Olivia calculates that this must be her routine; garden in the morning, nap in the afternoon. She tiptoes past her on the way to her bedroom while Tucker trots behind, his nails clicking on the wood floor with each step. "Some time we no can see da trut, just like we no can see da sky tru da clouds," Mrs. Capricci mutters with her eyes closed. Olivia stops dead in her tracks causing Tucker to bump into her legs. She waits for more confusing pearls of wisdom to spill forth from the woman. Instead, a slight snore escapes her mouth as her head falls to the side.

In her room, Olivia paces back and forth while Tucker's eyes follow her every move from the bed. Anxiety builds in her gut and she can't stay still. She picks up her phone and checks for messages—nothing. She scrolls through Facebook until the posts become one blur after another, and then she throws on a sweater, leashes up Tucker and heads for the river.

Walking north this time, the dike curves until she is walking west, the opposite direction of the park. She walks quickly, passing backyards on her left and then crossing State Avenue where it turns into North River Road, just before the bridge out of town. Soon, there are no more backyards along her route. A double dike had been constructed on this portion of the river long before she was born, leaving a wide expanse of land between the dikes, where local kids had built bicycle paths and jumps amid the trees and bushes. Olivia recalls countless days with friends spent on this tract of land they called "the obstacle course," challenging and being challenged to brave bike runs around hairpin curves, over thrilling jumps and down steep embankments. Olivia's eyes swing back to the Rio Grande and across it, to the bank on the opposite side that butts up against the golf course. She remembers with a giggle the time she and Brenda had planted pot seeds a few feet up the bank. They'd come to check on them every day, excitedly watching them as they grew into spindly stalks until one day when the river rose and swallowed them up. It was Olivia's one and only attempt to cultivate marijuana.

Some movement in the river startles Olivia. She spots a thin, naked body floating face-down in the shallow water just below her. Olivia panics, but then sees the floating body's head turn toward her, its face lifting from the water to catch a breath and then submerge again. In that moment, she sees that it's Carly. Tucker seems to recognize her, too. He tugs Olivia down the bank, whimpering as he runs, until she's forced to let go of his leash so she doesn't lose her footing.

Tucker reaches Carly first, splashing into the water and nudging at her arms. Carly rises and then sinks back onto her haunches in the two-feet deep water. "Tucker!" she says, as she wipes water from her face. "What are you doing here?"

"What are you doing here?" Olivia asks, as she stops short next to Carly's pile of clothes. "You nearly scared me to death!"

Carly doesn't return Olivia's gaze. Instead, she hugs her arms around her legs and peers out over the river. "I come here sometimes," she says, meekly.

Olivia's heart contracts. All the times that she, herself, came to this river to get free from the drama of her own family wash over her like a deluge. She sinks to the ground next to Carly's clothes. They sit there for a while, the two of them, both transfixed by some undefinable spot above the river, while Tucker, somehow knowing that this moment is not the time to play, sits perched on the water's edge peering at Carly.

"Can you turn around?" Carly asks. "I want to get out. It's getting cold."

"Of course," Olivia says, as she stands and faces the bank. "But I don't see a towel."

"I don't need a towel," Carly responds. "I use my sweatshirt."

From the corner of her eye, Olivia can see Carly grab her sweatshirt and then her jeans. She waits a minute and then turns back around, catching sight of a folded piece of yellow paper that has fallen to the ground. She bends down and picks it up. "What's this?" Olivia asks.

Carly is facing the river while she zips her jeans. When she turns to see what Olivia is asking about, her eyes catch sight of the letter and they immediately well-up with tears. "It's my fault!" Carly blurts out.

"What's your fault?" Olivia asks.

Carly wipes her face with the front of her too-big, wet sweatshirt. "Everything!" she cries.

Olivia looks down at the yellow piece of paper in her hand. "Are you talking about this?" Carly slowly nods her head. "Can I see?" Olivia asks. Carly shrugs her shoulders and then shakes her head in agreement. Olivia unfolds the piece of paper. The first thing she notices is that the letter is in Jeff's handwriting. She remembers it, even after all these years; his tight little chicken scratch.

Carly,

I'm sorry I wasn't a better father. I hope someday

you'll be able to forgive me.

I love you,

Dad

Olivia takes a deep breath and slowly refolds the piece of paper. This letter suggests that the rumors Tommy told her about Jeff committing suicide just may be true. "When did he give you this?" she asks.

"I found it in my dresser drawer a couple days ago." Tears stream down Carly's cheeks faster than she can wipe them away.

"This doesn't mean anything is your fault," Olivia says, as she puts her arms around the girl.

"It's my fault my mom drinks," Carly mutters.

"Oh, I don't think so," Olivia disputes her. "I don't think anyone can blame themselves for another person drinking or having to resort to any kind of vice."

Carly looks up at Olivia. "What's a vice?"

Olivia scrunches her lips and kicks at the dirt. "Well, sometimes life can be hard, Carly. You know that."

"Yeah."

"And some people need something to help them get through—to help them deal with how hard it is, ya know?"

"Yeah, I guess."

Olivia feels like she's botching this, so she attempts to change the subject. "How about Tucker and I walk you home? It looks like it's going to rain soon."

"Okay. Can I have my letter back?"

"Of course, you can." Olivia hands her the folded piece of

paper and Carly stuffs it in her back pocket. Carly slips on her sneakers and they climb the bank and walk in silence all the way to the bridge, where Carly splits off down State Avenue without another word said between them.

Mrs. Capricci is in the kitchen kneading dough on the table when Olivia and Tucker walk in. The smell of spicy green chili hangs thick in the air. "Sometime da young needa da old, and sometime da old needa da young." Mrs. Capricci says, like she's singing to the rhythm of her kneading hands.

"Which one am I?" Olivia asks, as she plops down at the kitchen table.

Mrs. Capricci swipes two fingers across her forehead to push a strand of hair from her eye and then scratches her cheek. The flour from her fingers leaves marks, as if she's got white war paint streaked across her tanned face. "Depend on da moment," the old woman replies.

CHAPTER TWENTY-ONE

PRESENT DAY

My God girl, you look good! Time has treated you well." Olivia says, as she hugs Brenda, squeezing her so tight her long-lost friend lets out a squeal. "Sorry, I guess I missed you more than I thought." Olivia apologizes. Brenda has barely changed. Her face may show a touch of age and she has a few wrinkles, but she's obviously taken good care of herself.

"Ditto. You're looking mighty good yourself," Brenda offers. "Stand back. Let me have a good long look at you." Brenda's eyes meet Olivia's, betraying a tenderness that only childhood memories can foster. They both burst into tears.

Sitting in the rockers on Mrs. Capricci's front porch, the warm afternoon sun beats down on them while the women trade stories, laughs and more tears about their lives, as if they haven't skipped a beat in all the intervening years. Brenda paints unflattering pictures of her three cheating husbands as she offers Olivia details about her marriages and divorces. She admits she too hastily married each of them because they were good in bed, not thinking through far enough to understand that it would mean they'd be good in bed with other women, too. Olivia, in turn, describes the rigid Italian family she'd married into, and the business that had torn the entire family apart. But, regardless, both agree life has blessed each of them with more than most.

Mrs. Capricci slides between them a tray with glasses of freshly squeezed lemonade. "Time, isa wait fo no one," she interjects. Having been told all about Mrs. Capricci and her conduct, Brenda shakes the old woman's hand and shares a grin with Olivia.

"We've got to be going soon, Mrs. Capricci," Olivia informs them both. And turning to Brenda she asks, "you game for a trip to Jeff's ranch?"

"Okay—what's up?"

"We're taking Dana to hunt for a life insurance policy. It might be a worthless trip. But I think it's worth a stab."

Mrs. Capricci smiles. "Wella, drink up den. You needa you strengt."

Brenda takes a big swig and jumps up. "Sleuthing! This sounds like fun! Let's go!"

Olivia chugs her lemonade, then trails after Brenda, shouting, "Thanks!" to Mrs. Capricci before she slides into Brenda's car.

Dana is sitting on the front steps waiting for them when they drive up. Olivia is taken aback by how pretty Dana can be when she tries. Her hair is combed, and she's added some mascara, a little blush and a smear of rose-colored lipstick that's glistening on her lips. She is dressed in a pair of gray capris and a pink cotton shirt, clearly not mourning attire.

"Dana, I don't know if you remember Brenda Garrison?" Olivia asks, after they climb out of the car and walk to the steps.

Dana looks Brenda up and down. "Who doesn't remember Brenda Garrison? Still got those boobs, I see."

"Yup, still got em." Brenda jiggles her chest. "Hope you don't mind if I tag along and bring my boobs with me."

Olivia laughs outright, but Dana smirks. "Don't know why you'd want to. It's probably going to be a wasted trip. But then, who am I to say?"

"Where's Carly?" Olivia inquires, hoping Dana hasn't left her alone.

"She's with a neighbor. She'll be fine."

They travel south toward Antonito, taking a right on Waverly Road. Dana doesn't waste any time diving into the details of her woe-begotten existence. "You know we're losing the ranch, too." Olivia and Brenda just let her talk. "The bills for the funeral are coming in. I don't have a rat's ass of an idea where that money's coming from."

They reach the turn to the ranch, a winding road that curves sharply south and then back to the west again. Sunlight flickers off a large dark spot in the road. "That's where he flipped his car," Dana points out, tears filling her eyes. "They say he lost control on an oil slick." All three women crane their necks to take in the scene as they drive by.

Pulling up to the ranch is unexpectedly eerie. There is no livestock anywhere; no cows, no pigs, no chickens, just dried up tumbleweeds blowing across empty fields. They sit peering out the window at the acres of fencing in desperate need of repair, and at the barn with its red peeling paint and doors standing wide open and empty. This ranch, if you can call it that, gives off the vibe of a miniature western ghost town. "Dana, where is the herd?" Olivia asks.

"I don't know." Dana replies, with her mouth hanging open.

"Didn't you wonder if someone was feeding the cows?" Olivia chastises her.

"Jeff had a ranch hand." Dana replies, defensively.

"It doesn't look like anyone's been here in some time," Brenda adds.

They all get out of the car and walk slowly up to the small metal building Jeff used as an office. A few tiny windows are caked with grime, making it impossible to see inside. Olivia walks through the open door and heads straight to the beat-up metal desk that sits in the corner, sliding open the top drawer. Dana, however, stands nearby, fixated on the family snapshots of Carly and Brian and Jeff's parents, all of them scattered haphazardly along the walls, held up by tacks.

"Holy shit!" Olivia exclaims. "It's right on top! Look, it's right here!" She taps her finger on a printed document she's pulled out of a drawer. Brenda and Dana move closer to see. "And it's current, too; doesn't expire until next March!"

"I don't believe it!" Dana grabs the policy out of Olivia's hands and falls back into the desk chair.

"Now let's just see if we can find his checkbook." Olivia resumes the search.

"Right here!" Brenda chimes in, as she pulls a check register from another drawer.

Olivia grabs it and flips through it, spotting an entry on April 19th to the insurance company. "Well, I'll be! It looks like he paid the premium. Dana, you might have something here."

Dana's reading the policy, registering disbelief. "A half a million dollars! He had a life insurance policy for a half a million dollars, and he never told me!" Dana's face is impossible to read. Olivia can't tell if she's happy or pissed. Then a broad smile breaks across her face, replacing the disbelief; it's a look like she's just won the lottery. "I'd say, this calls for drinks!"

They all pile back into Brenda's car, the atmosphere stepped up a few notches from what it was on the ride out. "Oh my God, what I can do with that money!" Dana begins to cite a few priorities as they occur to her. "I can keep the house and Brian can go to college and Carly—Carly—," she stops short. "—well, I can buy Carly new clothes."

Olivia is paying half attention as Brenda rounds the bend where the oil slick still lies in the road. She adjusts her line of sight back to the horizon and onto the yellow yield sign in front of them. Her eyes widen, and she leans forward to confirm what she sees. It's the exact same yield sign from 30 some-aught years ago, shot through with three bullet holes from Jeff's pistol; one delivered by him and the other two by Olivia. She notes to herself that it's just one of the inanimate objects they had target practice with back then, when Jeff was teaching her how to handle a gun. "Step on it, Brenda!" Olivia demands. "I think I need that drink, and I don't even drink!"

At Tommy's place, they all clink glasses, Olivia deciding on a virgin daiquiri after all. No need to make herself sick over seeing a yield sign.

"Cheers!" Tommy says kind of half-heartedly, clearly not sure that he should be toasting to Jeff's life insurance policy. "Oscar here'll take care of you. I'll be in the kitchen cooking up a dinner you'll never forget." Olivia watches Brenda's eyes trail Tommy's ass as he wanders off into the kitchen. Any sinful thoughts Olivia had about herself and Tommy are quickly replaced with the more honorable idea that single Brenda ought to hook up with him instead.

Dinner is, in fact, one she'll never forget; the best osso buco Olivia has ever tasted, served with mushroom risotto and baby carrots drizzled with honey. However, already on her fifth vodka, Dana barely touches her dinner. She excuses herself to make her way unsteadily to the restroom.

Olivia takes the opportunity to inform Brenda about what's nagging at her insides. "The police don't think Jeff's accident was an accident."

"What?"

"I know. Tommy told me they think it was suicide. What if the insurance company won't pay?"

"Oh shit. That'll kill Dana. She'll really have reason to drink then." Brenda scoots out of the booth. "I'll be right back, gotta go. We can talk about it later."

Olivia sits, contemplating the possibilities, when she spots Brenda heading back toward their table, dragging Dana by the arm. "Let. Me. Go!" Dana demands, shaking her arm free. "I'm f-f-fine!"

"I caught her taking pills, antidepressants. Not a good thing with this much alcohol. We should probably take her home. I'll let Tommy know." Brenda walks off, pushing through the swinging door into the kitchen like she owns the joint.

"I don't need no ba-a-a-bysitters. You two are pa-arty po-o-opers." Dana slurs, as she tumbles down into the booth flat on her back and begins to laugh uncontrollably.

"Oh Jesus." Olivia grimaces. "Let's go."

Brian peeks out from behind the swinging kitchen door, a look of utter embarrassment washing over his face.

"I'm n-n-not going n-n-nowhere, and you can't make me!"

It takes Tommy, Olivia and Brenda to get Dana into the car. Once there, she immediately passes out in the backseat. Brenda glances up at Tommy. "Thanks for a spectacular dinner. Who knew you could cook like that?"

"Well, you'd know if you came around more often," Tommy counters.

"Well, maybe I will," Brenda flirts back.

"Okay, okay, let's go," Olivia chimes in, rolling her eyes. "We need to get this woman to bed."

On the drive home, Brenda says, "I'll stay with her. She probably shouldn't be alone. Do you know what the deal is with Carly?"

"I heard Dana call the neighbor earlier and ask her if Carly could stay the night. I think she'll be fine. I'm not so sure about Brian. He saw the whole thing."

"I imagine it's not the first time, poor kid."

CHAPTER TWENTY-TWO

1979

Whenever she's in the house, Olivia's mother shadows her every move, clearly petrified to let her daughter anywhere near her father when they're alone. Olivia holds the knowledge of Cari's letters and the belief that Doris paid her to stay away over her mother's head with cleverly formed comments and contemptuous looks that say *I know what you did*. It's a game of cat and mouse that Olivia plays well, enjoying watching her mother squirm.

Grace appears at Olivia's bedroom door. She is home from college for the weekend, showing up without notice, dressed in skanky high heels, a way-too-short mini-skirt and a boob tube. It's 50 degrees outside, and Grace isn't dressed for the weather. Her eyes are heavily made-up with coal-black liner, and a smear of bright red lipstick coats her lips, while four-inch gold hoops hang from her earlobes. Olivia can't wait for her father to catch sight of how college has transformed his daughter.

"Nice get-up," Olivia remarks to her. "Where's Huggy Bear?" she asks, referencing the slick, urban, black character in the popular TV show, "Starsky and Hutch."

Grace ignores the insult and closes the door behind her. She drops down on Olivia's bed and pulls a roll of cash out of the pocket of her miniskirt. "Check this out, Oli." Grace fans out the bills, "Twelve hundred dollars!"

"Where the hell did you get that?"

"One week, and that's a light haul."

"What are you a drug dealer now?"

"Hell no! It's way better than that." Grace waves the money in front of Olivia's face, "I've cut you in, at least for this weekend."

"Cut me in on what? What the hell are you up to, Grace?"

"It's easy, a hundred a pop. I've got us booked for tonight and tomorrow night. You'll make a few hundred, easy."

"Are you talking about prostitution? Are you fucking crazy? That's what you've been doing at college, prostituting yourself?" Olivia stands up and starts to pace, her heart rate rising by the second. "Jesus Christ, Grace!"

"It's no big deal. I don't know why you're getting all worked up. Look what kind of money I'm making."

"It's not about the money, Grace. Fuck! I hope you're on birth control."

"No way, birth control makes me fat."

"What if you get pregnant—you stupid ass?"

"Already have. So, what? Abortions are nothing."

"Nothing? Nothing? There is seriously something wrong with you!" Olivia is visibly sweating now, and her heart is racing like a sports car in overdrive. "What did you mean, you have us booked? Here? In Alamosa—with people we know?"

"So what! It's just sex!" Grace rolls her eyes and begins to pick at a pimple on her cheek.

Olivia can't believe what she's hearing. "What people?" she asks.

"Just some guys from high school who stayed here for college. Well, and some other college guys we don't know. It's all set. You can't back out now."

"The hell I can't! You may be a fucking whore, but I am not!" Olivia can't think straight. Her head is swimming. Guys she knows. This'll spread all over town like wildfire. Images of the boys next door invade Olivia's brain. Their wadded-up 10-dollar bill, their bloody faces and bad breath, and that damned Grateful Dead t-shirt. Those boys have steered clear of Olivia ever since that day in their room. But Grace obviously didn't get the message.

Olivia storms from her room and out of the house, running to her car. She is crazed, seething with anger. Jeff's pistol is under the front seat. They were practicing today, shooting out near the ranch at a yield sign. He'd left the gun in her car when she'd dropped him off at home. Olivia grabs the pistol and runs back inside.

Grace is still on her bed, now filing her long red nails. When she sees the gun, she jumps up and backs toward the closet. "Olivia! What the hell? Where did you get a gun?"

"You fucking bitch! You may be willing to ruin your life, but there is no way you're sinking those skanky-ass nails into mine." Blind, barely containable rage overcomes her. Olivia's pistol practice kicks in and she pulls the trigger. The explosion in the small room startles Olivia out of her stupor. "Oh my God!" she cries, as she drops the gun to the floor. Miraculously, the bullet has just barely skimmed Grace's leg and hurtled through the middle of the closet door, into the black space where Grace had so wickedly abused Olivia for all those years.

Their mother immediately rushes in. Grace is on the ground, crying hysterically, clutching her leg with both hands. Without uttering a word, their mother grabs a t-shirt, wads it up, and presses it against the graze on Grace's leg, now glistening with bright-red blood. She guides Grace's hands to the makeshift bandage, indicating that she should hold it in place. As Olivia watches through a haze of hot tears, Doris rips an Eagles poster off the wall and tacks it onto the front of the closet door, covering the splintered bullet hole. Then, without hesitation, she shoves the pistol into a pillowcase, places it into Olivia's hand and guides her out the front door toward her car. Olivia obeys as if she is hypnotized, pulling out of the driveway just as their neighbor hurries out onto her porch to see where the sound came from.

With her body shaking uncontrollably, Olivia drives straight to Jeff's house. She honks the horn and he emerges from the front door with his hands in the air. "What's up?"

"Get in!" she yells through the closed window.

Jeff hesitantly slides into the passenger seat, looking back at his house. "Where are we going? What the hell happened? It's dinnertime!"

"I just have to drive! Just let me drive! We have to go somewhere!" She speeds over the single-lane bridge, past the golf course, and out of town.

"Olivia, what happened?" Jeff implores her, his voice now fearful.

"I shot Grace! I shot Grace! What the fuck did I do?"

"You what? You shot Grace? Is she okay?"

"She's okay! I just grazed her leg!" Olivia pulls over to the side of the road. "Oh Jesus, Jeff, what did I do?" Her eyes are wild.

"It's okay, baby. She's okay, right?" Jeff scoots over and Olivia slumps into his arms. "Did you shoot her with my gun?" Olivia slowly shakes her head yes.

They stay that way for what seems like hours, Olivia sobbing and shaking in his arms and Jeff consoling her, until the sun goes down and the moon takes its place in the sky. All the while, Olivia talks like someone possessed, bleeding out her family's grim history, exposing herself and them—against any previous better judgment—as she never has before. Jeff sits quietly, taking it all in.

Olivia feels numb, ruined, hopeless. And on top of everything, now her mother has something on her. Olivia knows her mother won't breathe a word of what just happened to her father or to anyone else. Neither will Grace. She can predict the smug look her mother will have on her face when she gets home—check and checkmate.

The entire scene seems beyond belief. Olivia's head is swimming as she tries to recall the details of what just happened, wishing she could take back that second of her life. Her eyes are closed when, suddenly, behind her lids, the man appears. It's the dark-haired, confident man with the long arms and the stretched-out hand. This time, though, his hand is intertwined with hers as they rock in rocking chairs, back and forth on a covered wooden porch. She can feel his blood pumping and the warmth of his skin against hers. Her eyes pop open. She rubs one hand in the other searching for the warmth, but it has abandoned her as quickly as it seeped into her subconscious. She becomes aware of her surroundings, first looking out through the windshield to see that the sky is a dark indigo and the moon is covered by clouds. She realizes that she is still in Jeff's arms, that her clothes are drenched in tears, and she is rocking herself back and forth. Although subconsciously she has always known it, in this instant, she is struck with the awareness that the man in her dreams, the man who reaches for her and holds her hand, isn't Jeff.

CHAPTER TWENTY-THREE

PRESENT DAY

I t's Sunday morning and Mrs. Capricci invites Olivia to accompany her on a mission. She's taking a load of vegetables along with an activated charcoal remedy to a friend, the poultice to be used to treat a skin infection. Apparently, the friend's daughter has been scratching far too actively at her mosquito bites.

Olivia enjoys the visit with Mrs. Capricci's friends. The little girl is close to Carly's age. A vibrant little toe-headed child dressed in a lavender sundress—unlike Carly's jeans and dreary gray sweatshirt. Olivia plays hopscotch with her on the driveway, while Mrs. Capricci instructs the parents on how to use the poultice. It's been a long time since Olivia has jumped into the air. She's amazed she can still make it through a hop-scotch board.

They take a different route on the way home, driving by Olivia's childhood home. Although Olivia tries to keep her eyes forward, she is drawn to the carriage house and the house next to it. Unlike the first day she was in town, when she sat in her car in front of her old homestead and recalled special moments she'd shared with her dad, today, it's the house next door that commands her attention. As they drive by, Olivia catches a glimpse of the gigantic bur oak tree in the back yard, the one that hung over the next-door neighbor's pool when she was a kid. Tears burn her eyes and she begins to shake.

"Perhaps isa time to talk," Mrs. Capricci softly urges her.

Olivia purges herself of her story, right there in the car as they drive across town. Like a person who's been given syrup of ipecac, the words gush from her mouth, unfettered. She confesses about Grace being abused and abusing her, about Cari running away and never seeing her again, about the letters she'd found in her mother's drawer, about shooting Grace. She flushes all of it, emptying herself. She can almost visualize it, all the crap from her childhood circling the drain like detritus before it falls away into the void. In the act of spilling it all out to this woman she's just met a few days ago, Olivia realizes that the only other people she's ever told any of this to are Marco and Jeff.

Mrs. Capricci pulls the car into the driveway, but the two women remain inside. It's not the time to move, to break the stream of the telling or disturb the toxic outflow of poison. Finally, Olivia pulls herself from her exorcism. "Forgive me, Mrs. Capricci. I don't know what just happened. I shouldn't have burdened you—"

"—Ahh, mia amore," the old woman interrupts her. "Disa no burden."

Olivia gazes at Mrs. Capricci through tear-filled eyes. "Thank you."

"I have someting to tell you," Mrs. Capricci says, as she covers Olivia's hand with hers. "We go inside. I make a tea and we talk."

While they sit at the kitchen table waiting for the water to boil, Olivia runs her fingers through her long brown hair while Mrs. Capricci wrings her hands as if they are the dough she was kneading a couple days ago. Once the ginseng tea has properly steeped and two hot mugs sit on the table before them, Mrs. Capricci begins to speak. "I knew you fodder, and I knew you sister, Carissa, too."

"You knew Cari?" Olivia sits up straighter. Pictures flash through her mind: Cari's eyes when she looked at Olivia in her dream, just before she was scalped by Doris, and Cari's tapestry carpet bag that, even to this day, Olivia can clearly see in her mind's eye.

Mrs. Capricci nods her head yes. "You see, da day Carissa ran away from you house, she came here to me."

"Why you?"

"We become friends, Carissa and I. Whenever she able, she walka da river. I always walka, too. Dat where we met. I tink we bonded because we bot Italian. Not many Italians in dis town." Mrs. Capricci averts her eyes from Olivia's and she focuses on her mug of tea. "I let her stay da night befo I call you dad. He come right away da next day."

"My dad knew she was here?" Olivia adjusts in her seat.

"He did."

"So, she was here the whole time? How did we not know that? This is a small town. One of us would have seen her." Olivia is becoming agitated at the idea that Cari was right under their noses the entire time.

"No, mia amore. Carissa, she a stubborn-head girl. She said she never again step foot in da same house as you mudder. She insist she go back east where she come from. Only problem was her mudder dead and bot her grandparents, too. She had nowhere to go." Mrs. Capricci begins to wring her hands again.

"So, what happened?"

"I had a friend who live in New Jersey. I call him and ask him to take her, and he did."

"My dad let her go live with some stranger in New Jersey?"

"Carissa no really give him a choice. She say she go wit or witout his blessing."

"So, who was this friend? Did you keep in touch with Cari?" Olivia's stomach is jumping with excitement at the idea that she may get to see her stepsister again.

Mrs. Capricci's eyes scan the kitchen walls and then land on Olivia's. "Da man who took Carissa in was Leo Alfieri, you husband's uncle."

"What?" Olivia jumps up from her chair. "How can that be?"

"Da world a smaller place dan we tink, Olivia."

"Are you telling me that my dad knew when I married Marco that he was related to Leo, the same man he sent Cari to?"

Mrs. Capricci shakes her head no. "I don't tink so. You see, you dad never go back east to visit Carissa. She say she no want him to. And I don't tink he ever meet Leo in person."

"He did meet him! He met him when he came to my wedding! I can't believe this!" Olivia paces the kitchen. "Was my meeting Marco a setup, or something?"

"No, no, mia amore. I no tink you dad ever put two and two togedder. Dat was years after …" Mrs. Capricci stalls for a moment. "… after Carissa die."

Olivia stops dead in her train of thoughts. "She died? How did she die?" Olivia's heart sinks into her stomach.

"She die of a drug overdose when she was 27. It broke you fodder's heart. He blame himself. I no tink he was ever da same after dat."

Olivia sinks back down in the kitchen chair and leans her head in her hands. "Did Leo know that I was Cari's sister?"

"I no tink so. You have different last names. After Carissa move, she go by Carissa Della Torre, her mudder's maiden name." Mrs. Capricci stands up to retrieve the teapot and refreshes both of their mugs. "Carissa only live with Leo fo a year or so. When she graduate high school, she move to Brooklyn. Dat's where she live befo her mudder die. Leo only saw her a few times after dat. And you fodder, he send money to Leo and fo Carissa to go to college. But Carissa never go. You dad stop hearing from her."

Olivia calculates the years in her head. She visualizes the letters she found in her mother's dresser drawer and the scene in the living room two years later when her father informed she and Grace that Doris had nearly bankrupted them. Cari would have been 27 that year. "How did my dad find out about her death?"

"Dey found Leo's phone number on her. Leo called you fodder."

"Did my dad or Leo go to Cari's funeral?"

Mrs. Capricci closes her eyes and shakes her head no. "Der was no funeral. You see, Leo was in Europe when Carissa die. And der was no udder contacts on her body. She was homeless and—and in bad shape. By da time Leo return da call, dey bury her in da potter's field."

"Oh my God! My poor dad. And poor Leo. I can't imagine!" Olivia hangs her head and begins to cry. "I can't believe Cari was buried in a potter's field. I can't believe any of this."

"I know, mia amore. It all hard." Mrs. Capricci strokes Olivia's hair.

"Did you ever hear from her?" Olivia asks through her tears.

"She call me a few times in da first years. But no letters. And den nudding."

Olivia's mind feels like a computer attempting to process and file everything she's just been told. But there are facts here that she can't seem to reconcile. "This all seems way too far-fetched to be coincidence," she says.

Mrs. Capricci shakes her head in agreement. "Sometime serendipity is da only explanation."

"But if my dad didn't, and Leo didn't, how did you put me and Marco and Leo together?"

"Oh, I very close to Leo. He mean a lot to me. I go to his funeral, and dat where I saw you."

"You were at Uncle Leo's funeral? I don't remember you."

"Der were many people der." Mrs. Capricci nods her head. "He a good man—loved by many."

"I remember." Olivia scans the crowd in her mind's eyes, but she has no recollection of seeing Mrs. Capricci. "If you recognized me, why didn't you talk to me?"

"Oh, you were consoling you husband. He very sad. I no want to intrude."

Olivia's mind is reeling. She is trying to figure this all out—trying to remember Leo's funeral and then thinking again about her dad. She grasps for any tidbit that he may have said or done that would have been a clue. And then she remembers her father's instructions to be buried in an unmarked grave. A shiver slides up Olivia's spine when she links his request to the fact that Cari had no funeral and was buried in a potter's field. It was his way of punishing himself for what happened to Cari. "Did my mom know about all of this?"

"I no tink so. Leo say he always talk to you fodder at his office."

"It all happened because of my mother. She was horrible to Cari." All the times she and Grace would listen from their bedroom to Doris berating Cari flash through Olivia's mind. Anger builds in her gut.

"You know, Olivia, I used to walka da river with you fodder often. Many time we sit togedder and talk of our troubles." Mrs. Capricci adjusts in her seat. "He tella of you mudder and her past."

"Her past?"

"Do you know dat her fodder left when she was only 10-years old?"

"No. She never spoke of her childhood—ever."

"Mmmm. He run away wit her older sister when her mudder catcha dem togedder one night. She never see eder of dem again."

Razor-sharp currents run through Olivia, causing the hair on her skin to lift. Fragments of Olivia's childhood come together as one in her consciousness, suddenly as clear as a freshly washed windowpane. "So, my mother thought her own history would repeat itself with Cari." Olivia sighs deeply.

"History repeat when we no let air to da wound."

She sighs again. There is so much for Olivia to 'give air to'.

"Isa sad ting when der is more history dat is secret dan a no secret." The old woman reaches for Olivia's hands and holds them in her own. "Once revealed in da open air, heartbreak no longer wear da crown of torns. Dat way, fogiveness become easy."

Olivia looks admiringly at Mrs. Capricci, soaking up all that this wise woman is telling her, a student and her teacher. But Olivia is still unsettled, and she poses to Mrs. Capricci "Do you forgive your son?"

"You see, der is nudding to fogive. Maybe he know someting I no know. He isa just living his history, and history, mia amore, is perfección." The old woman smiles. "And who are we to question perfección?" With that, she pulls one of her hands from Olivia's and kisses her fingertips, waving them off as if to say, accepting, "Farewell."

CHAPTER TWENTY-FOUR

PRESENT DAY

I t is late morning when Olivia and Tucker wander up the street to Dana's, Tucker getting sidetracked every time he spies a squirrel or a chipmunk. Olivia's body is tense, and her mind spent from the morning. She is desperate for relief, some way to free herself from the constant rearrangement of puzzle pieces that are twisting her in a knot. She doesn't go to Dana's, but instead walks to Cole Park, sits on a bench and calls Marco. "You aren't going to believe this," she tells him.

"Believe what?"

The story she had learned that morning spills out—every piece of information that Mrs. Capricci had shared with her. She speaks fast and breathlessly, as if dishing it all out to Marco will somehow make sense of it.

"You're right," Marco agrees. "It is hard to believe. But I've got to tell you, Oli, when I was like 13 or 14 maybe, Uncle Leo told me that he had a teenage girl living with him. He told me he was fostering her."

"This is crazy, Marco!"

"I know! And then I do remember that I asked about her years later and Uncle Leo told me that she died." Marco's voice grows solemn. "I'm sorry, Oli. I know you always hoped you'd see her again."

Olivia draws a deep breath. "I kind of lost that hope over the years. I mean, don't get me wrong, I'm sad for Cari. But to tell you the truth, I'm sadder for my dad. And what I learned about my mom and her childhood, that makes me sad, too. To be honest, it makes me want to contact her."

"Mmmm, I get that. Maybe you should."

"Maybe." Olivia is quiet for a moment and then she asks, "Can you believe it, Marco? Can you believe the freaky connection? I mean, who would ever imagine something like this could be possible?"

"Yeah, I know. But for some reason, it makes me feel, I don't know—smaller."

"It may make me feel like the world is smaller," Olivia replies. "But to me, it makes you seem larger."

"What does that mean?"

"I don't know. It's just how I feel—like you and me, we're part of something bigger. You know, I always felt like I came from this little town with few connections and that I didn't really—I don't know—matter. Maybe that's why I've always been so fierce about trying to make myself mean something."

"Oli, I don't know what you're talking about. You've always mattered."

"Thanks. You matter, too."

"Thanks." The air hangs silent between them for a minute. "It's going to take me a few to process all of this," Marco finally says. "It's kind of like a 'Lifetime' movie."

"I know, me too. I should go. I've got to go check on Dana. Brenda and I took her to Tommy's last night and she got drunk."

"Well, good luck with that," Marco says with a chuckle.

"Thanks. I'll call you later." Olivia stands up and then bends over, stretching her fingers to her toes. Sharing the conversation with Marco has given her some of the relief she needed. "Let's go, Tucker," she says before walking the couple blocks back to Dana's.

Tommy meets her at the front door with an unmistakable twinkle in his eyes. "We were just going to call you."

Olivia laughs and rolls her eyes sarcastically.

"What's so funny?" Tommy feigns innocence.

"Like I didn't know this would happen. But really, in Dana's house?"

"You dirty-minded woman. I just got here."

"Yeah, right!" She slides past Tommy into the house. Brenda is in the kitchen, cleaning as though the queen were about to arrive. "Well, look at this! I didn't know you had magic powers."

"You don't know a lot of things," Brenda giggles.

Olivia rolls her eyes again. "You two are too much. But it should've happened years ago. Maybe you could've saved each other a few divorces."

She and Brenda both laugh too hard at the joke. Carly peeks her head around the corner from the hall and stares at the two women like they have four heads.

"Where's Dana?" Olivia asks.

"She's still in bed; says she's got a headache," Brenda replies, as she gives Olivia a 'no-joke-after-her-antics-last-night' look. "You game for a picnic? We just sent Brian to the restaurant for food."

"Seriously? I can't think of anything better to do right now."

The five of them and Tucker squeeze into Tommy's SUV and drive 20 minutes to a hidden clearing by the river, where a picnic table and a fire pit made of large rocks are situated. An old tire swing dangles from a branch that overhangs the river, perfectly located just over a swimming hole.

Brenda leans into Tommy. "Did you bring this picnic table out here?"

"Sure did. Great spot, huh?"

"Yeah, great spot," Brenda purrs, clearly insinuating something other than a location for a picnic.

Olivia interrupts the love fest. "Okay, you two. Something in that basket is making my stomach growl. How about you feed us, Tommy?"

"Right on top of that, Oli." He winks at Brenda and smiles at Olivia.

They all sit around the picnic table watching Tommy and Brian work. It's like being front and center at an iron chef competition. Tommy has obviously taught Brian a thing or two about cooking. As he slices smoked turkey that he explains is fresh from his own mesquite wood smokers, Tommy reminds everyone that he gets up at four in the morning, three times a week, to kindle and nurse the smokers for what turns out to be hours. Brian, for his part, slathers homemade mango chipotle aioli on one stack of corn tortillas, and cranberry sauce on another. Then he layers the smoked turkey on top of the tortillas, along with slices of green apple and a pile of fresh romaine from Tommy's garden.

Tommy has set up two paper bags to hang off the end of the picnic table. "One is for food scraps, the other for paper waste," he explains. "I'm always looking for food for my compost pile, which in turn feeds my garden." He smiles proudly at his own good sense.

"You garden too?" Olivia asks, astonished at her old friend's hidden talents.

"Of course, I do. My mom had a big garden when I was a kid, and then, in culinary school, we grew a kitchen garden on the plot behind the school. Where do you think I get all those award-winning vegetables I serve the public?"

"From the food supply truck?" Olivia shrugs.

This time, Tommy, Brian and Brenda take a turn laughing at Olivia. "You've been living in the city way too long," Tommy chides her.

"Actually, I live in the country now."

"Well then act like it woman! Grow yourself a garden!" he admonishes her.

"Maybe I will."

"That sounds like a threat," Brenda chimes in. "What's this over here in the container?" she asks, while she pries open a lid. "Ooh! It's my favorite, potato salad."

"There's no mayo either, Oli," Tommy interjects. "Olive oil and lemon instead, with lots of fresh parsley from the garden, of course."

They all dig in, letting out a series of oohs! and aahs! between bites. Tommy beams from ear to ear, and Brian pulls a close second when they praise him, too. After lunch, they all gather around the tire swing. "Come on, let's see what you can do!" Tommy eggs Brian on.

It doesn't take another word for Brian to peel off his t-shirt, stick his toothpick in his pocket and grab onto the swing. He swings out above the river in a flash, letting go and tumbling over into a well-practiced flip. The onlookers roar and clap.

"Isn't the water cold?" Olivia calls to Brian.

"Nah, it feels good!"

Tommy shucks off his t-shirt and follows Brian's lead, but hits the water with a resounding slap from an inelegantly executed cannonball. It prompts even more applause from the ladies. "Your turn, Carly!" Tommy urges her from the water. "I'll stay out here just in case you need me."

Carly looks at all of them sheepishly and shakes her head no. "Come on, Carly!" Olivia pushes her with a smile. "You can do it!"

Slowly, Carly peels off her sweatshirt, the one she's worn every day since Olivia met her, and inches toward the swing. She has a tank top on underneath and when she raises her arms to the rope, a series of purplish lines scarring her inner arms reveal themselves in the sunlight. In unison, Olivia and Brenda snap wide-eyed toward each other, both recognizing them as obvious cut marks. They nod to each other in silence, mutually understanding that now is not the time to probe their cause.

Without any further encouragement, Carly pushes off and swings out over the water letting out a squeal just as she releases her hands from the rope. Everyone claps. A second or two later, she's pulled herself out of the water and gone back for more—no need for Tommy's protection. Brian takes one more swing and then passes the rope to his sister, who can't seem to get enough.

Discreetly pulling his sketchpad from his backpack, Brian strolls out of sight, while the adults gather in a semi-circle, sitting on rocks at the water's edge, watching Carly and reminiscing about old times.

"Remember sneaking onto the Foster's farm and skinny dipping with the high beams from Jeff's pickup lighting up the waterhole?" Olivia asks. "You know, we never saw that waterhole in the daylight. I wonder if we would've been so brave if we had."

"I doubt it." Tommy shakes his head back and forth. "Plenty of snakes in those manmade irrigation holes."

"No, really?" Brenda asks with a shiver.

"Yes, really." Tommy slides closer to her and snakes his fingers up her thigh.

"Stop!" She jumps up and darts away.

"Okay, okay!" He pats the rock next to him and Brenda sits back down, leaning her head onto his shoulder. Tommy puts his arm around her and hugs her in tight.

Olivia smiles at the couple. "I hope something comes of this. You two are great together. Try not to screw it up, will you?"

"Thanks for the vote of confidence!" Tommy complains.

Olivia shrugs her shoulders and raises the palms of her hands in a gesture that says "Well???"

"So, what's your husband like?" Tommy asks Olivia.

"He's a good guy. I couldn't have asked for a better father for my kids. He's a big kid himself. And he takes really good care of me. I'm a lucky woman." Olivia is stopped short by her own response. He is a good husband. She is lucky. She begins to question why she's been so hard on him—why she's been so focused on what he isn't, instead of what he is. She pulls a picture of Marco and her sons from her wallet and proudly shows them off.

Brian emerges from the woods and distracts her from her photo exhibit. His sketchpad is open and hanging by his side. "Hey Brian, can we see?" Olivia asks.

He looks down at his pad and then at the group. "Aw, what the hell." he says, as he flings the pad onto Olivia's lap. The sketch is of Carly on the tire swing. He's skillfully captured the expression of delight on her face, just as her hands let go of the rope.

"Wow, Brian! This is really good!" Olivia exclaims. Brenda and Tommy shake their heads in agreement. "Can we see the others?"

Brian looks down and kicks the dirt with his bare foot. "I guess."

Together, the three adults flip through Brian's sketchpad, one page after another. The sketches are of random people, some smiling, some beaming and laughing, even one of an old man holding his stomach, clearly in the throes of a deep belly laugh.

Brenda speaks first. "Brian, you've captured an essence of pure joy in every one of these. They're magnificent!"

"Holding out on me, huh?" Tommy jokes. "How come you never showed me any of these?"

Brian does the hem-and-haw thing again. "I dunno."

"Well, I guess we know what this guy should do for a living," Olivia says. "Have you shown these to your art teacher at school, assuming you took art?"

"Yeah, he keeps pushing me to apply for scholarships."

"You really should," Brenda encourages him.

"Yeah, maybe someday."

"It may be too late this year. But, there's always next year." Olivia points at Tommy. "It's your job, boss man, to make sure he does."

"Hey, I'll do what I can!" Tommy says, nodding in agreement.

Tucker, who's been occupied by minnows the entire time, suddenly decides he's had enough and takes off into the trees after a squirrel. Olivia jumps up to go after him. As she chases after Tucker, Brian's sketches revolve around in her mind. Her brain begins to sprint through scenarios: she can help him with applications, she can talk to people she knows, she can encourage him to enter contests. And she can find out why Carly's been cutting herself. She winds her way through the brush, calling Tucker's name until he finally lopes back to her, outsmarted by the squirrel.

When she returns, everyone is in the process of cleaning up and loading the gear back into the SUV. Olivia sits down for a quick rest and feels a familiar Pop! Pop! and Pop! on her ankle. She reaches down to scratch and stops short; three little hot blisters have appeared in a row. "Shit! Poison oak!" If it wasn't for bad luck, she'd have no luck at all.

Back at Dana's, Brenda says her goodbyes. She's got work the next day and wants to get home before it's too late. She lingers in Tommy's arms for a while, the two of them whispering to each other. Then she turns to Olivia. "This is the best time I've had in years. Let's not allow so much time to pass before we do it again, huh?"

"No way. Text me when you get home. We've got some girl talking to do." Olivia bear-hugs her friend and they all wave as she heads up First Street and turns onto State Avenue. Even

Dana, who has emerged from her bedroom looking like she's been run over by a bulldozer, waves Brenda goodbye.

Olivia and Tucker walk the few blocks home to Mrs. Capricci's, Olivia forcing herself not to bend down and scratch with every step. Once they reach the house, Mrs. Capricci knows just the remedy for poison oak. "Da inner bark of da bur oak tree," she explains, as she pulls a bag out of her refrigerator and goes to work, rubbing it onto the puffy blisters.

"Where did you get the bark?" Olivia asks.

"From you old next-door neighbor. He keepa me in stock."

"They're still alive? They were older than my parents."

"No, no, da younger son. He live der now. His parents pass a few years back. He was da one who come home to nurse dem, and den he stay."

"Really?"

"Why so hard to believe? He go away to college and become a nurse."

Olivia promptly envisions the younger son with the Grateful Dead t-shirt; the one who first put his hands on her in his bedroom. She had hated the Grateful Dead ever since. It's difficult to reconcile the boy who attacked her with the man who has become a nurse, providing remedies to an old healer woman. The itch on her leg immediately vanishes.

Before dinner, Olivia takes a breather to check back in with Marco. She describes the picnic by the river, Brian's artistic ability and the cuts on Carly's arms.

"That's frightening," Marco responds. "Did you ask her about them?"

"No, it wasn't the right time. But I will," Olivia replies. "So, I'm sorry I didn't ask when I called before. How was your weekend?"

"Beside the bizarre stuff you told me, different."

"Oh, how so?"

"Well, I golfed with this guy on Saturday who was pretty interesting."

"Oh, good, you got out of the house."

"Yeah."

"What about the guy?"

"He invited me to come to a meeting, a group really. So, I went."

"Last night? What kind of group?"

"They're called 'El Guardia Legado.'"

"That's Spanish, right?"

"Yes, for The Legacy Guard."

"Why did he invite you? You're Italian."

"My ancestors came from Spain, remember?"

"How did he know that?"

"Don't know. Never asked."

"So, what was the meeting like?"

"It's a bunch of guys primarily from the tri-state area who moved up here to Vermont at one time or another. They talk about the lost legacies of Spain. I guess it's a group that has other factions throughout the world. They search for lost treasures. I looked on the internet, though, and couldn't find anything."

"Maybe they're too old to use the internet."

"Funny."

"I'm kidding. It sounds pretty cool. Will you go back?"

"I think so."

Olivia processes her husband's news as she hurries into the kitchen to help Mrs. Capricci with dinner, which just so happens to be paella. They work side by side. Olivia chops vegetables while Mrs. Capricci prepares the various ingredients: chicken, chorizo, clams and shrimp. They get it all together in a huge pan, Mrs. Capricci instructing Olivia to add a healthy dose of her treasured saffron.

"Sometime da yin and da yang get all confuse, like da bees who come in contact wit da poisons dey put on da plants and can't finda der way back to da hive," Mrs. Capricci says while she stirs. "It can trow off da balance of da nature."

Olivia has no reply. Mrs. Capricci's words swing her thoughts from the confusing events of the day back to Marco and the idea that just maybe, for the last years, she's been playing the wrong role.

CHAPTER TWENTY-FIVE

PRESENT DAY

O livia is sitting on the branch of a tree watching a police sketch artist draw one facial composite after another. The unfamiliar artist is positioned in a chair facing her and as he completes each sketch, he props them on easels that stretch across the grass, as if they're suspects in a police line-up. Olivia cannot see the sketches directly. Instead, she scrutinizes their reflections in the glistening water of the pool beneath her.

Each sketch is a headshot, portrayals of photographs eerily familiar in the recesses of Olivia's psyche. The first is of her mother, Doris, in her youth. The sketch is drawn with black carbon on white paper, but her lips are oversized and bright red. They waver in the movement of the water until the red bleeds from her lips, washing away like a stain in a washing machine. The next is of her sister, Grace. It's a likeness of her high school graduation picture when she had gained weight and her face was bloated. As Olivia peers at the sketch, the lines expand, causing Grace's face to become rounder and more bloated until it no longer fits on the paper. She watches as the carbon lines trail off into the water, leaving the piece of paper blank. Olivia shivers and diverts her attention to the next sketch. It is of Cari, though the rendering is not from a photograph, but from the frozen moment in Olivia's recurring nightmare when Cari's hair is being held tightly above her, and her eyes are locked on Olivia's. It is difficult to pull away from Cari's piercing stare, until a stream of crimson blood flows across the paper covering Cari's right eye. The blood sends a jolt through Olivia's system, as she now sees that the sketch no longer depicts Cari's head intact, but, instead, shows that her bloody scalp has been sliced clean off.

Like a rubbernecker at an accident, Olivia can't help but move on to the next sketch that beckons her attention. The image is of the funeral photograph of Marco's Uncle Leo with his prominent hooked nose as the focal point. A large black beetle drops from the sky and lands on the sketch paper just below Uncle Leo's nose. The force causes the paper to bob up and down in the ripple of the water and the carbon lines of Uncle Leo's nose bob with it. His nose twitches and sniffs with intensity, like a dog on a foxhunt, until it sniffs itself right off the paper. Olivia's eyes shift from the water onto the next sketch. She smiles at the portrait of a familiar vacation photo of Marco, his eyes squinting against the sun, his sexy five o'clock shadow enhancing the fullness of his lips. Olivia's body becomes warm and relaxed, liquid-like on the branch of the tree as she stretches like a feline and lolls across the limb. Another piece of paper floats over and bumps up against Marco's sketch. It ebbs and flows with the water until it floats across the top of Marco's sketch, blocking the view of his face. The image is familiar, and yet it isn't. It is of a man, but Olivia can't quite *place him. Agitated that she doesn't recognize the person (and that the paper is blocking her view of Marco), she anxiously examines the eyes and the lines of the face until she makes a connection. But the association she makes is with a woman—Mrs. Capricci. Her mind tells her that she isn't correct. But she is tired of the effort and reaches her arm down from the tree to move the paper that has overtaken the sensual image of her husband. The pool of water is some distance from her and she is thrown off balance, teetering for a second before falling from the limb.*

It's Monday, and Olivia wakes with a filtered remembrance of a dream, overtaken by the anticipation that her car will be fixed today. She rolls over and gazes out the window into the sunlit garden. A hummingbird is flitting nearby, sticking its long beak in and out of a single orange trumpet-vine blossom that has grown up the side of the window and intertwined with the honeysuckle. She's not so sure she wants her car to be fixed yet. Then she won't have an excuse to stay. Suddenly, she realizes that she misses Marco. Her skin tingles with the thought of mornings when his strong, masculine hands glide over her body with a slow caress that awakens her senses. She's missing him, but her heart tugs in the other direction, toward the house down the street.

"What do you think, Tucker? Is it time to leave?" Tucker rolls over and sticks his legs up in the air to beg for some caressing of his own. Olivia succumbs to his adorable coaxing, rubbing his soft belly for a few minutes before getting up and dressing in her new daily attire of shorts and a t-shirt—clothing that's appropriate for the dirty mess she makes of herself in the garden.

She waits until the morning chores that she's so quickly come to love are completed before she places her call to the garage. The parts are delayed. It will be another week before the car is done. Olivia's pulse revs up with the news. She's got more time.

"It looks like I'm going to be here for another week," Olivia informs Mrs. Capricci. "But I'm guessing you already know that."

Mrs. Capricci throws Olivia her signature, knowing look, and continues to wash the vegetables they'd picked earlier.

"I really do have to get out of here before June, though. I can't be here when the pesticides get thick in the air. The crop dusters scare me."

"Dey shoulda scare everyone," Mrs. Capricci replies. "Isa crop duster wit isa poison dat kill ma dear husband."

"A crop duster? What happened?"

"He spenda much time in da fields digging fo da artifacts. One day, a plane come and dump a full load of dos vile chemicals on him. He go into cardiac arrest righta der in da field."

"Oh my God, I'm so sorry!" Olivia's heart fills with empathy at the thought. She knows such a thing would probably kill her immediately. Her body has a hard time when it's exposed to even small amounts of pesticides, never mind a planeload.

"Isa almost kill me dat I no could save him after all da udders I have healed. He go before I able to get to him." She bows her head, her lips moving in a short, silent prayer. "Isa da same poison our son helpa to develop." Mrs. Capricci stops scrubbing the vegetable that is in her hand and takes a deep breath. "Da universe, isa know no bounds. We take a, and it take away."

Olivia works at the counter peeling carrots and chopping cucumbers while she ruminates over the information that she's just been told; take and take away, take and take away. She suddenly realizes that her body has been improving every day since she's been here. She's able to fight off exposure much more quickly. In fact, in just one week, she feels stronger and healthier than she has in years. Her intuition tells her that all the fresh vegetables, healing herbs and pungent spices have begun to build a fortress within her. Admittedly, she now recognizes that she's been concentrating too much on what she shouldn't eat instead of what she should.

"Seven years isa take a to build a new body," Mrs. Capricci continues. "You feeda youself right, you brand new."

Brand new. Olivia turns the term over in her mind. It's been over four-and-a-half years since she was poisoned—halfway to brand new. Today she feels like it could be true. She is strong enough to help Brian and Carly, and maybe even Dana. The universe is providing her the tools; a healthier body, Mrs. Capricci, and no way to go home. *The Why* is there, too, an eternal tether that links her to an unknown mission, one that she is becoming more and more confident relates to Jeff's family.

After lunch, Olivia changes into a sundress, sits down in a rocker on the front porch and calls Brenda, hoping she's on her lunch break and can talk. "So, I'll bet you were on the phone all night with Tommy. Am I right?"

"Maybe," Brenda giggles. "I feel like a kid again."

"I'm so happy for you. But, speaking of kids, you saw the scars on Carly's arms yesterday, right?"

"Yes. What the hell? They're cut marks, don't you think?"

"Yeah, I think. But why would she cut herself?" Olivia ponders.

"I don't know. I doubt it was over Jeff's death, though. The scars weren't that fresh."

"Yeah, I didn't think so either. I wouldn't have let her go in the water if I'd seen open wounds."

"If you're thinking of broaching the subject with Dana— and if I know you, you are—try to make sure she isn't drunk."

"Then I may never get the chance."

Brenda laughs, but not in a 'that's-funny' kind of way; more like, 'you're probably right'. They hang up, both knowing Olivia won't waste any time, regardless.

Mrs. Capricci emerges through the screen door with her arms full. "I go to ma lawyer friend to take him da leftover paella. He has a big family."

"Let me help you with that," Olivia rushes to grab the large, olive-green ceramic bowl full of paella from the old woman. She is carrying it in one arm and a very large stack of paper in the other.

Once Olivia has safely secured the paella on the floor in front of the car's passenger seat, Mrs. Capricci climbs into her old white Ford Falcon, her short stature making it difficult for her to get settled in with an armload of paper. She stretches and carefully places the stack of papers on the passenger seat and quickly waves goodbye. Olivia notices that there is a blank sheet of paper on top of the stack. Mrs. Capricci clearly doesn't want her to know what they are. Olivia brushes it off. It's none of her business.

Now familiar with the short trek to Dana's, Tucker leads the way up the street, stopping to pee in the exact same spots he's previously marked as his. "Yoo-hoo, Dana!" Olivia calls through the screen door.

"Yoo-hoo yourself!" Dana fires back.

"I came to see how you're feeling and if you've made the call to the insurance company. Can I come in?"

Dana swings the door open and motions for Olivia and Tucker to come in. "I dunno what to say to them." The smell of alcohol flies right up Olivia's nose as she passes. Dana is once again dressed in old sweats and a dirty t-shirt. A fresh drink sits on the coffee table.

"Do you want me to make the call?" Olivia asks, annoyed. All this woman does is drink. She wonders if the reason Jeff did the things he did had anything to do with this shit.

On the call, Olivia gets routed from one half-witted person to another. She sits on hold for minutes at a time before she is finally told that Jeff's case is under investigation. The policy was purchased less than two years ago which would negate payment if the cause of death is determined to be suicide. There will be no determination until the coroner and police reports are released and the investigation is complete.

Just as Olivia is relating the news to Dana, there is a knock on the door. Dana doesn't budge from the couch. Olivia answers it. "Can I help you?"

"Is Dana home?" a man dressed in business attire asks. He looks nervous and is averting his eyes to the sides of the door instead of at Olivia.

"Dana, there's someone here to see you."

"Then let him in."

Olivia steps to the side and ushers the man in. He is carrying a briefcase and has a letter in his hand.

"Great!" Dana exclaims, setting her glass on the table. "What the hel-l-l-l do you want?"

"I'm here with the final notice, Dana. You have one week from today to evacuate the premises. I'm sorry. I did all I could to get more time. The higher-ups, they just won't budge." It is clear from the man's demeanor that he knows Dana personally and that he truly is sorry.

Dana hangs her head for a few seconds and then pops it back up. "Get out!" she screams. "Get the hell out!" Carly comes running from her bedroom, straight into Olivia's arms. The man drops the letter on the table and backs out of the house, mumbling over and over that he's sorry. Dana grabs her glass and downs it in one gulp. She stands up, somewhat unsteady, and marches into the kitchen.

"Carly, could you go out back for a little while?" Olivia asks. "I need to talk with your mother."

"Can I take Tucker?" Carly inquires.

"Sure, honey." But Tucker won't budge from Olivia's side. Like a policeman steadies his hand next to his gun when on high alert, Tucker butts up to Olivia's leg and shadows her into the kitchen. "Sorry, Carly. I guess he wants to stay with me." Carly's hopeful face slides into a frown, and she solemnly walks out the back door.

"So, n-n-now you've got my daughter wanting you-u-u instead of me, huh?" Dana slurs, sloppily. "I shoulda known I couldn't trust you."

"Dana, stop. I've done no such thing. You just scared her when you yelled. Jesus, I'm not a threat. I'm here to help you."

"Yeah r-r-r-right, help me." She pours another drink, throws it back and slams the glass on the counter.

"Dana, I have to ask you something. Can you just stop for a minute?"

"Stop what?"

"Drinking like there's no tomorrow."

"Huh! There i-i-i-is no tomorrow. Don't you have ears?"

"There's a tomorrow for your kids, Dana, whether you choose to see it or not. Which brings me back to my question; have you seen the cut marks on Carly's arms?"

Dana's eyes turn from stone drunk to blind outrage in the flash of a second. "Who the hel-l-l-l do you think you are?" She drops her hands behind her and they slam against the edge of the counter, as she attempts to steady herself. "You're n-n-not a member of this family! Don't think you-u-u have a right to know our s-s-secrets!" Spit flies from Dana's mouth, along with the words she struggles to form.

"Dana, stop. I'm not here to judge you or find out your family secrets. Believe me, we all have those. I'm just worried about Carly and about you. And Brian, for that matter."

"Fuck off!" Dana spits at Olivia.

"You need help, Dana, and you're fucking off the one person who is here to help you. Look around; do you see anybody else here?" Olivia sweeps her arm around and behind her. "There is only me and I'm not going anywhere. At the very least, I'm getting Carly help. You can be damn sure of that!"

Dana drunkenly thrusts her jaw out and glares at Olivia. But her attention is suddenly drawn to the floor, where a parade of ants has begun to circle her feet. She stomps up and down, almost comically. "Fucking ants!" Twirling unsteadily around and reaching under the kitchen sink, Dana pulls out a spray can and then lurches back up and around, losing her balance in the process. Her body pitches forward toward Olivia just as she presses down on the spray nozzle. A hard mist of ant spray covers Olivia from head to toe.

Olivia immediately collapses, falling backward toward the table where Tucker, sensing her fall, positions his body under hers to block it. Her head narrowly misses the table, but within seconds she is prostrate on the floor, shaking uncontrollably.

Brian is immediately there. He has come home and walked into the kitchen just in time to witness what has just taken place. "Jesus, mom! What are you thinking?" Brian kneels by Olivia's side. "What should I do?"

"Get ... me ... out." Olivia is struggling to breathe. Black spots swarm inside her vision, like flies on a porch screen. She fights to stay conscious.

Brian lifts her off the floor and rushes her out the back door, where he lays her on the ground in front of Carly. "Now what? What do I do now?" he asks in a panic. Tucker has followed them out and is hovering over Olivia, whimpering.

"Hose ... me ... off." Olivia says haltingly. She senses that both her left limbs have gone numb. She can feel the numbness creeping up and over the side of her head. She searches her brain—now difficult to access—for solutions. Think Olivia, she says to herself. What's the protocol? Remember the protocol.

Brian reaches for the hose, "Carly, go turn the water on, quick!"

Carly runs to the side of the house, while Brian pulls on the hose to get enough slack to reach Olivia. Once the water begins to surge in the hose, he sprays her down from head to toe, which causes Olivia to shake even more violently.

"Blanket ... warmth ... get me ... warm." Her quaking body begins to jerk and her arms and legs to flail. She is now in full-seizure mode.

Brian runs into the house and emerges seconds later with an armload of blankets and towels. He and Carly work fast to lift her to a dry spot and onto one of the blankets. They frantically dry her off and then layer the blankets on top of her.

Olivia's voice is shaking and hard to discern. Like a stroke victim, it takes all her strength to form words and get them out. "Carly ... lie ... down ... on me ... please. I ... need ... your ... body heat."

Carly understands, and does exactly as she is told. She covers Olivia's body with hers as best she can, pressing herself down to transfer heat. Olivia closes her eyes and breathes, concentrating on receiving the radiant warmth. Minutes pass before her shaking, jerking body begins to slow, its life-saving reflex transforming into a nearly audible, humming vibration.

Brian turns to his mother who is peering through the back screen. With Olivia appearing to be out of immediate danger, he launches an attack. "How could you do this? You know she's sick! You could've killed her! When are you going to realize you're a fucking drunk? When is it gonna be enough? When are you gonna stop?" Like a deer in a headlight, Dana's eyes grow full and round, her face contorts in shock. Even Olivia can see it from her position. With Brian, Carly and Olivia all staring at her, Dana turns and runs to her bedroom, slamming the door behind her.

Olivia lies still on top of a sheet on her bed while Mrs. Capricci works fast, covering Olivia's entire body in a velveteen mud bath of bentonite clay. "Isa aged volcanic ash dat draw da chemicals froma you body." The old woman softly educates her while she works. "Isa replace da oxygen to you cells and isa have no odor at all." She covers Olivia's newly slathered body with warm towels and sits by her side on the edge of the bed. Brian hangs just outside the door, scuffing his shoe back and forth on the wood floor.

"Once dis dry, you helpa me get her into da ba-tub," Mrs. Capricci instructs Brian. "You do a good, Brian." She stands up and reaches around the doorframe to pat Brian on the shoulder. Mrs. Capricci can see alarm in the teenager's eyes. "You no worry. She be cover in da towel." A low, rumbling cackle escapes from her mouth.

Olivia smiles inside. Brian's the one getting an education. She is proud of him and of Carly. "Where is Carly?" she whispers.

Brian arches himself around the doorframe, but still averts his eyes. "In the living room with Tucker."

"Okay," is the only word Olivia can muster the strength for. She lies like a metal rod, fighting back the poison that has invaded her body through her pores. The vibration has subsided but has been replaced with an aching throb that thumps like a drumbeat throughout her entire being.

What seems like only moments later, she feels her body being lifted and moved into warm bathwater that smells predominantly of sage. She hears whispers and the door closing, and then feels skillful hands work over her, cleaning her, massaging her, relaxing her taut body. She feels grateful.

Back in bed, Olivia is fed a stream of savory nutrients in the form of a soup that Brian and then Carly take turns spooning into her mouth. With each mouthful, Olivia picks up the scent of onions, garlic and parsley, and tastes a chunk of soggy bread. Slowly, she begins to regain small measures of strength and she smiles at Tucker, who is lying across her legs.

"Tucker saved you, right Brian?" Carly eagerly informs

Olivia, praising the beloved dog. "He blocked your fall, so you didn't hit your head. Brian saw it."

Olivia smiles at Tucker who is curled up next to her on the bed, peering at her, and then at Carly and Brian. "I think the two of you played a big part, too, don't you?"

Carly shrugs her shoulders. "I guess we did."

"Oh, you did. I don't think I can ever thank you enough."

Brian grunts. "It happened in our house, because of our mother."

"Oh Brian," Olivia says. "Don't blame your mom. She didn't know. All that matters is that I'll be okay." She can feel a drag in her speech and the familiar droop on the left side of her face. It happens every time she experiences a seizure like this.

"Yeah right, that's all that matters."

"How about we take one thing at a time, huh? Right now, I'm just happy you two are here."

"Whata I, how you say, chop liver?" Mrs. Capricci feigns insult as she ambles in to clear the tray. Olivia gives the old woman one of her own looks and they both share a little laugh.

Mrs. Capricci shoos the kids back home for the night and arranges a standing tray next to Olivia's bed. Next, she carries in a pot of steaming water laced with the strong fragrances of clove, rosemary and eucalyptus. "You clear you lungs wit da oils dat I make myself." She hands Olivia a towel to put over her head and motions for her to lean over the pot. "Breate deep into da lungs, swirl da air around and den swoosh back out." Olivia follows her instructions, repeating the process over and over, feeling the medicated steam expand her lungs. "Da clay remove da toxins from you skin, da food soak up da toxins from you insides and da oils release da toxins from you lungs. It take a all da parts to make a you clean again."

Olivia scoots down in the bed and imagines her body as parts of a whole, each part needing its own unique attention. She questions her stupidity over the last several years, recalling how she had only focused on one aspect of her health at a time. Her thoughts trail off and dissolve like a dust cloud on a dirt road, as she falls into a deep slumber.

ৡৣৄ

In the morning, Olivia is anxious to call Marco. He had visited her in her dreams that night. She was sure it was him from the familiar kisses he'd trailed across her neck. But the only clear image she had of the man was that of a phantom magician with a white-masked face and white-gloved hands. In a surreal scene, he had gently pulled and straightened each of her limbs which were twisted and bent, and afterwards traced a figure eight along her torso with a copper wand. Finally, he had sprinkled her with bursts of sparkling dust and recited mysterious incantations in Spanish.

Marco sounds cheerful when he answers the phone. "I was just thinking about you," he shares.

"And I dreamed about you all night," Olivia remarks. She doesn't tell him about the ant spray. She doesn't want to deflate either of their moods.

"Maybe it was the same dream I had," he purrs suggestively.

"Mmmm, maybe," Olivia responds. The exchange melts like butter over her. She wishes he were there by her side at that very moment.

"Did you get the SUV back?" Marco suddenly turns the

sublime back to the practical.

"No. The parts didn't come. It's going to be another week." She is feeling some regret now. The tug of war between home and Alamosa has begun to loosen its grip on the Alamosa end.

"Oh damn! What the hell is taking so long?"

"It's a small town, Marco."

"I know, I know. Are you sure you're okay out there without me?"

"I miss you, but I'm okay." Olivia hopes the drag in her speech isn't pronounced enough for Marco to notice. "I imagine the delay is for a reason. Jeff's family is in dire straits. I'm hoping there is some way I can help them while I'm here."

"If I know you, you'll figure it out. You okay?"

"I'm fine." She brushes the inquiry off. "I hope I figure it out." But Olivia isn't so sure. "What's up with you?"

"I emailed Mateo last night," Marco says proudly.

"Really? Wow! Good for you." Olivia is super-impressed.

"I haven't gotten a response. But I really don't expect one."

"What made you do it?"

"Well, I had lunch yesterday with the guy from that group I told you about, El Guardia Legado. His name is Eddie. I kind of briefed him on the story and he encouraged me to initiate the communication."

Olivia's stomach tightens. She feels like she should be upset that he never listened to her all the times she tried to get him to write an email to Mateo. But maybe she should simply be happy that he did it, no matter why. She takes a deep breath and chooses the latter. Her stomach relaxes. He's acting more like the man she married way back when. Maybe this group he's joined is just the shot he needs.

"Well, you have to start somewhere," Olivia agrees. "But it's going to take time, probably a few attempts before you rattle his cage enough for him to respond."

"Rattle his cage, huh? We both know the venom he can release. Don't scare me away now."

"I'm just messing with you," she replies. "But when he does respond, expect more spice than sugar. You know him; he'll need to vent."

"Yeah, I know him. That's what I'm afraid of."

"No need to be afraid. Things can't get any worse than they are now."

"I guess you're right."

Olivia hangs up just as the door creaks open and Mrs. Capricci, still in her nightgown, appears with a breakfast tray. Steam rises from a bowl of oatmeal that is finished with pumpkin seeds and blueberries, and it streams as well from the little red teapot that smells unmistakably of peppermint tea. "You stay righta where you are today. You needa rest to regain you strengt. And Olivia," her caretaker pauses for effect, "remember, sometime whata push us foward is just whata hold us back."

Olivia lifts a spoonful of the nourishing oatmeal to her mouth and blows on it to cool it down. As she swallows the first bite, she has the conspicuous sense that she's swallowing her medicine, too.

CHAPTER TWENTY-SIX

PRESENT DAY

She has bouts of long deep sleep interspersed with restless dreams that spawn a mix of familiar characters. Dreams about the river make appearances in between others, but the people in the river dream have now been revealed as people she knows. Her mother, Doris, is the desperate woman in the water; Mateo the detached teenager; and Carly the fretful young girl. The reasoning of any of it is still a mystery. Olivia tells Mrs. Capricci about her latest dream—not of the river—while she steams her face in a pot of water laced with oils of clove, lemon, cinnamon, eucalyptus and rosemary. "It was a massive graveyard with unmarked headstones. I saw Uncle Leo driving away in a golf cart with rakes and stuff in the back. And then I turned to see an open hole with a skeleton in the bottom. There was a man shoveling dirt on top of it and he looked like you."

"Dat make sense," Mrs. Capricci deciphers. "It come from what I tell you about Carissa living with Leo and den being buried in da potter's field." She strokes Olivia's bent-over back as she talks. "I'ma so sorry dat da trut is causing you such grief. I afraid of dat."

"It's okay," Olivia assures her. "I feel better that I know. Not knowing was much harder."

Mrs. Capricci barely leaves Olivia's side for the next two days. She feeds her and uses a myriad of healing techniques to expunge the toxins from Olivia's body. When Olivia is awake, they talk for hours, as if they are making up for lost time. Mrs. Capricci recounts heartwarming stories from her childhood in Italy and the tragic story of losing her parents to the Germans before she escaped to America with her husband. Olivia tells stories of her children growing up and, together, they share the heartbreak of sons that don't speak to them.

It's Thursday afternoon before Olivia feels strong enough to venture outside again. Both Brian and Carly had come to visit her the day before. But there's been no sign of Dana.

Mrs. Capricci shoos Olivia to the river. "Go now!" she demands, as she hands her a sweater. "Isa just what da doctor order."

Tucker, no longer requiring a leash, leads the way up and over the bank. Olivia walks slowly behind, stopping to admire a precariously tall cairn of stones someone has stacked on top of a large rock. The air has turned, and a cool breeze lifts and swirls off the water. Olivia is thankful for the sweater that covers her bare arms. Along the river's edge, she is careful not to get wet. Tucker, on the other hand, splashes about and frolics with the minnows.

She is walking north, and eventually comes to the bend that curves westerly. As she makes the turn, she immediately spies Brian sitting on a rock. His head is in his hands, his shoulders shaking, his anguish visible—even from Olivia's distance. Tucker reaches Brian first, nudging his arm with his snout. Brian glances up at Tucker and then at Olivia, while he wipes the tears from his eyes. "Hey," he offers meekly.

"Hey," Olivia dittos as she slides herself down next to him on the rock. They sit for a few minutes in silence watching Tucker play in the water. Olivia picks up a flat stone and skims it over the water. One, two, three skips. "I'll bet you can do better," she challenges Brian.

He searches for and picks up a larger flat stone, and skillfully chucks it across the surface of the water, skipping it seven times.

"Wow, a master!" she teases. "Maybe you can teach me."

Brian turns up the sides of his mouth in a weak grin, and his trusty toothpick peeks out. "What are we going to do, Olivia?" he abruptly blurts out, his plaintive voice breaking. Tears begin to stream down his cheeks again.

"It'll be okay, Brian. I've been thinking a lot over the last couple of days and I have some ideas." She lays her hand on his knee. "But first, I have some questions and I need you to be honest with me."

"Okay." He awkwardly brushes the backs of his hands across his wet cheeks.

Olivia pushes forward. "Why was Carly cutting herself on her arms?" Brian hangs his head and the tears begin to flow harder. "Brian, I need you to tell me. It's the only way I can help."

He takes his time, breathing deeply, and then he begins to let it out, haltingly at first. "It was … because of … my dad."

"What about your dad?"

"He was … he was … he was going into her bedroom at night."

Olivia's hands fly uncontrollably up to grip her chest. It was just what she thought but didn't want to believe. She puts her arms around Brian and hugs him while she silently bemoans how Jeff could've become such a monster. They sit awhile, Brian releasing his shame through his tears, before Olivia presses on. "How did you find out?"

He wipes the drips of tears away again. "She cried out one night. Both my mom and I ran to her bedroom. He was there, on top of her." His tears stop suddenly, like a faucet that has been shut off tight.

"What did your mom do?"

"She ran back to her bedroom and stayed there for days."

"Hmmm." Olivia exhales, gathering her thoughts. From what she's learned of Dana over the last week, she wouldn't have expected much more. "How long ago was that?"

"It was January, right after Christmas."

"Is that when your mother started to drink?"

"No, she always drank. It just got worse. And then—then she started with the pills."

"What did your dad do after that?"

"He barely ever came home. It was like he almost disappeared." Brian is staring out over the river as though he's looking through it, not at it.

"And then Carly started cutting herself?"

Brian shakes his head no. "It was before. I didn't see them until after, though. But she told me she'd stopped. I check regularly, and I don't think she's gone back to it." Olivia lets out a heavy sigh and Brian wipes his nose on the sleeve of his t-shirt. "I don't know who to be madder at, my mom or my dad. You know they think he committed suicide."

"I heard that. But the investigation isn't complete yet."

"It doesn't matter. I know he did. I've known since it happened. I don't know how. I just know."

"Hmmm, well then you're probably right. Our instinct typically knows the answers before our brain does." Olivia's instinct is telling her the same.

"I wish I'd had better instincts about what he was doing to Carly."

"Don't blame yourself. None of this is your fault. And even though I understand how you feel, being mad at either your mom or your dad won't get anybody anywhere."

"Then what will?" he asks, with no hope in his voice.

"Look, your dad made his choices. There's nothing anyone can do about that now. But the rest of your family is still alive. The best thing any of you can do now is look forward instead of back."

"That's pretty hard to do with no money and no house and a mom who's an alcoholic and a drug addict." He shrugs his shoulders in a gesture of defeat.

"I didn't say it would be easy, at least not in the beginning. But, it will get easier and you do have a future."

"Pretty hard to see one right now."

"Well, how about you just start with today? Your mom needs help and so does Carly. I think you're the strongest of your whole family, and they both need you right now."

"Huh, that's what you think. I don't feel so strong. If you want to know the truth, all I think about is going away to college somewhere, escaping all of this. And that's just selfish and," he shrugs his shoulders, "pretty much impossible anyway."

"It's not selfish and nothing's impossible. But first, I think the most important thing is to get your mom into rehab somewhere. And second is to get Carly into counseling."

"That all takes money. We don't even have a place to live."

"Let me work on it. I've got some resources and I'll see what I can do. Right now, though, I want to go talk to your mother. Are you going to be okay?"

"Yeah, I'll be okay."

Olivia gives Brian a strengthening hug and calls Tucker from the water. A gust of wind whips through her hair and lifts it skyward. She tames it with her hand and shifts her gaze to the trees above. A magnificent, red-tailed hawk that has been quietly perched on a branch above them suddenly glides down and across their line of vision. Olivia's eyes follow its flight as it wheels and soars up the river. Just before it moves out of sight, its head turns back, and its luminous eyes connect squarely with Olivia's, holding her gaze, both suspended, together, in a timeless moment.

Olivia leaves Brian on the bank and trails Tucker back to Mrs. Capricci's, thinking about what she'll say to Dana. But the hawk that swooped and glided before her continues to make a play for her attention. Suddenly, she remembers with clarity the red-tailed hawk that had floated in front of her that day on the bank, so long ago, after she had escaped from the neighbor boys' room. The day, she now recalls, she saw the old woman on the riverbank.

"Mrs. Capricci," she says, as she walks into the kitchen. "I have a question, and I wonder if you might know something about it."

"Yes, mia amore."

"Is there some significance to the red-tailed hawk?"

The old woman smiles and her eyes twinkle. "Oh yes, isa da great guide, a messenger of da spirit world. Isa make an appearance in one's life when one most needa to pay attention." Olivia narrows her eyes and scrunches her nose. "Do you justa see one?" Mrs. Capricci asks.

"Yes, a red-tailed hawk. Brian and I both saw it. It's not the first time, either."

Mrs. Capricci nods her head, as if she already knew the answer to her question. "Isa show itself to guide or warn and it keepa show itself until da message is receive. Isa sacred and respect all da way back to da ancients."

"Oh!" Olivia replies in wonderment.

"Pay attention, mia amore. Da red-tailed hawk, isa no show itself to justa anyone."

Olivia leaves the house with Tucker, scanning the sky with each step, searching for the red-tailed hawk. She ponders what the message it is trying to give her might be. It could be trying to tell her what she already believes: that Dana and her family are *The Why*. As she walks, Olivia begins to pray under her breath, hoping to find the answers to help this family.

As Dana's house comes into view, she sees a police car parked in front of it and two uniformed policemen knocking on her front door. Olivia picks up her pace and reaches the door just after Dana has ushered the policemen inside. Dana waits behind the open screen door to hear what Olivia has to say. "I was coming over to talk. Do you want me to leave or could you use some support?" Olivia offers.

A look of shock crosses Dana's face. "You're here to support me after what I did?"

"It was an accident." Olivia points to the policemen who are standing in the living room. One is holding a thick folder. "Did they say why they're here?"

Dana looks inside and then back at Olivia. "They're here to talk about Jeff." Dana motions for Olivia to come in. "Maybe, if you wouldn't mind?"

Tucker bounds into the house and heads straight back to the kitchen, where he finds Carly. "Hey Carly," Olivia calls. "Think you could take Tucker for a walk?" Carly just nods her head in agreement. She is clearly alarmed by the police officers' presence and rushes out the back door with Tucker.

Back inside, the policemen, Dana and Olivia introduce themselves and sit down. An older, gray-haired and softer-looking policeman named Bill seems to know Dana. He has a quiet demeanor and appears sympathetic. The other, younger policeman, Chuck, is all business. His shoulders are thrust back, and he sits like he has a rod running up his spine. Dana tucks the drink that is sitting on the coffee table behind a lamp on the end table, as if that'll hide the fact that she's been drinking. The tension in the air is spring-loaded.

Dana steals a quick glance at her drink and fidgets in her seat, "Oka-a-ay?"

Chuck lays the folder on the coffee table, opens it up and scatters the documents over the top. There are photographs, diagrams, receipts and reports. Bill sits at a distance, a little removed from the conversation, almost as though he's a trainee. Chuck picks up a few pages of the report. "Well, here, this analysis tells us that the brakes on Jeff's vehicle were in good working order." He attempts to hand the report to Dana, but she waves it away. He resumes. "These pictures here are of the oil slick his truck skidded on. And these here," he hesitates, "these are of quite a few empty quarts of oil we found a hundred yards or so from the site, hidden behind some thistle bushes. They have Jeff's fingerprints on them."

Olivia scrunches her eyebrows up and fidgets. Dana's face turns gray.

Chuck continues. "We have a receipt here that tells us they were bought two days earlier, over in Monte Vista. The clerk in the store identified Jeff's picture as the person who bought them." He drops the receipt and picks up what looks like a doctor's prescription. "The toxicology report found a high dose of sleeping pills in Jeff's blood stream. This here is a prescription from a doctor in Monte Vista who also identified Jeff. He'd used a fake name when he made the appointment, and he paid cash." Chuck shuffles again through the documents. "These here are invoices showing that he'd sold off all the livestock over the last few months. I don't know if you've been out to the ranch, but there are no animals there and the bank informed us that they have issued multiple foreclosure notices."

Dana shakes her head yes, confirming that she's been there and knows at least something about the bank's actions.

"So," he sums up, "they've ruled it a suicide."

"How do the sleeping pills fit in?" Olivia asks.

"Well, they believe he took them that morning, just before the accident. More than likely, he wanted to make sure that if, by chance, he lived through the car crash, he'd die from the pills. I don't know why, but I guess he didn't think they'd test, being that it was early morning and the oil slick, and all." Chuck turns his palms upward in an *I don't know* gesture.

Dana leans forward. Her face is taut. In a barely audible voice, she chokes out, "What exactly did kill him?"

"The accident," Chuck replies. "His body was ejected through the windshield when the vehicle rolled, and he was killed on impact." Both officers look to the floor. Dana begins to shake and tears stream from her eyes.

Olivia stands. "Thank you, officers. Is there anything else?"

"I assume Dana, that you know there's an insurance investigator doing his own investigation," Chuck says.

Olivia replies for Dana. "Yes, she knows."

"Okay then, if there's nothing else …" Chuck's voice trails off as he reshuffles the evidence back into the folder and both officers stand to leave. Bill, who hasn't said a word, juts out his hand to shake Dana's and Chuck does the same with Olivia.

"We're awfully sorry." Bill finally mutters.

Chuck mimics him, but with more strength in his voice. "Yes, we're awfully sorry."

The room is quiet for a while after the officers make their exit. Dana doesn't move from her spot, except to retrieve her drink from behind the lamp. Finally, Olivia breaks the silence. "So, Dana, do you have any idea why Jeff would want to commit suicide?"

Dana looks up, her eyes void of light. "Too many to count."

Olivia sucks in a full breath of air and forges on. "The other day when we went on the picnic, I saw cut marks on Carly's arms." She stops, expecting a reaction from Dana, but nothing comes. "You know about them, right?"

Dana's dark eyes become riveted on Olivia. "I'm her mother, aren't I?"

"Yes, I'm sorry. I didn't mean anything by that." Olivia stands up and begins to pace the room. "I saw Brian at the river today. He told me why." Dana's eyes look dead. She stares forward at nothing. "How long was it happening, Dana?"

Dana drains her drink and then begins to talk. "He said it started after his dad died last year. He said he couldn't help himself. He told me he was sorry. He blamed himself for his dad's death. He'd asked Jeff to fix a hole in the fence. It was winter, lots of snow and ice on the ground. Jeff kept putting it off. One morning, he found him on the ground out by the broken fence. He was already dead."

"So, he took it out on Carly! Why?"

"I ask myself that question a hundred times a day."

"Hmmm." Olivia shakes her head up and down and then back and forth. "He hurt so many people. I guess it would be hard to keep living with yourself." Olivia stops pacing and sits back down. "Dana, you know you don't have much time before you have to get out of this house, and you've got to know that Carly needs counseling." Dana sighs, defeated. "But I have to say this. You need to help yourself first. You need rehab, Dana."

Dana slams her empty glass on the table. "Fuck you!"

"Come on, Dana. How are you going to help your kids in this condition? It's just rehab, a month of your life."

"I don't need rehab! What the hell are you talking about? What I need is money!"

"Money's not going to help your drinking or your addiction to pills."

"I'm not addicted to pills! How dare you!" Dana gets up and vanishes into the kitchen. Olivia follows her.

"Dana, stop it. You need help."

"Like I said, fuck you!"

"Oh, and fuck your kids, too? Because that's what you're saying! You're choosing pills and alcohol over them! Can't you see that?"

"I'm not choosing anything over them! What about me, huh? What about me?" Dana pounds her fists to her chest. "What am I supposed to do? Who's thinking about me?"

"I am, in case you haven't noticed!"

Dana glares at Olivia. "Why are you here, anyway? None of this is any of your fucking business! Do you want my kids now? Wasn't Jeff enough?"

"Dana, I didn't have Jeff. And all I want for your kids is to see them get through this, and for them to lead decent lives in the future. You should want that too."

"Don't tell me what I want!"

"Well then, what do you want?"

"What do you think I want? I want none of this to have happened! I want Carly to be an innocent little girl again! I want the insurance company to pay!"

Olivia nods her head. "I can understand all of that, Dana. But none of it is possible. What is possible is for you to get your act together so that you can be there for your kids."

"I am there for my kids! You don't know anything about us! What have you been here for, a week?"

"It doesn't take longer than that to see what's going on here. You're in denial, Dana. That's typical for someone with an addiction problem. But if you think you're there for your kids, you are fooling yourself. They are hurting, and they need the only parent they have left!"

"Again, fuck you! I am not an addict!"

"Then what would you call a person who drinks herself into oblivion every day?"

Dana stares at Olivia with hatred. "You try living through this!"

"What? You think you're the only one who's lived through suicide and abuse? I had to live through both and at a much younger age than you! It's a choice, Dana. You can let it take you down or you can use it to pick yourself up." Olivia is in disbelief that she's just revealed such personal information about herself to Dana. Oddly, it gives her some relief.

The look on Dana's face softens a little, but more from weariness than anything else. She seems to mull over Olivia's words, questioning them with skepticism. "You were abused? By who?"

Olivia challenges Dana's skepticism. "My sister. It started when I was five and lasted until I was nine. She did it because she'd been molested." Olivia pauses for a moment to push past the pain that can cripple you, if you let it. "She committed suicide when she was 21."

Dana hangs her head. "I didn't know."

"How would you? My parents kept the suicide out of the papers. It was different back then, before social media." Where Jeff's death was concerned, Olivia had read the gossipy comments after she friended Tommy on Facebook. The townspeople were having a field day with the speculation that Jeff committed suicide.

Dana drags a chair out from the kitchen table and slumps down into it. "This world is such a mess. Everything is so fucked up. I just can't see past it all."

"You can't see anything through the alcohol, Dana. Don't you see, if you could just get sober, you could help your kids?"

"How? I have no money to help my kids with."

"Right now, all they need is you. And they need you sober."

The two women sit at the table in silence for quite a while. Finally, Dana gets up and grabs the bottle of vodka, and sits back down without pouring it.

"So, what about rehab, Dana? Will you go?"

"Even if I wanted to, I don't have the money."

Olivia shakes her head in agreement. "I'm sure there are state programs. Do you have health insurance?"

Dana gives Olivia the 'yeah, right' look.

"What about your sister or Jeff's family. Can they help?"

"No, please, not my sister. I can't ask my sister. And Jeff's family? No way. They hate me. If they knew, they'd use it as an excuse to take my kids."

The back door squeaks open and shut and Tucker barrels in. Carly stops at the kitchen threshold. "Hey there, how was your walk?" Olivia asks.

Carly steals a glance at her mother and then at Olivia. "Good. He likes the minnows."

"I know. He thinks he can catch them. But they're way too quick. Carly, can you take Tucker out front? I'll be out in just a minute. Your mom and I are almost done." Olivia waits for Carly to be out of earshot. "Think about it, Dana. But I need to make one thing perfectly clear. If you choose not to go to rehab, I'll petition the court to take your kids away until you do. Whether they end up with family or in foster care, either is better than with you right now."

Dana doesn't say a word. She is struck silent by Olivia's threat. Olivia scoots her chair back and marches through the living room toward the front door. The shaky clink of the vodka bottle against a glass is the last thing she hears before she exits Dana's house.

CHAPTER TWENTY-SEVEN

1980

The frozen earth in the valley has thawed enough to dig, and so a large mound of freshly shoveled dirt rests next to the hole, ready to be heaved back in. Attendance is sparse. Olivia scans the few faces she can see and then lifts her gaze south into the distance beyond, where a cluster of rolling tumbleweeds has caught her eye. Russian thistle, she thinks; dried up, broken from its roots, untethered and roaming free.

Olivia is missing classes. Sadly, she had been summoned home from college in northern Colorado for this. Her sister Grace has committed suicide—hanged herself with a rope tied around a branch of the big bur oak tree in the neighbor's back yard. Their parents hadn't even known Grace was in town. It seems that, with some premeditation, she chose the exact spot where she was to take her life and had quietly driven home from the mountains west of Denver, where she'd been living since dropping out of college, to finish her grim task.

Grace had left a neatly folded note inside a sealed envelope on the ground next to the trunk of the tree. The neighbor—the mother of the wicked boys—had found her, and had given the unopened note to Grace's father, who then phoned Olivia and read it to her, word-for-word. It was a confession of her sins. She wrote about the abuse she had perpetrated on Olivia in the closet, and about the prostitution. She admitted to having had five abortions, the first of which—remarkably—was at the tender age of 13. She disclosed that she had gotten pregnant by the older neighbor boy, but that it hadn't been rape. She apologized for taking her life but said she could no longer live with herself.

The funeralgoers disperse, all but Olivia's immediate family. It's clear that their father is the most broken up of all. Kneeling by the side of Grace's grave, he's silently crying, his hands clasped in prayer. Olivia chokes as a sob rises unexpectedly in her throat. She kneels by her father's side and puts her arm around his shoulders. They surrender to their grief and weep together. Her mother, Marilyn and Elizabeth back away and turn slowly to make their way to the waiting cars.

They say their goodbyes at the cemetery, Olivia and her father, hugging each other as if it will be the last time. Then Olivia is off down the road and out of town, having no desire to sit around her parents' house to endure the bewildered faces of her remaining sisters and the smug expression her mother would undoubtedly have on her face.

A week passes. Olivia attends classes and attempts to study, but her thoughts are never far from Grace. Drawn to know more about the last place her sister lived, Olivia interrupts her routine to set out on a journey to locate her home, speak to people who knew her and to touch and feel anything she may have left behind.

Grace had worked at a ski area over the winter, Olivia learns, living in a cabin near a creek that had no electricity or running water of its own. Olivia travels up the dirt road, winding and switch-backing until she comes upon the tiny one-room cabin that was Grace's last home.

Finding that there's no lock on the door, Olivia pushes it open to reveal a sparsely furnished room with a woodburning stove in the corner, a bed, a table, two chairs and a round woven rug. The space is dismal but for the view through the windows of the side of the mountain, still patched with snow, and the pine trees rising starkly along the creek.

Olivia walks around the room searching for something, anything, that feels like Grace. She lifts a blanket from the bed and buries her nose in it, picking up the lingering odor of wood smoke. She sifts through a small pile of clothes on the floor, bunching up each piece and pressing it to her face until she recognizes Grace's scent on an old gray sweatshirt. She holds the age-softened fabric to her nose and inhales several times. The smell—Grace's smell—permeates her being, and she falls to the bed and begins to cry.

She cries for Grace, for the pain she clearly suffered and for the short, tormented life she led. She cries for herself and for the sin and shame Grace had so vehemently heaped on her; Grace, in all her childish naiveté, believed she could exorcise herself of her demons by visiting them on her little sister.

A small wooden stool in the corner of the room catches Olivia's eyes. Its top is painted with a blue and red checkerboard, and, hanging from a hook on its side, is a string of wooden checkers. Olivia picks up the stool and clutches it to her chest. She imagines Grace, huddled by the fire on cold winter nights, playing the game by herself or with friends from the ski area. Olivia takes the checkerboard stool and the sweatshirt with Grace's smell still suffusing it and lays them gently on the passenger seat of her car. She knows she will keep them both forever.

Before she leaves, Olivia walks down to the creek and sits on a boulder jutting into the water. Chunks of ice line the far side of the creek, where no sun reaches. The rock-faced mountain rises steeply above the creek. Like a high castle wall, it looms as protection against the western winds. Olivia sits where she imagines Grace might have chosen to sit at times when she was seeking solace. Olivia envisions her sister feeling locked in, desperate, yearning for the sun to illuminate her dark and shattered soul. With her eyes closed, Olivia prays that Grace is in a better place, that her father will be able to release yet another daughter, and that she, herself, will be able to fill the sickeningly empty hole that has grown in the pit of her stomach.

She is thirsty, and so she stops at the end of the road, at The Pine Tree Tavern. Inside, it's bustling with locals who are sitting at the bar, eating lunch. Olivia slides onto a vacant barstool. Before long, a guy sitting next to her strikes up a conversation. He is maybe a few years older than Olivia, and handsome, with dark Italian features and even darker eyes that draw you in. Olivia learns that he works at the same ski area that Grace had. He says that he knew her and tells Olivia that she was friendly but a loner, most often choosing to stay in her cabin rather than venture out with the locals.

Olivia is grateful for these morsels of information about her sister, even though they sink bitterly, like spoiled pieces of fruit, into her stomach. Olivia's companion at the bar tells her that he's from the east coast. He describes himself as a vagabond who has biked through South America and hiked the Pacific Coast Trail. He is funny and interesting. She feels comfortable sitting next to him, listening to him spin his tales. His name is Rick, and he asks for her number.

CHAPTER TWENTY-EIGHT

PRESENT DAY

Mrs. Capricci is uncharacteristically away from the kitchen this morning when Olivia and Tucker amble in. Instead, they find her on the back stoop, dressed in her nightgown and robe. She seems hypnotized by the beauty of her garden and all the nurturing creatures so busily working their magic in it. A steaming mug of peppermint tea is cupped in her hands and another is waiting on the stoop beside her.

Olivia sits down next to her and warms herself with the mug. The air is cool, and gray clouds roll across the sky overhead. Tucker disappears around the side of the house to find his designated pee spot, but quickly trots back and drapes himself, blanket-like, over the women's bare feet.

Olivia finally breaks the silence. "It smells like rain."

"Ahh yes, mia amore, it come soon." The old woman looks

tired as she pats Olivia on the knee. "You know, people who take dey own lives, maybe isa be da only way dey find rest. We no be da judge."

Goosebumps travel over Olivia's skin. She presses her warm mug to her chest. A bee buzzes past her ear.

Mrs. Capricci scoots sideways on the stoop, reaches out and pushes a wandering wisp of hair behind Olivia's ear. "Fo some, isa take a lifetime to fogive. But who we to say which is da bigger sin, or if eder is a sin at all?" The old woman leans forward and kisses Olivia on the forehead, and then sluggishly rises and makes her way into the house. Today, her achingly slow movement reveals the consequences of age.

They eat breakfast in silence, both lost in their thoughts. A feeling hangs—palpable—in the air between them, akin to that of a mother and daughter who need no words to impart their love for one another. Sprinkles of rain begin to tap on the windows. "You go now," Mrs. Capricci instructs Olivia. "We no garden today."

Olivia is anxious to get to Dana's. Her mission is clearly laid out in front of her, and she has always been an avid follower of her own designs. Mrs. Capricci is resting in her chair with a blanket across her lap when Olivia emerges from her room to depart. "Can I get you anything before I go"

"No, no. I'ma good." Olivia bends to kiss this treasure of a woman on the forehead, leashes Tucker and reaches for the umbrella resting near the threshold. "Mia amore," Mrs. Capricci speaks tenderly. "Like Aristotle say ..." Olivia turns back so she can hear her words more clearly. "Da more you know, da more you know you no know."

Mrs. Capricci's wise pronouncement streams through Olivia's consciousness as she and Tucker hurry up the street. She is beginning to feel like all she might have ever thought to be true—all that she had held so tightly as pure fact—was just a mirage, like an oasis in the desert might appear to a hallucinating soul. But Mrs. Capricci has taught her that she can begin again. She assures herself that, this time, she will do a better job.

Dana is still in her pajamas lounging on the couch and staring at the ceiling. At least she doesn't have a drink in her hands. "Where's Carly?" Olivia asks.

"In her room."

Olivia speaks in a low voice, not wasting any time. "So, Dana, what's your decision?"

Dana glares at her for a minute before she speaks. "You aren't really giving me a choice, are you?"

"Sure I am. Whichever way this goes, it's you who's making the choice." Olivia, standing with her hands planted on her hips, clearly means business.

"Where would I go with no money, some crappy state hospital or something?"

"I don't know. I imagine some phone calls will enlighten us as to what's out there. Do you want me to start making some or would you rather I call the Department of Child Welfare?" Olivia is losing patience.

"No, please, no child welfare."

Olivia finds the phone and begins a round of calls: the local hospital, the health department, two clinics, the state department of health. Dana sits on the couch the entire time, looking like she's on death row, awaiting her last meal. After nearly two hours of evasive responses and a hundred miles of red tape, Olivia is on the verge of surrendering to alcohol herself. The goal, it appears, is to lead the uninsured through a maze until, frustrated beyond comprehension, they give up.

Wracking her brain for another solution, Olivia calls Brenda. "I need your help. Got any idea about rehab facilities?"

"Actually, I do. One of my kids did a stint in one. He's better now. They work."

"Great. Where is it, and do you know if they take charity cases?"

"It's right here in Denver. But it's a private facility, one of the best. I highly doubt it."

"Oh. Okay, well screw it. Dana needs help now." Olivia glances into the living room where Dana has begun her descent into oblivion. She is holding her first drink of the day like an old lady on a busy street clutches her pocketbook, close and tight. "I'll figure out how to pay for it. Can you get me the information?"

"Sure. Let me find it. I'll text it to you. And Olivia, if there's anything else I can do to help, let me know."

"Remember you said that," Olivia chides.

Carly has been playing quietly in her room all morning. She hasn't attended school since Jeff's death. Olivia needs a break, so she peeks through Carly's door and invites her to take a walk in the rain.

A few minutes later, cloaked in raincoat and galoshes, Carly handles Tucker's leash while Olivia holds an umbrella over them. They walk in the gutter, splashing as they go, neither concerned with how soaked they get. "So, Carly, I have something to ask you," Olivia begins, the question arising out of thin air. "Do you think you'd be okay staying at Mrs. Capricci's for a bit? Your mom needs to go away for a little while."

Carly stops splashing and looks up at Olivia. "Will you be there, too?"

"For a while, but probably not for the whole time."

"Oh."

"Mrs. Capricci is a nice woman. She'd take good care of you. You were comfortable when you came to her house, right?"

"I guess so."

"You'd be doing it to help your mom, and it wouldn't be for that long."

"How long?"

"I don't know; maybe a month."

Carly kicks at a puddle, splashing water out into the already drenched street. "What about Brian?"

"I don't know that either. I'm hoping he'll stay there too."

Carly hesitantly shakes her head up and down. "Okay, I guess, if Brian is going to be there."

Olivia smiles and grabs Carly's hand, swinging it exaggeratedly back and forth as they walk back to the house. When they arrive, Carly finds a towel to dry Tucker off and then escapes back into her bedroom.

The text with the information is waiting on Olivia's phone. She makes the call and finds out what the damages will be. It's a high price, so much so that it gives Olivia reason to retreat. But she books Dana for Monday, anyway. A promise to pay with cash seems to trump all else and, miraculously, there is an opening. They assure Olivia that Dana will receive the best treatment available.

She breaks the news to a skeptical Dana. "You're booked for Monday in a private facility in Denver. Don't worry about the cost. I'll figure it out."

"Monday?" Dana panics.

"Yes, Monday. I'll figure out how to get you there. In the meantime, you need to pack this house. You are aware they're going to lock you out in three days, right?"

"Humph, the bastards!"

"Dana, focus. When Brian gets home from school, tell him to come see me. You'll need his help. I'll get you a storage unit."

Dana eagle-eyes Olivia, "I don't get why you're doing all this?"

"Frankly Dana, I don't either. I'm surprised myself. But regardless, I am. You'd be smart to take advantage. I don't see any other help waiting in line."

Tucker gets up from the spot where he's been lying and begins to circle Olivia's legs. Olivia reaches down to pet him. "There's a lot of stuff in this house. I suggest you start working. I'll have Brian get you boxes." Dana sits frozen. Tucker circles again and then pushes Olivia's legs toward the door and whimpers. "What's the matter, boy? You gotta pee? You were just out." He circles again, nudges and whimpers some more.

"Okay, it's time to go anyway." Olivia snaps at Dana. "Do it now, Dana! I'm not fucking around!"

Tucker doesn't pee. Instead, he pulls Olivia up the street like he's on a mission. She struggles holding the leash in one hand and the umbrella in the other. "Jesus Tucker, what's gotten into you?"

Once under the porch roof and out of the rain, Olivia shakes the water off her umbrella, collapses it and leans it against the house next to the front door. Inside, Mrs. Capricci is in her chair, napping. Olivia dries Tucker with a towel hanging on a hook by the door and peels off her wet boots. She tries not to wake Mrs.

Capricci, but once she's unleashed him, Tucker rushes to position his wet head on the woman's lap and begins nudging her hand with his muzzle. Olivia draws nearer to scoot him away, but, as she does, her heart leaps into her throat. Mrs. Capricci's face is gray, and she isn't breathing.

Frantically, she picks up the old woman's limp wrist to check for a pulse but finds none. Olivia drops to her knees and weeps. Tucker burrows his head deep into the folds of the woman's belly and moans in despair. As she kneels sobbing next to Mrs. Capricci's body, Olivia feels as though she's watching a reel playing all the events that have happened since she came here, and all that she learned about this woman and Olivia's own family. Immense sadness engulfs her. In less than two short weeks, Mrs. Capricci had propped her up and breathed new life into her. And now there is a part of Olivia that doesn't believe she can go on without her.

Nearly an hour passes before she rises and spots a handwritten note on the end table beside them. It is positioned next to a business card. The note, written in a shaky hand, reads: *Olivia, you my shooting star. I be forever grateful. Please contact my lawyer. He know what to do.* Olivia picks up the business card. It's labeled 'Jonathan Farro, Attorney at Law' next to a graphic of the justice symbol of balanced scales.

CHAPTER TWENTY-NINE

PRESENT DAY

Olivia's first phone call is to Tommy, and while she waits for him to arrive, she phones Marco. "She's dead, Marco. Mrs. Capricci is dead." Her voice breaking, she conveys the news with the emotion of a close family member.

Marco calms her, soothing her through the phone line. "Calm down, Olivia. Take some deep breaths. What happened? Do you want me to come? I'll come. I can be there by tomorrow."

"No, it's okay. I'll be okay. I'm just—I don't know—in shock. I can't believe she's gone. I just met her, but I swear she was like a grandma or a mother to me. I can't believe I'm saying this, but I loved her!" Tears retrace their path down Olivia's cheeks again.

"From the way you talked about her, I can understand. She seemed pretty remarkable."

"Yeah, to say the least."

"I can come, Olivia. Maybe you should accept some help."

"I don't even know what's what yet. She left a lawyer's card on the table next to her. It was like she knew she was going to die. I need to contact him, and Tommy will help me with the rest. But Marco, there's something else I need to tell you." Olivia braces herself, "I've made a reservation for Dana at a rehab facility in Denver. She's supposed to be there on Monday, and ..." Olivia hesitates, "I told her we'd pay for it."

Marco doesn't skip a beat. "Okay. We can do that. If you think it will help her, we'll figure it out."

Olivia's taut muscles relax a little. "Oh, wow! I didn't know how you'd react. Thank you." This is a different Marco. He's usually not immediately on board with the situations Olivia gets herself into in her attempt to help people.

"Olivia, I trust you. Don't you know that? You've helped a lot of people in your life and I just happen to be one of them."

"Hmmm, thanks for saying that. Right now, I can use all the support I can get."

"How about you give me the lowdown on the rehab place, and I take care of getting them paid. Would that help?"

"Are you kidding me? Yes!" Olivia can't believe her ears. Marco has never so much as lifted a finger for anything related to paying a bill. He likes to act like he has a say in where the money goes but doing the work of managing the money has never been of any interest to him. She sees Tommy's car pull up out front. "I've got to go, Marco. I'll call you later."

Olivia is relieved yet charged up, sad yet full of purpose. The more intense the stress, the better she performs. She greets Tommy at the door, feeling torn between her immediate responsibility for Mrs. Capricci and her impatience to speak to the lawyer on the business card.

The police arrive, and then the coroner. Tommy is a gem. The two of them answer questions and make decisions. But Olivia is clearly preoccupied. Tommy encourages her to get to the lawyer. "I'll finish up here," he says. With no car of her own, she locates the keys to Mrs. Capricci's Ford and takes it.

The lawyer's office, as Olivia soon observes, is on the outskirts of town, in a small adobe building sitting on a side street, all by itself. Not having thought to call first, Olivia hopes the lawyer is in and has time for her. Entering through the front door, she is greeted by a tall, thin, professional-looking man wearing a white shirt and blue tie. Olivia surmises that he's in his late 50s. He extends his hand welcomingly. "Hello Olivia, it's nice to finally meet you. I'm Jonathan Farro."

"Hello, nice to meet you." Olivia returns the nicety as she shakes his hand. "But how do you know my name? And what do you mean by 'finally'?"

He smiles and ushers her into a small office room furnished with a desk and chairs and file cabinets that line the walls. There is no outer office or even a desk for a receptionist. It is just him. Mr. Farro motions to Olivia to sit in a chair in front of a large, scarred-up wooden desk. Moving around it slowly, he sits himself in a tall leather chair facing her. "Mrs. Capricci told me to expect you today. I guess I thought she'd spoken to you about me."

"No, she didn't say anything."

"Well, that doesn't matter. I'm assuming, since you're here, that she has passed?"

"Yes," Olivia tells him sadly. "Just this morning."

"I'm so sorry. I know how fond of you she was. I imagine you felt the same. But then, it was hard not to be fond of Mrs. Capricci." He smiles a warm smile, covers his heart with his right hand and bows his head.

Olivia gives him a minute to process the sad news. "I'm confused. I truly don't know why I'm here, or how you knew I'd be coming today. Maybe you could enlighten me?"

"You see, Mrs. Capricci was a very determined woman. She told me that she was ready to die and knew exactly when she would." He pauses for a moment for this to sink in to Olivia, who scrunches her eyebrows together in a quizzical expression. "I have been working with her over the last months," he continues, "to execute her wishes and her will exactly as she requested. All of the legalities have already been taken care of, albeit filing the final papers, and, as of today, we are free and, directed by Mrs. Capricci, to quickly proceed." He rises from his desk. "And when I say quickly, I mean right now, and tomorrow and Sunday. Mrs. Capricci was very specific."

"Right now, what?" Olivia asks.

He reaches for a stack of papers on top of a filing cabinet behind him and drops them on the desk in front of Olivia. He then pulls a second stack and sets them in front of his desk chair and sits again. "These are Mrs. Capricci's beneficiaries. There are 358 of them." He smiles matter-of-factly, patting the stack in front of him.

"Wow! Okay. That's a lot of beneficiaries. But I still don't understand."

"Well, let's see. I believe yours is on top here." He pulls away the blank page that covers his pile, "Yes, here it is right here, Olivia Alfieri."

"She's left me something?" Olivia is surprised.

"Of course. It's right here." He points his finger to the paper in the stack on his side, signaling her to view the copy in her own stack. Olivia peels the cover page away and picks up the sheet with her name on it. It reads: "To Olivia Alfieri, I bequeath the River Tapestry."

"The River Tapestry, what's that?"

Mr. Farro smiles and stands once again. He unlocks a steel door to a closet and pulls out a long and extremely weathered-looking leather tube of the sort that would hold drawings or a map in the old days. "I assume that this, my dear, is the River Tapestry. I gave my promise never to open it and I, being an honorable man, have held to that promise." He hands the tube to Olivia. "It is yours now."

Still in disbelief, Olivia asks, "the River Tapestry? What the hell is the River Tapestry? Should I open it now?"

"You can do as you wish. I told you, I am an honorable man. Therefore, Mrs. Capricci has entrusted these belongings to me. I tell no one more than they need to know."

Olivia slides the worn, brown leather tube-shaped sheath up and down in her hands. She can tell by the feel that it has been preserved, possibly with beeswax. One end has a leather cap fixed with a strap that buckles it down. And there is a long carrying strap attached to both ends. She is intrigued. "I think I'd like to open it now."

"Be my guest." He pushes aside the stacks of paper on his desk to clear a space for Olivia to open the sheath.

Olivia unbuckles the tarnished buckle, lifts the cap and peers inside the sheath. There are what appears to be layers and layers of paper and cloth rolled up inside. She reaches in, pulls out the contents and carefully rolls them open across the desk. At first glance, there only appears to be sheets of muslin and parchment paper. Olivia begins to peel them apart until, beneath one layer, she reveals a woven tapestry. "Huh!" Olivia gasps. "It's an actual tapestry!" The rich, unmistakable smell of cedar travels up her nose, and she is reminded of the fragrance that wafted out of her grandmother's coat closet where she hung her old dusty coats and kept her ancient canvas travel bags.

Olivia runs her fingers over the fragile fabric and notes that it is a bit frayed on the edges. The tightly woven coarse textile feels like it might have once been sturdy but has deteriorated over time. Olivia can see places where it looks like it could rip at the slightest handling. Finally, she pulls her hand back to admire the tapestry scene itself. She observes that there are many people in the scene, all of them dressed in clothing from centuries ago. The hair rises on the back of Olivia's neck and an electricity-like vibration courses through her body. She realizes that there is no mistaking it: her dreams of the river were leading her to this very moment and the scene laid out before her on this fascinating tapestry.

When she finally collects herself, she sees that the tapestry depicts a flowing blue river with a small cluster of people standing in a clearing next it. One is a tall man with longish brown hair who appears from his attire to be of nobility. He's holding the hand of a young girl with auburn hair, and, with the other hand, he is reaching toward an adolescent boy who clearly resembles him. Another figure is a dark-haired peasant woman and another a man dressed in a red guard's uniform. They appear to be celebrating, dancing merrily in a circle with smiling faces. Another figure, a woman, is dressed in a dark-green, full-skirted gown with a high neck. She is sitting on a rock overlooking the river, a distance away from the group. Peering down into the water, the expression on her porcelain face, seen in her reflection, is one of distress. The group of people is surrounded by an abundance of flora, and, high in a tree, overlooking them all, a hawk is perched. Olivia drinks in every inch of the tapestry, expecting at any moment the totality of it to coalesce and reveal its meaning. She examines it, skimming her hands across its surface without touching the fragile fabric. Doing so, she senses its energy, but its meaning is still eluding her. Finally, she looks up at Mr. Farro, who has been quietly standing by. "It looks old," she says.

"I'd say so."

"Do you know its significance or anything about it?"

"No, I do not."

"Hmmm." Olivia very gently lifts the tapestry and turns it over. A symbol is stamped on the back: a circle with six elements that connect in the center. She can make out a sword pointing down with a hand reaching up. The other four aren't as discernible. She thinks that one possibly is a lightning strike, one some kind of plant and the others she's even less sure of. Olivia recognizes the marking itself as the same symbol on an amulet that Mrs. Capricci religiously wore around her neck. In fact, Olivia had just removed the amulet that afternoon before the coroner arrived. For some reason, she wasn't sure why, Olivia had felt the need to put it in safekeeping. "Have you ever seen this symbol before?" she asks Mr. Farro.

"No, never."

Olivia picks up the leather sheath to examine it further. She hears something rattling at the bottom, so she turns it upside down on the desk and shakes it. An old skeleton key and a business card fall out, as does a flat round rock. Olivia picks up the key and studies it. "Do you know what this is to?"

"No, I don't."

"It doesn't make sense," Olivia says in frustration. Sliding the business card in front of her, she reads: "Peter Velazquez, Registrar, Metropolitan Museum of Art." The card includes the museum logo, the address of the museum in New York City and a phone number. Nothing else—no email, no website and no Facebook or Twitter logo. It's obviously old. "Do you know this man?" Olivia asks the attorney.

Mr. Farro shakes his head. "No, never heard of him."

Olivia exhales in frustration. "You mean you don't know anything else about this?"

"No, but I must say it's intriguing." He moves again to sit in his chair and pats his stack of paper. "Olivia, we do have some other business to attend to." He points to her stack of papers.

"What other business?"

"The rest of the beneficiaries. Are you prepared to receive them?"

"Receive what?"

"The beneficiaries. They will begin to arrive tomorrow and I'm sure the procession will last through Sunday, at least."

"Procession?"

"They are all bequeathed a possession of Mrs. Capricci's. She asked that you help me to locate each item as they arrive at her door."

"Me? How will I know what they are?"

"She said you will just know." He smiles the same quixotic smile Mrs. Capricci had shown to Olivia so many times over the past two weeks.

"How will all these people know to come tomorrow? I mean, Mrs. Capricci just died this morning."

Mr. Farro smiles. "Email, my dear. I have them all ready and waiting. With just a push of a button, they will know. They will all be instructed to print their individual documents verifying who they are and bring the document with them."

Olivia is overwhelmed. She doesn't understand any of it, not the River Tapestry, nor the key, the business card nor the soon-to-occur procession. She just shakes her head to confirm for the attorney that she will do as Mrs. Capricci requested.

"Just a couple more things, Olivia," Mr. Farro continues. "I will contact the funeral home and arrange for the body to be cremated. Ramone Belmonte has inherited the house and the property. He will also be there to help us tomorrow. He is a relative of Mr. Capricci's and will be the one to discreetly spread her ashes over her garden. She has requested that there be no funeral and no attendees to witness the scattering of the ashes, other than Ramone and his family and a handful of other relatives."

"I understand." Olivia carefully rolls up the Tapestry and its protective layers into a tight cylinder. She drops the flat rock into the leather sheath first, assuming it has been used to help keep the tube's round shape, and then slides the Tapestry in. She drops the key and the business card in her purse and scoops up the stack of papers. "Is there anything else?" she asks.

"I will notify Mrs. Capricci's son, Franco. If he shows up at the house and I am not there, whatever you do, do not let him in. Refer him to me."

Olivia exhales again with a long, slow breath. "Okay, whatever you say. It was nice to meet you." She returns Mr. Farro's firm handshake, takes the two steps to the door and swings it open, welcoming the breeze that rushes in. Desperately in need of a good dose of fresh air, she drives with her head half in and half out the window.

Mrs. Capricci's body is gone when she gets back to her

house, and Brian is sitting in the living room with Tommy and Tucker. "So, what happened?" Tommy asks.

"What didn't!" replies Olivia as she plunks the stack of papers on the coffee table. She begins to tell them about the meeting, focusing on the procession that's poised to begin. She has left the sheath in the trunk of Mrs. Capricci's Ford and decided not to discuss it with anyone until she speaks to Marco. She tells Brian about the plans for his mom's rehab and asks Tommy if there is any way he can take Dana to Denver. Tommy is happy to help. Olivia imagines he sees it as a good excuse to get to Denver to see Brenda. Brian, on the other hand, has a look on his face that suggests he doesn't believe his mom will actually go. "She's going, Brian. I promise."

"I'll believe it when I see it. Besides, how are we going to pay for it?"

"Don't worry about that. It's taken care of. All you need to think about right now is packing up your house." Olivia instructs him to get boxes, and hands him her credit card to secure a storage unit. She is functioning on auto-pilot. All she can think about is the Tapestry, the skeleton key and the business card of the man from the Metropolitan Museum.

As soon as she's alone, she calls Marco and spills the beans. He is quiet, thinking it through, but is ultimately confused just like her. "I think it's a good idea to keep it quiet. You don't know enough about it. Does the card have anything else on it?" Marco asks.

Olivia shuffles through her purse and pulls it out, turning it over for the first time. "Oh! There's writing on the back! It says: *Contact this man and he will enlighten you.*"

CHAPTER THIRTY

1980

Where do you disappear to?" Olivia asks Rick. "How am I supposed to know if you're dead or alive?"

"Don't worry so much." Rick brushes her off and flops onto the couch.

"That's not so easy when your boyfriend just vanishes for days at a time." Olivia knows inside her gut what he's doing. She's just looking for confirmation.

Rick switches the television on. "I always come back, don't I?"

"That's not the point." But Rick has already switched her off. It's his modus operandi.

Olivia doesn't know *exactly* where he goes. All she knows is that he leaves for a few days and miraculously comes back with money in his pockets. That can only mean one thing: he's a drug runner. She is close to cutting him loose.

"Hey babe," Rick says over the voices on the television, "we've got company coming tonight."

"What do you mean, 'company'?"

"I called one of my buddies from back home last night. Couldn't get hold of him, so I called his dad. He was pissed. It was four o'clock in the morning their time." Rick laughs, proud of himself. "But I still got him to tell me where he was, in California at some meeting. So, I tracked him down at his hotel and he changed his flight. He's coming here for the weekend before he heads back home to New Jersey. That's where he lives now, freaking New Jersey!"

"Where's he staying?" Olivia hopes he doesn't think he's staying here.

"Here, he can sleep on the couch." Rick pats the cushion next to him while he laughs at "Hawkeye" on a rerun of "MASH".

Olivia turns and stomps into the tiny kitchen three feet away. She knows it won't make any difference if she argues. Rick's head is as hard and dense as bedrock.

"We have to leave soon!" he shouts at her. "His plane lands in an hour."

"An hour! Really Rick, you could've given me some warning!" she shouts back. "And what do you mean, 'we'? I have to go to work in an hour." Olivia is clearly upset. She stomps around the kitchen, sticks her head out the window for air and then pulls it back in. She tells herself *this is it*. She'll give him the weekend with his friend and then she's kicking his ass out. She's got bigger plans. She's going to be a businesswoman. She's not going to college full-time and working full-time to be mixed up with a drug runner who doesn't care what he does with his life.

"Call in sick, babe. I promise it'll be worth it. We'll go to that Chinese restaurant you love so much."

She does love that Chinese restaurant and she hasn't been out to eat in a while. She can't afford it. It's not easy supporting an apartment when you're 19 years old and going to college. But dorm life isn't for Olivia. She had only lasted a week in what she refers to as "that playground for shortsighted morons." Maybe she will call in sick, she thinks, make Rick pay for a nice dinner before she kicks his ass out. She's not happy about his friend staying here, though. It irks her that Rick acts like he owns the joint when he doesn't even pay rent.

ॐ

"So, what does your friend do?" Olivia asks while they stand near the off-ramp, waiting for Rick's friend to deplane.

"He works for his dad."

"Doing what?"

"I don't know, sales I think. His dad owns a forklift company."

"Hmmm," Olivia replies.

The first thing Olivia notices about Rick's friend is his gait as he struts toward them with a confident swagger. "Is that your friend?" she asks Rick, with a tone of skepticism.

"Sure is."

Olivia's eyes take in this young stud's taut body, from the Converse sneakers on his feet to the wild and dark curly hair on top of his head. "Hey buddy!" Rick greets him, and they do the obligatory guy half-hug thing. "This is Olivia," Rick gestures to her, "And, Olivia, this is Marco."

Marco's deep-brown, almost black eyes pierce Olivia's like an arrow hitting a bulls-eye, holding them hopelessly fixed. He thrusts his long arm toward her, his hand extended, and she robotically shakes it. His grip sends a current of electricity through her, and she holds onto his hand much longer than she knows she should. Her heart skips madly and she feels her jaw slacken. It takes a few seconds and Rick's voice saying, "Let's go," for the normal rhythm of her heartbeat to return, almost as though a defibrillator has shocked it back to normalcy. She is still vibrating from head to toe, though, and she can't seem to shake free of the reaction—and, anyway, she's not sure she wants to.

ๆๆๆ

All weekend long, Olivia and Marco pussyfoot around each other, stealing glances behind Rick's back. On Sunday morning, before Marco leaves, they take a ride up to the mountain so that Rick can show him the ski area where he works in the winter. On the way back down the dirt road, they stop at Grace's cabin. Rick wants to look around inside to see if he might want to rent it next season. Olivia and Marco meander slowly toward the creek, pick their way over rocks that peek out of the water along its edge, climb two big boulders that are situated next to one another and sit down. Olivia lifts her face to the caressing breeze, closes her eyes and lets the brisk mountain air wash over her.

"It must be hard for you to come here," Marco says.

"Not really," Olivia replies, with her eyes still closed. "I can feel her here."

Marco shakes his head like he understands, picks up a loose

rock and skips it downstream. The thump it makes as it hits a dead log that's fallen across the creek pulls Olivia from her reverie of Grace and startles a hawk perched on a tree limb above them. The majestic bird launches out suddenly and wings its way down the creek.

"So, I was wondering." Marco drops his voice into a low and sensuous cadence. "You and Rick, you got something serious going on or what?"

Olivia peers into the dark depths of Marco's eyes and cocks her head quizzically. "What do you think?"

He slowly nods his head back and forth, and a grin forms on his full, inviting lips.

Ten hours later, Olivia's phone rings. Startled, she pulls herself out of bed where she's been sleeping next to Rick, and hurries into the living room to catch it.

"Olivia, this is Marco …" His voice is smooth and calculated, like he's been practicing the line all day. "And I think I'm in love."

CHAPTER THIRTY-ONE

PRESENT DAY

lone in Mrs. Capricci's creaky old house, Olivia sleeps in fits and starts.

They are all by the river, joyfully dancing in a circle. Marco is there, squeezing Olivia's hand. Rio holds her other hand and Mateo holds his. Dana, Brian and Carly grasp one another's extended hands lovingly, and Brenda and Tommy complete the circle. Mrs. Capricci sits on a rock by the river clapping to the beat of the old movie classic, "We're off to see the wizard, the wonderful Wizard of Oz, because, because, because, because, because ..."

The circle makes another revolution and Olivia looks over at Mrs. Capricci. But now, suddenly, she's sitting in her living room chair, encased in a giant translucent bubble. The bubble floats up and

over the river, just like Glinda, the good witch did. Mrs. Capricci's
sparkling eyes twinkle at Olivia and then suddenly her face turns the
light-gray color of bentonite clay. There is a thunderous pop as the
bubble bursts and Mrs. Capricci and her living room chair disappear
into thin air.

సా

Olivia opens her eyes in the dark room. Tucker is huddled
next to her, wide-awake and staring at her. She rolls over and
runs her fingers over his soft curly coat and attempts to go back
to sleep. Her mind is racing, though, darting from one thing to
another. She wonders with a stir of excitement what the River
Tapestry is all about and why Mrs. Capricci left it to her. And
more inexplicably, she wonders how the dreams she'd had before
she arrived here could be so closely related to the events that
have befallen her over the recent weeks. And on top of that, she
ponders the mystery of the skeleton key and if she will ever find
out what it unlocks.

She shifts to her left side. Maybe she can sleep if she doesn't
face the window. Not knowing what to expect about this "procession" that's supposed to happen tomorrow is making her anxious. She can't imagine who all these supposed beneficiaries are,
or how she'll be able to find all their inheritances. She rolls back
over to face the window again and fights for sleep as she fidgets
over what she's going to do with Brian and Carly while Dana is
in rehab. She certainly can't leave them here alone.

సా

Marco and Olivia sit by the creek near Grace's cabin. The air is crisp and the sounds of nature call all around them. It is breezy, and they quietly watch the water ripple as it slides over rocks, moving inevitably southward through the gorge cutting between the mountains. The wind picks up, blowing Marco's Red Sox hat off into the water. A hawk drops from its perch in the trees and dips into the creek, scooping up the hat. Airborne again, the graceful bird glides upstream toward them and stops, suspended just feet above them, its wings rolling and flapping in rhythmic movement. Olivia can see the creature clearly now—with the body of a red-tailed hawk, and the face of her sister Grace.

Rising before dawn, Olivia is gripped by a desire to visit Grace's grave. She commandeers Mrs. Capricci's car and drives to the cemetery, creeping along the dirt roads that wind through the gravestones. From the sound of the engine, rabbits scatter every which way to safety behind stones and an old mausoleum building. The dewy newness of the day is beginning to reveal itself in a wash of crisp blues and pinks slowly arising over the eastern horizon, a harbinger of the exquisite spring day that the valley is in store for.

The ground is wet with dew, but Olivia doesn't mind. She and Tucker plunk themselves down on the grass, Olivia Indian-style and Tucker stoic as a statue, between Grace's grave and the one next to it with the unmarked headstone. Seizing the moment, Olivia begins to narrate aloud the Cliff Notes of her life, beginning from the moment of Grace's funeral and moving through every turn and turmoil until she reaches this very day. It seems odd to hear the timbre of her own voice in this quiet place as she lays it all out, sharing it like a book on tape, a gift to Grace and their beloved father. And then Olivia finishes by thanking them both from deep in her heart for all that she, Olivia, has been able to accomplish, and all the love with which she has been so mightily blessed to receive and return. For she knows in this moment that, without the lessons she'd learned from Grace, and without the love and guidance of her father, she would never have become the woman she is. When she finally stands, her body feels taller and more erect than it has in decades.

Dawn turns fully to morning as Olivia drives back into town, making a stop before she pulls up in front of Dana's house. She grabs the bag she has sitting in the back seat and hurries to the front door, pounding on it.

"What the hell, Olivia? It's 6:30!" Dana chides Olivia through half-closed eyes.

"I know! It's time to get up! You have a lot of work to do!" Olivia barges past a startled Dana, Tucker fast on her heels, and claps her hands. "Brian! Carly!" she yells. "Get up!" Within mere seconds, Brian sprints down the stairs and Carly bursts from her bedroom, both as though they're responding to a fire.

"What happened? What's the matter?" Brian demands, rubbing his eyes awake.

"Nothing's the matter," Olivia says. "It's just time to get up! You all have a tremendous amount of work to accomplish and just two days to do it in. Come on!" She claps her hands again. "Get dressed. I brought breakfast from the Campus Café. Bacon and eggs and, of course, their famous cinnamon rolls." The sleepy family groans and disperses to get dressed. Olivia hustles into the kitchen and lays out the breakfast spread.

Dana sips her hot coffee and pulls a chunk of cinnamon roll from Carly's plate. "Hey, that's mine!" Carly complains, and covers her plate with her arms. Then she slips a bite under the table to Tucker and they all laugh.

"Okay guys, I've got to go," Olivia finally announces. "Dana, help Carly pack her bedroom first. She'll need a suitcase of stuff to last her for a while. You all will, for that matter. When you're done with Carly's room, send her down the street to Mrs. Capricci's. She can spend the rest of the day with me."

"Olivia?" Dana questions. "How am I going to go now? What's the plan for Brian and Carly? I mean, since Mrs. Capricci …"

"Well, I'm not sure just yet," Olivia interrupts. "But I'll figure it out. You're going, Dana," Olivia replies like a drill sergeant. "No lollygagging or second guessing," Olivia says sternly as she heads for the door. "Time's a wastin'!"

When Olivia pulls into the driveway, she's alarmed to see people of all ages and sizes scattered across Mrs. Capricci's front yard. They're young and old, some dressed casually and some in more formal, dark-colored attire, as if they're attending a funeral. Several women are wearing brightly colored dresses and wide-brimmed hats, and a cluster of scholarly looking folks are engaged in lively conversation. Olivia guesses they may have been colleagues of Mr. Capricci's. Outside the front fence, a few families with a gaggle of small children are gathered in a knot. They appear to be of Hispanic descent. The men in the group give off a worldly, weathered vibe, as field workers might.

Sitting on the front porch in the rockers and drinking coffee are Mr. Farro, dressed in a crisp white shirt and a pink tie, and Ramone, who's in shorts and a t-shirt. Olivia weaves her way through the crowd and up to the front porch. "I didn't know you'd be here this early," Olivia says apologetically to Mr. Farro. "I'm sorry I kept you waiting."

He and Ramone nod their heads in unison. "No problem," Mr. Farro replies. "We're just enjoying the beautiful morning." He raises his Styrofoam coffee cup to the sky in a signaling gesture. Without further instruction, the restless crowd begins to form into a line that begins at the front step. Ramone rises and, without a word, disappears around the back. "Looks like the natives are restless," Mr. Farro offers. Displaying no sense of urgency, he himself rises and strolls through the front door behind Olivia and drops an empty box on the floor. "Have each person sign the document they should have brought with them and place them in here. That way I can figure out who hasn't made it and contact them later."

"Okay. So, how do we do this?" Olivia asks.

"We just start with the first and move on from there," Mr. Farro instructs.

Olivia shrugs her shoulders and reopens the screen door, introducing herself to the first person in line and shaking her hand. "Hello, I'm Olivia." The thin, well-kept blonde woman of about 40 is holding a large empty box. She hands her sheet of paper to Olivia and smiles. "Hi, I'm Carlene. My mother was Mr. Capricci's secretary for 30 years."

Olivia nods and reads the document aloud: "To Carlene Langston, I bequeath all of my Cast-Iron Pots and Pans." Olivia looks up at Carlene quizzically.

Carlene answers her unasked question. "When my mother was dying of cancer, Mrs. Capricci gave me cooking lessons so that I could properly nourish my mother in her final months."

Olivia smiles and gestures for Carlene to follow her. "I've got this one," she tells Mr. Farro, who has made himself at home on the sofa. Tucker lies at his feet, with one eye open and one shut.

Next in line is a middle-aged man accompanied by what appears to be his 20-something year old son. They are both dressed in black. Their paper reads: "To Carlos Martinez, I bequeath my antique Barcelona Rocking Chair."

Again, Olivia looks up quizzically. The father speaks. "We live up the street." He points to a house a half a block away. "My son, Carlos here, came to Mrs. Capricci's the summer that he was six, twice a day, every day, for weeks. He had burned his hand with a hot iron. It fell on top of it and melted the skin and tissue clean to the bone." As though on cue, Carlos lifts his hand and proudly shows off the scar, a triangle with a v-point. "Mrs. Capricci rocked him herself every single day in her rocking chair, while she soaked his hand in an iodine solution." The son quietly nods his head in a gesture of loving appreciation. The two men follow Olivia into the living room where the cherished rocking chair sits like a prize waiting in the corner.

Next is a pretty, young woman in a cornflower blue dress that matches her big blue eyes. Olivia can tell she is shy as she slowly inches her paper forward: "To Marly Twill, I bequeath my collection of God's Eyes."

Olivia doesn't wait for a response. She knows exactly where they are. She spins around and heads for the kitchen, indicating that Marly should follow her. The sun is gleaming through the window where the god's eyes prominently hang—six in all. Fashioned from Popsicle sticks and yarn, each has an array of vibrant woven colors bursting from its center. While Olivia is pulling them from their hooks, Marly begins to explain. "My father, Mr. Twill, sold Mrs. Capricci her goat's milk. I'm his daughter.

When I was nine, I lost my brother in a combine harvester accident. He fell into the blades." Marly stops, her voice momentarily catching with the lingering memory of that horrific day. " A while after it happened, I started to come here after school. Mrs. Capricci taught me how to make god's eyes, and we'd sit here at the kitchen table, each making one. It helped me get through the pain." Marly drops her eyes and her face seems to darken. "I kept hers and she kept mine." Olivia hands the stack of treasures to the girl and hugs her fiercely. Tears fall from both women's eyes onto each other's shoulders.

And so, it goes for five hours, one beneficiary after another, each with his or her own remarkable story. At noon, Mr. Farro arises from the couch, where he has been sitting, bearing silent witness all morning. "I'll be back with lunch," he announces.

Olivia glances through the screen door as he goes. If anything, the line has increased in length. It now wraps around the yard, out the gate and down the block. She notices Ramone who's now in the front yard. Beside him are baskets overflowing with fresh vegetables and plant cuttings that he's dispersing to the crowd. Ramone has obviously been hard at work.

Olivia sits down with Mr. Farro and Ramone to a plate of chicken enchiladas, prepared Olivia-style, with guacamole on top. She doesn't ask Mr. Farro how he knew to order them without cheese. Forgetting Mrs. Capricci's lesson to eat slowly, she gobbles them down like she hasn't eaten in days. The moment she is taking her last bite, Carly appears at the door.

"Come on in, honey. Did you get your room all packed?" Olivia asks, wiping guacamole off her chin.

Carly replies solemnly, "Yeah, I guess so."

"Why the sad face? You're on the verge of an adventure,"

Olivia says reassuringly, attempting to turn Carly's frown into a smile. "You know I've moved 13 times in my life, and each time I discovered something new."

"Really, like what?" Carly's curiosity is piqued.

"Oh, like a new park, or a new hiking trail I came across by accident, or a new friend." Olivia's instinctual sense for the new life Dana and her kids need to create for themselves clearly doesn't involve Alamosa. Too much has happened here that they might not be able to overcome, especially if it's staring them in the face every day. There are too many ghosts.

"Oh!" Carly's eyes begin to brighten.

"There is so much to experience in the world, Carly. If you don't start now, you might miss something special." The corners of Carly's mouth turn up a little as Olivia rises from the table and cleans up the mess. "Are you ready?" Olivia asks.

"Ready for what?" Carly questions her.

"To assist me with the crowd. I'm in dire need of a helper." Olivia glances at Mr. Farro, who feigns inattention and retires once again to the couch.

When they resume, the next in line is a woman in her thirties, with a daughter around Carly's age. The mother is wearing a flowery purple dress and the daughter has on a pink one. "I know her!" Carly whispers to Olivia.

"Well then, introduce me!" Olivia urges.

Carly begins shyly, "Hi, Madison, this is Olivia. Olivia, this is Madison. I don't know her mother's name."

The purple-clad woman smiles and reaches to shake Olivia's hand. "Hi, I'm Beth Hargrove; nice to meet you." She passes Olivia her paper bequest: To Madison Hargrove, I bequeath my Corinthian Wind Chimes.

Olivia looks up and points to the lovely-sounding chimes that have soothed her these past several days. "These here?" she asks Beth.

Beth nods her head yes and launches into the story: "Madison lost her hearing a couple of years ago from an extreme case of the mumps. I was in despair. But then Mrs. Capricci showed up at our door out of the clear blue. We didn't even know her. We'd only heard about her. She brought Madison to her house for a week and nursed her with homemade soups and poultice compresses. The first sound Madison heard after almost two weeks of deafness was the music from those wind chimes." Carly and Madison exchange knowing glances. Clearly, the story had made its way around school.

Olivia pulls herself up onto the banister under the chimes and unhooks them, releasing an orchestra of bells into the air, causing the girls to giggle. Olivia jiggles the chimes a few times to entertain the large crowd, whose attention has been momentarily captured by the melodious sound.

At seven o'clock, although there is still a long line, Olivia calls it quits. She stands on the porch and asks the remaining beneficiaries if they would be willing to return in the morning at seven. She needs rest. Mr. Farro and Ramone depart with the crowd assuring Olivia that they'll be back at the same time tomorrow.

Picking up her phone to check for messages, Olivia sees a missed call from Tommy and returns it. "Hey there. I see you called."

"Hey there," Tommy playfully mimics. "How'd the day go?"

Olivia pushes out a heavy breath. "Long," is all she says.

"I'll bet. I swung by and saw the line this afternoon after I stopped by Dana's. You're one brave woman."

"Like I have a choice? But no, honestly, it was great—beyond great, actually. I've never heard so many heart-wrenching and heartwarming stories. That Mrs. Capricci, she was one hell of a healer."

"I can only imagine. She had quite the reputation in this town."

"I'm finding that out."

"So, I just wanted to let you know that I hired a crew to help Brian move all of their furniture into the storage unit tomorrow."

"Wow Tommy, that's great! How were they doing when you went over there?"

"Dana was three sheets to the wind. But they actually got quite a bit done. I credit Brian. The kid kicks ass. And now he's here at work."

"Okay, well, it's confirmation, I guess, that we're doing the right thing with Dana; and kudos to Brian."

"Most definitely," Tommy agrees. "Well, I've got to get back to it. I just wanted to check in."

"Thanks, Tommy, for everything."

"I think I should be thanking you. I hate to admit it, but you're teaching me a thing or two about friendship."

Olivia hangs up the phone with a smile on her face and turns to Carly. "Want to spend the night?"

Carly nods her head eagerly. "Can I sleep with Tucker?"

"You sure can. I'll call your mom and let her know."

Olivia tucks Carly into the bed in her room early, Tucker by her side, and makes up the couch for herself. She is most definitely not sleeping in Mrs. Capricci's bed. Just the thought of it is disturbing, and it seems disrespectful and even a touch sacrilegious. She remembers Marco telling her that he was going to one of his meetings tonight. But its two hours later back east and Olivia suspects he's home by now.

"I was waiting for your call," Marco says warmly, when he answers. "How did it go today?"

"It was amazing." Olivia pours it out, going on for too long to tell him every story she can remember.

"Wow!" Marco repeats over and over.

"I'm sorry for going on so. How was your night? Did you go to—what is it—El Guardia Legado?"

"Yeah, I went. It was pretty cool."

"How so?"

"They showed me some pictures of things they've found, like old books and coins and stuff, mostly from people's attics and garages. But, there's definitely something else going on. They do a lot of whispering and speak in Spanish off and on. I think they're hot on the trail of something they don't want me to know about."

"Sounds kind of like treasure hunters searching for lost booty."

"Yeah, kind of. And Olivia, guess what else?"

"What?"

"I emailed Mateo again."

"Oh, good for you!" Olivia is thrilled. "What did you say?"

"I talked about things we did together, like go to the Red Sox game and stuff. He hasn't responded. But I'm not giving up."

Olivia's heart is swelled with hope. "No, don't give up, Marco. You're on a roll. One of these days he's going to figure out that he's lost his best friend, too."

CHAPTER THIRTY-TWO

PRESENT DAY

T here is absolutely no way Olivia is going to get through this line of good-hearted, story-telling inheritance seekers alone. "Okay you two," she says commandingly, mustering some authority to give Mr. Farro and Ramone instructions. "Today, you're helping. I'm forming the line into three." There are no arguments against Olivia's directive from the two men. They pitch right in.

Olivia's first is a middle-aged woman with long, curly, dark-brown hair and emerald green eyes. Dressed in billowy white cotton pants and a turquoise tunic, her ensemble is finished with sparkly, beaded earrings that dangle from her earlobes. Her paper reads: "To Evelyn McQueen, I bequeath my Bloodstone Copper Wand."

Olivia raises an eyebrow in question, learning the day before that such a look serves to invite an explanation and a story.

"I used to be a stained-glass artist when I was younger," the woman begins. "My work hangs in buildings all over the valley, and even in Colorado Springs and Denver." Olivia can hear the pride in the woman's voice. "Over time, I began to get weak and sickly. No doctor could tell me why. I had to stop my work altogether and I believed I was going to die. Mrs. Capricci showed up at my doorstep one day. She had heard about my art and my illness and knew precisely what my problem was. I had lead poisoning. Day after day, she showed up at my house with hot soups and thick breads and treated me with what she called her 'bloodstone copper wand,' moving it over my body in figure eights while she chanted. She gave me essential oils and herbal teas and instructed me how to use them. Within a few short weeks, I was healed. I was never able to return to stained glass. But now, thanks to Mrs. Capricci, I am an energy healer."

The location of the copper wand suddenly pops into Olivia's head, along with a brief reminder of the dream she'd had the other night, the one in which Marco was a magician. The wand is on the mantel, among a collection of crystals. Carly follows Olivia into the living room, like a bear cub trailing its mother, with Tucker close behind.

Mr. Farro and Ramone shift back and forth from the front stoop to some previously unknown location in the house, neither finding it necessary to ask the location of any of Mrs. Capricci's treasures.

A maybe 40-year-old man with three small children clinging to his legs hands Olivia his paper: "To Juan Lucero, I bequeath my Cast Iron Smudging Cauldron."

"I was a migrant worker," he begins, in a halting English thick with Spanish. "I was heavily poisoned by pesticides in the lettuce fields one day. When the boss find me lying in the field, weak and sick, he fire me. My wife bring me here, to this house. Mrs. Capricci, she cover me in the bentonite clay and make me soak in a tub of herbs. Then, she use the cauldron to smudge yarrow over my body. She give us oils and soups and lend the cauldron to my wife, who continue to smudge me every day. I was clear and strong in no time. She even find me a year-round job at a local farm. My family and me, we owe her our lives."

Carly and Tucker have disappeared but show up a moment later with the cauldron. Carly has become a valuable little helper. She is assisting Mr. Farro and Ramone as well. And Tucker hasn't left her side.

At lunch, Olivia strikes up a conversation with Ramone. He is sitting just across from a picture of Mr. and Mrs. Capricci when they were younger. Olivia is amazed at the resemblance between Mr. Capricci and Ramone. "So, I understand you and your family will be moving in here?" Olivia asks.

"Yes, my wife and I will be. My daughter and her children live with us now. She lost her husband to the war." He bows his head in a moment of silence and Olivia does as well, joining him in a quick prayer for fallen heroes. "With my daughter's five growing children, our tiny home is full. I will give my house to her. My wife and I, we will be quite comfortable here. You see, I am a gardener who has little property to garden on. Did you know, Filomena taught me to garden? She gave me my first pair of garden shears. They are the ones I still use today."

For a moment, the use of Mrs. Capricci's first name confuses Olivia. "You know, I never asked her first name. I always called her Mrs. Capricci. For some reason, the person she was seemed to demand that respect."

"Yes, I know. Most everyone called her that. She asked me to call her Filomena years ago. I'm not sure I truly ever got used to it."

"She was quite a woman. No doubt, we are all very lucky to have known her. I only wish I could have had more time with her."

"The time you had is exactly the time you needed, Olivia," Ramone says.

Back at it, Olivia stands in front of a lanky 20-something-year-old man. A dirt-smeared baseball cap with the words "I'd rather be fishing" sits low across his forehead. He unfolds his crumpled paper and hands it to her. "To Anthony Lama: I bequeath my Kingfisher Walking Stick."

Carly smiles widely, twirls on her toes and disappears through the screen door with her faithful Tucker.

Olivia nods her head and moves forward to invite the story. Anthony follows her lead. "When I was fifteen and more foolish than I am now, I was in Sedona—in Arizona—on vacation with my parents. I jumped off a cliff in Oak Creek Canyon and landed on the rocks instead of the water and broke my leg. A doctor at the hospital there set it, but not correctly. It didn't heal properly and gave me tremendous pain. A year later, Mrs. Capricci showed up at our house with the walking stick. She instructed me to not take a step without it from the time I got out of bed until the last step before bed at night. My mother made sure I did as I was told, no easy feat with a hard-headed teenager. Less than three months later, I had no pain and was walking like I'd never broken my leg."

Carly appears with the walking stick. It is wood-carved and gleaming of polish. There are bright blue and orange feathers dangling from a leather cord that's fed through a hole in a knot near the top where the stick bends to create a handle. Anthony leans on the stick, genuinely pleased to have it in his hands once again. He uses it to walk up the path, through the gate and to his car.

It is nearly six o'clock when the last person in line steps forward. She is an old woman, less than five feet tall, with gray hair that's tied up in a bun. Her attire is that of someone in mourning: black dress, black shoes and a black shawl that she has draped over her head. She has a rosary in one hand and a picture frame in the other. She hands the frame to Olivia. Under the glass is the woman's paper: "To my beloved Grace Salvatore, I bequeath my Amber Amulet."

Tears well in the old woman's eyes and Olivia reaches out to hug her. They stand on the front porch, oddly comfortable in each other's arms, and release their grief.

"She'sa ma sister-in-law," the woman begins once they've pulled their bodies apart. "She gave me ma life back when I was justa fifty-five and diagnose terminal wit da pancreatic cancer." Grace takes a deep breath and continues. "She show up at ma bedside and place her amulet around ma neck. Der was a pouch attach wit da dandelion tea inside. I still have." She nods her head enthusiastically. "She keepa bring me more, and when I go back to da doctor a mont later, he say I am a clear. No more cancer."

Olivia is stunned by the story, but no more so than by every other story she has heard over the course of the last two days. They are miracles, one after another. She knows exactly where the amulet is. Olivia had placed it in the top drawer of Mrs.

Capricci's dresser. She wonders again what the amulet may have to do with the Tapestry, because they are both marked with the same symbol.

They all proceed into the bedroom: Olivia, Carly, Grace and Tucker. There, they sit on the bed for an hour or more, partly in silence, while Grace strokes the amulet lovingly and Carly and Olivia stroke Tucker. Every few minutes, this beloved sister-in-law of Mrs. Capricci's remembers a fanciful story that she imparts to the others in her animated yet broken English, each story illustrating the great love and respect the two women have felt for each other through the years.

Mr. Farro and Ramone have quietly slipped out. Carly and Olivia walk around the house, now stripped almost bare of Mrs. Capricci's precious healing treasures. Books, plants, lanterns and candles, glass jars of dried herbs, bells, butterflies in frames, a mortar and pestle, rattles and driftwood, a lamp and a chalice and so much more have vanished with the stream of worthy beneficiaries. With the weight of her role over the past two days, as well as the countless stories she's listened to intently and absorbed into her very being, Olivia's heart feels both full and empty. She realizes as she gazes around this magical nest of her benefactor that her time here is drawing near to its end.

CHAPTER THIRTY-THREE

PRESENT DAY

I was thinking, Oli, how about you bring Brian and Carly here for however long Dana is in rehab?" Marco suggests. His unexpected call has come at the perfect time.

Olivia's mind hasn't even gone there. She's been too focused on Mrs. Capricci's beneficiaries. "Well, that could work as long as Dana and the kids buy in. It's nice of you to suggest it. I hadn't even thought of that possibility."

"How else am I going to get you home?"

Olivia laughs through her reply. "Missing me, are you?"

"Hell yes! I keep thinking about coming out there to get you."

"Who knew what a couple weeks apart could do? You sound so much more—I don't know—sure of yourself than you have in years. I like it," she purrs.

"Get home then!" Marco orders. "And I'll show you how sure I can be."

"Yes sir!" Olivia feels a tingle deep down inside. It makes her long for Marco to touch her. She hangs up thinking about Mrs. Capricci's words on yin and yang and the balance of nature.

Carly has been playing catch with Tucker in the front yard. Tucker is no retriever, though he likes to be chased. "They're here!" she yells in through the screen door.

A caravan pulls up in front of the house; Brian, Dana and Tommy each in their respective vehicles. Tommy leads the way up the walk with Brian close behind, carrying two duffle bags. Dana lags a few yards behind looking like she's angling for an escape.

"We're off to Denver!" Tommy says. "We'll leave Dana's car at my house on the way out of town." Olivia's not so sure Dana won't take off as soon as she's got the chance.

"Right now?" Olivia asks.

"I don't mind driving at night, and Dana's check-in is 10 a.m. We're going to stay at Brenda's."

"I don't have to be there by 10," Dana argues. Olivia and Tommy both give her the 'yes-you-do' look. Dana falls into a chair, shrinking herself as if she thinks she can hide in plain sight. Clearly, she's still not on board with the plan.

"So, Brian, you can sleep on the couch. I'll bunk with Carly and Tucker," Olivia tells him. Brian nods his head in agreement and drops the duffle bags of gear on the floor.

"Okay, so let's say our goodbyes, we're wasting daylight," Tommy urges.

"Wait Tommy," Olivia stalls him, "I need to talk to Dana for a minute."

"Okay. But hurry it up."

Olivia steers Dana out onto the front porch and directs her into one of the rocking chairs. Olivia sits down next to her. "So, Dana, you asked me what the plan with the kids is now that Mrs. Capricci isn't a possibility. I've been thinking about it and want to know how you feel about me taking them back to Vermont until you're out and settled somewhere."

The caged animal look that Dana's been wearing turns to fear of another kind. "I knew it! You want my kids!"

"Dana, that is not true! Tell me, what else should I do for the next month?"

Dana glares at Olivia. She's not buying the story. "I don't know. This is all your idea. You could stay in a motel near the clinic or something."

"We could, but that would cost a lot of money, and I'm spending quite a bit already. Maybe you could cut me a little slack. I wasn't planning on staying out here this long, let alone another month. I'm kind of anxious to get back home."

Dana huffs. "At least you have a home to get back to. You just said until I get settled. Where the hell do you expect me to settle to?"

Olivia takes another leap. "I don't know, maybe Denver. I'll get you started, rent you an apartment or a little house. And maybe Brenda can help you find a job. She's lived there for a long time. I'm sure she'd be willing to help."

Dana hangs her head and sighs. She is contemplating this new proposal. Maybe it's something she can grab onto. Finally, she lifts her troubled eyes to meet Olivia's. "You promise you'll bring them back?"

"I promise, Dana. It's not that I haven't grown to love your kids, but they're your kids, not mine. I have my own."

"Well, they've never been anywhere. I imagine a trip across the country might help them get through all of this."

Olivia reaches for Dana's hand, squeezing it in reassurance. "I think it might. I'll take good care of them, Dana."

"Oh Jesus!" Dana begins to cry. "I've never been away from them. I don't know if I can do this."

"You can do it, Dana. Just keep your eyes on the prize. Those two kids in there love you and need you. When you get out, you can start all over with them. My advice is this: when you're in rehab, conjure up a new life for all of you. Make it great, the best you can come up with. I don't know, maybe Brian becomes an animator for the movies. He's talented enough. And maybe Carly grows up to be a vet or something. She certainly loves animals. And you, you can start a career doing something you love. Visualize it all. It's worked for me. How do you think I created the life I have?"

A glimmer of light sparks in Dana's eyes. "Sounds a little improbable that conjuring up something in your mind can make it happen."

"Don't knock it until you've tried it. Believe me, it can work. You just have to stay really solid with the vision; own it."

"I don't feel solid about anything right now."

"You will. Give yourself a few weeks. And whatever you come up with, I'll want to hear all about it, okay?" Olivia detects the trace of a smile forming on Dana's lips. "Okay?" Olivia urges her again.

"Yeah, okay. What the hell else do I have to lose?"

"That's the way. Now let's go tell your kids they're going on a road trip."

Both Brian and Carly stare at their mother when they hear the news. "Vermont!" Brian utters it like it's the arctic tundra, or something.

"Vermont," Olivia answers. "It'll be fun." Carly starts to cry and jumps into her mother's lap.

"It'll be okay, honey," Dana tells Carly as she strokes her hair and, at the same time, eyes Olivia doubtfully. " Just imagine all the fun things you'll see and do."

"We have another dog, Carly," Olivia chimes in. "His name is Boo. I'll just bet you'll fall in love with him, too."

Carly wipes her eyes. "Is he the same kind of dog as Tucker?"

"He sure is; a little goofier, though."

Carly looks at Brian for support and he continues with the same coaxing vibe his mother and Olivia have been sounding. "Sounds like fun to me, but what about graduation?"

"Oh, well, I didn't think about that. It's in a couple weeks, right?" Olivia questions.

"Yeah, the twelfth of June."

"Hmmm, I guess we could fly you back out."

"Or I could skip it altogether; I really don't care about walking across a stage."

"Well, we have time to figure that out. You may not want to miss your high school graduation." Dana and Carly shift their gaze back and forth between Olivia and Brian. Tommy transfers his weight from one leg to another and back again. He's obviously anxious.

"We'd better get going. It's nearly dark outside." Tommy pushes.

Olivia walks toward the door to try and prompt Dana to hurry up. "I'll keep you posted about every little thing," she assures Dana. "And as soon as you can take phone calls, I'll have the kids call you every day."

Dana reluctantly peels herself up off the couch with Carly attached and reaches out for Brian. The family embraces in a big bear hug. All their faces show fear now and Carly is crying openly. Strands of her hair stick to her cheeks. The angst in the room is palpable.

"I'll keep them safe," Olivia tells Dana. "And before you know it, you'll be together again." Dana clutches her children even tighter.

Tommy steps forward to try and move the show along. "So, we'll be at Brenda's tonight. I don't want to keep her up waiting too late." He hugs Olivia intensely. "In case you're gone by the time I get back, it's been great to see you, Oli. I'm gonna miss you."

"Ditto, Tommy. But, don't think you're rid of me. I've kind of gotten accustomed to having you and Brenda around. Maybe the two of you can come visit us in Vermont sometime."

"Maybe we'll do that." Tommy pokes her affectionately in the belly and moves on to coax the kids from Dana so that he can hug them. "We've really got to go, Dana."

Olivia braces her arms on Dana's drooping shoulders. "You can do this, Dana. I believe in you." The two women squeeze each other tight. They've run the gamut the last couple of weeks, moving from sworn enemies to what could possibly be considered friends.

Carly is still crying as she holds onto her mother all the way to the car. Dana's got to physically pry the young girl's hands from her to close the door. "It'll be okay, honey," Dana tries to reassure her daughter. "Olivia will take care of you. We'll be back together before you know it."

Carly's not convinced. "Don't go, mommy! I'll be better, I promise!"

"Carly, this isn't about you, honey. You're always good. This is about mommy." Dana bucks up for Carly, squeezing her hands through the open window. "It's going to make me better." Dana starts the car and blows kisses to Brian and Carly as she slowly inches the vehicle out into the street.

"Anybody hungry?" Olivia asks, once Dana and Tommy have driven away. Both Brian and Carly nod their head affirmatively, although their faces still look pale and frozen, as if they've just seen a ghost.

Brian drives them to El Charro and the three of them order enchiladas, tacos, rice and beans. When their food arrives, Olivia eats heartily, while Brian and Carly pick at their plates. Olivia tries to distract them from their somber moods by dropping a dirty brown penny into the small bowl of hot sauce that came with the chips. "Watch this," she tells them. "Just give it a few minutes." When they're ready to leave, she picks the penny out of the sauce. The copper is as shiny as a newly minted coin. "That's what it does to your stomach," Olivia informs them. "Can you imagine?"

Their eyes widen, and they shake their heads in disbelief. "Don't guess I'll ever eat that again!" Brian decides on the spot.

"Who knows," Olivia counters. "Maybe it's good for the digestive tract. You know, clean out all the crap." That gets a giggle out of them both, and they seesaw their shoulders up and down, unsure of which side of the argument to be on now.

Back at Mrs. Capricci's, after Carly and Tucker have bedded down for the night, Olivia lights the candles in the lanterns that hang over the back stoop. She urges Brian to join her as she gazes out over the garden that has changed her in so many ways.

"I think you'll love where we live," Olivia tells Brian. "We have five acres and a pond, and a private apartment downstairs that I think I'll put you in. Carly can stay upstairs with us." Olivia waits to see if she's won him over yet, but Brian just rolls his toothpick from one side of his mouth to the other.

"It will certainly be easier on me with you along to help me drive."

The corners of his mouth curl up. "You'll let me drive?"

"Sure, probably most of the way if you're game. I'm much better in the passenger seat than I am behind the wheel."

Brian nods. Olivia is sure he's relating her comment to her wrecking her car. "I know what you're thinking!" she jostles him.

"What? I didn't say anything!" he feigns innocence and begins to chuckle.

"So, what do you think about the whole trip thing?"

Brian peers through the backyard and up over the riverbank into the star-filled sky. "I think it feels like I'll be deserting my mom and, in some ways, even my dad. Although I shouldn't care what he would think."

Olivia hasn't given any forethought to what she begins to tell Brian. It just comes out. "Well, I think I know how that feels. You know, I lost a sister to suicide when I was 19." The noisy frog calls in the distance nearly drown out Olivia's low, softened voice as she tells her story. "It happened here in town. I was in college up north at the time. When I came home for the funeral, I felt torn between staying here for my dad and doing what I knew in my heart was right for me. I felt guilt over leaving my sister, too. Even though there was nothing I could do for her anymore. She made her choice and I had to learn to respect it." She pauses, briefly reliving the day at the cemetery with her dad. "God knows it wasn't easy. But, I've always felt like I made the right choice."

"I'm sorry about your sister," Brian says, uncomfortably

wringing his hands. "I think I know what you're talking about, though. I feel like my stomach is in a tug of war every day."

"Yeah? What's your war over?"

"It's going to sound selfish."

"I won't judge you, Brian."

"Well, damn it, I want to go to college, and not here, somewhere far away. But how can I now, even if I could get a scholarship or loans?"

Olivia sighs and thinks for a minute. "You know, Brian, it's been my experience that if you keep telling yourself 'I can't,' then you won't. Maybe if you just let yourself off the hook for a while, the answer will appear ... some doors will open."

"Huh! Easier said than done."

"I didn't say it was easy. Leaving my dad wasn't easy, but I never felt like he held it against me. I don't think, once your mom gets well, that she'll hold it against you, either. And your dad, well, who knows? He could be looking down on you and be proud of you for going after your dreams."

Brian, deep in thought, deftly maneuvers the toothpick around in his mouth.

"You know," Olivia continues, "there's a quote from Darwin that has guided me most of my life, and I believe it's served me well. It goes something like this: *It's not the strongest or the most intelligent that survive, but those most adaptable to change.*"

"Hmmm, I don't think I'm any of those."

"Well, how about we work on the adaptable to change thing?"

Brian smiles a weak smile. "I guess I can do that."

CHAPTER THIRTY-FOUR

PRESENT DAY

First thing the next morning, Olivia calls the repair shop and learns that her car will be ready at noon. She knows her next move hinges on getting her car back, so she is grateful and throws up a little kiss to the gods. She informs the kids that they'll be leaving tomorrow.

Some exercise will do Carly good, Olivia decides, so she sends the young girl for a long walk with Tucker. It's a warm day, and the last chance the playful dog will have to get his paws wet cavorting with the minnows.

Brian takes a trip to the storage unit to retrieve additional belongings he and Carly will need now that they're traveling across country. Olivia dives into her own suitcases, which are in dire need of reorganization. She separates her clothes into piles, clean and dirty, and puts a load of the latter into the washing machine.

Next, she opens the suitcase that houses her miscellaneous items, like a yoga mat she never used, a notebook she never wrote in and books she never read. She lifts a blanket that's laid across the top. Just underneath it sits a tapestry carpet bag. Olivia gasps and falls back onto the floor from the shock. There is no doubt in her mind, as she stares at the bag in front of her, that it is her sister, Cari's. She has envisioned it hundreds of times in her memories, never thinking she would see it again. Olivia scrambles forward onto her knees and caresses the tapestry fabric woven in a pattern of autumn-colored leaves. She lifts the bag and feels the weight of something inside. Olivia spreads it open and discovers an old wooden box, a treasure chest of sorts. She pulls it out of the bag to find that it has a skeleton lock. It's the size of an average jewelry box and bears a weathered family crest that's painted on the top. A blue and white checkerboard is in the middle of the crest, bordered by some type of ivy on the sides. Atop the checkerboard is a knight's helmet, boasting a sort of blue and white rope-like crown that is affixed to it. An unrolled scroll at the top of the crest reads "Veritas Vincit". Olivia has no idea what it means. But she is familiar with a single word on another scroll unrolled at the bottom of the crest. It reads "Alvarez," which causes the hair on Olivia's skin to stand at attention, and her brow to abruptly bead with sweat. She had learned years ago, through a family history search, that her Italian marital name, "Alfieri," is derived from the Spanish surname, "Alvarez."

Olivia is anxious to know what on earth this little wooden box is concealing. She surmises that Cari must have left her tapestry carpet bag with Mrs. Capricci when she moved to New Jersey, and that Mrs. Capricci must have stashed it in Olivia's suitcase before she died. But she has no idea what could be in the box. Olivia peeks back into the bag and notices something else. There, packed in a ziplock bag, is a bundle of syringes filled with a pinkish solution and, with them, a note. She doesn't know which to examine first, the ziplock bag or the treasure chest. She picks up the ziplock and reaches inside for the note.

Olivia,

> *Keep these syringes close at all time. The poison inside is from the seed of the rosary pea berry. When they injected into the bloodstream, they cause an immediate heart attack. It possible you may need them to save you life!*

"What the hell?" Olivia exclaims aloud. "Why would I need poison to save my life?" Poison almost took her life. She's suddenly immersed in the sensation of ants crawling all over her skin. She drops the ziplock bag and begins to scratch.

Olivia then turns her rattled attention to the wooden box and inspects the lock. It dawns on her that the skeleton key she found at the bottom of the leather sheath in Mr. Farro's office might be the key to this box. She hustles to her purse to find it.

The key fits perfectly in the lock. She turns it and opens the lid with nervous anticipation, having no idea what she might find. Inside is a stack of papers. Olivia carefully takes out the one on top and reads it.

Olivia,

> *I am honor to have been the holder of the River*

Tapestry since I was eighteen years-old. It serve me beyond any recognition I can ever imagine. Its value is immeasurable.

It is imperative that the River Tapestry remain in the possession of the Velazquez bloodline and that its safety is held in the highest regard. There are those who will not stop short at killing in attempt to take its custody.

The letters in this chest explain its heritage. Mr. Peter Velazquez is in possession of their translation. The destiny of this gift is now in you hands. You must remain clever and sometime ruthless.

Good luck and safe keeping.

Mrs. Filomena Velazquez-Capricci

Olivia is stunned by Mrs. Capricci's words on this piece of paper. Many questions arise and swirl like an eddy in her mind. What do the words mean? Why would someone kill for the Tapestry? And what does the Velazquez name have to do with the Alvarez crest? A shiver runs through her and a storm of unrest builds in her belly. The unknown importance of this treasure hits her like she's run into a glass door, and it shatters all ideas of safety she might have ever, so innocently, held. The thought occurs to her that never in her life has she possessed anything that someone would kill for.

Looking over her shoulder to confirm she's alone, Olivia

closes the door to the bedroom and locks it. Her fingers move gingerly over the delicate sheaf of remaining letters. She carefully lifts them out one-by-one, examining each before replacing them again in the same order that she found them. Incredibly, the first letter at the bottom of the pile is dated 1645. All of them are penned in Spanish, Olivia thinks, and maybe some are in Italian, but she can't be certain. They appear to be written in an array of different hands. She scans the words, recognizing few but the names "Velazquez" and "Alvarez" that dot them. She believes the words "el Tapiz del Río" must translate to "the River Tapestry," and she notes that the words "Los Seis Regalos" appear in nearly every letter.

Olivia reaches for her phone and types in "Spanish to English translation." When the answer materializes, she learns that "Los Seis Regalos" means "The Six Gifts." She learns, too, that she is right about "el Tapiz del Río." And "Veritas Vincit" means "Truth Conquers." Olivia can feel the blood coursing in her veins. Suddenly, she is both protective and fearful of this gift that has been bestowed upon her. She thinks about the fact that she's left the Tapestry in the trunk of Mrs. Capricci's car rather than bringing it into the house and hopes that it's a wise decision.

The front screen door creaks open and closed, alerting Olivia that someone is home. She gathers the letters and puts them back into the little wooden box, locks it and stores it back in its hiding place inside Cari's tapestry carpet bag, before checking to see who's come in.

It's Brian who is back, hoisting an armload of belongings. Through the open door, Olivia catches sight of a man striding up the front walk. "Brian, do you know who that man is?" Olivia asks him.

Brian peers through the door. "No, never saw him before."

Olivia flips the front screen door latch into place, knowing full well that the flimsy piece of metal won't hold against an intruder. Brian regards her quizzically as she locks the door but takes her lead and stands behind her in a protective stance.

"May I help you?" Olivia asks the stranger, when he reaches the door.

"I'm Franco Capricci; who are you?" The man's voice is gruff, and his large, burly stature matches it. Olivia catches his dark, darting eyes, which to her seem unfriendly.

"My name is Olivia Alfieri. You must be Mrs. Capricci's son?" Olivia scans the man's face for any similarity to Mrs. Capricci. She can't make the connection. Both she and her husband were short, small-boned people with refined facial features. This guy's face looks like a big pock-marked blob of dough.

"Yes. May I ask why you're in my mother's house?"

"I was renting a room here when she passed. She left instructions that I help to sort through her belongings so that they can be distributed to her beneficiaries."

"I'm her beneficiary! I'm her only child!" the man snaps at her.

Olivia inhales and wills herself to stay calm. "Her lawyer is Mr. Farro. I can give you his information. He asked that, if you show up, I direct you to him." A little "déjà vu" sensation floods over her. In her mind's eye, she envisions a snapshot of herself in the executive dining room after she's injected a sirloin burger with a heavy dose of pesticides. Considering his background that his mother spoke so despairingly about, she imagines this man taking a bite of his own lethal medicine, which summons a fleeting sense of satisfaction mixed with tremors of fear pulsing up and down her spine, knowing that supposedly, there are now poisonous syringes in her suitcase. The coincidence is too eerie.

The man's left eye begins to twitch rapidly as he absorbs what Olivia has just said. "Can I come in? I'd like to look around."

"I'd rather you not. Like I said, Mr. Farro will answer any questions you have." Brian steps forward and stands tall next to her.

The man claiming to be Franco Capricci grabs the handle of the screen door and jiggles it. "You've locked me out of my own house?" Brian grabs the handle in reaction and pulls the door tight against the frame.

"This house now belongs to Ramone Belmonte," Olivia bravely counters. "I'd appreciate it if you'd leave now." Olivia's voice sounds much stronger than her quaking body feels.

"Who the hell are you to tell me to leave?" The man shouts as he stares at Olivia threateningly. Like a strobe light suddenly stuck in the blinking position, the twitch in his eye picks up speed. He steps backward and moves off the porch. But just as Olivia thinks he is leaving, he turns and sprints around toward the back of the house.

"Brian, hurry! Lock the back door and the windows!" Olivia yells frantically. But Brian is already on it, moving quickly toward the rear of the house. Olivia suddenly spots Carly and Tucker on their way up the front path. "Carly! Get inside! Hurry up!" She opens the screen door and hastens them in.

"What's the matter?" Carly asks, startled by Olivia closing both the screen and the front door and locking them behind her.

"Nothing honey, it's okay. We're just taking precautions."

"Why?"

"Just instructions from Mr. Farro not to let anyone in."

"Who wants in?"

Before she can respond, the intruder makes an appearance at the front door again, unable to gain access any other way. Brian comes back in the room and stands beside Olivia. "She told you to leave!" he firmly says.

Frustrated, the man contorts his face and ratchets up his volume as he bellows through the door. "So, who's this kid?" Carly cowers behind Olivia as neither she nor Brian responds to his question. "Jesus! I'm not here to hurt anybody," the man utters, in a less threatening tone, rotating his hands palm-up in despair of his situation. "I just wanted to see if any of my old stuff is still here. And you know, maybe I'd like some of my parents' things. You'd think I'd be entitled, right?"

But Olivia's not having any of it. "Like I said, speak to Mr. Farro. Do you need his contact information?" she shouts through the door.

"I have it!" the man spits out. He stands on the front porch and drills his eyes into Olivia's through the glass in the door, making sure he drives his point home. "I'll be back! You can be sure of it!"

CHAPTER THIRTY-FIVE

PRESENT DAY

When they are certain the man has left, the three of them stand in the living room and stare at each other in disbelief. "What's up with that guy?" Brian asks.

"I imagine he thought he was going to inherit everything," Olivia responds. "And, uh, I can see why he didn't." She sits down on the couch and holds her head in her hands, thinking. She needs a plan, and quick. It doesn't take but a minute before she jumps up. "Okay guys, we're leaving today. Give me a minute and we'll go pick up my car."

"Today?" Brian and Carly say in unison.

"Today," Olivia responds with authority as she rushes to put her load of clothes in the dryer. "You two gather all your stuff and put it right here by the front door." For some reason, Olivia knows she's got to hightail it out of town. She needs to leave this house, its possessions, and Franco Capricci for Ramone and Mr. Farro to deal with.

Olivia retreats into her bedroom, retrieves the wooden box from the carpet bag, wraps it in a t-shirt to conceal it and then gently places it back in the carpet bag. Then she tucks the ziplock bag with the syringes into the side zipper-pocket of her purse. Positioning the leather handles of the carpet bag over her shoulder, she secures it between her arm and her torso, and slings her purse onto the opposite shoulder and secures it under her other arm the same way.

"You ready? Let's go!" she tells the kids, who follow her out the door. She's decided to leave Tucker behind. He's got a threatening bark and can be a good deterrent if someone tries to get in. She locks the door behind her. "We're taking Mrs. Capricci's car to go pick up mine at the garage."

"We can take my truck," Brian says.

"No, we'll take this one. You can drive my car on the way home and see how it feels, see if you think it's safe to drive." Olivia is not about to let the Tapestry sit vulnerably in the driveway with that lunatic threatening to come back.

At the garage, she pays Jeb, half listening to his speech about how long it takes to get parts for these damned cars today. "Thanks for everything." Olivia shakes his hand and tosses Brian the keys and a few bills of cash, never letting the carpet bag or her purse leave her side. "Carly, you go with Brian. Stop and pick up some tacos for lunch and meet me back at home, okay? And no cheese on mine."

"Okay, if you say so." Carly responds.

Brian doesn't ask any more questions. He just bites on his toothpick and does as he's told.

On the way back to the house, Olivia creeps down the side streets in Mrs. Capricci's car, keeping her eyes peeled for anything abnormal. A paranoia she began to feel earlier when the man showed up at the door has suddenly increased to a heightened level. Once she reaches the house, she sprints inside, leaving the Tapestry in Mrs. Capricci's trunk.

A few minutes pass, and Olivia is hastily folding her laundry when she hears the front door creak open. She is positive that she just locked it when she came in, and it's too quick for the kids to be back. They don't have a key anyway. Olivia hears Tucker bark and begin to growl. Lumps swell in her throat and her pulse picks up, but she finds the nerve to make her legs work and moves to confront whoever it is.

The man who earlier identified himself as Franco Capricci has already made his way to the kitchen with Tucker hot on his heels, barking and growling the entire way. Olivia stops short. She is on one side of the room and he on the other. "How did you get in here?" Olivia says. Tucker growls and stands ready to attack.

The man glares at her, unmindful of her question. "Where is it?"

"Where is what?" Olivia eyes her purse that's sitting on the kitchen table.

He takes a few steps toward her. "You know exactly what I'm talking about. Make it easy on yourself. Where is it?"

Olivia takes the two steps toward him and grabs her purse. The man pushes her shoulders and she falls to the ground. The purse slides from her grip as she hits the floor, butt-first. Tucker, growling ferociously, grabs onto the man's pant leg with his teeth and begins to pull. The man shakes his leg violently but can't get free of Tucker. He coils his arm back and punches Tucker hard in the nose. The dog squeals and shrinks back, stunned. The man swings around and catches Olivia before she can get up. Grabbing one of her shoulders, he pulls his other arm back and makes a fist. He is about to punch her, but Olivia acts first. With all her might, she swings her foot up and kicks him solidly in the groin. He cries out with pain and falls back onto the floor, doubling over and grabbing himself. "You bitch!" he screams.

Olivia scrambles for her purse, pulls out the ziplock bag and pulls it open. With shaking fingers, she manages to yank out one of the syringes. The man has raised himself to his feet and lunges at her again. She rolls evasively to the side and throws a kitchen chair toward him. He catches his foot on it and falls forward. Tucker has recovered and pounces on the back of his legs, ready to bite. "No Tucker! Stop!" Olivia commands him, as she rises to her feet. Tucker jumps off the man and stands at attention ready to attack. She has one of the syringes in her hand. The man is on the floor with his back to her, but she knows she won't be able to evade him for much longer. In a split second, she reasons that she has only two paths: she can either hit him on the head with something or she can use the syringe. She knows those are her only options, if she doesn't want to get hurt. The man attempts to stand up, yelling and cussing all the while. Olivia looks around frantically for a pan or something heavy to hit him with, but there is nothing within reach. With not a second to spare, she decides what she must do. Even though adrenaline is pumping through her system with ferocity, everything seems to move in slow motion as she thrusts the syringe toward the threatening man, stabbing it through his shirt into his upper back, and then pushing down the plunger.

Instantaneously, the man's body begins to jerk and shake violently as he clutches at his chest. Olivia and Tucker watch the terrible scene unfolding before their eyes, as he collapses to the floor, convulsing in a horrible, twisting rhythm. It's only a couple of minutes before his body stops moving entirely and he is lying perfectly still. Olivia's heart is in her throat, her ears pounding. She stares incomprehensibly at the man and then searches the room—for what, she has no idea. Everything is still moving in slow motion—her vision, her movement, her thoughts—until it occurs to her that Brian and Carly will be back any minute.

Breathe, Olivia, breathe, she tells herself. Think, Olivia, think! You had to do this. It was self-defense. He would have killed you! He would have killed you for the Tapestry! It occurs to her again that she is in possession of something people will evidently kill for. Mrs. Capricci's words written on the paper inside the bag of syringes have taken on an entirely new meaning and importance. She shakes her head to push back these frightening thoughts, so she can focus on her immediate situation. She still has work to do if she's going to save herself.

Olivia retrieves the syringe still hanging from the man's back, stuffs it into the ziplock bag and then jams the bag back in her purse. She quickly analyzes the scene. Other than a small tear in his pant leg from Tucker's teeth, it looks more like this man has had a heart attack and fallen onto the floor. She checks underneath him. There is no blood. He could have torn his pant leg anywhere. She hustles back to her bedroom and grabs everything she can. Tucker, meanwhile, stands guard over the body, clearly not convinced that this man won't come back to life. Olivia, her chest heaving with anxiety, lugs her bags to the front porch, stepping over the body as she makes her way through the kitchen. It takes her three trips. She wrestles all of Carly and Brian's bags outside and stacks them next to hers. Running around the house, she scans each room quickly to make sure she's got everything she needs.

"Tucker! Come!" Olivia shouts, and then races to Mrs. Capricci's trunk to recover the sheath with the Tapestry inside, which she mixes in amongst her belongings on the front porch. Just as Brian and Carly are pulling up, Olivia yanks the front door shut behind her, locks it and shoves the keys behind a pot of pansies.

"Hey, I would've gotten all of this," Brian says as he walks up the path carrying lunch. Carly leans down to pet Tucker, who is alertly standing guard on the front step. Olivia notices what she thinks is probably the man's car, parked a house away. She prays Brian doesn't notice it.

"I know. I just want to get on the road. How about we get this stuff in the car and eat lunch at the park?" Olivia attempts to convince Brian and Carly and herself that she is calm, all the while feeling like she could faint at any minute.

"Okay," Brian says cooperatively. Olivia is thankful that this kid is so agreeable. "Hey," he points, "I think that's that guy's car over there. Did he come back?"

"No," Olivia lies, "I haven't seen him. Maybe he's at a neighbor's or something." Brian glances around, shrugs his shoulders and starts to haul the bags. Before leaving the front porch, Olivia stops for a brief second and scoops up a cairn of river rocks. Using her shirt as a hammock to hold them all, she carries them to her car and dumps them into the back. Just knowing a piece of the river will be with her gives her a slight feeling of security, like that from a rubbing stone in one's pocket. Right now, she feels like she can use anything she can find to calm herself down. "You okay?" Brian asks. "You seem kind of, I don't know, nervous."

Olivia pulls in a deep breath. "I'm fine; just sad I guess. It was hard to come here and now it's hard to leave. I guess I just want to get the leaving part over with." She struggles with her emotions determined to keep her composure.

"Well then, let's go," Brian directs. "Follow me to Tommy's to drop off my truck and then we can go to the park." Olivia doesn't argue.

They make their way to Tommy's and then onto the park, where they sit at a picnic table. As soon as she sits down, her head swivels left to right and then right to left, checking every visible entry. While she keeps watch, Olivia wolfs down her tacos, but in her nervous state she feels like she's going to throw them right back up. She urges the kids to finish, takes Tucker for a quick walk and hurries them all back into the SUV.

Olivia smiles halfheartedly as Brian drives them past the old steam locomotive at the tip of Cole Park. It sits like an anchor for all the memories that tie her to this southwestern town. She appreciates the small doses of childhood joy it granted her, with its colorfully lit wheels that chugged brightly through snowy winter nights, year after year. The trickling Rio Grande flows slowly beneath them as they motor over the bridge leading out of town, east on Highway 160. Olivia sticks her head out the window and inhales deeply of the river air that so distinctly smells of her youth, holding her breath for as long as she can to ensure that the rarefied oxygen permeates her every cell. She'd wanted excitement, even prayed for excitement. She just didn't imagine it happening like this.

As the valley slips behind them, the past two weeks roll through Olivia's brain. She's regained old friendships with Tommy and Brenda, she's gotten Dana into rehab, and she met an old woman who has changed her life in countless ways. Grief weighs heavy on Olivia's heart for Mrs. Capricci, for the dried-up Rio Grande, for Jeff's broken family, for her broken family, and for Cari and Grace, who died much too young. Life seemed so innocent just a week ago. Olivia was being taken care of by an amazing old woman and she was helping a family through turmoil. Now, Olivia realizes with a shudder, Dana's problem with alcohol and money pales in comparison to the fact that Olivia has just committed murder.

Brian drives until dusk, the three of them barely speaking. They are each lost in their own individual battles of the mind, troubled over everything that has happened and the predicaments they find themselves thrown into. Olivia's thoughts have turned to the possibility of getting caught and going to prison. Scenes from the TV show, "Orange is the New Black," play out in her mind. She is most definitely not prison material. With her allergies, the food alone would put her body into such a state she'd be catatonic. Dread swarms over her. Sleeping in a cell, rarely seeing the light, eating prison food, single-file this and watch-your-fucking-ass that. She quakes at the thought. If Mrs. Capricci hadn't given her those syringes, this wouldn't have happened. But on the other hand, if not, she might be hurt or even dead. The idea that Mrs. Capricci may have had to use the syringes at some point enters her mind. Olivia ponders that possibility, creating alarming scenarios in her mind. One of them is Mrs. Capricci playing the survivor amid various victims, forever saving her own life by killing others with her syringes. That could be the future Olivia has in store for herself. She realizes the importance of keeping the syringes secret and vows to never let anyone find them—not even Marco.

Olivia directs them to a motel just off the highway, where she registers for two rooms. After feeding Tucker and getting him settled in one of the rooms, Olivia escorts the trio to a nearby restaurant, parking the car within view. She has yet to let the carpet bag or the car out of her sight. She wants to keep her eyes on where the Tapestry is hidden, tucked tightly into the crevice, up against the back seat. The syringes are still in her purse, tamped way down in the side pocket.

"So, you two have never been anywhere but Colorado, huh?" Olivia needs something else to think about besides the dead body in Mrs. Capricci's house and whoever else might be after the Tapestry.

"Nope, never," Brian confirms.

Olivia thinks for a minute. Maybe a side trip would be a good idea. She feels that maybe driving off the beaten path would be more confusing to any pursuers. If someone knows where she lives and decides to chase her across the country, they wouldn't think she'd go off track. She's just got to pray that no one shows up and confronts Marco before they get to Vermont. And who really knows what's happened since she'd fled Mrs. Capricci's house? The police could be after her. She feels like she needs a breather, a place to regain her equilibrium before she's confronted with questions from Marco, or the police or who knows who. Finally, she says, "So, how about we make a stop along the way?"

"Like where?" Brian asks.

"Like maybe Chicago. What do you think?"

"Chicago?" Brian and Carly say in unison, looking at each other quizzically.

"Yeah, Chicago." Why Chicago, she has no idea. Her brain is not working in its normal fashion. Maybe it's a good idea. Maybe it's not. Maybe she's a murderer. And then again, maybe she's not.

CHAPTER THIRTY-SIX

PRESENT DAY

That evening, Olivia sits on the outside steps of their motor hotel and calls Marco. She tells him about the treasure chest, the letters referencing the Velazquez bloodline and the Alvarez crest. She tells him about Mrs. Capricci's letter, leaving out the part that reads, *there are those who will not stop short at killing in attempt to take its custody.* She doesn't mention a word about the man she killed, or the syringes. "Do you think the Alvarez name has anything to do with us?" she asks him.

"I have no idea. How could it, though? I can't imagine there's any connection between Mrs. Capricci and my family. There have to be a hell of a lot of Alvarezes in the world." Marco ponders the idea for a minute. "Besides, you said she spoke about the Velazquez bloodline in her letter. I don't know any Velazquezes, do you?"

"I don't think so. The man at the museum has the last name Velazquez, though. But I'm really stumped by why she left me the River Tapestry and the box of letters. I guess I'll find out more when I go see this Peter Velazquez guy after I get back."

"So, when exactly do you plan on going to see him?"

"I'm thinking I'll probably go down the day after I get back. I can stay with Rio. I may as well get it over with. That is, if you don't mind being alone with Brian and Carly for a couple of days. And I hope you don't mind that we come home via Chicago. I'm thinking a little sightseeing would be a nice diversion for the kids." Olivia is desperate to blurt out everything that happened today. She is ready to explode. But she worries that Marco will think differently of her if he knows the truth. He's always had the purer heart. He's the one who's always given everyone the benefit of the doubt—everyone. It drives Olivia crazy. Alter boy, she's always called him. Olivia keeps the ugly truths to herself.

"I don't mind staying with the kids, and I guess going to Chicago would be nice for them. How long are you going to stay there?"

"Just a day. I figured we could see an awful lot if we just sightsee all day. But that probably means it'll take a couple extra days to get home."

Marco is hesitant but comes around. "Okay, I guess. But, I'm not very happy about you driving to New York alone again right after you get back home. Don't you think you should rest for a few days first?"

"We'll see how I feel. I just don't think I'm going to be able to really rest until I find out what this thing is all about. It'll just be for a couple of days."

"Let's talk about it when you get home. I don't want you

going into the city alone, though. If I'm not going, Rio will have to go with you."

"You know he will. He'll be just as intrigued as we are once he hears about all of this. Why don't you bring him up to speed? I can't talk in the car with the kids there."

"I'll call him tomorrow. Sleep well, my love."

"Oh Marco, I can't wait to get home to you. I miss you so much, more than you can imagine. I miss Boo, too, and who would've thought I'd ever miss those mountains." She does—she really does. She misses those soft-green, rolling hills and valleys. They seem so far away from everything she's been through, so innocent and less terrifying than the Rockies and all that lingers with them.

Olivia is restless after they hang up. She paces the cement balcony outside of their second-floor motel room, scanning the parking lot and the horizon for anything that looks abnormal. She's hidden the carpet bag in her suitcase and the sheath is in her motel room stuffed behind her suitcase. Brian had asked what was in the leather sheath, and she told him it was some papers Mrs. Capricci left her that she wanted to look at. She prays they'll all be safe. Without really knowing why, Olivia has taken on the safety of these items as if her life depends on it.

The light from Brian's television shines through his window. She thinks about knocking to see if he wants some company, but decides, instead, that she needs rest for the drive the next day. Carly is watching television with Tucker curled up next to her on the bed. Olivia goes into the bathroom. When she reaches for her toothbrush, she notices some droplets of blood in the sink and then looking down, she sees blood-soaked tissues in the trashcan. Her chin drops to her chest. The only thing she can think is that Carly cut herself again. She raises her eyes to the mirror and searches them for strength before she walks out of the bathroom.

"Carly, can we talk?" she says in a concerned voice. Carly turns her attention from the television to Olivia. "Can you turn that off for a minute?" Carly grabs the remote and clicks the power button, but she doesn't move from her position. Olivia takes a deep breath and forges ahead. "Carly, what you've had to live through hasn't been easy, I know." Olivia sits down on the edge of the bed and starts to pet Tucker. "When I was your age, I had some similar things happen to me." She looks at Carly, who doesn't utter a word. "When I found you at the river that day, naked and submerging yourself, it made me remember the times I did the same thing."

"You did?" Carly asks with surprise.

Olivia shakes her head in confirmation. "I was trying to wash myself clean." Olivia takes her time as she talks. "My sister had been molested when she was younger than you—and she used to take it out on me." Carly takes her eyes off Olivia and stares at the blank television screen. "The river always made me feel better." Olivia moves her hand from Tucker onto the comforter that covers Carly's legs. She slides her hand back and forth in a loving gesture before continuing. "The day we went to the river with Tommy and Brenda, I noticed some scars on the inside of your upper arms when you were swinging on the tire swing." Carly scoots back and sits up in the bed, pulling her legs in tight and wrapping her arms around them. "It's okay, Carly. We all find different ways to deal with the things that happen to us." Tears burst from Carly's eyes. "Can you tell me why you're hurting yourself now?"

Carly drops her head to her knees and begins to cry harder. Olivia waits while the young girl sobs. Eventually, she gets up to retrieve a box of tissues from the bathroom and hands one to Carly, who blows her nose and wipes her eyes. "None of this would have happened if it wasn't for me!" she blurts out.

"None of what?" Olivia asks.

"None of it! My dad wouldn't have killed himself and my mom wouldn't be in in rehab and we wouldn't have lost our home!"

"Oh Carly, I don't think any of that happened because of you." Olivia takes another deep breath and looks up at the ceiling for a minute before continuing. "I guess if you think you're to blame, then I am, too. Didn't you say that your dad called you Oli sometimes?" Carly nods her head yes. "But you know that your dad and I hadn't seen each other in over 30 years. Do you think I should blame myself?" Carly shakes her head no. "Then, you aren't to blame either. It was your dad that had the problem. And I can't imagine how hard it was for your mom. She had to know how he felt and once she found out about you and losing the farm and the house, it probably all scared her to death. I imagine she blames herself for everything and that's why she drinks." Carly tries to blink back tears that have started rolling from her eyes again. "You miss your dad, don't you?"

Carly talks between sobs. "I miss him so much. I just want everything to be like it was."

"I know you do." Olivia lays back on the bed and is quiet for a while. Thoughts of her own childhood intermingle with the tragedy of Carly's. She grasps for some words of wisdom— something she can say that will ease Carly's pain. But Olivia knows better. She knows that only time will take the pain away, and really all that time truly does is dull the pain to a resting position. It never fully goes away. For Olivia, it was meeting Marco that gave her new hope. It was her life with him and having children that created layers of healing tissue over the wounds. But like any injury, there's always a scar left behind. "You know, Carly, it takes time. But for me, I ended up having a good life, even after a painful childhood. I guess I just always kept looking forward, and eventually I found my husband and had my kids, and all that love overshadowed the pain. It can happen for you, too—and for your mom—and Brian."

Carly wipes her eyes on her sleeve and Olivia notices the bulge on her arm beneath her long-sleeve t-shirt. Carly sees that Olivia is looking and wraps her hand around her bicep to hide the bulge. "I don't know why I do it," she says.

"I know," Olivia says. "But there are probably safer ways to make yourself feel better." Olivia stands up, walks into the bathroom and digs around in her cosmetic bag. She sets a bottle of hydrogen peroxide, some cotton balls and some bandages on the counter before returning to the room. "I put some things on the counter in there. Could you please put some hydrogen peroxide on it, so it doesn't get infected? I can help you, if you want."

Carly slowly slides out of bed and slips into the bathroom without a word. Eventually, she emerges with a little grin on her face. "I guess that's better than a wadded-up tissue and a piece of tape."

Olivia nods her head in agreement. "How about we all sleep in the same bed tonight? You game?" Carly's grin grows a slight larger and she climbs into bed. Olivia changes into her pajamas, slides in under the sheets and maneuvers so that Carly can lay her head in the crook of Olivia's arm. Tucker circles until he finds the perfect spot where he wedges himself between their legs. Olivia flips the television back on and they fall asleep to "Chopped Junior." But Olivia is awake every hour on the hour, throughout the night. She gets up over and over to survey the parking lot through the blinds, and then paces the room and tries to fall asleep again. But her mind is racing. She is worried about Carly now, too.

ৡৡ

The next morning, Olivia drives. They are traveling on a trucker route, which has never been a favorite of hers. She creeps along in the right lane as one tractor trailer after another whiz past them, promising herself that she will find a good counselor for Carly during the weeks she's in Vermont.

"Why don't you pass?" Brian urges her.

"I hate to pass," Olivia confesses.

"Then let me drive or this trip is going to take twice as long." Brian rolls his eyes and chews on his toothpick.

"I'm not that bad; come on!"

"Yeah, you're that bad! This is killing me! Pull off at the next rest stop and we'll switch."

"Fine! Whatever!" Olivia changes the subject. "So, Carly, why don't you take out my iPad and look up some of the sights in Chicago? We can make a list of what we want to see."

"Okay."

"Can we go see Wrigley Field?" Brian asks.

"We can at least drive by. I imagine we'll do a lot of driving by. We only have one day."

Olivia switches seats with Brian at the next rest stop and,

once in the driver's seat, he maneuvers the car into the left lane behind a fast-moving tractor trailer and follows it all the way past Kansas City, where they finally pull off for the night. Same act, same play: Olivia has adopted the behaviors of a criminal on the run. She backs herself into booths where she can see every exit. She walks sideways down hallways, and clutches at her purse and the tapestry carpet bag like they've got gold in them. People have got to be suspicious. The kids keep giving her looks like they think she's crazy. At night, Olivia doesn't leave the motel room to call Marco until she is sure Carly is asleep and hasn't cut herself again.

On the phone, Oli tells Marco about what she found in the bathroom the night before, and about her conversation with Carly. "I think we'll need to get her into counseling right away," Olivia says. "She needs a professional to help her through this."

"I think you're right," Marco agrees. "It's hard to figure, though, how she could blame herself and how she could miss a man that did that to her."

"She misses the man he was before it all happened. And she blames herself for the fact that everything changed." Olivia thinks back to when she was young and always wishing that Grace was the person she was before she was molested, and that her dad was the same man he was before Cari ran away. "I can certainly understand wishing you could go backward," Olivia offers. "I imagine everyone wishes at one time or another, especially when they're young, that they could go back to their innocence. You know, before whatever it was that happened in their life shattered it."

"I guess you're right," Marco says. Olivia can tell from the tone of his voice that he's thinking about events in his own life.

"And I don't know why I said I don't understand how she could blame herself," he says. "Because I do."

The next day, Brian drives them all the way to Chicago. While in route, they spend hours listening to the country music station, "The Highway." Olivia sings along quietly to The Cadillac Three's "White Lightning." In fact, she did see white lightning. She saw it twice when she was three, when she had nearly drowned. Olivia had held it inside of her for over 50 years, like a ball of white fire burning in her gut. She'd gone to Alamosa in search of *The Why*, or at the very least to find a way to be useful. She'd thought she'd done that in helping Dana and her family and in her efforts to fulfill Mrs. Capricci's wishes. It's not the first time she's thought she was helping someone just to have it turn around and bite her in the ass. But nothing she's ever done in the past compares to killing someone with a poisonous syringe— even if it was in self-defense.

The trees on the side of the road pass by in a blur. The signs on the highway appear and disappear before she can read them. Her senses are heightened, but her reflexes are slug-like. She feels as if she's drowning in a sea of misunderstanding, and a tidal wave of questions is weighting her down, pulling her under. They swirl in her brain like the whirling blades on a fan. What the hell is all of this about? What the hell is the River Tapestry? Could she have done things differently? Should she have gone to the police? Please let them think it was a heart attack, she silently pleads. Please don't let there be an autopsy. Please don't let them link the man's death to her.

They rest for the night, this time in a nicer motel in a suburb of Chicago instead of on a trucker route. Olivia makes sure that there is a window that opens and that the room hasn't recently been renovated, and she still lugs her own bedding in and her oxygen tank, just in case. Once they're settled, Olivia texts Brenda to make sure she hasn't been contacted by the police. "Got any idea when the kids can call Dana?" she asks as a disguise for what she's really fishing for.

"Not sure. It could be a week or so. How's it going on the road?"

"Good. How's Tommy?"

"Lol, you know, he's ... good."

Olivia takes a deep breath. From Brenda's response, she can feel comfortable that there were no police calls there. Olivia promises to let Brenda know when they get to Vermont, and Brenda promises to let her know when they can call Dana. "I miss you already," Olivia texts.

"I miss you too, girlfriend. It's too bad we live so far apart."

"Yeah, the story of my life. I live too far from everybody. Maybe I'll just become a traveler." Olivia contemplates a life on the run.

"Sounds good. Travel out this way again soon."

"I'll have to come to bring Brian and Carly back. We'll see each other then. That reminds me, could you start searching for an apartment or a little house for Dana and the kids? I think it might be a good idea for them to stay in Denver, don't you?"

"Yeah, I think that's a great idea. I'll get right on it."

"And while you're at it, maybe think of any job openings you think Dana could possibly be good at. She'll need a job."

"That's harder. But I'll see what I can do. I'll need to talk to her first to find out her skills."

"I have no idea. But she's got to be able to do something."

Sleeping in motel rooms has become a chore for Olivia. She mostly tries to figure out ways to trick herself to sleep. Nothing works. She crawls out of bed the next day feeling like she just walked out of a tomb. Her symptoms are returning. A migraine lies in wait.

Consuming caffeine through a couple of hot teas and then iced tea, Olivia wills herself to smile and act nonchalant as they tour the city, like newbies at an amusement park. They drive and park and drive and park from one landmark to the next. Olivia has left the carpet bag with the wooden box of letters in her suitcase and has pulled the blanket tightly over the sheath for protection in the back of the SUV. Still, she worries about them throughout the day. The words, *there are those who will not stop short at killing in attempt to take its custody* keep a vigil in the back of her mind. Compounding her distress, Olivia is hyper-aware of the syringes inside her purse that she holds tightly underneath her arm. They have power. She imagines them burning through the leather and into her arm. She imagines every policeman she sees taking her down, stripping her of her purse, finding the syringes and booking her for murder. She knows that if she is caught with them, she is totally fucked.

They park in various public lots on numerous streets to take pictures at every landmark they can find, from Wrigley Field and the Willis Tower to the Big Bean in Millennium Park and the Navy Pier. They walk up and down the Magnificent Mile, stopping to read many of the stones along the facade of the Tribune Tower and to peek in the windows of the high-end designer shops. Olivia, on auto pilot, barely remembers going from one to the next. She can hear herself laugh and she can feel herself put one foot in front of the other. But it's all a blur.

Contrastingly, Brian and Carly are in awe of it all. Their faces are lit up the entire day. And Tucker tags along everywhere they go. Standing on a corner in downtown Chicago, Olivia loses sight of Carly for just a minute and panics. But as it turns out Carly has just run back to look in a window, and she quickly reappears. It takes Olivia a minute to regain her composure.

"You okay?" Brian asks, concerned.

"Yeah, I'm okay. Sorry. I just—you know—don't want anything to happen while you're under my watch." Olivia takes a few deep breaths while she strokes Carly's hair.

Finally, Olivia suggests that they take Tucker to the motel for a rest and then find a place for dinner. The side trip hadn't worked like she thought it would. She has yet to yank her mind from its turmoil. Every worrisome development one could possibly dream up has made its way into Olivia's thoughts: she's been on trial in the courtroom, lived for years in jail. She's been attacked over and over by Franco Capricci clones, and each time she's forced to use another syringe.

After they find a restaurant, Brian and Carly's faces are soon covered in deep-dish pizza residue, while Olivia pushes a salad around on her plate.

"We don't know how to thank you for all of this," Brian blurts out to Olivia, with obvious sincerity.

"Yeah, we don't," Carly chimes in, around a mouthful of pepperoni.

"Just seeing you happy is thanks enough," Olivia replies honestly. Carly suddenly drops her pizza onto her plate and wraps her arms around Olivia in a big bear hug. Brian smiles at the sight of his little sister showing emotion. The young girl's affection gives Olivia a moment of relief from her fretting. She realizes that she's forgotten that, to the kids, this is all a new experience, something special. All those landmarks, the travel, restaurants and motels; for these kids, they're like windows into the way other people live their lives. Olivia chastises herself for being so preoccupied and promises to focus more on them.

Later that night, after they walk Tucker around the parking lot, the kids fall into bed exhausted. Again, Olivia waits until Carly is asleep before she goes outside to sit in the car and call Marco to recite the day's activities, albeit with little enthusiasm. She goes on and on about how she wishes they could help Brian with college. "He's so talented," she tells Marco. "And it would certainly help him have a better future, but I know it's probably out of the question."

"Who knows?" Marco responds. "Maybe he can get a scholarship."

"Yeah, who knows?" Olivia replies, but with pessimism in her voice.

"Olivia," Marco says, "I have something to tell you. But I don't want you to think too much of it. I just think you should know, though."

"What is it?" Olivia sits up straight, her mood shifting quickly to concern. She imagines the police have contacted Marco.

"Well, when I came home from downtown today I found that Eddie guy from El Guardia Legado snooping around the back of the house. He said he was just checking to see if I was in the backyard. But, I didn't buy it. He was acting kind of fishy, like he'd been caught in the act, or something."

"What do you think he was looking for?" Olivia eyes the car and then scans the area. She has her own potential stalkers to worry about.

"I have no idea. I just thought you should know."

"Will you go back to another meeting?"

"I think so, if for no other reason than to try and find out what he was looking for."

CHAPTER THIRTY-SEVEN

PRESENT DAY

Brian pulls the SUV into Olivia and Marco's dirt driveway just after 10 on Saturday night. As they exit the vehicle, Tucker bounds out of the back seat toward an Adirondack rocker on the front porch, into Marco's waiting arms. Boo leaps crazily all over Olivia, licking her face, and then moves on to Brian and Carly, who immediately fall for his loving demeanor.

"Do you call him Boo because he's white like a ghost?" Carly asks.

"That's exactly why," Marco replies.

The commotion dies down after the introductions are over, the bags are piled in the house and the SUV is safely lodged in the garage, with the sheath still blanketed in the back. Olivia and Marco march the kids all around the house, showing them where everything they'll need is and where each will take up residence. The look on Brian's face tells Olivia he's feeling pretty grown-up about his newly renovated, fully furnished "apartment" accommodations.

"We'll explore the property in the daylight. Right now, I think it's time to settle in." Olivia turns and speaks directly to Brian. "I want to thank you, Brian. I don't know where you got your driving skills, but I'd say you'd pretty much qualify as a professional now." She then turns to Marco. "He probably drove 90 percent of the way."

Marco fist-bumps Brian. "I don't blame you. I usually need a tranquilizer when she's driving."

Olivia gives Marco a playful shove. "Hey! Don't you two guys start ganging up on me, or Carly and I'll have to show you a thing or two, right Carly?" Carly tentatively nods her head in agreement.

"Ooh, we're scared!" Marco jests.

Brian clarifies Olivia's former statement. "And it was more like 99 percent of the driving."

"Whatever! Go to bed." With a broad smile on her face, Olivia shoos Brian down the stairs to his new digs and ushers Carly into her bedroom at the end of the hall, kissing her on the forehead once she's crawled under the covers. "Sleep well, sweet one." Tucker curls up at Carly's feet and Olivia gives him a quick scratch on the ears before she closes the door behind her. Boo has his nose on the ground shoved up under the door that leads downstairs. He's sniffing for Brian. "Come sleep with us, Boo. I missed you," Olivia says. "You can accost Brian tomorrow."

"So, are you going to show me the infamous River Tapestry and the box of letters?" Marco asks, when Olivia walks back into the kitchen.

"Well, I've been thinking about it," Olivia replies, as she lingers with a cup of peppermint tea Marco has prepared. She finds it funny that Marco has fixed her the very same tea Mrs.

Capricci had just days earlier. It's not like they were ever in the habit of drinking it before. "I really don't know if we have any idea how to handle them. They're so old. How do we know if the oils from our fingers will damage the cloth or if we should be handling the letters in some special way? I think I want to talk to this Peter guy at the museum before we handle them again. Don't you think that's a good idea?"

"So, you're going to keep me in suspense?" he says with a grin on his face.

"Marco, a couple of days won't kill you." Olivia is struggling with all the secrets inside. She wants to tell Marco that she's afraid people may be after her because she now has the Tapestry. She wants to tell him about the syringes, and that she believes she killed someone. The fact that she's the only one who knows is eating Olivia up.

"Okay," he reluctantly agrees. "So, does that mean you plan on leaving again soon?"

"I'm thinking tomorrow afternoon I'll drive to Rio's, and then Monday morning I'll go to New York City. I'll come back home that afternoon."

"What do you mean, I'll? You're not going into the city alone."

"I'll be okay, Marco. I'm a big girl."

"No. I told you before, either Rio goes, or I do."

"You have to stay here with the kids. How would that look if I left them alone right after we got here?"

"You're leaving them with me, and I'm a stranger?" Marco teases.

"Well, you are strange," Olivia laughs. "But you're no more of a stranger than I am, really."

"Hardly. It's not that I don't want you to go, just not by yourself. No way."

"Okay, fine. Rio can go with me." Olivia had been hoping to keep some of this danger stuff under cover. That's likely not to be the case if Rio accompanies her. But then again, the meeting could be benign. She tells herself that the museum guy can't possibly know about the syringes or what happened in Alamosa, or can he?

Marco eyes her with skepticism, like he doesn't believe she'll stick to her word. "I called Rio and told him. He wants to go with you. So, don't try anything once you get there."

"So, how was your meeting tonight?" Olivia deftly changes the subject.

"Odd," says Marco, following the bait. "A couple of the guys, including the one I caught in the backyard, were obviously buttering me up. But, strangely, some of the others treated me like I was the enemy."

"It always takes a while to find your place in a new group. You know, jealousies and shit?"

"Yeah, I guess. I did overhear something intriguing, though."

"Oh yeah, what?"

"Well, when I was coming out of the bathroom, before they could see me, I heard a couple of the guys talking about a sword like it was the Holy Grail or something. One of them said he thought they were close to finding it. But as soon as they spotted me, they got quiet and the rest of the night they pretty much spoke in Spanish. Those were the two that were treating me like the enemy."

"Hmmm, a sword, huh? You sure these guys aren't The Knights of Templar or something?" Olivia laughs and pokes Marco, making like she's jousting.

"Funny!" he counters, grabbing Olivia by the wrist and twirling her around. "It's so good to see you. I missed you. And Boo was beside himself."

"Oh, just Boo?" Olivia flirts.

Marco's look turns to smoldering heat and he leads Olivia to their bedroom where he kicks the door closed behind him. He pushes her onto the bed, just like he used to do decades ago when they were young. Her heart leaps. His mouth devours hers as he rips off her clothes. Olivia is keenly aware of the frantic pounding of her own heart. Their lovemaking is ancient and fresh, solid and soft, confident and playful. Secure in Marco's embrace, her troubles melt away into the sheets beneath her. She takes all the fear and all the confusion and all the pent-up angst she's been carrying for days and—like alchemy—transforms it into pure passion. She feels as if she's undergoing a metamorphosis, as though she has fully shed a skin and is free of it. She convinces herself that the past of Alamosa is behind her and the idea that she'll ever be booked for murder is ludicrous. She finds herself able—as she has always been—to put the past in its place, which is, after all, in the past. She turns her focus instead to the future. She is going forward into an exciting new adventure. Lifting herself up, she rides Marco like a wild stallion. They are young again, on top of the world, with all the possibilities of life before them. Olivia, without a doubt, feels like she's on the precipice of feeling, thrillingly, brand-new.

The sky is a soft blue with high wispy clouds that look like an intricate lace overlay. Olivia spends a moment examining the sky, and then moves her eyes back to the quartet of men climbing the

steep hill across from the rock ledge where she sits dangling her legs over the edge. Marco's Uncle Leo is in the lead, maneuvering his way with a walking stick. Olivia squints so that she can make out the bright orange and blue Kingfisher feathers that dangle from the carved piece of wood. She attempts to remember who it was that gave him the walking stick, but the memory is evasive.

Uncle Leo slows down and stops to rest. Marco takes the lead, positioning his feet carefully on one foothold after another. But soon, his momentum wanes as well, and his sons quickly pass him. Olivia can hear laughter in the distance, and she watches intently as Mateo turns his head around and yells, "No worries, old men! We'll meet you at the top!" He fist-bumps his brother, Rio, and the two quicken their pace, climbing with a vivacity displayed only by the young.

Olivia's heart is torn between her pride for her children and the melancholy she feels for their father and great-uncle. She remembers the first time Rio beat her up one of those manmade rock walls. He was 14 years old and Olivia was 39. It hit her hard. She imagines that Marco and Uncle Leo feel similarly right now.

A fly buzzes around her and she waves it away. It lands on her leg for just a second and then whizzes off. She reaches down to scratch her leg and when she does, her feet come into view. They aren't hers, though. They are the hairy, taloned paws of a black bear.

It's a struggle to pull herself from sleep as she plays tug-of-war with a dream. Her body is ready to wake, but her subconscious grapples with itself, seeking some form of clarification it never receives. Without knowledge or control she gives in, and the dream fades away.

CHAPTER THIRTY-EIGHT

PRESENT DAY

Olivia speeds down the highway after a morning of walking mountain roads with dogs and kids and her long-lost but newly found lover, Marco. They had lingered over breakfast, explored the pond, and she had built a rock cairn on her front porch with the rocks she had taken from Mrs. Capricci's.

"Screw those chauvinistic men, if they think I can't drive!" She proclaims to herself out loud. After all, she's made this drive a hundred times. Her thoughts turn to her mission. She'd confirmed with the museum that morning that Peter Velazquez will be in on Monday, but there were no guarantees that Olivia will be able to see him. He works via appointment only. But Olivia is willing to take her chances.

The highway becomes a chessboard. She positions herself

strategically so that she can see every car around her. Speeding seems to work best. The faster she goes, the more likely she'll outrun anyone who may have the desire to follow her. She most certainly doesn't want to lead some ill-intentioned stalker to Rio's house. The hours of driving give her time to think. She gets off two exits early, winds her way around the back roads, and circles the block three times before she feels it's safe to pull into her son's driveway. Olivia tells herself that she's just got to be smarter than anyone who might be following her.

Rio and his family have held up dinner, and they all eat a lively meal with Olivia's three-year-old grandson, Leo, holding court. Watching his every move is even more delicious than the meal itself. The antics of this light-hearted little boy allow Olivia to release the tension of the drive. Looking at her grandson is like seeing Rio as a toddler all over again. The image she recalls of Rio when he was that age is difficult to distinguish from this expressive little curly-headed boy. Leo winks at her before dropping morsels of chicken on the ground for their dog. He uses his fork to mold the mashed sweet potatoes on his plate into the rough shape of a spaceship and then switches to tapping his fork on the table in a rhythm only he recognizes. Olivia is reminded once again, with a stinging twinge of regret, why she's sad they live so far apart. The night is a perfect capsule of laughter and joy to hold in her heart until the universe grants her another.

The next morning, Rio drives her through the congested Lincoln Tunnel into New York City. He maneuvers Olivia's SUV adeptly between lanes and they eventually pull into a parking garage near the museum. Olivia, dressed in a blue suit, pulls the tapestry carpet bag from the backseat, and Rio retrieves the leather sheath from underneath the blanket in the far back. On the walk up Fifth Avenue, Olivia clutches the carpet bag underneath her arm, keeping one eye on the sheath Rio carries and the other to size up each person they pass. Every few steps, she looks behind her, bothered that she keeps imagining seeing the man from Colorado who identified himself as Franco Capricci stalking her every move, when she knows that's impossible after she stuck him with the poisonous syringe. Everyone on the street looks suspicious.

"Mom, what's up? You're acting like a criminal on the run."

"I'm just nervous I guess." Rio only knows what Marco told him, which, of course, isn't much less than Olivia knows, except for the not stop short at killing part and, of course, the syringes that are still in her purse.

They find their way through the maze of the museum to where the offices are located, and Olivia explains who she is to the receptionist. A mere two minutes later, the courteous young woman informs them, "Mr. Velazquez will see you now." She leads them down the hall and into a luxuriously appointed corner office with windows that look out over the city.

"Welcome. I've been expecting you, Olivia. May I call you Olivia?" A tall, impeccably dressed man with distinguished looks, gray-blonde hair and blue eyes extends his hand.

"Of course," Olivia says as she shakes his hand. "This is my son, Rio."

"Please call me Peter," he says as he shakes Rio's hand before directing his guests to sit in two leather chairs positioned across from an enormous mahogany desk.

"You've been expecting me?" Olivia inquires with some surprise.

The handsome man with captivating eyes nods his head yes. "Filomena contacted me a few months ago to let me know that either you or your husband would be coming to see me." Olivia's brain shuffles backward. That had to be before she began having the river dreams.

Olivia shifts nervously in her chair. "Well, obviously, Mrs. Capricci held you in the highest regard. I imagine that means we can trust you?"

Peter smiles, flashing a set of perfectly straight, bright-white teeth, and nods his positive reply.

"Well then, maybe you can inform us about the River Tapestry? And then, there is this box of letters." Olivia begins to struggle trying to remove the box from the carpet bag. But Peter holds his hand up to stop her.

"There is no need to show me. I am very familiar with these articles. You see, I am a relative of Filomena's. She brought the letters to me decades ago to have translated into English. I hold those translations in a secure location offsite."

Olivia nods her head in understanding and settles the carpet bag back under her arm. "To be honest, I'm extremely confused about all of this."

"As anyone would be," Peter confidently assures her.

Again, Olivia nods in bewildered agreement and looks over at Rio for support. He takes her lead. "Mr. Velazquez, obviously, my mother has been directed to you for a reason. You must know the meaning and value of the Tapestry?" The look in Peter's eyes confirms Rio's question. "Could you please enlighten us?"

CHAPTER THIRTY-NINE

1644

Buen Retiro Palace, the summer residence of King Philip IV of Spain, is in utter turmoil. Servants and handmaidens lurk behind doors and around corners, fearful of a confrontation with their king, who has been roaming the vast halls for hours, bellowing in despair. Queen Elisabeth is locked in her quarters, inconsolable. She is devastated by the possibility that they may be destined to lose yet another child.

Their red-headed six-year-old daughter, Maria Theresa, had been playing in the expansive gardens, frolicking around the ponds, as she is known to do. Her mother, who had dismissed the nanny from her charge for the afternoon, had trouble keeping up, and lost sight of her daughter for a moment. Yet that moment was long enough for little Maria Theresa to be lured by a bush on which hung several clusters of white berries with black dots in the centers, like eerie eyes. She pulled off a cluster, plucked a handful of berries and popped them into her mouth. The young girl chewed briefly and swallowed. The bright pink stems and remaining berries were found lying on the ground at Maria Theresa's feet when her mother, huffing and puffing, hastened to her side.

"¡Oh querido!" Oh dear! Queen Elisabeth had shouted in distress. The nanny, who had been secretly trailing them, rushed to her sniveling charge, scooped the young girl into her arms and ran back to the safety of the princess's quarters.

Immediately, the child began to scratch at her burning throat and, within an hour's time, the temperature on the brandy thermometer the nanny used to gauge the level of fever had spiked. The palace doctors were summoned and, one after another, each attempted to treat the child, all without success. Maria Theresa clutched her stomach and wailed in pain. The staff's eyes bulged in terror at the sight of the child's limbs: her tendons began to spasm uncontrollably, causing her legs and arms to jerk violently into unfathomable positions. The king was informed by the medical team that there was nothing further they could do to help his beloved daughter.

But the nanny, Olinda Velazquez, thinks she knows of a remedy. She has seen it used before, by her cousin's father. With the help of a guard, her brother-in-law, Hernan, they frantically run to the garden and begin to search around the ponds for a stalk of marshmallow plant. Locating it, they run at a breathless pace back to the palace kitchen. The kitchen cooks stand back and gawk, bewildered by Olinda's actions. But the head chef, Olinda's father, Benito, assists her and Hernan as they mash the leaves and roots of the marshmallow plant with a mortar and pestle and then boil them to extract the plant's oddly fragrant oils. Then, oils in hand, the nanny, along with her father and Hernan, run to Maria Theresa's side and force copious spoonfuls of the substance down the child's throat, repeating the process over and over again. Within a short time, the princess appears revived, to the tremendous relief of the king and queen.

A week later, Diego Velazquez, the leading artist in the court of King Philip IV and uncle to Olinda, is commissioned to paint a portrait in which the royal family, along with Maria Theresa's saviors, Olinda and Hernan, are to be depicted—a courtly celebration of the healing of the royal daughter.

There are musicians playing Maria Theresa's most-loved songs and tables laden with her favorite foods. Holding hands, the attendees dance in a circle next to the Rio Manzanares. They are all smiling and laughing; all but Queen Elisabeth. She separates herself from the congregation to sit on a rock next to the river, where she hangs her head above the water. From his position on an outcropping just above the river, the painter, Diego, has an unobstructed view of the queen's reflection in the clear river below. Wanting to include the queen in his painting, and unable to see her face directly, he paints her dismal expression as seen in her reflection.

Weeks pass, and Queen Elisabeth continues to sulk. She is inconsolable for having been so remiss as to allow her young daughter alone near poisonous berries. The queen rarely leaves her quarters and eventually doctors are summoned to diagnose her ailment. They find nothing medically wrong. Their only prescription is for the queen to spend time with her daughter, which she can't seem to bring herself to do.

Three months later, Queen Elisabeth is dead from heart failure, never having recovered from the deep sense of remorse she had fixed upon her own culpable heart.

CHAPTER FORTY

PRESENT DAY

You see, the chef, Benito Velazquez, was Diego Velazquez's brother," Peter Velazquez explains to Olivia and Rio. "He was in the room when the healing of the king's daughter took place. He had the king's painting weaved into a tapestry and made a gift of it to his daughter, Olinda." Pushing the button on his desk phone, Peter leans forward and says, "Francesca, please bring us some tea and coffee?" He gestures to Olivia and Rio for a preference.

"Tea is fine," Olivia replies. Rio nods in agreement. "Okay," Olivia says, "that tells us how it came to be. But why is it so valuable that people are willing to kill for it?" Rio's eyes grow big and round, and he turns his head to his mother in an expression of disbelief. This is the first he's heard of any danger connected to the crazy series of events his mother has been at the center of. Olivia feels Rio's eyes burning into the side of her face but doesn't turn to meet them. She silently chastises herself for not having been more careful with her word choice.

One of Peter's eyebrows raises at the question. "The letter translations will bring light to those questions. I will courier them to your home tomorrow. Please write your address here." He pushes a pad of paper across his desk to Olivia.

Olivia scribbles her address on the paper while continuing with questions. "I noticed when I was looking through the letters that each one references something called 'Los Seis Regalos.' I looked it up and found that it means 'The Six Gifts.' Can you tell us more about that?"

"Of course, Los Seis Regalos. The River Tapestry is but one of these six highly treasured gifts. The translations will explain more about them, but not all. For ultimate enlightenment, the possessor of one of the gifts must go to what's called the 'Stone.' But not just any possessor. For one to be taken to the Stone, the possessor must be in the Velazquez bloodline."

"And this 'Stone'—what is it?"

"That, Olivia, I cannot say, for I have never been in possession of one of the gifts. The Stone—whatever it might be—is only accessible by a possessor."

Olivia slumps back in her chair and attempts to process Peter's words. Peter is silent, awaiting her next question. Rio impatiently shifts and re-shifts his body and unconsciously taps the arm of his chair. Finally, Olivia sits up straight again, another light having been switched on in her brain. "Why me? I'm not a Velazquez," she questions.

"Ahh, not you my dear. Filomena merely trusted you to transfer possession to a rightful Velazquez descendant."

"And that is?"

"Either your husband or one of your sons."

Both Olivia and Rio's mouths drop open. Olivia shakes her head in disbelief. "Marco is a Velazquez descendant?"

"He most certainly is. You see, Olinda married the guard after his first wife, her sister, died. His name was Hernan Alvarez and they had two children, a son and a daughter, and so on and so forth."

"But our name is Alfieri, not Alvarez," Rio says.

"It was changed when your ancestors moved from Spain to Italy," Olivia clarifies. She puts her hands to the sides of her cheeks and begins to mumble to herself, quietly reiterating all that they have just learned.

Rio recovers more quickly. "What's this about people willing to kill for it?"

Peter directs his answer to Rio. "There are many, for its value is immeasurable."

"So, in dollars, it's worth what?" Rio wobbles his head from side to side, in a questioning gesture.

"Like I said, it is immeasurable. But, if you're asking what dollar figure you may be able to gain for it, I must strongly advise that you dismiss the idea. This is a gift, and it is imperative that it remain in the Velazquez bloodline." He pauses long enough for his point to sink in. "But if you decide that parting with it is your only option, I can probably raise three million, which I'm sure is much less than it is worth. However, if you choose to sell it to me, it will stay in the bloodline. Still, I do not suggest it. Filomena had every opportunity to leave the Tapestry to me. But, instead, she chose to give it to your family."

Olivia and Rio both draw deep breaths and take sips of their tea, which had been quietly served by Francesca during a break in the conversation. Olivia speaks next. "And the Stone, is its location in the letters?"

Peter shakes his head no. "When your family has read the translations and you decide whether or not to keep it, we will speak again." He rises from his chair, an indication that the meeting is over.

"One last question," Olivia says. "Is it safe to handle the Tapestry and the letters?"

"I suggest you not take the letters out of the box or touch them with your bare hands. Wait for the translations. As far as the Tapestry is concerned, be very careful. It is old and fragile. Handle it only if you must and then, only with clean cotton gloves."

They shake hands at the door and as Peter reaches for the handle, he looks gravely at both Olivia and Rio. "Do not belittle the importance of this gift. It is not only a great treasure of Spain, but also of the entire world's. It has been kept safe by your ancestors for centuries and is now yours to keep safe for future generations."

CHAPTER FORTY-ONE

PRESENT DAY

R io and Olivia walk hastily toward Olivia's SUV, not wanting to speak until they are alone inside the privacy of the car. "What do you make of all this, Rio?"

"I think something we could never have imagined has just happened to our family," her son says.

"No shit! So, what do you think we should do?"

"Wait for the translations."

"I mean, keep it or sell it?"

"Are you crazy? We're not selling it!" Rio regards his mother disbelievingly. "I only asked its value because I was curious. But I can see now why Peter says it's invaluable."

Olivia sighs. "I know, I know; I guess I just still have Dana and her family on my mind. The money would go a long way to help them."

"Mom. Stop it. Don't act like we don't have resources. We can get Dana back on her feet and figure out how to help pay for Brian's college and Carly's therapy, or whatever." Rio casts his mother a look of disappointment before he pulls the SUV out of the garage. "Dad's been keeping me in the loop."

Olivia hangs her head. "I'm sorry I haven't kept in touch over the last few weeks, Rio. I've been a little busy."

"I know. It's just that, well, you've always told me everything. That's how you say I've learned so much so fast." He puts his hand on her shoulder and squeezes it. "I guess I've just been missing you, that's all."

Olivia reaches over with both arms and hugs her son. "Rio, I've missed you, too. You have no idea how much. Last night, being with you and your family really knocked me for a loop. It's harder than you can believe living so far away from you. And with Mateo not speaking to us; well, it's just hard."

They drive in silence through the city, the tunnel and onto the turnpike. "It's your father's, you know." Olivia softly says.

"I know," Rio confirms. "But we're not selling it."

"Okay, okay, I get it! I can't wait to read the translations. I still feel like we're totally in the dark."

"Will you call and let me know what you find out?" Rio asks.

"Of course, and I've got to tell you that I've just been thinking; you know how you always asked me why we named you and Mateo Spanish names? Well, I still say it was totally intuitive. But I knew it was something we had to do. I didn't even understand it then. But now I'm thinking that it really was my intuition. Somehow, I knew you were supposed to be, or are, Spanish."

"Pretty strong intuition. Freaky mom," Rio says.

"Yeah, I'm freaky alright!" Olivia pauses before continuing. "Rio, I want to tell you something else about intuition because I know you understand it. A couple of weeks before I went to Alamosa I started having these dreams about a mom and a son and a daughter by the side of the river. I had them a few times, and when I found out about Jeff dying I took them as a sign that I should go. For some reason, I felt like the river was The Rio Grande. But now I believe differently." Olivia looks over at Rio to make sure he's listening. "From the time I was a young girl I had these dreams—daydreams, really—about a man who was always saving me. When I grew up and met your dad I was convinced without a doubt that he was that man. I still am. But now I'm beginning to believe that Mrs. Capricci somehow planted those dreams in my head, just like I think she planted the river dreams in my head a few weeks ago. I think she always had me pegged as the way to get to your father, whom I think she had hand-picked decades ago."

"I don't know how people can plant dreams in your head, Mom."

"Neither do I, but you didn't meet Mrs. Capricci. If there exists a kind of magical person who can do that, well, it would be her."

"Well, it is weird that you went there for a funeral and ended up with the River Tapestry, and that it's linked to Dad."

"Right?"

"You sure you're okay to drive home by yourself?" Rio asks as he pulls into his driveway. "I'm a little worried about this danger shit. Why didn't you tell me about that?"

"I don't know. I guess I didn't know how serious it is." Olivia knows damn well how serious it is. She fucking killed someone over it.

"Just be careful, okay?"

"I will." Olivia gets out of the car to change seats, hugging Rio like she can't remember when, crying like a baby while they say goodbye. "Thank you so much for going with me."

"Thank you for taking me," Rio says with conviction. "I'm honored! I don't know about you, but I feel like it's all kind of a dream or something. Don't you?"

"Yeah, but honestly, I'm hoping we don't wake up from this dream. It's way beyond cool."

"Yeah, way beyond. Safe travels, Mom."

Olivia is on autopilot as she drives up the parkway, not budging from the left lane as she pulls onto the congested New York State Thruway. She has suddenly become expert at scanning the rearview mirror for tails. She imagines her vehicle as an armored car, heading north, encased in a force field. All she can think about is the Tapestry and keeping it safe. Every inch of her house and property come into her mind, like hiding places in a treasure hunt. But Mrs. Capricci didn't keep the Tapestry in her house. She kept it at Mr. Farro's office. Olivia scrambles to think of someone she trusts that much. Rio is the only person she can think of and, because he's her son, she determines that he's too close and would be put in the same danger. So, she discounts that idea. Olivia imagines burying the Tapestry underground somewhere, in a cache or something, but it would have to be sealed against the moisture. They'd need an expert to help them with that and that would mean involving someone they don't know. Every scenario she conjures comes to a dead end. She begins to think about the syringes and the letters and where to hide them, wondering again if Mrs. Capricci ever had to use the syringes. She figures so, if she felt compelled enough to leave them for Olivia with the strong message she sent with them. The fact that Marco is a Velazquez from way back enters her mind. The story of how Mrs. Capricci knew this about him picks at her brain, along with the question of how the old woman could have possibly lured Olivia to Alamosa through her dreams.

These questions, and the story of the Tapestry itself, invade every crevice of her thoughts and wind their way into the recesses of her heart. She calls to her mind the characters from 1644 in detail, everything from the color of their hair to the style of their clothing, bringing them to life. Hernan, the guard, takes on the appearance of Marco. Marco! She's only an hour from home when it dawns on her that she needs to call him. She's made it all the way to Vermont Route 7, just past Manchester, when she picks up her cell phone, noticing for the first time several missed calls from Marco. She had put her phone on mute when she'd gone into Peter's office and never turned the ringer back on.

Olivia punches the number for home. "Oh Marco, I'm so sorry I haven't called. I didn't even notice what time it was. I can't stop thinking about the meeting and what Peter told us."

"Well, thank God you're okay. I was worried to death! I spoke to Rio and he told me when you left. I thought maybe your phone died and you didn't have the car charger, or something."

"I'm sorry. It didn't even dawn on me what time it was until I got all the way to Manchester. I didn't mean to make you worry. Are Brian and Carly alright?"

"They're fine. Brian is out by the pond sketching and Carly is watching a movie. They've been asking about you."

Olivia smiles at the thought of these two kids being concerned about her. She's grown to love them in the past few weeks.

For some reason, she feels that she and they are significant to one another's life now. And then there's also this innate responsibility she feels to keep them safe. She chalks it up to motherly instinct. "That's sweet. They're good kids, aren't they?"

"Yeah, so far, so good. They've both been pretty quiet since you left. So, come on, tell me, what did you find out? The suspense is killing me!"

"Rio didn't tell you?"

"No, he said he thought you should be the one."

"That Rio—always could keep a secret." Olivia's heart swells with pride. They did *something* right, she thinks. Rio has proven himself to be a man of integrity. "Well, I'm not sure where to begin." Olivia begins to recount every detail she can remember, every word that Peter spoke. The words come out fast, her voice rising and falling with suspense, and her monologue sounding like the trailer to a thriller movie. Marco is transfixed by the information. When Olivia finally comes up for air, silence ensues while both of their minds attempt to process what's just transpired between them. Marco has a lot to take in. Obviously, there is more to his family heritage than he ever dreamed. And Olivia has also finally shared with Marco the danger Mrs. Capricci expressed over possessing this gift. Still, she holds secret her incident with the man who claimed to be Mrs. Capricci's son; the man she presumes she killed. Olivia resolves to never allow that secret to escape her mouth.

"Are you okay?" Marco asks. "What kind of danger are you talking about?"

"How do I know?" Olivia lies. "Everybody just keeps talking about danger. Like the letter that said, in so many words—*people will kill for the Tapestry.*"

"We really need those translations and you really need to be careful. I'm worried about you now," Marco intimates. "And when you get home, we've got to find a damn good hiding place for the Tapestry."

"I'm thinking we hide it underground in a PVC pipe, or something, on our property somewhere. What do you think?"

"It's an idea. But, possibly, the moisture wouldn't be good for it. The thing has made it through a few centuries, so we know it can be done. I certainly wouldn't want to ruin it now. We just need to be smart, that's all."

"Yeah," she replies, "we need to be smart and we need to know more in able to be smart. Let's hope the translations will tell us enough to at least help us understand the whole thing. I imagine the Stone has some final information of some sort and Peter said that the translations still don't tell you where the Stone is. He did indicate that he can get us there, though. I wonder if it's in Spain. It would be totally cool to go to Spain. We could do it, Marco! We could go to Spain to visit the Stone, whatever the Stone is."

From murder and mayhem to sleuthing for treasure in Spain, Olivia is now envisioning herself as the character in an action film. But a jolt of fear prompted from recent experiences overcomes any excitement and reminds that when you wish for excitement, you ought to be careful what you wish for.

"How about we take this one step at a time," Marco says. "This is all too crazy, don't you think? We've just been given a treasure from 1644. I mean really, who'd a thunk it?"

"Yeah, who'd a thunk it?"

"And you say it's only one of six treasures, right?"

"That's what Peter said. It's one of 'Los Seis Regalos.' That's got to be what the symbol that's marked on the back of the Tap-estry represents. It's the same symbol that's engraved on Mrs. Capricci's amulet. I wonder what the other five gifts are. My guess is that one is a sword because there is clearly a sword in the symbol. Maybe we can find out what the others are if we go to Spain. Or maybe the translations will tell us."

"I hope they tell us something," Marco says. "How are we supposed to know what to do with the Tapestry? I mean, maybe there's something special we're supposed to do with it." Olivia listens to Marco take a deep breath. "I'm going to have to think about everything my dad or my Uncle Leo ever said. But then again, who knows if they ever even knew about any of this."

"You're right, I guess. But I got the impression Mrs. Capricci was close to your Uncle Leo. I mean, she sent my sister, Cari, to him, and she went to his funeral. And from what Peter says, they were related. You know that means you and Mrs. Capricci were related, right? I'm still having a little trouble processing that."

"You! I'm having trouble processing any of this! But you know how you talk about Mrs. Capricci being, I don't know—magical?"

"Yeah?"

"Don't you remember Uncle Leo being kind of like that? I mean, it always seemed like he knew things nobody else knew."

"You're right; if anyone was magical, it was your Uncle Leo." Olivia scans the horizon and conjures up images of Uncle Leo and Mrs. Capricci in her thoughts. "Both he and Mrs. Capricci; they're hard acts to follow."

"No joke."

"I just hope it's not simply a tapestry we're supposed to keep hidden in a leather sheath for the rest of our lives," Olivia says.

"There's got to be more to it than that."

"Yeah, there's got to be." There is a long moment of silence between them while they contemplate the possibilities. "So, guess what? I got an email from Mateo today," Marco says, out of the blue.

"You did?"

"Well, he responded to another email I sent him last night."

"And?"

"He told me to stop emailing him."

Olivia snickers. "It's just like him to say that. But, hey, they're words, right? It's a message. He's really saying don't stop emailing. You know that, right?"

"I guess."

Olivia is suddenly struck with an understanding that hits her like a crack of lightning from the sky. "Oh my God, Marco!" she gasps, sucking in air like her lungs have suddenly been squeezed shut. "The Why; I know what it is! Oh my God, I know what The Why is!"

"What, Olivia, what is it?"

"And to think I've spent my whole life searching for something I could never have found! Or maybe I did find it and just didn't know it! But I didn't find it completely. It still had to find me!" Olivia is dumbstruck by the revelation and how damned long it took her to figure it out.

"What are you talking about, Olivia? You're not making any sense."

"Don't you see, Marco? All these years, ever since I can remember, it was all about you. It was all for you! The man in my dreams from the time I was a child—he was planted there to lead me to you. Holy shit!" The events of Olivia's life stream through her consciousness. "Don't you see? Every time I was saved from death, I was saved for you!" Olivia's heart is racing as she impatiently honks at the slow-moving woman driving in front of her. "Marco, it's obvious now. I'm just a messenger, a courier, a pigeon, a hawk!"

"Olivia, stop! You're not *just* anything."

"Yeah Marco, I'm just the ... the baton passer, the means for Mrs. Capricci to get the Tapestry to you!" Now that she knows, and knows for sure what *The Why* is, Olivia feels disappointed, deflated, done—like she's been punched in the gut. The question of *The Why* has driven her unstoppably for more than 50 years and now, in a mere second, the drive has vanished. For Olivia, even this new excitement over the Tapestry pales in comparison to her search for *The Why*, because *The Why* has been lurking in her heart and mind for nearly her entire life. A recognizable feeling envelops her, the feeling that she is being smothered by Marco's family. Having spent a lifetime being married to the son of a domineering Italian man and working in the family business for decades, there have been years when she literally felt like she'd never get out from under that family's spell. Fidgeting in her driver's seat, a battle stirs inside of her. The intrigue of the River Tapestry and the part she's played in its story wages war against the irritating fact that she feels like she's been bred for the sole purpose of delivering the Tapestry to Marco. Something Mrs. Capricci once said about Marco flashes through her thoughts: *Maybe he no find his purpose yet*, she'd said. All these years, Olivia has been obsessed with *The Why*, her own why. She's never once thought about Marco's why.

In the rearview mirror, Olivia notices the man in the car behind her driving too close for comfort. He's so close on her tail, in fact, that she can see his face, and he looks eerily familiar. The hair rises on the back of her neck. She doesn't know what to be more distressed about: the possibility that someone may be following her or the fact that her whole life's purpose has been to dispatch a gift to Marco. And now that she has dispatched that gift, there's nothing left for *her* to do. A flash of irritation travels up her spine.

She is driving on a two-lane highway and the woman in front of her is continuing to move at a snail's pace. Olivia throws her head back in despair and flips her blinker on. "I'm going to pass this freaking woman!" she says to Marco. "She's driving like a fucking slug and I just want to get home! I'm shaking, and I swear my heart is beating so fast it's gonna pop!"

"No Olivia, don't! Just wait, be patient." Marco discourages her.

"Huh? Patient? I've been patient for 50 fucking years!" Olivia pulls out into the oncoming lane. There are no cars coming in the opposite direction, so she guns it, passing the woman and then steering back into the right lane. Suddenly, she sees an animal scramble onto the road in front of her. It's a large black bear and its staring straight at her. Olivia's heart literally skips a beat. She blinks, and then blinks again. The dark-black eyes of the bear seem to drill directly into her own. Her natural reaction is to jerk the wheel to the right to avoid hitting it. When she does, the SUV goes airborne over an embankment and touches ground in the field below where the velocity and sudden redirection of the vehicle causes it to flip over and then over again.

In the microseconds that her vehicle takes to tumble across the field, Olivia feels as if everything is happening in slow motion. Images, sounds and emotions engulf her: the first time she saw Marco when he walked off that plane and looked at her with those bottomless dark eyes; the warm sumptuous taste of their first kiss; Mateo taking his first wobbly step and falling forward into her waiting arms; Rio clinging to her leg for dear life, like a baby kangaroo searching for protection in its mother's pouch. And then the sound of her grandson, Leo's, first giggle when Marco blew raspberries onto his bare belly. And all those years ago, her proud father running along by her side as she launches off on her two-wheeler bike, solo for the first time.

CHAPTER FORTY-TWO

PRESENT DAY

Marco pulls up to the crash site. Police cars and an ambulance are blocking the road. He has been praying for Olivia the entire way here. But in his heart, he knows that she's gone.

He eases himself out of his car and slowly walks to the ambulance where he can see Olivia's covered body. Marco climbs inside, lays himself across her and weeps until the EMTs have got to physically lift him off and gently steer him out of the ambulance. A policeman guides him to the passenger seat of his cruiser where he tells Marco what they know. They have a witness. Olivia had just passed the woman and another car was passing behind Olivia. Then, for no apparent reason, Olivia jerked the wheel to the right and flew off the highway. Oddly, the man passing behind her kept going and never stopped.

"That's all the woman said?" Marco asks, craving more information. "Are you telling me that the car passing didn't push her off the road?"

"According to the woman," the police officer responds, "she didn't see that car get close enough to your wife's car to hit it. As a matter of fact, we have yet to find *any* evidence telling us why your wife went off the road."

"Did the woman get the license plate of the other guy?"

"No. She did say that she could see it was a Vermont plate, though."

"Is there anything else?" Marco asks. "I'd like to walk out to the car to see for myself."

The officer looks up and down the gray light of the highway. "We're waiting for the tow truck. It's going to be dark soon." He pauses for a minute before adding, "For some reason, the airbag in your wife's car didn't deploy. They found her in the field. You want me to go with you?"

"No," Marco looks at the ground. "I just want to ..." He doesn't finish his sentence, but instead shakes the policeman's hand before he slides down the embankment and walks out into the field. Olivia's SUV rests right-side-up next to a maple tree near the bank of The Mill River. As he walks, Marco is overtaken by the feeling that, any minute, Olivia will open the door and climb out. But he knows it is only wishful thinking and that his mind and his heart are playing tricks on him.

Marco squeezes the handle and the door pops open. Inside, Olivia's purse is on the floor of the passenger side and, after fumbling around in the backseat, he finds the tapestry carpet bag. He pulls them both out of the car, positions the straps over one shoulder and walks around to the open backend of the SUV.

The leather sheath that holds the Tapestry is lying, uncovered, in the crevice up against the back seat.

Marco reaches in across the caved-in back of the SUV, wraps his hand around the sheath and is suddenly hit by a force that is beyond his comprehension. It feels to him as though he's just touched an electrified wire that's zapped him from head to toe. The intensity of it propels him backward from the vehicle and knocks him to the ground. The sheath is still secure in his grip, but his eyes are shut tight from the impact. Lying there, he feels the inexplicable sensation of a blended mirage of trees and plants, flowers and herbs, instructions and formulas, diagrams and illustrations, medicines and remedies, ancient belief systems and tenets of modern science funnel into him. It's as though a lifetime's worth of education has suddenly and instantaneously crash-landed in his brain and is now vouchsafed in a zip drive of knowledge that surpasses that of any recognized scholars of botany and naturopathy. In that instant, he has become a different person, someone gifted with enormous insight, while at the same time stripped of the very essence of his former being. His heart aches unbearably. Yet, ironically, he feels brand-new.

A distinct rustle in the woods nearby pulls Marco from his reverie. His eyes shoot through the trees and across the small river. The light is low, nearly gone, but Marco is sure of what he sees. Just at the edge of the water stands a black bear. But Marco's already traumatized body doesn't shake with fear at the sight of this majestic creature. Instead, he feels a peaceful stillness encompass the space where the river runs between himself and the bear. A moment passes before Marco slowly rises to his feet to steady himself. His movement causes the bear to turn toward him. Suddenly, the sounds of birds, the crackle of chipmunks and the distant whir of vehicles on the highway become inaudible over the pounding of his heart. A last flicker of daylight illuminates the buckle of the miraculous leather sheath in Marco's hand and then trips across the river, where it catches the whites of the bear's eyes. Marco draws in a long slow breath as he watches the bear nod in his direction, as if it's acknowledging his presence. And then, with a touch of melodrama, the bear slowly rolls its head away and lumbers south, into the dusky shadows of the river.

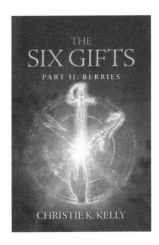

READ ON ...

For Marco Alfieri, the repercussions of past mistakes have frozen him in place, wrapping him in guilt. But a healing gift is his first ray of light – and hope. It enables him to put his troubles aside to comfort a lost and grieving family that has literally landed on his doorstep. The unconditional love he receives from them gives Marco the strength and courage to begin to mend his own broken, estranged family. In the midst of all this turmoil, he's given a stack of cryptic letters that introduce him to legendary ancestors he never knew he had. The letters prompt him to board a plane to Spain in a quest to unravel the mystery of "The Six Gifts," their remarkable origin, and their enigmatic destiny.

Read more about the entire series at www.christiekkelly.com

CHRISTIE K. KELLY

Born in Greeley, Colorado, Christie K. Kelly spent her formative years in the San Luis Valley of southern Colorado, surrounded by the majestic Rockies. She met and married her husband, Michael, and they had two sons before Christie returned to school and earned an accounting degree from Western International University in Phoenix, Arizona.

Christie later moved to New Jersey, where she helped her family start up and manage a flourishing material handling business. The business's success has allowed Christie to indulge her true callings—painting and writing.

In 2007, Christie and Michael were nearly fatally poisoned by methane and hydrogen sulfide gases in their own home. In the aftermath, Christie was inspired to use this near tragedy as the basis for a series of fictional novels called "The Six Gifts."

Today, Christie K. Kelly and her husband are blessed with two grown sons and five grandchildren. The couple makes their home in the Green Mountains of rural Vermont with their two goldendoodles, Charlie and Dylan.

www.christiekkelly.com

CHRISTIE K. KELLY

**THANK YOU FOR READING
THE SIX GIFTS PART I: SECRETS**

To receive special offers, bonus content, info on
new releases and more, sign up for my newsletter at
www.christiekkelly.com/newsletter.

And … it would be humbly appreciated
if you would take a few moments to post a review
on Amazon.com.

Connect with Christie K. Kelly at
www.christiekkelly.com

Also, on the following sites as ChristieKKelly: